# King of Cups

# Phoebe Woods

# Contents

For my family—moyners!

I thought
the fall would
kill me
but it only
made me real
*Ocean Vuong, "Skinny Dipping"*

·)) ● (C·

I can't undo all I have done to myself
what I have let an appetite for love do to me.
I have wanted all the world, its beauties
and its injuries; some days,
I think that is punishment enough.
Often, I received more than I'd asked,
which is how this works—you fish in open water
ready to be wounded on what you reel in.
*Maya C. Popa, "Dear Life"*

# Chapter One

Her goddamn piece-of-crap car struck at the worst moment. With the sun boiling the inside of her ancient Corolla and melting her makeup, thus destroying any professionalism in her appearance, and already late for the appointment that was supposed to fix everything—Eloise's car would not start.

"Hello, consequences of my own poor choices." Eloise bumped her forehead against the steering wheel, her frayed bleached hair coming free of her bun with the motion. This drama was for no one's benefit but hers, as Eloise was alone in her car, and her Southie side street—baking in the August sun—was abandoned in the heat.

*Just get an Uber,* her former best friend Monique would have said, back when they still talked, *and stop whining,* and she would have been right, but unfortunately an Uber was not possible right now. Eloise had no money in her account, and in fact it was overdrawn—thus the urgency of this appointment.

That fact alone was a cold shot of reality. "You have no choice," Eloise told herself, muffled by the steering wheel that was mashed against her bottom lip, "and you know what you need to do, so just do it." Then she let out a huff and mopped her face just as she remembered she was wearing foundation.

This was getting ridiculous. "Enough already," she muttered, and took out her phone.

"This is Hollis Davies." Her older brother always answered the phone in a clipped, you-have-interrupted-me voice. Of course he had her in his contact list, but he got a kick out of pretending he was too busy to check the caller ID.

"Holl." Eloise shifted on the molten, cracked leather seat. Sweat was dripping down her back, making the polyester lining of her H&M blazer stick to her skin. "How busy are you right now?"

"Busy like I have a job," Hollis said. "Let me guess: your car won't start, and you needed to be somewhere ten minutes ago."

"Got it in one." She allowed herself one last moment of hesitation before glancing at the time on her phone and blazing forward. "It's a new client—a new potential client, so someone I need to impress," she corrected quickly, "*and*, fun fact, it's someone affiliated with the Bruins."

"Wow, they have come to the right private eye," Hollis said grandly, trying not to laugh. "Local Bruins expert: Eloise Davies."

Hollis and Dad knew everything there was to know about Boston sports, while Eloise—the lone girl of the family—knew nothing and cared less. She had witnessed her brother and father cry real, actual tears over the trajectory of a ball or puck, and she would never share that emotion with them.

"Yeah, yeah, har har. Can you just help me?"

Hollis sighed theatrically into the phone. His days were peppered with conference calls and dire reports for the FDA, so in all fairness his schedule was less flexible than that of an aspiring private investigator.

"I know you're busy," she added.

"I'll help," he said at last. "But it'll cost you, because you only ever call me when you need something. You're doing The Visits for two weeks, and you have to actually *do* them, okay?"

"Of course I will," Eloise promised, like a liar.

Twenty minutes later, Hollis's tidy blue Ford Fiesta was prowling down the narrow Southie street on which Eloise lived, putting in mind a guest squeezing through a crowded party. Hollis, likely clad in a crisp button-up picked out by his live-in girlfriend Lily, would definitely be smirking through his aviators at her.

The Fiesta rolled to a stop and Eloise closed her eyes, steeling herself. She despised having her chaos revealed to anyone because once they saw it, it was all they saw about her. She had already called the client, a shrewd-sounding Krystal Taylor, to let her know she would be late, apologizing profusely. Krystal had been understanding—but not nearly receptive enough to relieve Eloise of the sense that she had already, somehow, lost control of this too.

"Ugh, thank you, you are a lifesaver," she said in a rush as she ducked into the car. Hollis's Fiesta was pristine, unlike her Corolla, and still smelled like mint and aftershave and new car, even though he had had it for years.

"I'm the best," Hollis reminded her as he pulled away from the curb.

When Eloise checked her face in the sideview mirror, she cringed. She looked like hell. Twenty panicked minutes of trying to start her car, followed by waiting in the broiling sun in polyester suiting, had not done anything to make her look less like a trashy college student on her way to her first interview. Sometimes, her wavy bleached hair (naturally auburn, though it had not been that color in a few years) came out cool and edgy, like the Debbie Harry picture that had inspired it. Sometimes, like today, it looked cheap. Eloise tried to flatten the puffy waves.

Whatever. She was not one to ruminate or worry for too long.

"You *are* the best," she agreed, sending her brother a sidelong glance. Anyone would be able to tell that they were related: both smaller in stature, with pale, freckled faces and dark eyes, and auburn brows that quirked asymmetrically as they talked. They also both looked younger than they were. Hollis had just turned thirty-six and still got carded (Eloise told him it was his height); and Eloise, at thirty-three, still got asked where she was going to school (Hollis told her it was her bad hair).

She knew that she ought to make an effort with her brother. They had only recently come back from not speaking for a few months, and she had weakly resolved to be better with him, even if she did not actually feel any more warmly toward him and got the sense that he had not quite forgiven her for their last disagreement.

"So... no lunch meetings today?"

"Just one, but I canceled it," Hollis said. He rolled down his window to let in the August air, which rose from the streets of Southie in shimmers.

"Thanks," she muttered, ashamed.

"Forget it. So you're meeting her at the Fairmont? Snazzy," Hollis marveled. "Is she paying?"

"If we decide to move forward, then yes. It'll be charged to her account," Eloise told him in a lofty voice, but in truth she was making this up as she went.

No previous client had bothered with an intake meeting like this. Eloise had no office location, so they usually spoke over the phone or email. If they met in person it was brief, to exchange photographs or documents. Eloise flitted in and out of their lives and their problems like a ghost, and most had such vague, confused expectations of private investigation that it was up to her to guide the process. Meanwhile, Krystal Taylor had insisted on an initial meeting, demanding the details of payment upfront, and Eloise got the impression that she had been taking notes as they had spoken over the phone. She had never felt so official, and she was wondering how often Krystal Taylor hired private investigators.

Eloise had been at this work for a year, ever since she had unexpectedly left her job as a bench chemist for one of the forensic drug testing labs in Massachusetts. It was only unexpected in timing; Eloise had been thinking for years of starting her own private investigative business, and though Dad and Hollis said she was a flake about her career, this was one decision that she had given significant thought. It had started in her mid-twenties as a passing fancy—she had had to testify in court regularly for her bench chemist job, and had been exposed to multiple private investigators over the years—and had grown increasingly sophisticated, until she was looking up how to get her own LLC and whether she would need to have a lawyer on retainer. For years it had all just been *Research* in her mind, without any clear goal or expectations—a recurring daydream whose details she would idly flesh out on long car rides, or on nights when she couldn't sleep.

The real shift had happened a few years ago on her thirtieth birthday. Eloise had gone to the Bee Hive in the tidy, twinkle-lit South End with Monique, keenly aware of the state of her life as she turned 'dirty thirty': single in a way that seemed permanent, with her job hobbling along, barely breathing, barely a career. She didn't own a house, she didn't have children, and she had no five-year plan—and though she often felt piercingly lonely, the idea of a relationship was laughable, for so many reasons.

And then, several cocktails in, with the live jazz blaring too loud for conversation, Eloise had had a moment to look at the couples around her and it had dawned on her.

Some of them had seemed happy, some seemed bored; many had seemed like they were going to argue on the way home. And Eloise had realized that was a life path that was going to be hard for her to walk, because to be wrapped up in someone else's life meant sacrificing your own. The very idea of it chafed. She didn't have enough life of her own to just hand over to someone else yet. She hadn't *done* anything yet—at least, not anything she was proud of. She was not yet the person she was supposed to be—she was not yet the person she hoped was hiding inside of her.

*I have to try it*, she had thought vaguely through the cocktail haze, too drunk to define for herself what *it* was just yet.

Three years and some change later, that sense of just-do-it optimism was in short supply. She was beginning to agree with Hollis and Dad: maybe she *was* just a flake. Maybe there was no better person hiding inside of her. These days, there was a permanent knot in her chest that made it hard to breathe. She rarely went out because it seemed like everything cost money, and the hours spent alone in her costly apartment were doing bad things to her.

"Man, usually you can't shut up," Hollis pointed out, drawing her back out of her own head. They rolled past brick buildings and drowsy sycamores that were turning brown in the summer drought. "Are you on your period or what?"

(One of Hollis's idiosyncrasies was his total lack of awkwardness about biological functions, even those of women. Eloise attributed it to his scientific education and an early addiction to the Discovery Channel. Eloise herself had never had the attention span for that. While Hollis was sprawled in front of the Discovery Channel, mouth agape at whatever was happening with the apes, Eloise had been poised in the bay window of their twin home, studying the comings and goings of the neighbors and drawing all kinds of conclusions about them—wondering about their lives, their wants and their disappointments, their hidden flaws and their secret longings.)

"No," Eloise said, flattening her curly bangs again. "Just worried about this."

"Oh. Well, don't worry," Hollis said cheerfully. "I mean, you should be worried, because your business is *ridiculous* and I honestly don't know how you make any money, and you're absolutely not moving in with me and Lily if you can't pay rent—"

"Thanks, Hollis, I'm aware," Eloise said loudly.

Hollis backpedaled a little. "You can always go back to the lab, right?"

(Hollis remained unaware of the circumstances under which she had left her stable, 'real' job. He still thought she had simply quit, and she had no urge to clarify.)

"Yeah," she lied vaguely. "Totally can just do that."

"So there you go. No need to worry. If this doesn't work out, you just do the next thing," he said with a shrug.

"You're right. It'll be fine."

Hollis's trajectory had been neater than Eloise's, and since graduating from a Human Factors master's program at Tufts, he had hopped from pharmaceutical company to pharma-consultancy with a detachment that Monique had insisted was male by design (*pump and dump*, she had called it). Eloise, by contrast, had been hired by the forensic lab a few years after graduating, and had stayed there until leaving in, more or less, flames.

Hollis seemed to sense that this had been a useless thing to say; she could feel him looking at her.

"So, the Bruins, eh? Now, here's the million-dollar question, El-lie—" His voice took on the broad, expansive tones of a gameshow host. "What sport do the Bruins play?"

In spite of it all, Eloise had to laugh at that.

"Shut up. I know all about the Bruins now," she informed him. "After I got the call, I spent hours researching them." She tapped her ancient tablet, where she had made all of her notes, to wake it up.

"Oh, really?" Hollis snickered. "Alright, tell me—and no cheating—when was the last time they won the Stanley Cup?"

"Er, 2011," Eloise recalled, dutifully covering her tablet screen, "but they're usually in the playoffs, and made it to the conference finals last year, and—um—"

"Lost," he finished for her, "to whom?"

"Tampa Bay."

"Yes—which was devastating for reasons we can get into later," Hollis said patiently. "And who are their star players?"

Eloise closed her eyes. "So there's the captain—Lavesque—"

"It's pronounced La-veck, but yes, Jacques Lavesque is the captain, and the best player on the team—especially since Andrei Koslov was traded a few years ago," Hollis corrected eagerly. "You should remember his name because I have his jersey, and it's *signed*, and if our apartment was burning down it's literally what I would grab first. Lavesque's played with the Bruins his whole career. Face-off lead in the league, and guaranteed hall-of-famer," he continued, unable to hide his boyish admiration. "He is also a total class act. Like, not at all your typical pro athlete."

"Yes, I noticed that, actually," Eloise recalled. "He and his perfect wife and sons are all over social media. They really *use* his Mr. Perfect image, don't they?"

Lavesque had surprised her. Hockey players always looked like lumbering bumblebees to her, bulky and hairy, buzzing gracelessly around the ice in their striped uniforms. When she had Googled the Bruins' roster, she had been taken aback. Lavesque looked, to Eloise's overactive imagination, like he should have been cast in some gritty medieval drama on HBO, with his broken Gallic nose and carved jaw. He had a good smile, too—it was real and asymmetric, and his eyes crinkled at the corners like he liked you, no matter who he was talking to.

Fascinated, she had kept scrolling. His wife, with her thick brown locks and bright brown eyes, had a fresh-faced beauty that was made real by a gummy smile. She looked like the actress you would cast to play the nice popular girl, the one who deserved to be prom queen. They had two beautiful little boys, and Eloise had seen dozens of shots of their family out and about in Boston, interacting with fans like they were delighted and flattered every single time.

"Because he *is* Mr. Perfect. He's my hero," Hollis agreed. "It'll kill me when he retires. I don't know when he plans on retiring but it's got to be soon. He's aged like a fine wine, but I think he's like, thirty-six, and even the best of them tap out near forty."

Then he glanced at Eloise. "Also, he's seriously a god to Boston sports fans. Maybe not quite Brady levels? But close. So if this has anything to do with him, you shouldn't take the job because Boston will literally riot."

"Got it—will incite Boston Tea Party part two; will become most hated woman in Boston," Eloise pretended to write on her tablet. "So he's the best one?"

"Yeah, he's overall a better player than Andrei Koslov was. He definitely has carried the team, but the Bruins do have a few other good players. It's basically Lavesque's line that does all the work, to be honest." Hollis grinned again. "Can you name anyone else on that line?"

"Alright, let me think—there's the tall skinny redheaded guy—"

"Pelletier, pretty decent player and an all-around good guy," Hollis rattled off, "and—?"

"Um... Short guy, head-butts people?"

"Henry Burnap, known as Burnie. Only player older than Lavesque on the team," Hollis said proudly. "He is a *great* defensive forward and he's won the Selke a bunch of times. Wins all the speed tests, too, and I think he might be the shortest guy in the NHL. We love representation."

At five-six, Hollis was surprisingly not sensitive about his height, and usually the first to make fun of it.

"The line used to be Koslov-Lavesque-Burnie, and it was a god-damn *iconic* line, but then Koslov got traded to Tampa Bay, and, obviously, went on to win the Stanley Cup with them. It's a really sore spot for Boston, just so you know."

"If Koslov was so good, why'd he go?"

Hollis shrugged. "Who knows? He was a huge pain in the ass. The most temperamental player ever. It's a shame, because Lavesque doesn't play *quite* the same without Koslov on the ice, but Koslov started a lot of fights. I also kind of remember seeing something on Twitter about homophobic slurs, racism, that kind of thing," he reasoned, earning a cynical laugh from Eloise.

"Anyway, there are other good players, but that's a good start," he relented. "Do you know what the case is about yet?"

"Absolutely no idea. The woman is in Bruins PR and it looks like she runs the show, but she was pretty aloof on the phone and refused to share any details. I don't even know if it's related to the Bruins organization," Eloise admitted. "It could be a personal thing, but she did ask for my *utmost* discretion."

"You need to text me what it is as soon as you get out of there, because I can't even imagine what it could be," Hollis wondered.

"We'll see," she said with a shrug.

The Boston Public Library was in sight now. The Fairmont was across Copley Square, shadowed by the dun-colored Romanesque triumph that was Trinity Church. Traffic was choked around the square and moving at a snail's pace, so Eloise leaned in and bonked her head against Hollis's—this was as affectionate as they got—and then scrambled out of the blue Ford Fiesta before traffic could move again.

In the glass of the Fairmont, she checked her reflection: an awkward figure in an ill-fitting black suit and chunky loafers, her bleached curly hair coming free of her pixie bun, tote bag slipping down her shoulder and her sunglasses askew. *Eloise Davies, private investigator*, she said in her head, and straightened up. *Hollis is right*, she told herself. *If this doesn't work out, you just do the next thing.*

(Never mind that she had been ghosting things—jobs, friendships, relationships, commitments—all her life, always ready to move on to the next thing the minute something didn't work out. Her private investigative work was the first thing—the only thing—she had ever held onto, the first difficulty she had ever pushed through, the first commitment she had honored even when tested. If there was anyone who knew how to move on to the next thing, it was Eloise.)

She walked between the two massive golden lion statues, and passed through a blast of air conditioning and was reborn into a new world, one of palm fronds and crystal and fusty red carpet. The Oak Long Bar + Kitchen was waiting behind a broad door paneled with frosted glass, and her immediate impression was of warmth and wood and light, and a cheerful noisiness that came with eating lunch out in the summer. Eloise stood on her tiptoes and scanned the room.

Krystal Taylor had described herself to Eloise via text: she would be 'the one with the braids and Gucci loafers and probably on the phone.' Eloise clocked her immediately beneath one of the large Palladian windows. The Black woman was tapping rapidly on a brand-new iPad and, as promised, wearing AirPods and deep in conversation. She was dressed in a simple black T-shirt and jeans, her elegant legs crossed at the knee, and long braids cascaded over her slim shoulders. The iconic horse-bit on her loafers caught the light just beneath the table. As Eloise approached, she noticed the tiny diamonds that glinted in Krystal's ears, and a Cartier love bracelet flashed as she typed. She had a frisée salad and a barely-touched glass of white wine set aside.

"Hi, Krystal?" Eloise called just as Krystal looked up, fixing Eloise with shrewd eyes. "I am *so* sorry about the car trouble—"

"It's fine, I was able to catch up on emails. I've got to go, talk later," Krystal interrupted, swiping her iPad closed. She took her AirPods out and snapped them neatly into their case. In the time it took Eloise to set down her own tablet and doff her tote bag, Krystal's pristine iPhone had buzzed three times with messages, adding to Eloise's sense of sloth around the woman.

"Here's the menu. I got the chardonnay; it's acceptable," Krystal added, fetching a menu from the seat beside her.

"Oh, wonderful, thank you," Eloise blustered as she took it. Composed, pulled-together women had always unnerved her. She pretended to scan the menu but it was pointless—she would not know a good chardonnay if she was drowning in it, nor could she be certain she would be able to pronounce many of the wines on the list without sounding like she was trying to be funny. "You know what? I'll just copy you."

They were an island of silence surrounded by bubbling laughter and the clink of silverware. Eloise cleared her throat and set down the menu. "So."

"So." Krystal aligned the edge of the iPad with the napkin she had re-folded. "You're probably wanting more details."

Eloise watched her tidy. What was it like to be a Black woman in an environment so traditionally male and white as the NHL? How had Krystal landed in Bruins hockey, and how did she handle it? She was clearly in a position of power and influence; Eloise had internet-stalked her enough to be intimidated by her resumé, and had not even had enough time to read through all of the articles detailing Krystal's impact on the Bruins organization.

"Yes, I am," Eloise said, "but I don't have a set way of doing this. Just start wherever you feel comfortable."

Krystal swept her braids over her slim shoulder, a movement that Eloise guessed was a nervous tic.

"I do the Bruins' PR," she began bluntly, like she was expecting Eloise to contradict her, and Eloise wondered how many times she *had* been contradicted. "I don't know if you're a sports fan, but I'm sure you know that Boston sports is a cult, and the fans worship

Boston athletes. I take my job very seriously." She looked thoughtful. "It's not all Twitter posts and puppies, you know. It's reputation. It's consistency. It's developing a brand for each of these men and protecting that brand, because it all adds up to the brand of the Bruins, right? And ultimately, that adds up to the brand of the NHL, and that is what pays our salaries."

Eloise was scribbling notes with her stylus.

"So you're saying you get to know the players really well," she guessed.

"They tell me what I need to know to do my job. Sometimes that means understanding that they've got a little partying problem, so we lock their Twitter and Instagram so they can't post stupid things when they're drunk. Sometimes it means finding them the best media coach possible. Sometimes it means finding them an English tutor, or a therapist, or a pet Bernedoodle. All I ask is that they be transparent with me."

"And someone's not being transparent?" Eloise intuited.

"To say the least. There's actually more than one who is just straight-up *lying* to me, but—" Krystal tapped her manicured nails on the white table cloth. "One of them—"

She inhaled through her nose, looking deeply put-upon. "I just can't believe it. After all these *years*—but you know what? It is what it is. He's very private," she reasoned to herself, "and I *respect* that, but after all this time, the one thing I ask of him—"

She halted and shuddered in fury. "Sorry. You ever just want to kill a man?"

Eloise let out an unexpected cackle, then covered her mouth when other patrons glanced at them. Krystal snickered, visibly pleased that she had made Eloise laugh.

"Yes," Eloise said when they had composed themselves. "Generally, to be honest. There's always at least one on my hit list."

"Glad I'm not the only one with a list," Krystal muttered wryly. She exhaled, her posture a little looser now, and toyed with her water glass. This had been bothering her.

"So there's two cases?" Eloise probed, trying not to sound hopeful.

"No, it's just one. I would love to set you on Lavy and find out what this nonsense is, but he has his shit together," she said firmly, splaying her hands as though trying to convince Eloise. "He has never given me a real reason to be worried, so I can't justify it. It would be a betrayal of trust. He told me not to worry, so..."

"You mean Jacques Lavesque?" Eloise asked in a low voice. She thought of the man with the breathtaking wife. "What did he do? My brother will be personally devastated if it's bad," she put in.

Krystal gave a knowing, indulgent smile, though it vanished quickly. "Obviously this is all under some kind of NDA."

"It stays with me," Eloise promised. "Part of the job."

"So, he might be separating from his wife," Krystal explained, "but he told me that no one else can know about it, and he won't tell me why."

Eloise didn't want to diminish what was obviously causing Krystal a significant amount of distress, but she could not help but wonder why Krystal cared about Jacques Lavesque's marital status or found this to be important. Maybe there were feelings there? Krystal was certainly beautiful and confident; it would not surprise Eloise if the woman had tension with one of the players, especially a man who seemed so engaging.

"But that's not the reason I want to hire you," Krystal clarified. "That man has given his life to the organization and I have to trust that he would never do anything to jeopardize the brand, especially after all this time. Most of the players wouldn't. The problem"—she paused, checking that the tables on either side of them were still vacant—"is Kyle Hearst."

"I'm not familiar with him," Eloise admitted as she scribbled his name. Krystal sighed.

"Brand new rookie, nineteen years old. A baby in every respect. We just got him from the Providence Bruins. He hasn't grown up yet, even if he does have some serious talent. He's a local Boston boy and has too many old friends, if you know what I mean."

Her eyes narrowed into that shrewd look again as she considered her words. "He had some drug trouble back in the day, and that nonsense never goes away with these guys. I tried to tell them he was going to be a bad investment—just another Koslov without the size or speed or outrageous talent. Koslov really struggled with the alcoholism for a while, and it was a *mess*. Though I heard he's sober now. Good for him, good for Tampa," Krystal mused, "because when he's bad? He's *bad*."

There was that name again, like a shark lurking in green, shadowed waters. Eloise remembered the roster picture of a man with a brutal-ly-carved face, black hair, and clever brown eyes, but once she saw that he had been traded to Tampa Bay, she had moved on.

"So you want to find out if Kyle Hearst's got drug trouble again?"

"That—or if there's other nonsense going on." Krystal looked un-settled again. "There's *something* going on with him. I keep tabs on him through social media, and there are a lot of freaks in his pictures. Doesn't socialize with anyone else on the team, doesn't show up to any of the team events, isn't really making friends even though the other rookies are a bunch of human golden retrievers. And look, if you sign with the Bruins, you're part of a family. That's just how the team is run. Most guys are thrilled to be part of such a legacy, and they're so used to the professional side of things, and they know it's not a choice. It's part of the job. You just put in your time and do it with a smile, because you don't get those millions for free, you know? And Lavesque knows where his money comes from so he sets the tone and everyone falls in line."

*Mr. Perfect*, Eloise thought again, though she kept that to herself. If she were a gambling woman—and she was not, because she was deeply broke—she would bet money that Mr. Perfect had cheated on his beautiful wife with their nanny, or something like that.

"Got it. And Hearst's not falling in line?"

"He's not," Krystal agreed, "and Lavy told me not to worry about it—he insists that Hearst's just immature. But I don't like the guys in his pictures and I don't like that my gut is telling me there's something messed up about Kyle Hearst. We're going into a tough season, and I want to know ahead of time whether he's going to be Andrei Koslov 2.0 for me or not."

"Tough season?" Eloise probed.

Krystal studied her then. Eloise saw the moment she made the decision to hold something back.

"There are going to be some changes coming," she said evasively. There was a cool resolve about her, like she was preparing for a fight.

"Does it matter to this case?" Eloise asked.

"No," Krystal said confidently, but the twist of her mouth and the dart of her gaze said, *maybe*.

·)) ● ((·

"So? Did Lavesque kill someone? Are you gonna be rich?" Hollis wanted to know later that night. Eloise had Kyle Hearst's Instagram open on her old laptop and was scrolling through it yet again as she pinned the phone between her ear and shoulder.

"Yes, he murdered the president, and I'm a billionaire," she said distractedly as she screenshot a few images of Hearst.

He looked so much like any local Boston boy, with his thin Irish lips and grown-out auburn hair flattened beneath a backwards Sox hat, that she wanted to laugh. He really was Just Some Guy. You could have gone out on any given night, to any shitty pub in Southie, and found him in the corner drinking Sam Adams and bitching about the Pats.

"You know I can't share any real details," she added, feeling guilty—Hollis *had* canceled a meeting to drive her.

"Can't you at least give me a hint?"

"Nope. You're too smart. You'd figure it out, and then this woman would kill me."

She paused on an image from a few months ago. Based on the caption it looked like the day Hearst had signed his contract, and featured Hearst with Lavesque. Both of them were in suits, and Lavesque was smiling at Kyle, who was flushed at the attention. He wore his suit like it was his First Holy Communion, too big in the shoulders and plain like it had been picked out by someone else. This was the one picture where the Sox hat was missing and his auburn hair looked oddly flat, his ears soft and vulnerable, without it.

"I don't know how I'm going to figure this one out," she admitted.

"Can't you just do it through cyberstalking? Isn't that how you usually get these done?"

Eloise studied the image, then advanced to the next one, a shot of a lake at sunset. Kyle Hearst was shirtless, slouched in a beach chair at the shoreline and holding a can of beer, though the actual logo was hidden by his hand, so he could plausibly deny it was alcohol—*a clever kid*, she thought—and a cigarette in the same hand. Vivid tattoos snaked down his pale, muscled arms. In the corner of the image she glimpsed the muddy pattern of fatigues that were tucked into scuffed combat boots.

"I don't think I can. He is either totally not *online*, or he's careful as hell about what he does online." She scrolled through the comments but, like every other post, none jumped out at her, and he had not replied to or interacted with any of them. "I think I'm going to have to go in. Like, in person."

"As in, meet the players?"

"Meet them. Get to know them." She closed Instagram and on a whim Googled Lavesque again. "Have you heard anything interesting about the rookies this year?"

"No," Hollis laughed. "Unless they're number one or number two draft picks, I don't think anyone hears much about them at all, and Boston never gets high picks anymore because they're too good. Is this about a rookie?"

"No, just wondering. Trying to understand the team dynamic."

She navigated to Lavesque's Instagram. The latest picture was a lovely shot of the back of a little boy's head as he surveyed his work on a sandcastle, the soft ash-brown hair curly and sweet. The picture bore no caption, but was geo-tagged as Nantucket.

"Anyway, I should go."

"Alright, fine. Lily's making dumplings, anyway, so I have better stuff to do," Hollis teased, and they hung up.

Eloise stared at Lavesque's Instagram—then closed it hastily, like someone had caught her.

Lavesque was not the one under investigation, and it was none of her business why Mr. Perfect's marriage was ending.

# Chapter Two

J acques used to love Nantucket.

His wife's family's Nantucket 'cottage' was not a cottage so much as a six-bedroom haven that overlooked the Sound, with its own private staircase down to the beach, and a vast deck with a pool wreathed by striped umbrellas. To access the house, you took a crushed-shell driveway whose dusty ruts were made by one of the Jeeps that the family left on the island because it 'just made sense.' The house even had a name—it was called Thatch, a tongue-in-cheek reference to the fact that it was listed as a cottage.

Jacques had loved the house since that first summer he and Rachel were together, back when he had just signed with the Bruins and she was still in college. They had been together for six months when she had suggested, during sex, that they visit her parents' *other* house. Drunk on tequila, his mind on other things, he had uttered 'Yeah, sure, whatever you want,' and had not thought to regret it until the next morning when he remembered that he was probably not the man that this trust-fund girl's parents were hoping she would bring to Nantucket.

They had taken the ferry together, the sky an auspicious blue, the Sound glittering like so many diamonds. When they arrived on Nantucket, her parents had picked them up from the ferry in one of their rattiest Jeeps, with one of the golden retrievers (this one named Jeeves) sitting in the back seat like he did this all the time. They had looked like an ad for *something*, and Jacques could still remember thinking that he was not cool enough to know what the ad would be.

But Jeff and Milly, tan and white-teethed, had been as delighted with Jacques as the golden retriever was, and all of his fears had dissolved. For the first time, Rachel—always the one to put others at ease—had been the nervous one, and Jacques had been charmed by her new shyness. Her father had teased her as they loaded their suitcases into the Jeep, and Jacques had caught her eye and thought *she's the one*.

In the Hathaways' whitewashed kitchen at Thatch, they had sat around the island, drinking wine into the small hours of the night with the French doors open to let in the sea breeze. Jacques had felt like he was home.

He had been so afraid. Would they be stuck-up? Would they look down on him, on his career and his tattoos and his upbringing? His lack of education, his thick and unglamorous accent? Would they judge him for not knowing wine, for never having skied despite coming from Canada, for not caring about art, for having no interest in higher education?

But they hadn't judged him. They hadn't even seemed to notice that he was from a different walk of life, a trait that Jacques soon came to associate with generational wealth. They happily told anecdotes about their maids and boarding school educations as though everyone had those, and interpreted Jacques's confused laughter as amusement. That first night, the golden retriever Jeeves had leapt onto Jacques in delight and he had spilled wine on the ivory sofa. Milly had just laughed it off—and she had meant it.

They had put Jacques in one of the guest rooms that night, with a vast heirloom cane bed done in crisp white linens. Rachel had sneaked in so they could lay there together, tangled and drunk and happy. Jacques had fallen asleep with his fingers wound in her glossy fine brown hair, head swimming with costly wine and the mingled scents of sunscreen and sand.

That night he had dreamed of years of summers at this lovely house, with these lovely people as his family—and then his dreams had come true.

They had even had their engagement party here. The Hathaways had hired a chef, and a billion of the family's closest friends had gathered on the back deck, traipsing in and out of the French doors with flutes of Veuve (what they called 'party champagne' because the cost meant so little to them, a fact that had taken Jacques years to get over). Rachel had worn a white dress that he could still remember taking off her that night, the white so bright against her summer-freckled skin. He had been high on the end of a good season and everyone had wanted to talk to him about it.

Jacques could still remember looking out at the sea—navy that night, and dotted with pinpricks of golden light from boats—and unable to fully absorb his own luck. Andrei had been there that night, brooding in the corner and working on getting shit-faced. Some of Rachel's cousins had surrounded him, giggling and in awe of his massive, brutal physicality, like kittens gathered round a lion. Jacques had caught his eye over a head of expensive hair and Andrei had grinned at him, and for a moment it had felt like the old days, even though things were already changing between them at that point, and everything had seemed golden and happy.

Right now, though, nothing felt like the old days. Jacques was relieved to be leaving this custardy island, with its insistent hydrangea and its tedious flags. When you were on this island, every night was another happy hour, another twilit deck of people who knew Rachel from art classes or study abroad and who pretended not to want Jacques's autograph until the drinks had flowed sufficiently for them to admit they did. He did not begrudge it; he had known what he was signing up for when he signed with the Bruins, but lately he found that his face didn't do the Media Smile as easily, and gracious banter didn't come as naturally.

Jacques always followed through on his responsibilities, and this inability to fulfill his responsibilities only seemed to add to the anger he felt lately. Everything about his life was crumbling. To have it happen on this island that he associated with dreams and family and granted wishes made it all the worse.

But then yesterday Krystal had sent him that magic text, freeing him from it: *We need to talk.*

He had been out on the deck with the boys, taking a break from playing with them in the pool. Peter was old enough to splash by himself with floaties; Luke still needed to be held. Jacques had heard his phone *ping* with the tone he'd given to everyone associated with the Bruins, and had reached for it immediately.

*You need me back in town? On Nantucket,* he had typed, aware of Rachel hovering inside with her mother, looking out those lovely French doors at him and the boys.

(They had not actually spoken privately since he had arrived two days ago, because he still could not stand to look at her. Rachel was giving him a wide berth, as though this were a passing storm that she could weather if she simply gave him enough space. She did not believe him when he'd said he was only coming for the boys.

(And maybe it *was* just a passing storm.)

*Ugh, do not say 'on Nantucket,' you know how much I hate that,* Krystal had texted back.

He had laughed, watching the three dots appear. *It's better if you come into town,* she had added. *Not really phone call material, honestly.*

Peter was sitting on a lounge chair by then, absorbed in his Batman and Joker toys, but Luke was draped on Jacques like a barnacle, already asleep. Just a few weeks ago, this would have been a perfect moment; he would not have answered his phone right away, and would have resented Krystal for interrupting his limited vacation.

He could still glimpse that old world, but now it was on the other side of soundproof glass.

His mother had always told him, in her hoarse voice, that life turned on a dime—for better *and* for worse, she had warned—and it was only now that forty was closer than thirty that he really got what she meant. She had done tarot readings for the local women in their town for extra money, and he could still remember how she had talked about the Wheel of Fortune: what goes up must, inevitably, come down.

*I can be there tomorrow morning*, he had tapped out, running the fingers of his free hand through Luke's fine brown hair. He had closed the window and opened a new one to check the ferry schedule.

Today was a Thursday and the weekend crowds were already pouring in with their suitcases and their goldendoodles and their white jeans. One of the workers on the ferry had joked 'You're going the wrong way!' to Jacques as he'd boarded with his duffle bag slung over his shoulder. He had laughed indulgently with him, guilty that his laugh was not genuine, and had been relieved to find the ferry mostly empty. He had taken a seat in the corner, leaning his head against the tinted glass and watching the docks of Nantucket slide out of view.

What could Krystal want? It was unlike her to be vague with him. He had known her as long as he had been with the Bruins; she had been his first friend in the organization, before even Burnie. He knew he was a product to her—she had seen his potential immediately, and had painstakingly developed him into what he had become—but over the years they had become real friends, too.

Still, he also knew what she expected of him, and what the Bruins organization expected of him. He was not delusional about his contract, about the unwritten responsibilities contained between the lines of that contract, which had only grown as the years had passed.

(That contract was up this year, but there was no question that he would keep going until something forced him to stop.)

*You can't fuck up*, Krystal had told him all those years ago, sitting him down in a private room after he had signed the contract. *You can't get mad. You can't fight. You can't lose your temper with the media, you can't do weird shit on the internet. You can't be impatient with fans when they stop you on the street, and you can't be caught doing messy shit in clubs. You've got to protect the brand.*

*You're the generational talent*, she had told him. *You're going to be the face of the Bruins for years. You're going to end up in the hall of fame. Kids are going to buy your jersey, have posters of you on their walls. You've got to be perfect.*

*I know*, he had said, and he had meant it. *I know this is my job too.* He had reminded himself that he was intensely lucky, and that when he had signed his name on that contract he had been handed his dreams. It was the age of the NHL trying to rebrand itself into something bigger and better, back then, and perhaps the Bruins thought they were getting another Connor McDavid or Sidney Crosby out of him, another wholesome Canadian good boy with milk-white virgin skin and a safe smile.

(Never mind that he had already been covered in tattoos and had showed up to Draft Day with his nose broken by his own brother, with his English clunky and staccato and, even to his own ears, painful to listen to.)

Maybe this vagueness was Krystal's way of punishing him for not divulging details on the separation, but Jacques had not yet told anyone. He hadn't even told his own mother. Every time he went to speak of it, his throat closed up and he found himself mute with anger—not that he had ever been close enough to his mother to tell her much. The circumstances of his childhood and the way he had broken his nose had barred that door forever; theirs was a tepid ceasefire that they maintained because neither saw the point of a fight, and he was so busy these days.

He turned off his phone, mostly to avoid notifications from Rachel, and soon the ferry was pulling into the Hyannis harbor. Jacques spotted Krystal waiting for him as soon as he stepped onto the gangway. He saw the gleaming black Audi, with its owner leaning against the door, slender arms folded over her chest, wearing large round sunglasses as glossy and black as her car.

"Not the Mercedes today?" Jacques teased when he reached her, gravel crunching underneath his suede sneakers. Krystal arched her brows before pulling him in for a hug.

"Please. I know you like the Audi better," she dismissed. Jacques stuffed his bag in the pristine back seat, and then dropped into the passenger seat. "And you need a haircut. It's getting too floppy on top," she added as she started the Audi.

"Good to see you too, Krystal."

Jacques studied Krystal, trying to determine how hard to push her, as they pulled out of the port authority. "So? What was this thing you wanted to tell me in person? We are in person now."

"Yes. Yes we are."

Krystal didn't elaborate further, just drove, so Jacques stayed quiet. You had to let Krystal come to you sometimes.

She did a double-take when they reached the light, lowering her sunglasses to look at him more closely. "Lavy. You look *terrible*."

"Insomnia," he dismissed. He had been sleeping in the old guest room that Milly and Jeff had once put him up in all those years ago, and it was still bizarre to sleep apart from Rachel. On the first night, the boys had exploded into the bedroom to say goodnight and Rachel had lingered by the door, hugging her long cardigan around her slim form, smiling apologetically like he was a guest that the boys were harassing.

Sleep had not been possible after that, and the next night he had heard Rachel and Milly talking late into the night beneath him—not the words, but the rhythm of their voices, and he had known they were talking about him.

He had lay there wondering if Milly and Jeff thought him immature or petty for all of this. It had shamed him, and you couldn't sleep on a shamed conscience. It was not a way he often felt; he was so careful to act according to his principles that it had been a while since he had gone to bed with a guilty conscience.

And then every time he felt bad, the whole cycle would explode into motion again. The betrayal. The defensiveness. The anger. The grief. The sense of loss.

Trees were blurring past his window now, bringing him back to the present.

"We have not even discussed the separation," he explained, recognizing that until he gave Krystal *something*, she was going to remain mad. "I have a lawyer, but I do not know what will happen next." It was easier to talk about it like it was something out of his hands, like it was something to be determined by someone else.

"And you didn't consider consulting me for a lawyer?" Krystal exploded. "Damn it, Lavy, this is literally the *point* of me." She paused. "And we're supposed to be friends. I'm picking you up from the Nantucket ferry, for god's sake, because I don't want you going into this meeting blind."

"I haven't talked to anyone about it, Krystal. Burnie and Pell don't even know," he told her. "My own mother doesn't know. Don't be offended."

"Well, why not? You know you're not getting through this kind of thing without help—"

"I don't want help," he said, a little more forcefully than he should have.

Krystal scoffed. "I know you're private, but you had better give me a heads-up before any shit hits the fan, alright? I'm letting you off easy because we've known each other this long. But the *minute* the process starts—"

"*If* the process starts, believe me," he promised her, "you will be the first to know."

They sat in silence for a few miles, the air thick with tension. He had been waiting to be a father and a husband all of his life, and it was all crumbling. *There it goes again*, he thought tiredly, feeling the cycle of emotions start in his throat.

"So what is this meeting?" he asked at last.

Krystal took a long swig of her sweating Dunkin iced coffee, a branding choice to hide that she was in fact a New Yorker and would have far preferred bodega coffee. She drove, and drove, and finally sighed.

"There's no way to prep you for this or make it go down easy," she muttered. "And you better believe I wish there was a way to make this easier. I know you've given everything to this team, and you deserve better. *I* was pissed when they told me—pissed enough that I went and bought this *stupid* Hermès scarf out of sheer rage. It has horses on it."

That made him laugh, as he suspected she had intended.

"Come on. Just tell me," he said.

"Alright. But you didn't hear it from me, and you've got to act surprised when they tell you."

She swept her braids over her shoulder in a move to steel her resolve. And then she said the words that changed everything.

"They're bringing Andrei back."

·)·)●(·(·

Eloise was crouched in a hydrangea bush of all places, trying not to flinch every time a bee hummed past her ear, when her phone pulsed with a call from her latest client.

She dropped down, the bush rustling around her. It was the only spot that afforded her a view of the back door of the lovely Beacon Hill house, and she was hoping to catch her target leaving—hopefully being seen out by his alleged girlfriend.

"Krystal," Eloise said under her breath. "Hi. So sorry. I'm a little—I'm in the middle of something, so I can't talk for long."

"You did a pretty convincing social media job," Krystal said approvingly, making Eloise grin. "I mean, I wouldn't *hire* you, but I wouldn't question it, either."

"So? You want to go for it?"

Eloise sat back up, balancing her camera on one knee to steady the shot. When Krystal didn't speak right away, she rushed to fill the silence. "You could say you're doing me a favor. Maybe I'm a family friend and this was all you could come up with to help me. I'm like an informal intern, and if anyone looks into me, you can just say that I *obviously* need some help because I have nothing going for me. It'll give me a chance to interview the players, hang around them a bit, ask some personal questions, and when I'm done, no one will question it when I disappear."

"The only one smart enough to see through it will be Lavy," Krystal said thoughtfully, "and probably Pell and Bouchard, but none of them would ever say a word about it." She paused. "Well, and—and this is so confidential, the ink isn't even *dry* yet—but Koslov, too."

"Koslov?" There was activity inside; Eloise checked her camera again. "The big alcoholic Russian guy? The homophobic racist one? Isn't he on another team now? Tampa Bay or something?"

"I don't know that he's specifically homophobic or racist, but yes. That one." Krystal sounded grim. "He's coming back for a year for a Cup run and he is *smart* and gets a kick out of poking holes in things.

If he felt like calling you out, he would. We'll just have to keep you out of his line of sight," she reasoned.

"Would he even notice?" Eloise mopped some sweat off her brow. "This is going to sound like I'm fishing for compliments and I promise I'm not, but I don't really stand out, especially to men. It's kind of why I can even do this job. If I'm not interviewing him, will he even notice I'm there?"

"Koslov has a nose for trouble," Krystal hedged, and Eloise was relieved that she didn't try to reassure her about her appearance, "but maybe you're right. So long as you don't try anything with him—"

"You mean *flirt*? Krystal, you met me. What would you estimate that my flirting capacity is? Because it's zero. Also, by the way," she continued, flinching as another bumblebee buzzed past her ear, "I can't say I have much of a thing for hockey players—or 'mean as hell' racists, either."

"You'd be shocked at the Koslov effect," Krystal said darkly. "All I'll say is this: he could be on trial for murder and if there were enough women on the jury, he'd get away with it."

"Wow. That makes me want him even more," she said dryly, and was rewarded by Krystal's laugh. A shadow appeared in the window of the back door. "Gotta go—we'll talk later?"

"Yes. It's on," Krystal said, and they hung up.

The door swung open, and her target appeared: a tall, thin middle-aged man in custom suiting, and Eloise snapped a picture of him just as he twisted to say goodbye to his girlfriend inside.

Another bumblebee buzzed past her ear and this time she did yelp, just as he was getting into his BMW. He paused, looking around, and she held her breath until he lost interest and ducked back into the car.

The silver BMW backed out and when it had rounded the corner, Eloise slumped down, relieved, and sent the picture to her client. And then, because she was sweaty and hungry and tired and needed some motivation, she checked her bank account to stare at the negative number.

She needed that money—badly.

# Chapter Three

One week later, Eloise Davies had transformed into Eloise Morris: aspiring social media strategist and part-time employee staffed in the supplements aisle at Whole Foods. Eloise had enjoyed putting together her disguise for this one—the clear pink plastic glasses were a recent thrift store acquisition from the last time she had felt like she had money to spare, and she had not gotten to use them yet.

"You look like a flake," Hollis's girlfriend Lily told Eloise thickly through a mouthful of Greek yogurt. She was draped on Eloise's unmade bed, watching Eloise prepare to go to the Bruins' practice rink.

"So, unlikely to catch the attention of a hockey player?" Eloise guessed as she pulled on a T-shirt printed with cartoon handlebar mustaches.

"Don't be hurt, but you look like you have a Tumblr account," Lily said before licking the foil top of the yogurt. "So yes. Very unlikely. Also, that shirt looks like it's from 2010. Where did you even get that?"

"Forever 21... in 2010," Eloise admitted. She turned to assess her appearance in the mirror. She had chosen a long mustard skirt, an ancient pair of Converse, and a khaki messenger bag to pair with her mustache top. "Ideally I'd be outrageously hot and seduce the dirt from them, but we work with what we've got."

"You *are* outrageously hot, in your own way," Lily said absently, setting aside her yogurt to dig through Eloise's closet.

"Thanks, Mom," Eloise joked. She watched Lily produce a black sleeveless dress, her round face lighting up.

"What is *this* and why have you never worn it?" she demanded, shaking the dress so that her thick black waves shook with it. "Oh my god, wait. This is *designer*. Why have we not discussed this purchase? Why was there no fashion show?"

"Put it away," Eloise groaned. "I got it on sale in that runway section at TJ Maxx a few years ago and then didn't return it in time, and it was too much money to just give to Goodwill. I feel like such an asshole for even buying it in the first place. It gives me guilt every time I see it."

"Why would you return it?" Lily held it up to Eloise. "It looks like it was made for you. It's so... simple. It would make *you* shine."

Eloise snatched the dress from her sister-in-law (in feeling if not in letter; Lily and Hollis's perennial New Years' resolution was to get married, and in the eighteen years they had been together, they had yet to pick out a ring. Lily always said that she had been Dr. Zhou for simply too long at this point and that becoming Dr. Davies would hurt 'her brand' but Eloise suspected it had more to do with the fact that a wedding would cut dramatically into their restaurant budget).

"It's just not me, okay? And besides, it's too dressy to wear to this anyway," she insisted, hanging the dress where it belonged: in the very back of her closet, well-hidden by all of her surveillance clothing, all odds and ends that had been picked up at thrift stores so that believable disguises could be assembled easily. "Focus, Lilian! I need to know if the look is complete."

"Yes. You look like someone who needs reluctant occupational favors from distant friends," Lily reassured her as she dropped onto the bed again. "Also, *occupational favors* sounds like a euphemism," she reflected with a shudder. "I would totally give you a sympathy interview, anyway, and I wouldn't think anything of it."

"Good." Eloise flattened her bangs. "Alright. I've got my disguise. I've got my cheat sheet. I've got my tablet."

Eloise turned to Lily and adjusted her glasses. "My name? Is Eloise Morris? And like, I'm an INFP? And a Ravenclaw?"

"I am begging you to stop," Lily laughed. "Maybe you *do* have a Tumblr account."

"At the very least, I had a WeHeartIt account at some point," Eloise said. Sensing Lily's doubt, she pressed on. "It's probably not necessary, but I always feel like this stuff is easier if I'm not *me,* you know? Not that anyone is going to notice me either way. I'm not exactly in their target demographic."

Lily was looking at her funny. "What?" Eloise probed curiously.

"It's just..." Lily hesitated, glancing at the closet full of strange clothing that had belonged to other people. "You ever think you get into disguise too easily? Like, you're too... *comfortable* in your disguises?"

"You think I'm a chameleon. You think I should be nominated for the Oscar. You think I'm the next Meryl, and honestly I would have to agree—" Eloise began, but halted when Lily rolled her eyes.

"Ugh. Never mind," she dismissed irritably. "You Davies kids can never resist your dumb jokes, and I am not in the mood."

Hollis was watching baseball on his phone, sprawled on the couch with one arm behind his head. He glanced up and Eloise posed in a faux-curtsy, splaying the mustard skirt.

"You look the same as you always do," he decided, looking back at the game. "Yo, why don't you have any food in your fridge? I think Lily got the last edible thing out of it."

Eloise turned away from them both. "Oh, I haven't felt like going grocery shopping. It's too hot," she said vaguely, pretending to be absorbed in looking through her messenger bag.

"You're a goddamn disaster," Hollis muttered before cursing loudly at something happening in the game.

Lily ripped Hollis from the couch, demanding that Eloise get in touch and share how it went as soon as possible, and Hollis begged her for an autograph from Lavesque as Lily was dragging him away. Eloise stood on her front stoop and watched, in the late August sun, as they got into Hollis's beloved Ford Fiesta and drove down the street.

She tried to ignore the squirming shame at being the sort of person who didn't have food in her fridge. Hopefully Hollis hadn't given it too much thought. He was smarter than he acted, that she knew, but he could also be oblivious and right now she was counting on his male tendency to miss subtle things. She had already billed Krystal the first invoice but it hadn't gone through yet, and the money she had made from her last case had all gone towards paying her rent this month. Her account was back to that ugly, negative number and she had awoken with a start in the night and opened her banking app, face lit by the glow of her screen, and had stared at the number in weary dread.

This whole thing was getting harder and harder to maintain. Right now, Krystal was her only client, and she had no others in sight. Eloise had been telling herself all summer that all of the rich people, most likely to hire her, were on Nantucket or at their beach houses for the season. Boston emptied of its rich locals in the summer and the tourists descended, wearing Harvard tees and walking four and five across on the sidewalks, and none of them would need to hire her. If she could only hold on until autumn... perhaps then her business would pick up again... but she had told herself that last season, for different reasons, and no clients save for Krystal had magically appeared...

*Never mind*, she told herself as she locked her door. *I'll worry about that later. Warrior Ice Arena—here I come.*

It was a complicated, sweltering journey via public transportation. It had rained earlier in the day, and steam rose off the streets; summer had come late this year and now it was making up for lost time, rendering the T almost unbearable with smells. As she swayed with the train, Eloise reviewed the cheat sheet on her tablet. She had memorized names and faces, numbers and positions, and key Bruins history, though she would not have expected Eloise Morris to remember all of it.

She was beginning to feel nervous, actually. She locked her tablet and wiped her palms on her long mustard skirt, her stomach writhing like she had had too much caffeine and not enough food. Were it not for the matter of her bank account, she might have just ghosted Krystal and the Bruins.

Her phone buzzed with a new text from Krystal. *Are we still on?* With clumsy fingers she typed *yes almost there.*

She got off the train at Boston Landing, an industrial no-man's land after the bustle and brick of the Back Bay, and gulped in the fresh air after the sour fug of the T. The concrete was wet here, too, and more steam rose off the pavement as she walked past a newly-minted apartment building. Blue signs pointed her in the direction of the Warrior Ice Arena, making it clear that this was the main attraction of this strange, in-between place. She passed a New Balance store and glimpsed her reflection in the windows: squinty in the sunlight, her bleached hair worse for the humidity, and long mustard skirt undulating as she walked. *It's just a disguise*, she reminded herself.

(And, by the way, Lily was wrong. Eloise was not 'too comfortable' in her disguises. She was never comfortable at all—not in her own skin and not in anyone else's. After all, underneath it all there she was—a trespasser no matter where she went, an interloper who had never learned to root in any soil, a witch forever in exile.)

At the end of the block she saw the sign for Athletes Park and a discreet Bruins logo, just as Krystal had described. Krystal stood beneath the logo in a sliver of shade, wearing enormous sunglasses and AirPods, talking and pacing, looking somehow cool and composed even in the heat. She glimpsed Eloise and lifted a hand, Cartier bracelet winking in the sunlight.

"What is *that*." Krystal had hung up and was staring, aghast, at her outfit. "What Salvation Army hell did you have to burrow into to find all of that? Are you trying to make a point?"

"Actually, I owned it all already," she admitted, and laughed when Krystal's eyebrows shot up.

"I guess you meant it when you said you didn't care about hockey players. Most women would have shown up in their tightest jeans and best hair." Krystal turned and pulled open the door, leaving Eloise to feel a little stung by her words. A blast of air conditioning hit them both, making Eloise newly aware of how sweaty she was. "Come on in, they're just free skating now. It's the perfect time to slip in."

Eloise stifled another burst of nerves. She wished that they would all be preoccupied with their practice—too occupied to notice her.

"So," Krystal whispered as they walked a long hallway, "there's going to be some *news* released today, if you recall what I'm talking about, and most of the players don't—oh, hey, Pell!"

A gangling man with a poof of ginger hair, reminding Eloise of a stem of broccolini, emerged from what she guessed was a gym. His grey T-shirt was drenched with sweat and he was mopping his beaky, freckled nose with a towel. He dropped the towel and smiled good-naturedly at Eloise.

"Pell, this is Eloise. She's going to be doing an internship with me this season. Eloise, this is Matt Pelletier."

"I'd shake your hand, but I'm pretty sweaty," Pelletier told her. He was still a little out of breath from whatever he had been doing in the gym. "Is this your college internship or something?"

"Something like that," Eloise said with an unnecessary, nervous laugh. To his credit, Pelletier merely nodded, giving no sign that he found her response weird.

"Nice, nice," he said seriously. "So, you want a tour of the arena?"

"Oh, that'd be amazing. Thanks, Pell. Just show her around—I need to call Scott back," Krystal said, touching Pelletier's freckled bicep. She nodded to Eloise with a meaningful look. "I'll meet you on the ice later, alright?"

Eloise went to give a thumbs-up and nearly dropped her tablet.

"Whoops. I'm obviously just as coordinated as you are," she joked, righting herself, her face flushing. She was not normally a clumsy person, but she had not had anything to be nervous about in so long; she had forgotten what it felt like. Pelletier laughed and gestured for her to follow him.

"You'd be surprised. I tried surfing this summer and humiliated myself. My wife told me I looked like a dying scarecrow—totally what I was going for—and my daughter has brought it up every *single* day since then. 'Remember when Daddy looked stupid?' It's humbling."

Eloise laughed louder than she had meant to as they entered the gym, but her laugh caught in her throat when she saw it was not empty—in fact, it was filled with men.

The gym was smaller than she would have expected. There were a few cardio machines, and a long stretch of green turf beneath a bank of windows that overlooked the street. A short, lean man with a shock of spiky brown hair was sprinting on one of the machines—*Burnie*, she recalled, the one who won all those trophies—and he slowed down, peering at her with interest. Up close, his eyelashes were thick and dark, giving him a permanently intent look.

"Eloise, this is *Henry*—"

"Shut up, Pell," he interrupted, pressing a button to stop the machine and mopping his face with a towel that bore the Bruins logo. "'Sup. I'm Burnie."

"Hi, I'm Eloise," she said with a wave.

"She's interning for Krystal," Pell tried again, and Burnie cackled.

"Yikes. The fuck you do to deserve that?"

"Don't say that, the walls have ears," Pell whispered, giving a paranoid glance at the door. "Krystal always *knows*."

"I'm not afraid of Krystal."

A soft laugh caught Eloise's attention. A broad, bald Black man was stretching on the other side of the room, shaking his head. He was the starter goalie—maybe named Bouchard?

"You should be," he said with a thick French-Canadian accent. He nodded to Eloise. "Marcel," he said with a flash of very straight white teeth.

"We're the *elite* players—why are you just standing there?" Burnie exploded, startling Eloise. "Write that down. It's key intel!"

"Don't write that down," Pell counseled her. "We're just the Olds. And Burnie's the oldest. That's why he's on the old man elliptical."

"Shut your face, you freckled fuck," Burnie fired back as he resumed sprinting, "and don't come bitching to me in ten years when you're creaking around like a grandma. I protect my joints and that's why I'm gonna be skating circles around your lanky ass when I'm eighty."

*"Moving on,"* Pelletier said. "Over here in the corner we have Ilya. Ilya, say hi."

A stocky blond man sitting on a weight machine took out an earbud and waved vaguely at her.

"Ilya is not a man of many words, but still waters run deep," Pelletier confided, earning an eye-roll from Ilya, who put his earbud back in and resumed his workout.

"Pelletier—is a man—of too many words," Ilya grunted as he benched.

"I like him best when he's silent," Pell said, but both men were grinning. "Alright, the hell with these guys. Let's go to the ice and meet some of the *youths*."

"Bye, Intern," Burnie called after her, followed by Marcel hissing, "You can't call her that. She has a name, just don't ask me what it was—" and then the gym door swung shut.

There was an awkward silence; she could tell Pelletier was trying to think of something reassuring to say.

"Don't worry, I would not expect any of them to remember my name," she said as they walked.

"Bouchard—that's Marcel—is kind of aloof. I'm pretty sure he doesn't know who any of the rookies are, and by the end of the season he still won't know," Pell told her. "Lavesque insists he's just an introvert. Also today it was supposed to just be the rookies that come in, but Lavesque said he was going to be here to support them, and then everyone else felt pressured to come too, and I think Marcel didn't really want to come in because the children annoy him. Personally, I like seeing them. It's kind of like getting a new puppy, you know? They're all dumb and helpless—it's sweet."

They reached the rink and were hit by a blast of cold. Distantly, Lady Gaga's "Poker Face" was playing, barely audible over the clack of stick on puck and the hush of blades on ice. Goosebumps prickled along Eloise's skin and she clutched her notebook and tablet in front of her.

In their practice jerseys and helmets, the players were indistinguishable, save for one man at the far end of the rink who was helmetless and had a precise undercut, balancing his stick across his shoulders as he watched a rookie fire pucks into the net with rapid precision.

"And there's our captain," Pell said, nodding to the helmetless man. Her stomach dropped. *Mr. Perfect.*

(She had decided late last night, after compulsively visiting his Instagram yet again, that her fascination lay in the fact that she had nothing in common with him. With his composure and his popularity and his easy grace, he was like a different species to her. She could identify with most people but she could find nothing in him, and she kept looking at his Instagram in the hopes of finding some way in.)

From here, it looked like the rookie was Kyle Hearst—her target—but she couldn't be sure.

"I'm guessing you're here to meet Lavesque? You don't have to be nervous, he's really easy to talk to," Pell reassured her now, drawing Eloise out of her rumination and reminding her of her mission.

"I'm not here to meet him, actually." Eloise and Pell walked to the edge of the rink. "I was hoping to profile one of the rookies to start."

Pell brightened.

"That's a really good idea," he said warmly. "Anyone in mind? Travis is always happy to talk," he reflected, "and he's fun, too. You'll like him. He just came out openly, like to the NHL, and he did it in a really cool way. The social media team made a whole thing of it during Pride month, and it was really nice."

"I'd definitely love to talk to him, but I thought I might start with someone named"—she halted, pretending to consult her notes—"Kyle? Krystal mentioned he was brand new and that he's from Boston."

"Oh, yeah, Hearst is the freshest blood," Pell agreed. He nodded to the rink. "He's the one with Lavesque. Come on, I'll introduce you." He noticed her hesitation. "Don't worry, it's just the rookie skate. No one will be bothered if you're on the ice."

Pelletier hopped onto the ice and turned back to help her. The Cons—not a shoe she typically wore—provided no traction on the ice, so Eloise shuffled along, highly aware of the players who stopped to stare at her. Now she wished she had worn a less distinctive disguise, because she looked completely out of place. Pell waved at a red-faced man in a hat and whistle that she assumed was one of the coaches; if she remembered correctly he was named something like Duffy. He frowned at Eloise and her maxi skirt before losing interest.

"Yo, Lavy!" Pell called when they reached the other end of the rink. Lavesque still had the stick balanced casually across his shoulders, and was gliding absently around Kyle. He looked up at their approach and smiled. "This is Eloise, Krystal's new intern."

Just as her eyes met his striking slate ones, her skirt caught under her shoe and she slipped with a yelp.

"Whoa—" Lavesque caught her tablet before she could drop it, and handed it back to her after she had caught herself.

"Thanks!" Eloise said in a strangled voice, straightening her skirt and tucking the tablet under her arm.

Up close and in person Jacques Lavesque seemed more human than he had online: he had a few faint scars marking his skin, little fingernail-sized nicks, and a red line on his cheek where presumably something had scratched him earlier. The points of a tattoo that must have stretched across his upper back peeked out of the edge of his practice jersey, and the ink looked faded, tired. His smile was more blazing in person, though, all the more so because it was so directly aimed at her.

"No idea why you haven't made maxi skirts a standard part of the uniform yet—they're obviously great on the ice," Eloise joked nervously. He laughed as though it had been clever.

"Next season, probably," Lavesque said with a grin. "You know, I think Pell would look very nice in one. And yours is even yellow, like the Bruins yellow. I would expect nothing less of Krystal's intern."

Behind him, Kyle Hearst was peering at her and she caught his eye.

"She wants to profile Kyle," Pell explained to Lavesque. "You guys got it from here?"

"Absolutely, and thank you," Eloise said. "I really appreciate you showing me around."

"No problem. All I ask is that you mention I'm extremely hand-some and funny when you profile me," Pell said, and then with a self-deprecating laugh and a wave, he turned and walked over to the group of rookie players, leaving Eloise with Lavesque and Kyle.

"Keep going," Lavesque told Kyle with a nod. Kyle wordlessly turned back to the pucks scattered in front of him.

Lavesque was a head taller than her, so Eloise had to crane her neck to meet his gaze. He smiled at her again. "So you are profiling the rookies?"

His accent was harsher and more staccato than she had expected; she could hear the effort and care with which he chose his words and was reminded that this was his second language. The full force of his attention upon her was blinding; she almost wanted to squint.

"I—yeah, well," she tried with an unnecessary shrug, "enough's been written about you guys at this point, right? You, and Burnap, and all..."

"Very true," Lavesque agreed. He touched her arm lightly, fingertips brushing her bare skin, and she was quick to pull away. Physical contact was not an experience she had very much these days, and the casual touch was startling, flustering her more than she would have liked. "Come on, let's move to the edge of the ice," he said, nodding toward the boards, glancing down when she pulled her arm away. "I think Krystal will kill me if her intern gets hit with a puck on her first day, and Connor is not too precise when he shoots."

She shuffled alongside him with care as he glided to the edge of the rink, gesturing over his shoulder for Kyle to continue what he was doing. They reached the boards and leaned against them.

"You know, you should talk to Travis," Lavesque said, pointing to one of the players on the ice, who was—for whatever reason—skating in circles around another player and making loud cooing noises, like a pigeon. The other player looked torn between annoyance and entertainment, and Lavesque tried not to laugh. "He just—"

"Came out, right? Pelletier mentioned," Eloise said. "It's really brave of Travis to do that."

"You can just call him Pell, you're on the team now," Lavesque coached her with a wave of his hand. "And it *was* brave. He has a really interesting perspective on the sport, and he is very easy to talk to. You should also interview Connor," he added, pointing to the player that Travis was circling.

"I would love to talk to them too," Eloise said as graciously as she could, "but I have to admit I'm most curious about Kyle Hearst."

"You are from Boston?" Lavesque guessed, studying her. "You sound a bit like it. Not like Kyle, he says things like *summah*, and *packie*, and—"

"Oh my god." Eloise exploded with laughter, forgetting her nervousness. "That might be the worst Boston accent I have ever heard."

Lavesque flushed even as he laughed with her. She felt like she had found the first crack—but she wondered if it was a vulnerability he had wanted her to find, drawing her attention to it purposefully. *Manipulative*, she thought as their eyes met again. *He knows how to draw people in.*

"How long have you even lived in Boston?"

"Only eighteen years," he conceded with a grin, still pink, "but I did my best, alright? I love when Kyle's accent comes out," he added. "I love the Boston accent so much. It never gets old to me."

"So he's the only local on the team?" Eloise guessed, glancing back at Kyle, who had finished shooting all the pucks and was idly circling on the ice, watching Travis and Connor as they went through a drill.

"Well, Boston is home to all of us, but yes, the rest of us are from somewhere else. Burnie and Pell and I are all from Canada, obviously, and Ilya and Sekelsky are from Russia, and of course, Novak is Czech, and I think Connor is from Delaware or Maryland," he added with an uncertain frown, counting off on his fingers.

Was he *trying* to pull her attention away from Kyle?

"Kyle must feel a lot of pride to be playing for the Bruins," she tested, watching Lavesque. "Being *from* Boston, I mean."

"We all are. Boston is everything—it is legacy, and tradition," he said passionately. "It is a huge honor to any player—"

"But especially to Kyle, right? I would love to hear *his* take on it," she insisted. She noticed now that his slate-blue eyes had little flecks of brown, if you looked closely enough. Another tiny little flaw, another tiny hint at his humanity. Now she realized they had been studying each other, his gaze lingering on her glasses, and she looked away.

"Good luck. He is not much of a talker," Lavesque said with an innocent shrug. "The rest of us can't shut up, so it is probably for the best that we have a quiet guy or two," he added ruefully. "But I bet you probably have, I don't know, techniques or something to get us to talk when we are difficult. You probably went to school for this, right?" He put his weight on his stick, tilting his head as he looked down at her.

"I didn't, which is why this internship matters so much to me." He seemed to like taking care of people, so she decided to put that to the test. "Krystal seems like a harsh grader, so to speak, and I really want to do well. She's so connected, and so influential."

Lavesque nodded seriously.

"She is very impressive," he agreed. "I would be intimidated too. I'm curious about why you're doing it. I mean," he added quickly, looking embarrassed, "that came out wrong. I meant, I am wondering what draws you to public relations, and social media, and all of this."

She couldn't tell if it was an act or not. He was looking at her like he wanted to know. She could not remember the last time someone had asked her a question about herself and had sincerely wanted to know the answer. *Definitely cheated*, she decided, taking in those flecks of brown in his eyes.

"I—" Eloise hesitated. The best lies had a grain of truth in them, and she wanted to move off this topic and get back to Kyle. "I love people-watching," she admitted at last, "and I love people. I love understanding them, and I love finding out the truth about them—the stuff you don't see immediately."

It was true enough, and whenever she had enough to drink and enough of her natural cynicism melted away, she could admit it was a large part of what had lured her to private investigative work in the first place.

Lavesque nodded, looking thoughtful.

"I can see that," he said seriously. "I am the same way. So your first project is to show people who the younger, less-known players are?"

"Exactly. So if you love people—you've already told me things you like about the other rookies—" she tried, but stopped when a massive, tall figure in a sloppy grey hoodie and shorts stepped onto the ice, followed by a number of men in suits, making everyone on the ice halt in their tracks.

Lavesque did not turn right away, and she glimpsed the way his smile dropped—just for the briefest instant—before he pulled himself together again (she saw, too, the instant he rearranged his features) and glanced over his shoulder.

Eloise had read enough about the Bruins, looked through enough pictures, to identify this man on sight—and of course, Krystal had foreshadowed it.

There was Andrei Koslov, standing at the edge of the rink.

# Chapter Four

"That's Andrei Koslov," Eloise said, watching Lavesque closely, but after that brief reveal of his true feelings, he was not giving anything else away. Koslov was looking in their direction, between Lavesque and Eloise, but they were too far from him for Eloise to interpret his expression.

"That is him," Lavesque said simply. They watched Coach Duffy skate over to Koslov and the men in suits—head office, she guessed—leaving the other players to stare.

Kyle had glided over to them and wrenched off his helmet, revealing reddish-brown waves that were flattened to his skin with sweat, as well as a tattoo on his neck that looked like a crude drawing of a fork. He glanced at Eloise again, giving her a quick once-over—not like he was checking her out, but like he was scanning her—before turning his attention to Lavesque.

"Koslov?" Kyle asked in a low voice, bumping into him a little. He said it like *Kazlav*; Lavesque had not been kidding about his accent.

Lavesque's face gave away *nothing*. He seemed, if anything, pleasantly indifferent—but Eloise knew what she had seen in that brief glimpse. He was anything but indifferent about this, and she had found another crack in the wall; this time, she guessed, one he had not wanted her to find.

"Yes, that is him. He is joining the team for this season. He was signing the contract today." Lavesque looked back at Koslov and the others, but they were already leaving the rink. "I'm sure you'll have a chance to meet him today at some point."

Kyle watched Andrei Koslov go.

"In a *hoodie*? Seriously, dude?" he asked at last. "You sign a contract for ten million fucking dollars, and you do it in a hoodie?"

Lavesque laughed easily.

"I had to bribe you to take off the Red Sox hat for yours," he reminded him. He rapped Kyle's leg with his stick. "Come on, back to work."

"I got through all the pucks," Kyle complained. Eloise was trying to commit his fork tattoo to memory without getting caught staring, but he looked at her out of the corner of his eye self-consciously again, forcing her to look away.

"Maybe now would be a good time to—" Eloise began, but they were interrupted by the coach returning to the ice and signaling for Kyle to join the other players.

Now she and Lavesque were alone once more.

"How do you feel about Koslov returning?" Eloise asked, just to break the silence. She had read enough to know that Lavesque and Koslov had once upon a time been like brothers, that once upon a time it had been impossible to speak of one without the other—but notably they were not anymore, and had not even acknowledged each other's existence in the Stanley Cup playoffs last season. It sounded like Koslov had been more or less forced out of the Bruins organization last time. There were dozens of think-pieces online about it, but none that explained why Koslov had left. Eloise assumed it had something to do with the racism or homophobia that Hollis had referenced, but it was hard—and disappointing—to imagine a team captain liking and befriending a man like Koslov.

"It is the right choice for Boston," Lavesque said. "Andrei is a great winger, and he brings a lot of skills to the team that we are frankly missing right now. He contributes significantly no matter where he is and we are lucky to have him back." The line was canned even if he sounded perfectly genuine, but after that look on his face, Eloise knew this was a blatant, bare-faced lie—a *no comment* if she had ever seen one.

"I heard he's an asshole," she tossed out experimentally, watching him, but again he was a wall and this time the crack was not exposed. He smiled.

"He is a professional athlete," Lavesque said graciously, another skilled evasion. "But maybe you can reveal something about him that the rest of the world has not seen yet," he added, fidgeting with his stick. When he looked down, the collar of his practice jersey shifted, revealing more of his tattoo—it looked like the points of a crown—and she flushed when he looked up, catching her staring. Embarrassment and awkwardness lingered. She toyed with acknowledging it, but decided against it.

"I should go. It looks like you guys are starting to actually practice," Eloise said hastily, gesturing at the rookies and Coach Duffy. They both laughed, then looked away.

"You can watch the practice, if you want," Lavesque said quickly, almost apologetically, pointing to the yellow stadium seats, where a few people were sitting in clumps, drinking sodas and watching or texting. "We usually have at least a few people watching."

Right, because she totally wanted to reinforce the incorrect notion that she wanted to stare at him and his tattoo some more. Eloise dismissed it with a hasty wave.

"Don't worry about it. I'd better find Krystal. Thank you, by the way, for taking the time to chat."

"No, thank you, it was interesting and I am looking forward to talking to you more," he said so smoothly, so genuinely, but the way his face had looked when Andrei Koslov had stepped onto the ice was imprinted in her mind's eye now. *He hates him*, she realized.

"Yeah, me too," she said awkwardly. "Anyway. Um. See you."

"Yes, see you," he said, and then he was skating over to center ice and she was picking her way back to the edge of the rink, lost in her own embarrassment and defensiveness.

God. Why did she have to look at his stupid tattoo like that? It had made it weird; it had cast the conversation in a light that was not true. He was probably used to female attention—she had seen plenty of thirst threads on Reddit and Twitter in her research on the Bruins, and Lavesque was a *very* frequent focus—and he probably thought she was just another thirsty fan, daydreaming about catching his attention, even though he was not personally her type and she was not someone who lusted after athletes or celebrities, especially ones who had probably cheated on their wives, and *ugh*—

She rounded the corner into the tunnel and smacked into grey jersey, dropping her tablet—she had the stray thought that this might finally be its death—and losing her glasses in the process. She stumbled backwards in shock, narrowly avoiding stepping on the fake glasses.

Andrei Koslov—broad-shouldered and black-haired and almost ugly—was looking down at her impassively.

"Um, sorry. Let me just—" She crouched down, mustard skirt billowing around her like a mushroom, as she scrambled to snatch up her tablet and glasses. Koslov had put on ice skates—she supposed that was why the floor was rubbery, to manage players walking around with blades strapped to their feet. "Sorry, I apparently am a disaster today and probably should have been paying attention to where I was going."

"Probably."

His voice was softer than she would have guessed, and more melodic. He probably had a decent singing voice but he didn't look like a man who would ever voluntarily sing. She looked up—and up, and up. She crouched there transfixed, mostly with an animal confusion. It was like she had encountered a panther in a grocery store. He was just so *big*.

"Yes, well, live and learn, I guess, though at thirty-three it seems a little bit late to learn to look both ways before crossing," Eloise rambled, trying to recover as she clumsily rose from her crouch. God, but she was rusty at human interaction. It had been so long since she had last interacted with people; for months and months she had really only viewed life through the lens of a camera or the screen of a laptop, and clearly she had only gotten weirder.

Koslov made no move to help her. He simply regarded her as she got to her feet, as though she were an amusement put before him and he couldn't decide if she was funny or not. It might have been a look of interest or embarrassment or anything else, but his features were too hard to read. He had none of Lavesque's subtle animation—his nose and jaw might as well have been carved from stone, like he was a rough draft of a statue and his features needed refining, and the dark circles beneath his eyes gave him the sickly look of an invalid who had not moved much. *Alcoholic*, she remembered, though according to Krystal he was in recovery.

"You are Taylor's intern," he observed. The only part of him that had any liveliness or animation was his eyes, a light, leonine brown that was almost hazel. He watched her awkwardly put on her fake glasses again. It took her a second to realize he was talking about Krystal. *Of course, he would know her as well as the other players do.*

"That's me. I'm going to profile the rookies first—stuff like their hobbies, why they got into hockey, that kind of thing—and then later I'll interview the more seasoned players."

She flashed a grin, feeling like she was some absurd Vaudeville entertainer with a cane and top hat, wheeling around on a stage before him. "So, can I count on you for an interview at some point?"

*Jesus.* Why did she say that? She sounded ridiculous. Koslov considered his words.

"Maybe. If I feel like it. If you have interesting questions."

She opened her mouth, not quite sure what was going to come out of it, but Krystal and the coach came around the corner. Krystal's eyes subtly widened as she approached.

"There you are! Coach is going to pull together the players for a huddle so we should skedaddle," Krystal explained hastily, glancing at Andrei. "Let's get coffee."

Before Eloise could say anything, Krystal's hand had closed around her arm and she was frog-marching her down the hall, half-dragging her away from Andrei Koslov.

·⁾⁾●⁽⁽·

"He calls you Taylor," Eloise remarked.

They had decided on Kohi Coffee, a clattery white-tiled coffee shop that was clean and close to the ice arena. They faced each other at a long bleached-wood table, with an untouched pastry apiece. Eloise was dying to wolf hers down—she had become very aware of food—but Krystal had not taken a bite yet and it seemed rude.

The woman was distracted, glancing around and checking the screen of her Apple Watch compulsively, like she was on the run from something.

"What? Oh," Krystal said vaguely, "Andrei has always hated me and wants to make it *so* clear that he doesn't respect me like the rest of the guys do." She checked the screen of her watch again. "Sorry, I'm a mess. We released the official statement that Andrei signed for a year," Krystal explained. "I need to get a grip and just *stop* obsessing."

She ripped off her watch to bury it in her fine leather tote.

"Does that bother you?" Eloise tried not to think too hard about the delicious-looking scone before her. "Him not respecting you, I mean."

"Not anymore. I got over Andrei years ago, but it did take a while," she said. "We could have had it all, you know? He's magnetic. Big Leo energy. He's fascinating to look at. He's *massively* talented, and he's really fun to watch on the ice... and he's funny, too, when he feels like it. He could've done incredible things for our brand, especially in counterpoint to Lavy's friendly charisma. But at heart he is a dick. He pretends he can't speak English whenever the media ask him questions that he doesn't like, he shows up late—or not at all—to media engagements, likes to mess with the guys who seem insecure... Whatever."

Krystal glanced at her bag, then shuddered again. "Whatever!" she repeated disgustedly, throwing up her hands before massaging her eyes. "I have had enough Andrei Koslov to last me a lifetime and the season hasn't even started."

"Well." Eloise toyed with the sleeve on her coffee cup, sensing that they needed to change the subject. "I tried to talk to Kyle, but Lavesque would not let me near him."

That did the trick. Krystal dropped her hands from her eyes, regarding Eloise with a shrewd look that Eloise did not like.

"I saw you two talking," she said slowly. "Looked cozy."

"He's very friendly and really kind," Eloise said evasively, noncommittally, taking a page out of Lavesque's book as she watched Krystal finally break off a piece of scone, "but also, he was definitely guarding Kyle. Did you tell him about me?"

"No," she said simply. "He'd be so disappointed in me."

"I mean... would it be that bad?" Eloise wondered. Krystal's brows shot up.

"Yes. That man has principles, and woe betide the person who violates them. Seriously. Plus he just seems on the edge of something lately and I'm not giving him any excuses to do something stupid."

"What do you mean?"

Krystal's attention was slipping back to the watch in her bag, but she forced it back to Eloise.

"He hasn't *said* anything, but something's different about him this season. He's not the same old Lavy that he's always been. And this is the last year of his contract. Of course he wouldn't retire, there's no reason to and he's as healthy as ever, but *something* is off about him."

"Could it be because he's in the middle of what's probably a devastating separation?" Eloise pointed out. Krystal waved her hand.

"He's had trouble with Rachel before, and I wouldn't have known except she told me about it," she said. "I am not taking this too seriously; he committed to her and there's no way he'll actually break that commitment."

"She told you? You must be close."

Krystal took a long swig of her coffee, rolling her eyes.

"No, that girl just talks too much when she's drunk," she said disgustedly. "Gets all sloppy and weepy. Suddenly wants to be Best Girlfriends Forever!" She put on a high-pitched valley girl voice before rolling her eyes again. "Clinging to you in the bathroom, telling you that you're *like, actually so pretty*, that kind of thing."

Eloise tried not to laugh as she pictured a supremely unmoved Krystal trying to break free of the drunken embrace of a pretty brunette.

"She's so well-behaved most of the time, like she's the Kate Middleton of Boston, and then you get enough white wine in her and it all comes out. You wouldn't know it because normally she's so pulled together, and she's also damn successful. But underneath it all? That girl is a mess."

Krystal took another delicate bite of her scone. "Believe me, Lavy doesn't let it show when he's going through it with her. Something is different."

"So we won't tell him," Eloise summarized. She massaged her temple. "Well, I need access to Kyle without Lavesque there to stop me. I can't just tail him everywhere he goes, because I can't afford to," she admitted.

Krystal looked thoughtful as she chewed. "I'll set up interviews with you and all the rookies," she decided. "Casual ones so they're not on a schedule. We'll shuffle him in there."

"Alright." Eloise nodded to Krystal's bag. "Do you want to take a minute and check your social media?" she teased, and Krystal snatched her phone out of her bag. Eloise watched the emotions on Krystal's face as she scanned her alerts, scrolling and scrolling and scrolling.

"Well? Is Boston furious or delighted to have Koslov back?"

"Both." Krystal shrugged, but her movements were tight and stilted. "Mostly furious."

She laughed at something on her screen. "And Burnie wants to know if he officially has to invite Andrei to the pre-season party he and Steph are throwing. Yes, Burnie," Krystal said as she typed, "of *course* you have to invite him. Not that Andrei will go. He already stopped going a few years before he left the team. He never does anything for anyone else."

She set down her phone. "Alright. Let me arrange some interviews. I'll try to work it out so that it doesn't take up all of your time."

The two women finished their food, making idle chitchat for a few minutes, and then ventured back into the sunny humidity.

"Good luck," Eloise said as they stood on the sidewalk. Krystal laughed.

"The worst is done," she said with a wave of her hand. "I'm going to have an early glass of wine tonight, put the phone on airplane mode, order sushi, and rewatch the first season of *Scandal*."

"That sounds perfect," Eloise said with perhaps a little too much longing. She couldn't remember the last time she had done something so decadent.

Just as they were each raising their hands to wave, Eloise paused. "Oh, wait. One question. Do you know what the tattoo is that Kyle has behind his ear?"

Krystal frowned. "No, I never noticed he even had one," she admitted. "All the guys have tattoos, except Pell and Andrei—Lavy's got two full sleeves and a bunch on his back and legs. I've stopped paying attention. I can ask?" she offered, looking skeptical.

"No need—I can ask when I interview him." She waved now. "Thanks again."

On the train back, Eloise felt strangely drained yet anxious. When she tried to recollect what had happened that morning, it was like digging blindly through a child's toy chest: all color and chaotic edges and unfamiliar shapes.

Hollis had texted her about Andrei Koslov signing with the Bruins again, and Lily had texted to ask how her 'disguise' had gone over, but Eloise didn't feel like talking to anyone. She put her phone on 'do not disturb' and let herself sway with the train, her headphones blasting heavy metal.

Why was Jacques Lavesque *so* protective of Kyle Hearst? Was it the same reason that Krystal wanted Eloise to look into him? Or was Lavesque like that with all of the rookies? And why had he looked like *that* when he had seen Andrei Koslov step onto the ice? Were the rumors about Koslov true, or had she over-interpreted a stray look that meant nothing?

(And how had he betrayed *none* of the stress going on in his personal life?)

She didn't want to let herself get stuck on Lavesque, so she unlocked her phone screen and, thinking of Kyle's tattoo she had glimpsed, typed in 'fork tattoo' in Google Images. Predictably, she saw plenty of detailed tattoos of actual forks, but none that looked like what she had spied behind Kyle's ear just before his hair had covered it. There had been something eerie about it, something pagan and strange.

*Pagan tattoos*, she tried, but she found nothing that resembled the tattoo.

Maybe it was nothing. *Probably* it was nothing. Eloise thought of the glimpse of ink on Jacques Lavesque's neck, peeking out from his jersey, and for some reason her face felt hot and she locked her phone screen again, cringing in her seat.

*So embarrassing*, she thought, though she could not specify why she was so embarrassed.

# Chapter Five

Sunday rolled around all too soon, and with it came the prospect of a Visit. Eloise awoke with a knot in her stomach, but that might have simply been hunger.

Her laptop and phone were both buried in her blankets around her; she had been up late researching the Bruins, scrolling through Kyle Hearst's Instagram and, when she needed a break, think-pieces on Andrei Koslov's return to Boston, and had fallen asleep at her laptop. She fumbled for her phone, dismissed the low-battery warning, and scrolled through a half-dozen texts from Hollis.

**Hollis [7:36am]:** ur doing the visit today right

**Hollis [7:36am]:** u said u would

**Hollis [7:37am]:** u CANNOT back out of this ok

**Hollis [7:37am]:** its YOUR turn

**Hollis [7:52am]:** i always do them and u said u would and u keep making excuses

Eloise groaned and closed her eyes as she fell back into her pillows. Hollis was always transactional about duties and chores; when they were teenagers, he had drawn up a chore chart that hung on the refrigerator, and absolutely lost it if she did not do precisely her share.

**Eloise [8:12am]**: yes I am doing it

**Eloise [8:12am]**: psycho

She plugged her phone in, disentangled herself from her blanket, and searched her cabinets for something that could count as breakfast, but pickings were slim.

What she wanted more than anything was to walk to a Pret a Manger and devour a scone and an iced coffee. She used to do that all the time. It had always been a little indulgence, but it hadn't murdered her bank account and she had not thought of it as anything but a treat to shore her up for another boring week to come. She stirred her expired oatmeal and tried not to think about scones and iced coffees and whether she had ruined her own life.

She ate her oatmeal and showered, feeling defensive and argumentative. Something about Hollis's texts niggled her in a way that had her slamming doors and running over her older brother's faults in her head. Eloise yanked appropriate clothes out of her closet, but all of her 'appropriate' clothes were pieces that she used for her disguises, and when she put them on she felt like she was playing a part once again—the part of a daughter who had her shit together; a part that she could not begin to truly embody, not when her bank account looked like that.

The journey to her childhood home in Chestnut Hill that was half an hour by car was nearly two hours via public transportation, and she was uncharacteristically angry the whole time. The instant oatmeal—expired, but could oatmeal expire?—was sitting funny in her stomach (perhaps that was her answer) and she looked repeatedly at Hollis's texts, composing scathing replies in her head that she would never type.

By the time she reached Boston College it was nearly eleven. It was a glorious day—it was finally less humid and the season was turning—but her old stomping grounds felt mocking in all their glory: the Tudor houses, the lush lawns, the shiny cars, the wide streets. None of it had ever belonged to her, and it had certainly never wanted her to belong to it. Even before she had bleached her hair and rejected the nine-to-five path, Eloise had not fit in here. They had lived in a cozy twin, purchased with her mother's money, and when her mother left, the money had too. It had nearly killed her father to finish paying for that house, and now that he had paid it off, there was no money left for him to leave it.

And as she approached the twin, you could tell. Hollis did his best to mow the lawn and weed the garden, but there was a pervasive shabbiness that couldn't be masked by the wreath from Target that Lily had hung on the door, or the freshly-mown grass. The house needed work that no one could afford to do, and the car that sat parked in front was a little too old to really fit in with the rest of the street.

Eloise stopped halfway down the block, regarding her childhood home. Her father was in that house, sitting alone in front of the television, waiting for a game to start, in the sitting room that looked exactly the same as it had in the nineties—albeit faded, shabby, lonely.

(This was the danger of loving too much, as her father had. Love was a crypt; love was a black hole out of which nothing could return, least of all yourself; love was a cup from which she would not drink.)

She just had to go in and spend some time with her father. That was all there was to it!

*its YOUR turn*

She glimpsed her reflection in one of the nearby shiny cars and then, blood pounding in her ears and eyes burning, she turned and began marching back toward Boston College station, breathing in heavily through her nose, but the ride back to Boston brought no relief because she was hungry, and there was no food left in her cabinets, and she had no money to buy food, and there was no one she could ask for help.

*Maybe it is time to give this up*, she thought, and Boston turned blurry with her tears.

·☽☾●☾☾·

Rachel and the boys were on Nantucket for the weekend, so Jacques could have gone home without having to encounter his wife at all. He wanted nothing more than to stay in his own bed, to shower in his own shower, to live out of a closet rather than a suitcase.

He even considered doing it, because he was so tired of that hotel smell, tired of pillows that weren't right, tired of key cards and suitcases and walking past the bar, with its champagne and chandeliers, each night.

But when he imagined alighting the front steps and passing the potted plants that Rachel had set on each step, when he imagined unlocking the door and seeing *that* wreath, a lump rose in his throat. He could not stand the thought of it.

So instead he found himself lying in bed in the hotel on top of the coverlet, listlessly reviewing the divorce papers that his new lawyer (a textbook 'Masshole' even if he had custom suits and a Harvard education, though Jacques liked him even more for that) had drawn up.

*An expensive tantrum*, his mother had called it when he had finally told her about the separation over the phone last week, in her hoarse French croak. He had known she was smoking, though he could not see her. She was in her mid-sixties but she sounded like she was in her nineties.

*Not like you, is it?* she had mused, and then added, *But maybe it is. We both know you've never been able to forgive people.*

He knew she was missing a key piece of information that might have equipped her with more sympathy—she did not even know why he and Rachel had separated—but on the other hand, he couldn't be certain that having all of the information would make his mother more generous toward him.

Jacques closed his eyes and let the packet of papers from Anthony rest on his chest, then had a flashback to how he'd held Peter, then Luke, on his chest when they were infants, relishing their weight on him, their silky-soft heads grazing his chin. He cast the packet beside him on the hotel bed.

Maybe it *was* just a tantrum. Rachel's parents thought of it that way. Jeff had invited him out for golf a few days ago, and luckily Jacques had been genuinely busy and unable to join. He knew that around the seventh hole, Jeff would have slyly broached the subject. *So, you and Rachel...* By the thirteenth hole, Jeff would be musing on marriage—he might share some bullshit anecdote about him and Milly—and then they would get a beer. Just as they were parting, Jeff would take him by the arm, flash his teeth, and remind him that Rachel was still his 'little girl.'

The invitation to play golf had inspired both anger and guilt in Jacques and he was grateful that the invitation had come over text. It had given him time to stifle his feelings and politely decline with an honest explanation. Jeff had sent a *no worries* back, but Jacques could picture Jeff and Milly analyzing it over wine in their gleaming kitchen, reasoning (like everyone else) that once Jacques cooled off, this would just be an embarrassing and uncomfortable memory. Rachel seemed to think so, too. Even Krystal was barely taking it seriously.

Jacques had been on the verge of telling Burnie a few times, but he couldn't face Burnie's reaction, which would be along the lines of 'good fucking riddance, divorce her ass' with a little more profanity sprinkled in. Burnie had always disliked Rachel. He had agreed to be best man at their wedding—Jacques had known better than to ask Andrei, even though it should have been him—but had made it clear that he thought Jacques was making a mistake. Jacques was afraid that if he told Burnie, he'd end up drunk and savagely disparaging Rachel (he was *so* angry) and when he went back to Rachel—because that was the likeliest outcome; because that was the *right* outcome—his longstanding friendship with Burnie would be fractured.

Pell, on the other hand, would be gracious and kind, and would listen empathetically. The idea of all that kindness frustrated him. Jacques wanted someone to fight with him, to throw fragile things at him; he wanted someone to yell at him all of the accusations that were bouncing around in his head so that he might fight back against those accusations with substance and ferocity. He did not want to be treated with kid gloves; he wanted bloody battle.

His phone started pulsing; when he lifted to check the screen, a picture of Krystal in her massive Prada sunglasses, looking furious, greeted him. In spite of his mood he laughed and answered. "Hello?"

"You sound alone. Are you alone?" she asked. "Why are you alone?"

He could hear a football game on in the background—Krystal's true passion. She had never intended to work in the NHL, had always aimed for the NFL, and he knew it was a source of pain for her as she had always found hockey to be a silly sport in comparison. Her office was plastered with Patriots paraphernalia, and two years ago Pell had given her a picture of a sweaty Tom Brady in a heart-shaped frame. (After Brady had been traded, Burnie had drawn X's over Brady's eyes on the glass in black permanent marker, as well as devil horns and buck teeth.)

"Yes, I'm alone."

"Missing your boys, aren't you?"

As soon as she said it, he fixed his gaze on a point on the ceiling.

"Look, I wanted to call because it sounds like you've got a problem with my intern."

"Intern? You mean Eloise?" Jacques sat up, massaging his neck. "I have no problem with her. What do you mean?"

"She said you wouldn't let her near Hearst." He could hear Krystal uncapping a beer. "And she had a great idea to interview all the rookies and do a thing with them. She's new to this, and she really needs the experience, alright? So maybe you could back off a little? I promise she's nice."

"Kyle is not ready for *any* interviews, even with our own people. He needs a lot more practice, and you know that," he pointed out, going to the windows to open the blinds. Brilliant late-September sunlight flooded the stuffy hotel room, casting his open suitcase and messy desk in high relief. He normally was not messy; he could still remember sharing hotels with Andrei and the two of them laughing at how Jacques's half of the room always looked like it had just been cleaned, possessions arranged with pride, and Andrei's always looked like a pigsty.

*I want to go home.* He wanted to close the blinds. *But I can't go home.* He willed himself to not close the blinds and sink back into silent anger. *But I should just go home.* "I didn't know you were taking on interns. Aren't you too busy? Why not have Lori or someone else manage her?"

"Yeah, doing someone a favor. Long story," Krystal explained without really explaining. "So she's going to be around for a while. She's not out to get anyone. I promise."

"She does not seem like your type," Jacques said, watching the traffic that wreathed Copley Square. A bunch of dressed-up girls were on the Square, taking turns to photograph each one as they posed. He thought of Eloise, with her long skirt and her fake glasses that looked like a cheap disguise. *Pretty eyes,* he had noticed in the moment, but then he had been distracted, thrown by her laser-like interest in Kyle, and then the way she had looked at him—again, laser-like—when Andrei had come onto the ice.

Krystal laughed.

"Actually, you know what? I really like her," Krystal said with mirth. "You'll like her too, once you get to know her. She wasn't even cowed by Andrei when she ran into him, which is unusual for women.

She's smart, and kind of unexpectedly spunky? She keeps surprising me."

Jacques resisted the urge to probe; he was not entirely sure where the curiosity was coming from.

"Anyway, I've got a preseason game to watch. You should go out tonight, alright? Don't go getting weird on me."

Jacques laughed, but it was forced. "Alright, I promise," he lied, and they hung up.

He went to the bed and picked up the divorce papers that he'd had Anthony draw up. He thought of the sleeping weight of Peter and Luke on his chest, he thought of moving the palm of his hand over their soft downy heads.

*An expensive tantrum*, he told himself. He shoved the papers in the shallow desk drawer.

# Chapter Six

Already the weather had turned since the last time Eloise had gotten off the train at Boston Landing, and tart, golden September had somehow emerged from August's ripe, over-sweet humidity.

September was when everyone fell in love with Boston, and every year Eloise took pleasure in watching the city come back from summer. It was easy to be on the T again, and each train was packed with professionals back from their holidays and clad in new suiting; everyone was planning their cookouts in their Patriots jerseys; suddenly there were ads for Salem everywhere, promising witchcraft and mystery just beyond the brick and saltwater brine of the city's limits.

But this time none of it mattered. Eloise took in these signs of Boston returning to life and resented them. She had been applying to jobs—all of them, haphazardly and capriciously—in between researching Kyle Hearst, mapping out the places he frequented and the people he spoke to, all the while knowing that she should have given up on this case weeks ago.

She had even toyed with just ghosting Krystal, until the woman had called her to tell her she could come in today, all breezy plans and blunt questions, and Eloise had been unable to admit that it was time to give up on her dream. Now she was here, walking past the New Balance shop and the Kohi Coffee just like she had so recently, this time knowing that it was all ending.

Krystal had instructed her to come to the rink so she could interview the rookies in the bleachers during practice, and Eloise had agreed, resolving that she would interview Kyle, report to Krystal that there was nothing deeper to learn about him, and then go back to dealing with her life—one job application at a time.

Her exit strategy was in place—such a familiar thought; she had run from schools and relationships and friendships and jobs since she could walk—but it felt like surrender rather than freedom, grief instead of relief. She had not even bothered with one of her disguises, instead choosing clothing at random, and had left the fake glasses at home. There was no point.

She was just now realizing how much this meant to her, but no one knew that she had dreamed of this and no one knew how much it meant to her, so she had no one to tell that it was ending. She used to ride her bicycle late at night past innumerable houses and apartments, glimpsing the inside of each one and thinking that there were stories within each one that might never be told. She always thought it should be someone's responsibility to at least know each story even if they never told it. Now she was one of those untold stories, a lone figure at a kitchen table underneath a bald light.

None of the players had arrived yet for practice but various staffers in Bruins gear were buzzing along the halls, too busy to pay any attention to her, and she was glad for it. Eloise made her way toward the ice, prepared to huddle in a seat and wait.

The rink was empty, save for a lone figure doing swift laps with an effortlessness that made Eloise stop at the boards and stare. A practice net was askew at one end; a little pile of pucks had been arranged at center ice, waiting to be hit. The sunlight streamed in from the wall of windows that overlooked the ice, casting gold panels that the skater wove in and out of absently—the way Eloise might bounce her leg at her laptop while she worked.

Eloise stared. She had never seen anyone move so beautifully, so effortlessly. Her skin prickled with goosebumps at the sight, at the awareness of being near talent that she would never possess. He sped up into something like a run, just for the hell of it, and then slowed into an easy glide, so obviously lost in thought.

And as the skater turned at the other end, she realized it was Jacques Lavesque. He had not spotted her yet; he wore a look of intense rumination, brows knit together. He lightly hit a few pucks into the net, but this was as absent as his skating. The fiery precision with which he hit the pucks did not matter to him at all.

She wondered if he had come here early to think; she wondered if his marriage was ending or if he and his wife had decided to reconcile. When she had met him last she had gotten no hint of any personal distress at all, but today his walls were not up yet and even if his movements were lovely—

His mouth twisted mutinously, a sudden burst of feeling, and then he abruptly fired a puck so hard at the boards that it made her jolt and gasp. At the noise he turned and saw her before she could slip away and give him his privacy. She gave a sheepish wave—one that she hoped read as *don't worry, just passing through*—but he glided over to her anyway.

"Eloise," he called with an apologetic laugh as he reached the boards, bumping against them lightly. He looked softer today: his stubble was growing in, softening his jaw, and the practice jersey he was wearing was wrinkled; it strained at his shoulders like it needed to be tugged straight, like he had pulled it on in a hurry.

The awkwardness of their last encounter stood between them like the boards—low enough to see over, tall enough to be in view.

"Krystal asked me to come early," Eloise explained quickly, before he could get any ideas that this had anything to do with him, or his tattoo, or his neck, or anything like that. "I'm going to watch you guys practice and interview some of the newer players as they have time. I totally did not expect to have company this early and I'm sure you didn't, either, so please do not mind me and please go back to your skating."

"Do you skate?" Lavesque asked, instead of skating off like she had told him to.

"God, no. The last thing I need is blades strapped to my feet, trust me," she dismissed. "I was just wondering what it must feel like to be able to skate like that. I really can't imagine having that much confidence in anything. You looked so free."

He was grinning. That didn't bode well.

"You cannot be an intern for an ice hockey team and not skate," he teased, stepping off the ice to join her on the rubberized floor. "Come on, there's plenty of time before anyone else gets here. I'll show you."

"I—wait—"

She scrambled to follow him. He walked fast, even in skates, and she tried not to peer at his neck, where the edges of his tattoo peeked out of his jersey. It was definitely the points of a crown, like she had guessed last time, and it was definitely an older tattoo.

"I am certain we have skates for you," he was saying as they reached the locker room door. He shouldered it open for her, and she squeezed past him, her shoulder brushing his chest, causing her to pull back quickly. "Mackenzie comes on the ice all the time and I am sure she just borrows skates."

"You seriously don't have to do this," Eloise protested as they strode through the locker room together. He gave her a sidelong look.

"Of course I do. I told you, we cannot have an intern who cannot skate. What would people say? It would be very embarrassing."

He came to an abrupt halt and she bumped into him; she backed away, face flushing at the contact, as he leaned into a room. "Dan isn't here yet?" he wondered under his breath. "He is not usually this lazy. Come in."

The equipment room had a long bank of cabinets and stacks of large plastic containers, full of jerseys and shorts and helmets and padding. Across from these, there was a workstation scattered with tools and blades. Eloise would have been afraid to touch any of it, but Lavesque moved about the room like he owned it—and he may as well have—opening and closing cabinets rapidly as he hunted.

"Here, these look right. Try these on," he instructed, producing black skates from a cabinet on the end that looked like a catch-all, with old skates and other equipment that had yellowed with age.

"What—here? Oh. Okay."

She set down her bag and, thanking whatever higher power that her socks were black and therefore not as embarrassing as they could have been, slipped off her boot. Gripping the side of the cabinets, she jammed her foot into the skate. "It's close enough," she said as Lavesque dropped down into a crouch.

"Yes, good enough," he agreed, pressing his fingers into the skate to feel for her foot. Before she could stop him he was helping her to lace up the skate, and they each had to rock back to avoid banging their heads.

"Sorry. I'll do this one, here. This is how tight it should be," he said, his grip tight around her ankle. "You need good support here so you can move more quickly."

"Yeah, I'm gonna be really speedy. Gotta prepare for that," she joked.

"You talk fast so you might skate fast," he said. "You seem like a fast person in general."

When Eloise was laced into her skates, Lavesque rose from his crouch. "You can leave your bag here, it'll be safe," he said, tapping the countertop. "No one goes in here except Dan and he won't touch your bag."

"What—not Dan's style?" she asked, trying to distract herself from her overall embarrassment and fluster. Lavesque gestured for her to follow him back out.

"Dan is too busy for anything that isn't hockey equipment," he said. "You'll see when you meet him. He is the most organized person I have ever met in my life."

"You know, you're talking about him like he's, like, a Michelin-rated chef or something," Eloise observed as she followed his effortless strides on the rubberized floor. "Are you like this about everyone?"

"Well—basically yes," he admitted as he led her down a side hallway, and through the locker room, which smelled strongly of cleaning fluids, rubber, and sweat. "And here is our locker room. I recommend that you avoid it during practice unless you want to see some bad tattoos," he counseled her as they passed the tidy stalls.

"Like yours?" It was out before she could stop herself, and Lavesque paused in the hallway leading to the ice, glancing back at her over his shoulder, raising his brows. Eloise had thought it would be a safe way to establish that she had not been staring in lust. "Sorry," she said, "sometimes I think I'm being funny and I come across like a jerk instead."

"Don't worry," he said easily, "I'm used to trash-talk. I just don't tend to hear it from people half my size." He started walking again and they reached the ice. "And my tattoos are mostly art."

"Mostly?" She hesitated at the edge of the rink. "Also, I'm not *half* your size."

Lavesque set his helmet on the bench and glided onto the ice, turning back to face her so that he was skating backwards.

"Hmm. I don't see you winning any fights with me any time soon," he assessed, looking her over. "Come on, the ice isn't going to hurt you."

"No, it's just going to make *me* hurt myself," she countered, inching toward the ice and gripping the boards for stability.

"The longer you wait, the more likely you are to have an audience," he told her, "and when Burnie gets here you will get some trash-talk of your own. Come on, skate onto the ice." His voice was firmer now as he gestured for her with a brisk motion, showing a little of the command that had put him into a leadership position.

"Ugh. Fine."

She set a blade on the ice, still gripping the boards. Admittedly, the idea of Henry Burnap screaming trash-talk at her in that seagull shriek of his was motivating. "Also, I distinctly remember reading that you've never gotten into a fight, so maybe I *would* win."

He was there, grabbing hold of her arm and pulling her before she was ready. She scrambled at first, skates sliding beneath her, but he held her steady, pulling her toward center ice, and it allowed her to align her skates and regain her balance.

"Not on the ice," he admitted. "I'm a hockey player, not a boxer. There you go—you're skating. Do you feel free yet?"

He was teasing her, but her mind had snagged on *not on the ice*. She glanced up at him, at his broken nose, but his blue-grey eyes caught hers, distracting her from the question she might have asked.

"So free." She forced out a laugh, looking down at her skates as they inched along the ice, his grip firm on her forearms.

"You have definitely skated before," he decided as he watched her.

"Well, if that's your takeaway, I'll count myself lucky."

He released her and let her glide on her own, looking like he was trying not to laugh.

"Eloise," he said patiently, "that was an invitation for you to tell me when you have skated before."

"Jacques," she countered in the same condescending tone, the sounds of his name self-conscious in her mouth, "respectfully—I decline your invitation."

"That is okay," he dismissed carelessly, gliding in a circle around her. "I will find another way in. Don't reach out like that, you will lose your balance," he corrected suddenly as she began to wobble, holding her arms out like a penguin. "Reach for your knees instead."

"Thanks," she muttered, righting herself once more and creaking along the ice as he followed. "So is that how you do it—how you bond with other players?"

"By getting to know them? Yes, that is how it's usually done," he said with a laugh. "Do you have some other way of bonding with people?"

"No, my way is the same, I guess," she hedged, glancing at him. "So if you love everyone so much—tell me what you love most about some of your teammates. Like Pell," she added casually, so that he would not think she was digging specifically for Kyle.

Now he was smiling as he skated and considered her question, that fond smile that she had seen in so many photographs.

"I—well, there are so many things to love about Pell," he began, "but he always sits with the newer players on the bus and plane, and all, and he pretends to sleep, but really he's listening in on their conversations."

"To get to know them?" she guessed.

"No, just for gossip, and he usually texts me and Burnie what he learns," he explained. "And Burnie is, you know, my best friend so I could go on for many hours, but one thing that most people don't know about him is that he knows every Disney princess and has very strong opinions on them, because of his daughters. There was a media thing where they had us trying to name the Disney princesses, and we all failed except Burnie. If you really want to get him riled up," he added slyly, "ask him what he thought of the live-action *Beauty and the Beast*."

"How did you do on the princess test?" Eloise wondered, picturing Burnie shouting each princess's name and then correcting the interviewer.

"I failed it," Jacques said with a wave of his hand. "I didn't have a television when I was little and I am not sure I would have watched it anyway, and my boys don't care about Disney. Luke could never sit still through a whole movie, and for Peter, if it's not trains, Batman, or dinosaurs, it might as well not exist."

"You were too busy with hockey, I'm guessing." They skated through the panels of morning sunlight coming in through the windows. She was getting the hang of it now, feeling more confident with each stride, and it was not lost on her that Jacques was matching his strides to hers, watching the movement of her skates.

"No, I just was usually in my own world," he said. "I was very quiet when I was little, not social at all." He paused. "'Oh, me too, Jacques!'" he said in a high voice, trying not to laugh. "Or, you could say something like, 'oh, I wasn't like that at all, I was very outgoing,'" he suggested. "You know, like a normal person."

"I need you to know that you are truly terrible at voices and mimicry," Eloise said, trying not to flinch, or tremble, or any other embarrassing thing, as he set a hand on her back, guiding her in an arc as they rounded the edge of the rink. "You sounded like a dying bird there and I *know* I don't sound like that. My voice is actually kind of deep for a woman's voice."

"Another diversion," he observed, shaking his head. "Okay, I will try another way. I will get you eventually."

"That sounds ominous," she remarked as he dropped his hand and they settled into skating the length of the rink again.

"It should. I always win face-offs," he pointed out.

"Oh, there we go. I've been wondering where you were hiding your pro-athlete ego, but it's there," she teased, grinning when he smiled. "Okay, what about the rookies? What do you love most about them?"

Jacques looked thoughtful for a moment.

"You know, most rookies are very intimidated by the older players, and it takes them a very long time to interact normally with us, but Travis was able to from the very beginning. He respects us for sure, but he is not so intimidated by us that he can't talk to us normally, or practice with us. And Connor is very emotional and takes everything very seriously," he explained so lovingly, "and everything matters very much to him and it's nice to see so much passion."

"What about Kyle Hearst?"

They glanced at each other. This time when they hit the end of the rink and arced along the boards, she did not need his guiding hand.

"Very nice," he said with a nod to her skates. "Kyle is so private, I don't know much about him yet because he hasn't let me," he hedged, "like some other people I could mention..."

"This is a really sore spot for you, isn't it?"

They glided to a stop and faced each other.

"Just *one* personal fact," he tried.

"No," she shot back, and then they were laughing and she did not know why, because it was embarrassing that she was this filled with glee at the fact that someone wanted to know anything about her.

"Okay, now Andrei Koslov," she tried, and felt a swooping sensation of guilt when his smile dropped. "Because I am struggling to find something about him to love, and I've read plenty that you used to be close with him," she added hastily.

His mask was firmly in place now.

"Unless it's too sensitive. Maybe I went too far—"

"No, it's okay," he said, but the pleasantly neutral expression—his *'no comment'* face—was still firmly in place. "I did know him really well. I know he is not a very likable person, but there is plenty about Andrei to like."

"Such as?" She began skating again, and he followed.

"He is very good at languages," Jacques said. "When we first played together, his English was much better than mine, and he was always correcting me on things. Like I would say I played 'good' and he would tell me it's 'well' and, you know, stuff like that. And he taught himself French when he was a kid. He lived with his uncle and cousins and one of their books was this red book of French vocabulary and grammar, things like that, and he picked up a lot of it and sometimes we'd talk in French, just little things, and he was always trying to get me to correct his French so he could get better at it."

"That's—that's actually really sweet," she admitted. It was hard to imagine Andrei Koslov reading, studying something, taking criticism graciously and changing based upon it—but not hard to imagine that Jacques Lavesque had pulled that from him. "I—"

She wanted to explain that she had not meant to catch him off-guard, that she had not meant to strike him when he was vulnerable, but it was too late: other players were spilling onto the ice now, arriving for practice.

"INTERNS ON ICE!" Burnie bellowed, the first in the rink. Unlike Jacques's swift grace, he skated like he was running, with abrupt strikes of his skates into the ice. Pell, his gangling height accentuated next to Burnie's stocky form, was close behind him, moving with a disconnected fluidity as he adjusted his helmet.

"I have figured it out—Eloise is going to be a d-man," Jacques explained to them. A third player studied Eloise warily as he approached, and she recognized him as one of the rookies she had seen last time. He looked about twenty, and reminded her strongly of a young Prince William, with his flushed pout and thick yellow-blond waves.

"Good, maybe she can replace Connor BONEHEAD Kennedy," Burnie said loudly as the Prince William dead-ringer reached them. "As long as she can spot the puck she's already an improvement."

"Come on, Burnie," the rookie, Connor, complained, but he was looking at Eloise as he spoke.

"This is Krystal's intern, Eloise," Jacques told Connor. "You probably saw her on the first day of practice."

"Yes, and I don't want to replace you—I'm sure I'm much more of a bonehead than you are," she promised Connor, recalling what Jacques had said about him taking everything too seriously.

"Uh, um, that's fine, you're probably not a bonehead," he stammered, avoiding her eyes.

"Jesus. Have you ever talked to a woman before, Bonehead?" Burnie asked, face twisted in disgust.

"The word 'bonehead' is losing all meaning," Pell complained. "Bonehead. Bonehead. What does it even *mean*? Besides Connor, I mean."

"Assholes," Connor muttered, turning and skating away from them to do a lap around the rink.

Burnie was staring at Connor like he had found a mythical creature.

"I think you have a fan," Jacques observed to Eloise, elbowing her. "Connor is not normally shy."

"Congratulations—you are now the owner of a completely useless puppy," Burnie said after he had recovered. "That kid can't do shit."

"He is fascinating," Pell said under his breath, eyes trained on Connor. "Did you know he has a pet goat, and also he's in an open relationship with his girlfriend from high school?"

"What?" Burnie scoffed. "That's fucking optimistic of him. The girlfriend, not the goat. He can't even make eye contact with an intern." He glanced at her. "No offense, intern."

"None taken. Usually I'm the weirdest one in the exchange," Eloise said, holding up her hands, "so that was refreshing."

"Yeah, I kind of figured," Burnie said casually, indifferent to how this might be hurtful. "Yo, you're coming to my party, right?"

"Um—"

It was not lost on Eloise that these men were going out of their way to be nice to her; that Burnie, for all of his blunt words and cursing, was inviting her to a party because it was the kind thing to do (or perhaps because he *was* actually intimidated by Krystal). "Party?" she settled on after a pause.

"Yeah, every year Stephy and I host a rager to kick off the season," Burnie explained distractedly, examining the tape on his stick. "Was Dan drunk when he taped this? Do I have to do everything around here? I cook, I clean..."

"Oh, you're coming. It's great," Pell said. "The rookies always get shit-faced and you learn so much about them."

*"And,"* Burnie interjected, "sometimes we do karaoke and last year Lavesque got drunk enough to *sing*."

"I was wondering when you were going to use that against me," Jacques said, but he was smiling.

"What did you sing?" Eloise asked him.

"You'll have to get it out of someone else," he said with an innocent shrug. "Perhaps your new puppy will tell you," he added, nodding to Connor who refused to look at them as he skated past, his face tomato-red.

"Man, I had no idea he had a thing for indie chicks," Burnie marveled. "No wonder he's the only rookie who doesn't get nervous around Mackenzie."

"Mackenzie is a reporter for ESPN," Pell explained to Eloise, "and it's like a rite of passage at this point to have a crush on her. She is—and I'm just being honest—outrageously hot."

"I'm pretty sure she's gay so they're wasting their time," Burnie said, "but also, she's a butterface."

"On that note—let's get you off the ice before Connor melts," Jacques said hastily.

Burnie and Pell skated off together, with Burnie complaining about something Connor did at their last practice, leaving Jacques and Eloise to skate to the edge of the rink. There was a group of players amassing by the bench and Eloise watched as Jacques easily interacted with each of them: high-fives and waves, little inside jokes, claps to the shoulder. They all seemed to brighten and bloom as he passed.

"Thank you," Eloise said, following Jacques back through the tunnel. The locker room was half-full of players in various stages of undress, and Eloise hurried past them as she heard wolf-whistles and catcalls.

"Nothing to thank me for," Jacques said over his shoulder as he knocked on the door to the equipment room. A tall, skinny guy with a loping energy and large Adam's apple straightened as they entered. His ash-brown hair was carefully combed into a side-part, reminding Eloise of picture day in second grade.

"This is Dan. Dan, this is Krystal's intern, Eloise," Jacques said, gesturing to her.

"Hi Eloise, where did you get those skates?" Dan demanded in one breath, looking down furiously at her feet.

"Calm down. I stole them for her," Jacques reassured him. "We are putting them back now."

"Oh. So *those* are where those women's shoes came from," Dan realized, looking back at where Eloise's boots were lined up by the cabinets.

"Do you routinely find women's shoes in here?" Eloise wondered. Dan looked deeply pained.

"You have no idea what I find in here sometimes," he said darkly, but he didn't elaborate. Jacques grinned at her when Dan turned back to his work, arching his brows in mutual entertainment.

"How is Jamie? She started school this week, right?" Jacques asked Dan, leaning on the counter as Eloise changed into her boots. Dan softened slightly.

"She's good, just adjusting to her non-mermaid life," he said dryly.

"Always a difficult transition, yeah," Jacques agreed solemnly, and the two men laughed together. Eloise watched how Dan relaxed, how his shoulders dropped a little, and by the time she and Jacques had left the room, he was humming to himself. This time when they passed through the locker room it was empty of players, their gym bags and water bottles and clothes scattered around.

"But seriously, thank you for skating with me," she tried again as they reached the rink. There was a new energy to the place now—it was full of players in alternating practice jersey colors, the box lined with assistant coaches and water coolers and bottles of Gatorade, and pop music was playing.

"No, thank you," Jacques countered with a smile, skating backwards onto the ice as he donned his helmet again. He was about to say something but the coach, Duffy, accosted him, and Eloise waved him off before turning back to the seats to scan for a place to sit.

"There you are," Krystal said, catching Eloise's attention. She emerged from the tunnel, clad in a Bruins zip-up fleece that she wore with the elegance that another woman might wear a Max Mara coat. "I hear you got a skating lesson from Lavy."

There was something in Krystal's tone that Eloise decided to ignore.

"Yes, and I also got invited to Burnie's 'rager.'" She made air-quotes as she walked with Krystal to the other end of the box, and followed her in climbing over the seats to the row behind it. "Where's Andrei?"

"Late, I think," Krystal said darkly, glancing back at the rink. "And so it begins. His usual nonsense."

"Is he back to partying?" Eloise guessed.

"I doubt it. According to my friends in Tampa, he's sober for good. I think this is just a little stunt—if he's late, it's on purpose," Krystal said. "You can sit here. I told the kids they had to talk to you so they know to come over."

Eloise dropped into one of the yellow seats. From this vantage point she could see all of the rink, and she watched the players for a moment.

And like a sonic ripple, every head turned toward the entrance of the rink as a broad form lingered at the edge of the ice, putting on his helmet. *Andrei.* The hairs on the back of her neck prickled as she looked for Jacques, but he barely glanced in Andrei's direction before turning his attention back to the player he was talking to.

He was completely hidden. He gave nothing of how he really felt away—from the end of his marriage to his feelings about Andrei Koslov rejoining the team.

"There he is," Krystal said under her breath, crossing her arms. The two women watched as the coach skated over to the edge of the rink, presumably to give Andrei a talking-to, but Andrei pushed past him.

He moved differently—like molten liquid, pouring himself along the ice in an inexorable rush, easily slipping between other skaters and looping around cones, both fire and flood. It seemed impossible that someone that tall and broad could move with such grace.

"He's something," Eloise admitted.

"You see him skate and you're like, *damn,*" Krystal agreed softly, shaking her head. "I told you—we could have had it all, if he only had let me."

Krystal left to take a call, allowing Eloise to watch the team move through drills together. The whole thing was a held breath: Jacques still had not acknowledged Andrei, and the cool silence was painfully obvious. As Pell had alluded to, Jacques set the tone, and everyone followed his example. Andrei was an island, isolated from everyone else, and Eloise would not have cared except she thought of the little red book of French phrases, and suddenly she did care.

Andrei finished a drill and skated to the edge of the rink to get water. He paused, lifted his gaze, swung it to her corner of the bleachers—and lifted his gloved hand in a small wave.

She lifted her hand and gave a small wave back. He nodded—and then swung his long legs over the boards and began making his way toward her.

# Chapter Seven

"You again," Andrei observed when he reached her. He dropped into the plastic yellow seat beside her as he yanked off his helmet, his jersey brushing her sleeve with the movement.

He took up so much *space*. The yellow seat creaked uneasily with his weight; when his knees pressed the back of the seat in front of him, the plastic squeaked in protest.

Eloise resisted the urge to shift over to give him more room—there was a stubborn part of her that refused to give in to man-spreading, particularly when it was this intentional—but all the same she felt herself cringing away from him.

"I'm interviewing the rookies today," Eloise explained when she realized he wasn't going to say anything else. Andrei rested his elbows on his heavily-padded knees and looked back at her over one broad shoulder, inscrutable as a sphinx.

"No glasses today." He studied her face in a way that gave her the urge to check her skin.

"They were fake. Just a fashion statement." She could *feel* the players and the coach and assistant coaches looking at them and she wondered if Jacques was, too. "Shouldn't you be practicing with everyone else?"

Andrei shook his head, pale lips curving.

"What are they going to do?" he asked her lazily. "They paid a lot of money for me, traded players so they could afford me, dragged me from Tampa. They need me more than I need them." His voice was like his movements, pouring from one word to the next like something liquid and smooth, yet she sensed the effort of that too—the effort of a second language. Eloise wondered how he had learned English, and imagined him lying on a mattress as he held up the little red book of French phrases.

"Wow. I'd love to have one tenth of your confidence."

"They can't do a Cup run without me," he continued, ignoring her. "They have one more Cup run in them before they need to rebuild, and it will go hard for them. Jay is getting old, and Burnap *is* old. They are the only good players, and they are excellent but they are old. You can have a good car, take good care of it, but it will still die. What are they going to do—build a team around Wet Blanket Pelletier? Around Mr. Hairstyle Novak?"

He scoffed and shifted his legs, knees brushing the seat in front of him again. Eloise had the sense of being crammed in a closet with him, the air and the walls too close, too warm. *He calls Jacques Jay.* The nickname seemed important. He wanted her to know his relationship with Jacques was different than anyone else's. To Andrei he was not Lavesque, or Lavy, or Cap, or any of the other nicknames she had seen given to Jacques. In this context it felt like he was trying to take Jacques down a few pegs, but perhaps she was reading into it.

"Some people think you're old."

She was fairly certain that Andrei was actually older than Jacques. He looked it—he did not have that glow of health that Jacques and the other players had.

"I'm old, yes, but I'm a Cup winner," Andrei pointed out.

"They're Cup winners too."

"Not in years. They *were* Cup winners—they are losers now."

He settled against the seat, elbow knocking hers. Something about him was like a metronome, a bloody beating heart. Glowing eyes in the brush, a revving engine behind you. She sensed that even this act of sitting with her was a form of tiny rebellion, of troublemaking—a little stunt, as Krystal had called it.

"So you *did* say you'd give me an interview if you felt like it, and you obviously do," Eloise reminded him. "So what do I need to know about the rookies before I interview them?"

Andrei considered her question as the two of them surveyed the rink.

"You know—Travis Martin, Connor Kennedy, Kyle Hearst..."

"I know who the rookies are."

He sounded offended. It seemed like he was sincerely contemplating the question as he studied the players on the rink, but Eloise was still tensed, prepared for something harsh.

"Travis Martin is very average," he decided. "He will be a fourth-line player his whole career. He should go back to the AHL if he wants recognition. Same with Kennedy. He is too stupid to play NHL hockey."

"Tell me how you really feel," she marveled—though she noted that he said nothing about Travis being gay. Maybe he was too clever to let his homophobia show in this setting, or perhaps he was not homophobic at all.

"You asked," he reminded her. "And I told you. That is what you need to know about them."

"Okay, then." Eloise considered her next move. "What about Kyle Hearst? I heard he was a hasty investment."

"Taylor told you that," he guessed shrewdly. "Once in a while, she is right. Hearst is much better than the others. He is very fast, very precise. He learns, too. Watch him during practice today, he is watching everyone and learning their tricks, like Jay does. I understand why he turned heads. If you know players you think he's another Jay. But he doesn't have it."

"What's *it*?"

"The need to win."

He was looking at her again, giving her that sense that she had something on her nose. "We all have it. Even your good friend Prince Jacques. He seems so nice, showing you how to skate, right? Patting everybody on the back, joking with everyone—oh, ha ha, let's all be one big happy Boston family! But he would cut off his own leg before losing."

He shook his head. "Kyle Hearst cares about something else more than hockey. And that's why he is a waste."

It was almost like he knew that this was what she was looking for. She met Andrei's eyes—the only pretty thing about him—but she could read nothing in them, nothing but disdain and spite.

"What about you? Do you care about hockey more than anything else?"

"Yes," he said, looking away. "More than anything else."

"So what do you think *is* the most important thing to Kyle?"

"Who cares?" He was smirking again. "He is just a local boy who got lucky. He made it this far because a few dumb men in suits think he is the next one. If he were not on the Bruins he would be bagging groceries, wearing a hard hat and standing around a construction site. Holding up signs, or whatever."

Eloise could not help but laugh disgustedly. "Oh, really—and what would you be doing? Investment banking? Neurosurgery?"

"I would not do anything but hockey." He grinned at the look on her face. "You are like Jay—you get mad when people are not how you think they should be."

"No, I get mad when people are classist, actually," she said before she could stop herself. "I'm not a receptacle for you to come and say shitty things about your teammates or demean people who have been kind to you," she continued, aware that the words came out clumsy. "And maybe you think you have some kind of charm with women so maybe you think I'll find this cute or something, but—"

"Who told you that?" He looked genuinely curious. "I have no luck with women."

He paused, with a sidelong look like he was recalling an inside joke. "Almost no luck," he amended.

"God, I wonder why!" she said, and was surprised yet again when he laughed. He had a reluctant laugh, she noticed, like he was afraid to show his teeth or smile fully, like he was ashamed to find something funny. The self-consciousness was unexpectedly human.

"Look." He nudged her, pointing to a group of players at the edge of the rink, their helmets close together as they talked. They were looking up at Eloise and Andrei. "They know they are supposed to come up here and talk to you because Taylor told them to, and they are scared of her. But *I* am here, and they are scared of me. What are they going to do?"

Eloise watched Jacques skate over to them. He touched Kyle on the shoulder, nodding in Eloise's direction, said something, and then skated off again, and they watched the three young players make their way over to them.

"Last chance to tell me something juicy about them," she said quickly. "Bad tattoos? Embarrassing phobias? Weird hobbies?"

Andrei thought for a moment, watching the rookies pick their way towards them.

"You are most interested in Hearst," he concluded, but he continued before she could correct him. "He has a tarot deck in his gym bag."

"A tarot deck," she repeated in shock.

"Yes. A tarot deck," he said with a slight grin and a shrug. "He does not let anyone see it. I am not supposed to know about it. I think he would get very mad if you brought it up."

Andrei got to his feet, letting her questions linger—how had he found out about the tarot deck, and what did he think of it? He climbed over the seats with ease. Kyle, Connor, and Travis all squished to one side, eyes averted, to let Andrei pass. Even from here she heard him snicker disgustedly at their deference.

"Kyle," she called when they had recovered from Andrei. "You first?" she offered, hoping that it sounded encouraging.

Kyle shrugged but climbed up to her row obediently, with Travis—fresh-faced and freckled with loose waves; he looked like the lifeguard at your local pool with whom you might have been in love at age eleven—and Connor watching with interest.

After Andrei, Kyle seemed child-sized though he was at least six feet tall and not a small man by any means. He sat smaller than Andrei, conscious of the space he took up, avoiding her eyes as he shifted his weight, trying to get comfortable in the hard plastic seat without jostling her. His reddish hair was dark with sweat and curling around his jaw and the nape of his neck, and the edge of that tattoo—just a single line of ink—was visible.

"So." He bounced one leg. "Krystal said you wanted to interview me?"

"Yes, just for fun," Eloise reassured him. "Nothing serious."

"Alright." He rubbed his nose, leaving the skin blotchy and red. "Lavesque told me it was good practice. And he said you're funny so it would be easy."

"Oh." She flushed, even though she knew he had not been paying her a compliment—merely reassuring himself with Jacques's words. "You two seem close," she said lightly, scrawling Kyle's name on her tablet. Kyle was still bouncing his leg, watching the rink with slumped but taut posture.

"Yeah, he was my hero growing up," he said, "like every other kid in Boston, I guess." *Bah-stan.*

"Did you have a poster of him when you were younger?"

"Nah, that's Martin." *Mah-tin.* She had to stifle a grin. "My dad couldn't afford stuff like that. I wouldn't've asked for it."

"It all went to hockey stuff?"

Kyle shook his head. "He wasn't working, so I got my own hockey stuff. Babysitting, mowing lawns. My gramma bought me stuff sometimes. It's one of the reasons Lavesque gets me," he said, looking at Eloise for the first time. "Like he had to figure out how to pay for it all too. He wasn't farmed to play hockey by his parents like the rest of them."

*So how did you figure it out?* she wondered, because she doubted that babysitting and mowing lawns could begin to make a dent in the costs of hockey.

He paused. "Also, my little brother had some issues. Like health stuff. I wasn't gonna roll in and ask my dad for money when my little brother's all fucked up."

Something in his voice had caught on *my little brother.*

"You haven't really shared this stuff before," she observed.

"Not exactly gonna put it on blast that my family was broke and sick."

"My dad's broke, too," she confessed. Marcel, the goalie, and another player dressed in goalie pads were stretching, and they watched them together. From here the other goalie—perhaps named Harper, though she could not quite remember—looked squat and bearded and genial, a bit like Jack Black.

"Sucks," Kyle said with a shrug. "You're probably not making shit at this gig, are you? Can't imagine you can help much."

"No," she admitted with a laugh that she hoped wasn't too revealing. "How is your little brother now?"

Kyle didn't answer right away. His blue-grey eyes followed Jacques in an assessing, watchful way—noting each movement, committing it to memory.

"He's not sick anymore," he said. "He's fine."

"Are you two close?"

"I don't really want to talk about it," Kyle said suddenly. "And Lavesque told me to just say when I didn't want to talk to you about something and that you'd be okay with it."

"Of course. It was a personal question," she said quickly. "We can shift gears. Favorite movie?" Eloise tried to inject some levity in her tone, an acknowledgment of the silliness of such a question after what they had just talked about, and Kyle laughed reluctantly.

"Uh. *Home Alone*," he said after a moment. "Those old movies are underrated."

She cringed. She had forgotten that she probably had T-shirts in her closet that were older than Kyle.

"Favorite candy?"

"Snickers," he decided. "But I also like those dots. The ones that come on the paper strip."

"And... which team are you most excited to play against this season?"

"The Maple Leafs," he said after a moment's thought, though he did not elaborate.

"One more," she coached him, earning a half-smile, self-conscious as it was. "I noticed last time that you had a new tattoo on your neck—are you open to sharing what it is, and if it has any special meaning?"

His hand clapped to his neck as he blushed.

"Uh, it's just—like a symbol thing," he stammered. "Like an ancient symbol. It's embarrassing. Whatever. I don't even know why I got it, it's kind of—I dunno."

"What does it mean?"

"It's personal." He flattened his hair over it. "I thought you couldn't see it," he muttered.

"Yeah, sure, I totally see that that might be private," she said hastily. "Any other tattoos you're comfortable sharing?"

"Yeah, a dragon on my arm," he said more easily, reminding her of the one she had glimpsed in his Instagram photos, "and a Celtic cross on my back, and I got the Bruins symbol thing on my chest, over my heart," he added, touching his chest like he was pledging allegiance. "I got that one this summer," he said with a little pride, "after I signed my contract."

"You must have a high pain tolerance," she noted, pretending to take notes, then set down her stylus. "And there—you're done!" she said, doing jazz hands. Kyle laughed. "Lavesque would be proud."

"He's so good at this stuff," Kyle said in a rush. "He just always has a good answer. He told me it's just practice, and showed me some of his early interviews and I felt a lot better. He was a mess, he was so awkward. Like one time he just flipped out at an interviewer." He covered his face, laughing. "I couldn't even watch, it was so fucking bad. So maybe I'll get less weird."

"I'm sure you will," Eloise reassured him, resisting the urge to probe on what interview he was talking about. Jacques Lavesque was not the one under investigation here.

Kyle pushed off his seat, visibly relieved now that he was done.

"Ask Kennedy about his goat," he confided, "but don't ask about the girlfriend. You don't wanna know."

"Goat? Thanks... I think?" She laughed with Kyle as he made his way back down, motioning for Connor to go next, and then snatched her tablet and, quick as she could, drew Kyle's tattoo from memory.

Connor was almost there; there was no time to try Googling the symbol, so she saved the sketch and quickly switched her screen.

"Um, sorry about earlier," Connor mumbled when he reached her, his face the color of a pomegranate.

"Not at all, it had to be weird seeing someone so bad at skating on a professional hockey rink," she joked. Connor plunked down beside her, not as aware of her personal space as Kyle had been.

"You weren't that bad," he tried. "So, uh. How does this work?"

"Well, I just had a long talk with Kyle about tattoos," Eloise said, writing Connor's name on her tablet, "and was wondering if you had any."

"No, Mom would *kill* me," he said, aghast. "But if I did get one, it would be a goat. On my shoulder, like right here." He gestured to the outside of his arm.

"Do all of the guys have tattoos?"

"Most of them, not everyone. Pell and Koslov don't, but Lavesque's got a lot. He's got a map of the T, and some guy's face, and this weird tree, and this dude, it goes all up his back, but he doesn't really take his shirt off much so I haven't gotten a close look…"

He trailed off, ruffling his golden-blond hair. "Kyle's dragon *is* cool. The cross is lame, though. A lot of guys around here have that one," he added, "but I guess that's Boston for you."

It was very obviously a dig at Boston. Eloise couldn't remember where Connor was from but she was certain it was not a Catholic place and he wanted her to know that.

"It's funny that so many of them have a cross," Eloise said, "because I feel like, right now at least, anything Celtic or really Christian is kind of loaded."

"Yeah, it is, but you gotta remember," Connor coached her, gesturing to the rink, "these are really dumb guys. Like if you showed them a kanji character and told them it meant *badass*, or something, they'd get it inked, no questions asked, and it could literally mean *toilet*. They wouldn't even check."

"Good point," Eloise said neutrally, and Connor frowned.

"You're thinking of how Burnie and Pelletier called me Bonehead," he correctly guessed, "but the thing is, I had an *education*. A lot of these guys didn't even really finish high school. Pell and I are the only ones who have a college degree—well, soon I'll have a college degree."

"Pell has a degree?" she asked, intrigued.

"Yeah, it's something boring like civil engineering. *I'm* majoring in econ," he said pompously, "and minoring in psychology. I've got a 4.0, too."

"That's really impressive," Eloise said, thinking of her own dismal GPA. "So you think some of these guys are just getting crosses and things like that because it looks cool?"

"Pretty much. None of them even read the news, except Bouchard but he just reads the finance stuff and the horoscopes. He always really appreciates my input on finance stuff," he added.

Eloise recalled Pell saying that Marcel Bouchard rarely kept track of the younger players' names. She bit her lip to hide a grin.

"Like, I'm the one who has to explain current events and even then they really don't care. I don't get it. My dad and I always talked politics at dinner every night."

She had to redirect; Connor kept straying from where she wanted him to go.

"So are you close with the other rookies?"

"Yeah, we're all good friends. Travis is really cool. I'm teaching him golf," Connor said, brightening, "and he knows I'm cool with him being gay. You wouldn't think it's a big deal anymore, but with these guys it is."

Eloise wondered who he meant when he said 'these guys.' She surveyed the rink.

"It's good that he has you as an open ally. What about Kyle?"

"We're friends." Connor shrugged. "But Kyle doesn't really hang out with anyone outside of practice, and he's really bad about replying to texts. He totally disappears between practices. I've been to everyone else's place but his, and Travis said he's never been, either. He kind of just clings to Lavesque and ignores everyone else. He won't even add me on social media and didn't even want to give me his number. I was like, dude, we are literally on a team together, I could just get your number from one of the coaches."

He frowned at Travis approaching. "Travis, why are you here? We're still talking," Connor complained as Travis came up to their row and perched on the edge of one of the seats in front of them.

"Saving her," he laughed, handsome brown eyes crinkling at the corners. "Are we talking about Rebecca or Horny the goat?"

"Neither, actually," Connor said with great dignity. "We were discussing Kyle and his tattoos. And also how no one on this team gives a damn about politics."

"I thought we were going to be asked things like our favorite movies and stuff." Travis examined his helmet, and rubbed at a spot on it. "Or what Hogwarts house we think everyone would be."

"*No one* wants to talk about Harry Potter," Connor grumbled.

"You're just mad 'cause I said you'd be Hufflepuff," Travis said easily. He flashed a grin at Eloise. "I sorted everyone. People might think Krystal is Slytherin, but I think she's actually a Hufflepuff because she likes nice things so much. You need to tell me what you think since you're working for her—"

"No one cares about Harry Potter," Connor insisted loudly, hitting Travis in the shoulder with his stick. "It's a *kid's* series and J.K. Rowling is *problematic*—"

"Connor is really nice," Travis told her, "but you need to understand that he also has a copy of *The Invisible Man* in his gym bag, positioned exactly so that you can always see it—"

"Because I'm *reading* it," Connor interrupted.

"You probably are, that's the really weird thing," Travis reflected. "So why are we talking about Hearst? He's the quietest one on the team. He doesn't do anything, his socials are all empty except for like, blurry shots of him and his weird friends. No one knows anything about him. He just talks to Lavy and goes home," he summarized, swinging his legs.

"His tattoos are kind of intense," Connor put in. Travis nodded.

"Yeah, when he gets traded to, like, Dallas or whatever in two years, I wonder what he'll do about the Bruins tattoo," he said with a grin.

"I was wondering about the fact that so many players apparently have Christian tattoos," Eloise explained.

Travis tilted his head in thought. He had a bright, almost birdlike energy to him, like a cheerful robin.

"Well, I dunno about the rest of them, but Kyle's really religious, like he touches the cross on a chain he has before he goes on the ice. Oh, and when I shared a room with him back in Juniors, I woke up in the middle of the night one time and he was praying. Like, kneeling on the floor and everything. I think he actually goes to church, too."

"He seems like he hangs out a lot with his friends based on his Instagram," Eloise tossed out casually. Travis and Connor glanced at each other.

"Yeah, but not with anyone *we'd* go near," Connor said. "Anyway, back to the interesting stuff. My favorite movie is *Atonement*—"

"This is his mating dance," Travis explained to her. "It worked on Rebecca, apparently, and probably on Horny—"

"Shut up, Martin," Connor said, turning red again. "What's *your* favorite movie—*Harry Potter*?" he sneered, but it didn't have the requisite cruelty to it.

"No, those movies were terrible," he dismissed, pushing at his lazy, dark blond ringlets. "I've thought about this a lot and think it'd have to be the Charlie Brown Christmas movie."

"Why are you *so* dumb," Connor wondered for Eloise's benefit. "And *why* is Coach waving to us? Krystal told him we had media."

"I'm sure I don't count as actual media," Eloise said quickly. "You guys should go, I'll catch you after practice."

"Yeah, you should, we barely got through anything," Connor complained. Travis was grinning.

"Yeah, she really needs to know what hipster candy you'll say is your favorite," he teased, bumping into Connor as they got to their feet. "Really valuable insight."

Eloise watched them make their way back to the ice, arguing pleasantly, feeling like she had been caught in a storm of teenage boy. Still—she had learned more than she had ever expected she would. Eloise wrote as fast as she could, trying to capture every detail before it faded.

# Chapter Eight

E loise had planned to pull Krystal aside after practice and break the news to her—that this investigation was over—but Krystal never showed up at the rink again, and something held Eloise back from simply texting her and asking where she was. She sat there for a while after the rink had emptied, staring at the empty ice and running over all that she had learned.

*You know what you have to do*, she told herself as she shut her tablet full of the notes she had so furiously captured, *so why aren't you just doing it?*

She put her ancient tablet in her bag, but she still didn't get up. Her phone vibrated with an email and when she opened it, she was surprised to see a polite confirmation of receipt of her resumé, rather than another canned rejection. She scrolled through the email and wondered why she didn't feel more excited.

*You know what you have to do*, she told herself again. But she did not want to. She pulled out her tablet and studied the drawing of Kyle's tattoo, and then opened Google on her phone and searched *rune tattoo hate symbol*. None of the results matched Kyle's tattoo exactly, but the look was so similar, and there was something about his shame surrounding the tattoo that had struck her...

*Not with anyone we'd go near*, Connor had said, and Travis had obviously agreed. Eloise opened a new tab on her phone and Googled 'tarot deck' and scrolled through the results, her skin prickling at the strange illustrations.

Maybe Kyle Hearst was just a religious boy who had taken a rebellious interest in the occult. Maybe it was his way of managing the stress of his home life, of having been plucked from his normal world and placed in this world of professional athletes. Eloise shut her tablet and stuffed it in her bag, and forced herself to her feet.

*You know what you have to do*, she told herself as she picked her way out of the stadium seating, *so why aren't you doing it?*

She went down the stairs to the entrance, lost in thought, and as a result encountered a familiar figure before she could slip away and avoid the confrontation. Jacques Lavesque was standing by the door, scowling at his phone, mouth twisted in frustration. He was wearing a slightly wrinkled Bruins T-shirt and gym shorts, a gym bag slung over his shoulder, his hair sweaty and mussed.

(It was a fight with the nanny, she decided, though of course this was fanciful; she did not even know if they had one at all.)

"I swear to god I'm not following you," Eloise said when Jacques looked up from his phone. Once again she watched him slide his mask on, smoothing out his frustration like a key sliding into a lock. "I was just leaving."

"Oh, yeah? Did you have good interviews?" he asked pleasantly as she descended the remaining steps.

(How had he done it? How had he stuffed his anger away so easily?)

"Yeah... With Andrei, too, surprisingly," she admitted. She saw it then—the briefest flash of frustration, of anger, though he was quick to smooth it away again. She reached him and they faced each other.

*Prince Jacques*, she recalled Andrei saying so disdainfully, and then she was thinking of how alone Andrei seemed, how isolated, and how Jacques had so obviously frozen him out. It had seemed more validated, more understandable, when she had thought Andrei really was bigoted, but in their conversation all she had really seen was a deep resentment for Jacques and some elitist notions that she guessed were the result of growing up in poverty. From this side of that conversation, Jacques's behavior seemed petty.

And just like earlier on the ice, she realized she had only brought up Andrei because it was clearly an effective weapon, and she wondered, as their eyes met, why she felt like she needed a weapon against Jacques Lavesque.

"He's not as bad as I expected," she added.

"Ah, you got that from one conversation," he said lightly, but the sarcasm was not lost on her and she stared at him in surprise—and some anger of her own. It was the doubt that got her—that he doubted her ability to understand people, that he doubted her conclusions.

"Yeah, actually, I did," she fired back with a caustic laugh. "Is that hard to believe? It's my job."

"I think it is a little stretch to think you know someone after one conversation," Jacques said with a shrug, his voice still light, "but you know, you're right, it is your job. I don't really know much about it."

Oh, but the condescension was breathtaking, and she laughed again in disbelief, watching him try and fail to control his anger. She had the stray thought that Andrei might have corrected his English—*it's a bit of a stretch, not a little stretch*, he would have said.

"Oh, more 'no comment' bullshit, nice," she blurted, and that seemed to be the thing that finally made him snap. His face and neck flushed, and she felt her own face grow hot in turn.

"What?"

"You obviously wanted to say something else," she said defensively, "but just so you know, when you do that, you're not actually hiding anything—"

"Just so *you* know, I can tell you are trying very hard to get me to say something bad about Andrei," Jacques interrupted with a laugh of his own, "you are not subtle, and no matter what fake glasses you wear, you are not under the radar—"

"I'm not *trying* to get you to say something bad about him, I'm trying to understand," Eloise countered. Her hands were shaking and she fisted them. She was exposed, raw, burning in the sun. "But this is obviously a sore subject for you, so maybe I should—"

"No, you started this and you worked very hard to do it," Jacques interrupted furiously, "so why don't you see it through?"

Her eyes stung like the room had filled with smoke; her throat tightened as she watched his shoulders rise and fall as he drew in a deep breath, watched his jaw drop.

"I—"

There were voices and the shriek of sneakers on tile, and Jacques and Eloise each froze. Eloise looked over her shoulder, her heart pounding, and then blinked furiously, trying to erase her feelings from her face.

Pell and the squat backup goalie she had seen earlier—Harper?—spilled from the hallway to the locker room, both dressed in Bruins T-shirts and shorts like Jacques. They had been laughing about something.

"Eloise!" Pell greeted brightly. "Harper, this is Krystal's intern."

"Ah, Bonehead's one *twu wuv*," Harper concluded immediately. Up close he looked less like Jack Black, and was burlier and broader, with black hair and a black beard. If Jacques was the warrior-king in a period piece, Harper would be his blacksmith. "And Lavy! We were just re-traumatizing Dan, and now we're getting some lunch."

Harper pointed at Eloise with two finger-guns, and wiggled his shoulders in a little dance. Even though it was a joke, Eloise could tell he was a good dancer. "You coming? I heard Bonehead told you his favorite movie was some chick flick and I have questions."

"No—I really have to get going, but thank you, that's really nice of you," Eloise said quickly.

"Ugh. Fine," Harper grumbled. He was oblivious to any tension, but Pell was looking between her and Jacques, ginger brows knit together. "What about you, Lavesque—burgers?" Harper prompted.

"Ah, I should get going as well," Jacques declined with a half-smile. The only sign of his fury that remained was a light flush across his cheeks, and a tension to his shoulders. "I have two boys who have decided that today is pizza day."

"*Every* day is pizza day, unless it's burger day," Harper reasoned. "Fine. Pell and I will have a romantic date of our own without you guys."

Harper had already moved on, but Pell was still looking at Eloise and Jacques closely.

"You guys alright?" Pell asked.

"I'm great! I got so much great material and everyone was so nice, really," she reassured him. "But I've got a train to catch, and lots of information to synthesize, and you all have burgers and pizza to get to, so—so anyways, I'll see you all later."

"Later, gator," Harper said, saluting her. Pell waved a little limply, looking unconvinced.

"See you," she said to Jacques, avoiding his eyes.

"Yes—see you," he said, avoiding hers too.

·)) ● ((·

Eloise rode the train from Boston Landing in agony over Jacques Lavesque.

She wanted to rip her skin off, she wanted to pace up and down the train screeching like a pterodactyl; she wanted to drink tequila until her face melted off. She had gotten some email replies about her job applications, but she couldn't even comprehend them because of the immediacy of her agony and her fury.

He was right—she had been out to get him, one way or another, since their first encounter. She was mad at him—mad that he wanted to get to know her, mad about whatever he had done to end that beautiful marriage, mad that he was freezing out Andrei Koslov, perpetuating Andrei's isolation and bitterness. She was unfairly mad at a man she did not know, for things half-imagined and half-interpreted.

And yet...

*Why don't you see it through?*

Why had he said *that*?

She pressed her forehead against the window and squeezed her eyes shut the whole way home. Ghosted faces and burned bridges swam in her mind's eye. She never stuck with anything, never saw anything through—except when she did, and then it ended in personal disaster for her.

By the time she got back to her apartment, the outrage had receded, leaving a dulled anger in its place. She unlocked her door and stood in the entryway, still clutching her bag. Her apartment seemed too small to contain all that she was feeling, but she could not afford to go anywhere else.

Her apartment was a mess, and out of sheer spite she set to work collecting all the empty mugs and random forks and plates, loading the dishwasher as she mentally rewrote their encounter—except when she tried to imagine a victorious end, the idea of storming off after delivering a devastating blow didn't feel satisfying. He had been so obviously upset already, and she had known that. She had seen his moment of weakness—his fury at whoever he was fighting with over text—and subconsciously had struck.

Something about it was niggling her, like there was a detail she had overlooked, one that was begging to be examined. Eloise stood at her kitchen sink, staring out the window at the opposite building's white siding, turning over a mug printed with stars in her hand.

She set the mug in the dishwasher and closed it, then dropped onto her sagging couch and opened her laptop. She went to Jacques's Instagram and scrolled back—and back, and back, nearly ten years, to when Andrei had last had a presence in his pictures.

There they were, younger and greener, the picture quality as unpolished as their hair and clothing. Pelletier and Burnie were in these pictures too—Pell so *young*, with shorn hair and a coltish posture; Burnie looking precisely the same—but Andrei was, in the early days, always the one who stood closest to Jacques, their comfort with each other obvious.

She closed Instagram, and Googled until she found an early interview, one from the year that Jacques had signed with the Bruins. It had gotten little attention, eventually buried by the YouTube algorithm.

Eloise pressed 'play.'

"So what does your family think about your hockey career?" the interviewer, off-screen, asked a nineteen-year-old Jacques Lavesque.

His clothes were too big for his body, his nose a little too big for his face, and notably already broken. There was something so adolescent about him, so unformed, so *green*. You could tell he was headed in the direction of becoming a charming man—his eyes and smile were beautiful—but he was not charming yet. He was awkward, all mismatched parts. His posture was wrong, his hair was bad. He was wearing a Bruins jersey over a collared shirt and tie, and it made him look even younger. He was a long way from the man whose face would be emblazoned upon the side of Boston Garden.

"Um, they are supportive, I guess."

His accent was thicker, his words more halting, lacking the fluid confidence that he had now. He grimaced against a nervous laugh.

"Now, I know this next one is a painful topic," the interviewer began in a gentler tone, "but you lost your brother this year, right?"

Jacques swallowed, looked to the side. He glanced warily directly into the camera, giving the unsettling effect that he had made eye contact with her. He was too seasoned to make such a mistake now; she wondered if he even saw the cameras anymore.

"Let me guess," Eloise said bitterly to the screen, "no comment?"

"Yes, in January," he said shortly, tearing his gaze from the camera.

"Mm. Do you think your brother would be proud of you, knowing you've signed with the Bruins?"

"I do not know how to answer that," Jacques said stiffly, turning red, showing some of the temper she had glimpsed today. Maybe this was the interview that Kyle had been talking about. "I cannot ask him, obviously. I really do not know what he would think."

It was a terrible answer, bullishly refusing a sound bite where the interviewer had been leading him to one.

"Of course," the interviewer said hastily. "Your mother has worked as a psychic, right? Has that influenced the grieving process at all?"

She saw the moment Jacques decided to swallow a harsher, blunter response.

"Probably," he said with an aloof shrug. "That is just a side job, it is not her whole life. It is very hard to compare something like that."

"Right, that makes sense, and—" There was a crash and a curse, and Jacques leapt off his stool, hastening to catch something.

"Here. Sorry," Jacques said, handing the interviewer something.

"No need to be sorry, it was my fault—I should have secured that better before we started," the interviewer laughed.

"No, I am sorry for being short," Jacques clarified, visibly calming down, an early sign of the graciousness he would develop. "You were just doing your job, and I agreed to answer your questions. But it is very painful for me to talk about this."

"Completely understandable," the interviewer rushed in. "We can talk about something else. I have so many questions for you. So tell me—you and Andrei Koslov both signed with the Bruins. How does it feel to be on a team with such a close friend? You two were on the same AHL team. You've really grown up together. You're like brothers."

"Very—it's, um—" Jacques looked up, clearly trying to translate, biting his lip. "It is complicated, because I want to be the best player on the Bruins," he said at last with a self-conscious smile, "and now I know I will not be."

"Koslov said something similar about you," the interview noted. "What do you think makes Koslov such a valuable player?"

"He is... a very intuitive player, he can read my mind somehow," Jacques explained, gesturing with his hands, "and of course, he is so fast, it's hard for people to know what he will do next."

"He is certainly *unpredictable*," the interviewer agreed with a laugh. "When I asked him a question he didn't like, he just pretended to not know English... in English."

"Yes, he does that sometimes," Jacques conceded with an exasperated laugh.

Eloise paused the video. Something was beginning to come together in her mind, a connection that she had not made earlier. She could not believe she hadn't thought of it before.

Her apartment was silent; the only noise was the distant hum of traffic beyond the cheap windows. *jacques lavesque brother*, she Googled. The first result took her to Jacques's Wikipedia page.

Personal life [edit]
Lavesque is of French-Canadian descent. His father passed away when Lavesque was a young child[13], leaving his mother Adele to raise Lavesque and his older brother, Olivier, in their remote town outside of Quebec City. Lavesque has described his childhood as comfortable, uneventful, and 'quite snowy'[17].

Olivier Lavesque passed away unexpectedly on January 17, 2006[13].

   Lavesque and his wife Rachel Hathaway have two children, Peter and Luke[21].


   Eloise clicked through to the article on Olivier Lavesque's death, but it contained no details and no images, and she could not find any further information elsewhere.

   She chewed her lip, deep in thought. *kyle hearst bruins*, she Googled next, and scrolled through his considerably shorter Wikipedia page.

### Personal life [edit]
Hearst is from Boston and grew up in the Dorchester neighborhood. He has one younger brother, Patrick, and an older sister, Colleen[1].


   Eloise searched some more, but she couldn't find anything on Patrick Hearst—she couldn't find him on social media, even after scrolling through everyone that Kyle was following on Instagram, diligently clicking on each one and exploring their account.

   Her phone vibrated a few times. Hollis called and she watched her phone buzz along the fabric of her couch, displaced by the vibration. Hollis's contact photo was a picture of him dressed up in a Bruins jersey—Bobby Orr—when he was four or five. Eloise had chosen it primarily because he was clearly mid-meltdown, mouth huge and cheeks red and wet, and the fury of it always made her laugh.

   She watched the screen go dark again, then light up once more with a voicemail. She didn't have the energy to hear what she knew would be a tirade right now; she put her phone on 'do not disturb' and turned it screen-down on her couch.

   The truth of it was that she was at a crossroads. Her bank accounts and her cabinets were empty; yet if she pivoted to one of the jobs she had applied for, she would have to let go of the detective work which came with an unpredictable schedule and the need for flexibility. If she did this, she would have a steady income, and soon maybe even enough money to fix her car. She could rebuild her life, piece by piece, and start fresh, and leave this battered dream behind.

And yet...

*Why don't you see it through?* Jacques had asked so harshly. He had merely commented on her conversational style; he could not know he had struck precisely at the heart of something far thornier, far stickier and messier, a bloody sticky mess beneath shadowed stairs—the thing both most integral to her and yet most private about her.

*Not all of us have your commitment*, she wanted to argue. She wished she could fight him further on this, make him understand that there was something inherently different, inherently *better* about him. *Not all of us are like you.*

Some of us, she thought, were more like Andrei: brittle and messy and hurting. Not everyone was capable of maintaining that perfection, and Eloise had seen over and over again that it was best to leave while you still could, if you weren't strong enough to finish what you had started. In mountain climbing, they called it 'turnaround time' and it was very often the difference between life and death.

*Or else*, she thought, *you end up in a blood feud with a former teammate, and caught in a text message battle with what was probably your soon-to-be ex-wife when you should be getting lunch with your teammates.* Jacques Lavesque might have climbed Everest but he was alone up there, with no clear way to get back down again.

On the other hand, it was Jacques's face on the side of Boston Garden—no one else's. She could picture it easily, having gone past it so many times in the last decade: in massive, grainy black-and-white, his unmistakable light eyes looking out over the highway. She had never thought about who she was looking at, or just how long those eyes had looked out over route one and the Bunker Hill bridge. And every Halloween, how many little boys would don their tiny Lavesque jerseys for decades to come, like Hollis and his Bobby Orr jersey thirty years earlier? How many boys like Travis Martin had had his poster on their wall? If there was anyone who had the 'it' that Andrei had spoken of, it was Jacques, because you did not get to the top of that mountain by accident.

And then she was thinking of Kyle, who maybe reminded Jacques a little of himself, and thinking of all she had learned about Kyle today. *He had to figure out how to pay for it too*, Kyle had said, and sharing that had meant something, had revealed something.

*Why don't you see it through?*

Once again she had the sense of a detail overlooked, a thing her instinct had picked up on but which her mind had not yet processed. There was *something* there, glimmering just beyond her grasp. She opened her tablet once more and studied the sketch of Kyle's tattoo.

Maybe it wasn't time to turn around and abandon this investigation—maybe not quite yet. It was instinctive, based on nothing but a gut sense. She just needed a little more time. Then she'd give up; *then* she would turn around.

*how to apply for snap benefits*, she Googled.

# Chapter Nine

"This is Turbo," Peter informed Jacques, holding up a crumpled paper straw wrapper, "and this is Jill," he added, holding up his blue plastic cup.

"Oh, she looks like a Jill," Jacques agreed, making a show of studying the cup. "Are they friends?"

"No," Peter said without further explanation or context, and Jacques tried not to laugh.

"That is one ugly Jill—no wonder they're not friends," Burnie said absently. "I wouldn't be friends with her either."

Burnie had Jacques's other son, Luke, on his lap, and Luke's large brown eyes were trained in silent fascination on Burnie's shock of brown hair, his short beard, his animated face. "Turbo can totally find cooler friends. Right, Luke?" Burnie asked, jostling Luke, who didn't take his eyes off Burnie.

The table between them was covered with a lunch mess, Batman and train toys, crumpled napkins, and empty plates. No one in the pizzeria had recognized them yet, helped by the fact that neither of them wore Bruins gear and they were in a quiet part of town.

Burnie was like a dog on the hunt. Completely indifferent to the fact that Luke was now smushing his cheeks and lips, he kept talking.

"So *where* is Rachel again?" he asked in a muffled voice as Luke tried to cover Burnie's mouth with his hand. "I haven't seen her in like two months."

"She's been busy with work," Jacques said. *Oh, more 'no comment' bullshit?* Eloise asked in his head, and he let out a hot breath.

"Okay, well, Stephy is convinced that you two are getting a—" He mouthed the word *divorce* and then continued normally, "Or something, so make sure Rachel shows up to the party so she can stop asking me. Cut that out," Burnie told Luke carelessly. "See, I'll do it to you. You don't like it when I do that, right?"

He covered Luke's face, smushing his cheeks, and grinned when Luke began to cackle and shriek with delight.

(Burnie had twin daughters, Luna and Bella, who had inherited both Burnie and Stephanie's individually legendary confidence. They would have ruled the pizzeria by now, clad in costumes and shrieking. Burnie was a surprisingly competent parent, unbothered by chaos and usually in control, and he found Luke and Peter mild-mannered and easy in comparison.)

"Sure," Jacques said. Burnie was staring at him with narrowed eyes.

"What's up with you?" he wanted to know. "You've been like a teenager today. You're never moody. Who do you want me to kill?"

"Ah, it's nothing." Jacques shifted Peter's weight on his leg. He studied the way the sunlight fell on the sidewalk outside. He massaged the bridge of his nose, feeling the bump where it had been broken all those years ago. He could not remember the last time he had been so ashamed of himself. "I was—I was a jerk to Krystal's intern. It was really bad, I was really out of line."

"What—Blondie? Why?" Burnie was baffled. He stole some of Peter's untouched pizza, cramming it into his mouth and chewing loudly.

"I don't know." It was a lie. He did know, but there was no way he could explain it to Burnie. "She was sort of poking me about Andrei."

"Oh, gweat. Is she anower Kozzy fangirl?" Burnie asked thickly through a mouthful of pizza. "Whaf ish it wiff that guy ang women? Why do they love him?"

"She told me off for not including Andrei more," he explained with a shrug, knowing fully that this was a misrepresentation.

"Man, she does not seem dumb like that," Burnie marveled after swallowing, shaking his head. "Hope she knows the lion's not just a big cat."

"I like lions," Peter put in. Burnie tore off more of Peter's pizza.

"You *think* you like lions, because in pictures they're cool," he corrected, pointing at him with pizza crust, "but if you met one on the street I promise you wouldn't like them."

Burnie chewed thoughtfully as Peter drew what Jacques assumed was a lion on one of the napkins. "Did you tell her that you've probably known Koslov longer than she's been alive and you might have sound reasoning for not being all buddy-buddy with him?"

"I don't think she's that young," Jacques reflected. "Krystal said she wasn't a college intern. I think she's closer to our age."

"Huh. Once you hit forty they all look the same."

"You're not forty yet," Jacques said with a grin.

"Almost," he said. "Close enough, anyway."

"Do you think I should be bringing Andrei in more?" Jacques asked, knowing the answer he would get. "Am I wrong?"

"*No.* You are never wrong, got it?" Burnie absently wiped Luke's face, which had pizza sauce on it. "The guy's a mess, and he's not even that good anymore. He's not as fast as he used to be—remember how *fast* Koslov was in the old days? He used to be faster than me, and then the dude turned thirty and it went away. And besides, he doesn't have that *thing* he used to have. You know, that bit of magic. I hate to admit it, but he had magic, back in the old days."

"I'm not as fast anymore," Jacques pointed out.

"You're like wine, dude. You've only gotten better with age. Some guys are like milk and Koslov's one of them. It's over for him and I still can't believe we traded Mäkinen *and* Simpson to get him. Koslov is not worth those two. We should've got Connor Mc-freaking-David for them. Tampa Bay's gonna beat us again this year and Coach'll just want Mäkinen and Simpson back, but it won't matter because I'll have gone insane from a whole year of Koslov."

Privately, Jacques thought he might go insane by the end of this season as well, but he didn't share that with Burnie.

"Daddy, Uncle Burnie ate my pizza," Peter said quietly.

"You *let* Uncle Burnie eat your pizza," Burnie cut in. "You totally could've stopped me but you're too nice."

"You want more pizza?" Jacques asked Peter, tilting him on his lap so he could read his face better.

"No, not really," Peter said solemnly. He slumped against Jacques's chest. "When is your vacation over, Daddy?"

"Vacation's been over, kiddo," Burnie said, unwittingly saving Jacques. "Hockey's *back*."

"Daddy's on vacation," Peter insisted. "He's at a hotel."

"Kid's gonna be a writer," Burnie muttered, shaking his head. They began cleaning up the table; Burnie pretended to be a lion for Luke after showing him Peter's napkin drawing, and in the ruckus Peter looked concernedly at Jacques.

"Mommy said you were at a hotel," he accused.

"I'm right here with you," Jacques teased him, even as his throat tightened. "I can't be at a hotel."

*Oh, more 'no comment' bullshit?*

They left the pizzeria and emerged in the bright early autumn sunlight. "Thanks, man, for coming with me," he said to Burnie as they walked down the street to their cars. "I know it was short notice."

"No problem, dude." Burnie shrugged. "I was in the mood for pizza and Batman." He pointed threateningly at Jacques. "Text Stephy and tell her Rachel's coming, okay?"

"Sure, definitely," Jacques said. *Oh, more 'no comment' bullshit?* He crouched down next to his sons. "Wave goodbye to Burnie, okay?"

"BYE, UNCLE BURNIE!" Luke screamed, flailing his arms.

"BYE, LUKE!" Burnie copied him, also flailing, drawing interest from passersby. Peter was a little more reserved, waving at Burnie as he frowned, squinting in the sunlight, his ash brown hair, so like Jacques's, turned blond by the sun.

"Come on, now we have to get in our own car," he told them, lifting Luke up and taking Peter's hand in his free one.

They spent the rest of the afternoon at the Public Garden. Luke was fascinated by the ducks, happily oblivious, but Peter was still in a mood. Normally Jacques would have asked him what was wrong, but he knew Peter was unsettled by his lie, and he didn't have anything better to tell him.

*An expensive tantrum.* It wasn't just costing him money.

At five o'clock it was time to take the boys back to Rachel. Luke was sleepy; Peter was still quiet and discontented. When Jacques looked in the rearview mirror, Luke was asleep in his carseat, little mouth hanging open, but Peter was still frowning, staring out the window.

Jacques pulled up in front of the brownstone. Frail yellow leaves were scattered across the sidewalk. In the front window, a candle was flickering, one of those hundred-dollar ones that Rachel preferred. He glimpsed her slim silhouette there, too; she had been watching for them. He pressed his forehead against the steering wheel for a moment.

"Why are you doing that, Daddy?" Peter asked from the back seat.

"My head hurts," he said, drawing in a deep breath and sitting up straight again. "It's called a headache."

"Mommy said she had a headache today too," Peter noted.

"I bet she did," Jacques muttered disgustedly, thinking of the texts that he had gotten from her today, and he got out of the car.

He heard the heavy front door open as he was negotiating a cranky Luke out of his carseat. He didn't look up as he heard the clack of Rachel's boots on the sidewalk. She would have just gotten home from work. She worked at an art nonprofit—which was only successful because she helmed it—and dressed immaculately for it, all silk blouses and dark jeans and unusual gold jewelry, and shoes that made expensive noise when she walked.

"Mommy!" Peter called over Luke's complaining. Rachel opened the other passenger door to get Peter out, filling the car with her heavy perfume. Jacques glimpsed her soft brown hair, blown-out and curled, swinging as she reached for Peter, bracelets clinking together.

"Mommy, Daddy has a headache too," he said in his musical voice.

"Wow, how about that," Rachel said warmly. Over the seats their eyes met, but Luke was wriggling and complaining so Jacques was forced to look away. "Did you have fun with Uncle Burnie?"

"No. He stole my pizza." Peter paused. "And Daddy was mean to someone because of Andrei. What's Andrei?"

"Daddy would never be mean to anyone," Rachel said firmly. "And Andrei's a hockey player, isn't he?"

She was looking at him again; Jacques had gotten Luke out of his carseat.

"Yes, he is," he said before slamming the door.

Rachel's older sister Emma was there when Jacques entered with a fussy Luke in tow. Emma was a less beautiful clone of Rachel: her brows were permanently arched in a look of disdain, unlike Rachel's, which had an opposite arch to them, giving her a beseeching, entertained air—a *can you believe this?* type of simpatico that made people fall so in love with her. Emma was sitting on the ivory sofa by the fireplace with a glass of white wine. She got to her feet when Jacques entered, unfolding her long legs leisurely and setting her white wine on the marble-topped coffee table.

"Haven't seen *you* in forever," she greeted, air-kissing him like he had merely been on a long road trip. "Rach asked me to stay for a few days."

"Thank you, that is helpful," Jacques said as lightly as he could, avoiding her eyes.

There was a lot of business with the boys, and it was a half-hour later when Jacques was finally on the sidewalk again, unlocking his car. Rachel hurried after him, crossing her slender arms over her chest in the chilly evening, long waves cast about by the wind. He turned away from her.

"So that's where we're at now? You don't even reply to texts anymore?" she asked his back in a thick voice as Jacques looked down at his key.

"How could you send me a text like that when you know I was at practice?" He could not look back at her. "How old are you? Are we teenagers?"

"Because it was true." Her voice broke. "Jacques, can we stop with this now? It's killing me. Seriously. I'm starting to go crazy and think you're really going to..."

He couldn't erase the look on Peter's face from his mind's eye. If he gave in he could make it all go away. He could keep going, just a little hobbled by what he knew about who his wife had become.

And yet. "I miss you so much," she said thickly. "This isn't us."

That triggered something.

"Isn't it?"

He looked back at her—brown eyeliner running a little, brown eyes wet. He watched her swallow. "I guess it's not, because usually I just let things go."

"Oh, my poor long-suffering husband," Rachel choked, laughing acidly, changing instantaneously. The wind picked up her hair more and it swirled around her. "Because it's all *my* fault, right?"

"In your text, you said it was," he fired back.

"Yeah, and then I thought about how I sent my husband a text that said I was crying at work, and he didn't even reply. And I thought, hm, maybe *I'm* not the problem here."

Enough of this.

"I'm done," he said shortly. *Oh, more 'no comment' bullshit?*

Jacques walked around the car, blood pumping in his ears. Rachel was crying in earnest now, angular shoulders rising and falling. Before she could say anything else, he got in. His heart was pounding again as he turned the key. He did not look in the rearview mirror as he pulled away from his house.

When he got back to his hotel room, he dropped onto the crisp linens and closed his eyes.

He could faintly hear Boston rush-hour traffic beyond his window, and the soft noises of adjacent hotel rooms, and his loneliness intensified. He wanted to be home with his boys. He did not want to be in this fucking hotel room. He missed his wife, yet he knew that the person he missed was who she had been in the beginning, that first time he had fallen into bed with her—and where he had thought she was going.

It was like watching a movie about different people, to remember their first morning-after: the shy way she had pulled on his hoodie, the giddy silence of getting breakfast together. They had not been those people in so long, but he hadn't realized they were changing, that he no longer knew where they were going, until he had looked around and realized that everything looked different from how it should.

Jacques could still remember the first time he had noticed something different. It had been a car ride home from a party the summer after they'd had Peter. It had been a good party—Pell and his wife

Juliette had thrown it, and their parties were always fun. They were not the ragers that Burnie and Stephanie threw, but always comfortable and pretty. He couldn't remember the occasion but it had been something low-key and happy.

They had bid everyone goodbye, among the last to call it a night as usual. Jacques's face had hurt from smiling and laughing all night. The door had swung shut behind them, ensconcing them in darkness as they walked to the car, gravel crunching beneath their feet, too loud in a silence that should not have been there at all.

Nothing was really wrong. It was just that before, they would have been happily dissecting the party and comparing conversations; their chatter would have filled the car; he would have taken the long way home just so they could talk some more, even though they would not have to share each other with anyone else once they got home. As he started the car, he caught himself trying to remember the last time they had talked that much, and could not pinpoint it. *Cut that out*, he'd told himself. *You're just tired.*

"Did you have a good time?" he had asked at last, after they had gotten in the car. Rachel was staring out the window; he could only see a sliver of cheekbone when he glanced at her.

"Yeah!" Her voice had been casual, lighthearted, breezy.

"Everything alright?"

"Just peachy," she had said, looking down at her phone. "You?"

"Great, yeah. It was a good party."

"*So* nice," she had distractedly agreed, texting rapidly.

He had felt like he was driving someone's teenaged cousin home. He could not think of a single thing to say, a single thing he even *wanted* to say, and had no sense that Rachel intended to say anything to him either. *Not a big deal*, he had dismissed. They had been under so much stress lately, with Peter, and his career, and they hadn't been out in so long... And Rachel was going through some sort of postpartum thing that she refused to acknowledge... This happened all the time, he had told himself.

Still. It had stuck out to him; a tender tooth that he would eat around, telling himself it would get better in a day or two, so long as he let himself forget about it.

And the rest of that year, every time someone else referenced discontent in their marriage—even Pell, most easygoing man in the world, mentioned tension with Juliette—Jacques privately felt relief. *See? You were worried for nothing. This is normal.*

Maybe he *should* have shared, the way Pell and Burnie did. They never made it sound serious—the fights sounded terrible but were always mentioned in passing, minor details that didn't seem to factor into the larger picture of their marriages. Jacques had never spoken of his marriage to them, partly because he knew Burnie disdained Rachel so violently, partly because he did not have the amusing cycles that they seemed to have with their wives. And soon, their problems could not be neatly packaged into an anecdote anymore; their problems required too much prior context to even explain. *Well, it all started two months ago, and...*

He knew Rachel had drunkenly unloaded on Krystal a few times, but they had never spoken of it, and as far as he knew, Krystal had never shared his marital problems further.

And it hadn't mattered. Not really. He had been fine with it all. He had decided, hadn't he? That sunny morning on Nantucket, he had looked at Rachel and decided she was the one. He had decided.

As the anger at Rachel subsided, the shame from how he had behaved this morning with Eloise crept back in, and he covered his face with his hands.

*Why* had he done that? Every time he had looked at the seats (and *why* had he looked so much, again and again?), she was laughing with Andrei, allowing him to lean in close, visibly flushed by the closeness, and it annoyed him because it disappointed him. She had seemed, as

Burnie had put it, too smart for that—but this was petty and it should not have bothered him. He was supposed to be more than that, he was supposed to represent something more than that. After all, he had decided that too, hadn't he? He had decided to be that person. Krystal had held up the papers and he had signed on the dotted line. He was expected to be more.

**Jacques [6:37pm]**: hey can you give me eloise's phone number

**Jacques [6:37pm]**: i was rude with her today and owe her an apology

Before he could add any justification, his phone buzzed with a call from Krystal.

"What did you do?" Krystal wanted to know immediately. He could hear frosty music and low chatter in the background; he guessed she was at some designer shop or boutique.

"I lost my temper—she caught me at a bad moment," he said.

"I can't imagine you doing that," Krystal brushed it off. "You never lose your temper anymore. You're just overreacting to something she's probably forgotten about."

"No," he said firmly. "I was out of line. I would like to call her and apologize."

"Wow. Must've been bad. I can apologize for you. Or you can just wait for the next time she swings by the arena."

Did she not want to give him Eloise's number? Jacques sat up a little.

"It was really bad. I'd rather not wait," he said.

"What did you even say?"

"She just asked me a few questions about Andrei," he said. "It was completely my fault," he added before Krystal could assume that it was Eloise's fault, or decide to reprimand her. "I was pissed off about something else and bit her head off for no reason."

"Let me check and see if she's comfortable with me giving out her number," Krystal said at last. "She's really private. I don't even think she has social media."

"Really? A social media intern doesn't have social media?" he asked skeptically.

"It's best practice—she's smart. I don't have any personal social media either, as you know," Krystal said immediately. He heard her say something sharply to someone else, then sigh. When she spoke again her voice was lower, more private. "Anyway, has it started?"

His stomach dropped. Jacques looked at the desk, in which the papers were stored. *Should I? Is that the right thing to do?* Krystal was another person who had known him for over a decade, who supported him fiercely, yet somehow he couldn't turn to her for advice, either.

"Not yet," he said. She let out a breath. "I don't know if anything will get started."

"Alright."

"Yeah." He rubbed the back of his neck. "Anyway. Let me know about Eloise."

"Yeah, sure. Night."

"Night."

Jacques plugged his phone into its charger, which had been neatly coiled next to the bedside lamp by the housekeeping staff, and opened his laptop. What had Eloise's last name been...? M-something? He searched his email until he found the note from Krystal, notably sent *after* Eloise had first shown up at the practice rink.

*eloise morris boston*, he typed into Google, which returned nothing save for a locked Twitter account that listed her as a 'media strategist' and 'freelance writer,' and a Wordpress site that listed a communications degree from some university he'd never heard of.

She was nowhere else. No school records, no public records, and though he located the university she had listed, he couldn't find any proof that she had attended.

*Eloise*, he thought, studying the lack of Google results, *I don't think your last name is Morris.*

# Chapter Ten

S pend enough time alone in your apartment and you will eventually face yourself and your wrongs at odd hours. Eloise knew this dance so well. Every step she took further into her research on Kyle Hearst, the shame followed like a shadow. Ghosted faces and burned bridges; they all were visible in the corner of her eye.

"I could apologize," she had said at two in the morning on the first night, staring at a dusty corner of her ceiling that was not illuminated by her cheap white lamp. *No, no, very bad*, she had thought with a shudder. An apology would require looking into the face of something, a jagged quarry whose mouth she had been skirting for years.

"He thinks I'm an asshole," she said in the silence of her apartment the next morning, as she stood at her kitchen sink and ate stale cereal. She was testing the notion. *Why don't you see it through?* "Jacques Lavesque thinks I'm an asshole."

*You kind of are*, her empty apartment and silent phone said. But he was wrong. *She* knew why she had acted the way she did. He didn't know her at all and couldn't judge her.

She had gone back to her research on Kyle, stabbing at her laptop keys furiously. She kept seeing the wreath on her father's door, the one Lily had put there; she kept seeing Monique's face; she kept seeing the cardboard box that she had filled with odds and ends from her lab bench on the day that she had left the job. She had packed it in the quiet of the lab, her colleagues' backs to her.

The screen had blurred before her eyes and she had kept working, trying not to see the wreath, the box, her ex-best friend's face. Even as she called Krystal to talk through the case, there was a growing notion in her mind, one that could not be ignored: she had reached a place she had never wanted to be going at all.

When she had texted Krystal her request late that night, she had not known what to expect, but when she woke with a start this morning, sprawled on her couch with her laptop on her lap, she hadn't expected Jacques Lavesque's contact information in a crisp text, without question or comment. Krystal was so clearly protective of Jacques that Eloise had expected a struggle, and questions, and maybe even radio silence.

"Goddammit," she swore, setting her phone aside and getting up to shower. Part of her had assumed Krystal might simply refuse, and then she wouldn't have to do the thing.

The text carried a physical presence in her apartment, as though she were house-sitting an unfamiliar pet. She checked her phone again as soon as she was done showering, as though she might have imagined the text, dripping water on her phone screen and warping the pixels. The text remained unchanged, but her anxiety only increased.

*Why don't you see it through?*

She didn't have to do it yet. She could just do it whenever. She didn't even *have* to do it—he wasn't expecting to hear from her. He probably didn't even want to hear from her.

And yet. *Why don't you see it through?*

In addition to *that* task, she had some other plans for the day: she planned to visit Kyle's current home, an unglamorous apartment in Upham's Corner, and then his childhood home further south in

Dorchester, where his family still lived. Seeing where Kyle lived might trigger some fresh line of thought or inquiry. Plus, it was an opportunity to be out in the world, away from her apartment which seemed to be haunted by all of the mistakes she had made with people.

She dried her hair, scowling at her phone.

There would be no consequences if she did not do this thing, aside from the shame of knowing she could have tried. This was entirely self-imposed. And what if he answered, and she just made things even weirder? That was a distinct possibility.

*Why don't you see it through?*

Days later, that still hurt. Days later, she still wished she could yell at him, *that's not all of me.* For certain, it was some of her. She was old enough to admit that. She didn't want it to be all of her, though.

*You know what you have to do.*

"Fuck it," she muttered to her reflection. "Gonna just do the thing."

She finished getting dressed, and got a glass of water, and crouched on the edge of her sofa, holding her phone with clumsy cold hands. And, scrunching her eyes shut, she dialed Jacques Lavesque's number. Practice would not have started yet. She might catch him. She covered her face, listening to it ring.

"Hi, you have reached Jacques Lavesque," came that musical, staccato voice, warm like he was smiling as he spoke. She heard a child's happy shriek in the background, and then Jacques's soft laugh. "You can probably tell I am unavailable at the moment, but I will give you a call back when I can."

*Beep.*

"Hi. This is Eloise. As in, Intern Eloise."

Her mouth was so dry but she felt too clumsy to risk drinking her water.

She licked her lips instead, swallowing. "So, Krystal gave me your number, and I promise I won't do anything weird with it. I mean, I promise I won't share it with anyone else."

Her face burned. *Get to the point.* "I was totally out of line on Monday, and totally out of line the first time we met, too. You are a person, with feelings, and you are entitled to your privacy on those feelings, and I have no right to dig into things that are probably complicated and personal. I... have a lot of growing to do."

She did not know how else to put it. "Um. So. I'm probably running out of room on this voicemail, but that's it, really. I am so sorry for how I behaved. Anyway. Have a great day!"

She flung her phone across the couch and buried her face in the cushions and groaned into the fabric. Her phone buzzed and with a shriek she lunged for it, but it was just a promotional email from Credit Karma, which, she thought, was hilariously optimistic of them. She slumped into the cushions, turning her phone over again.

When she finally had accepted that Jacques would not be likely to return her call soon (if ever), she got to her feet, donned her jacket, and decided to focus, once more, on Kyle Hearst.

It was easier to feel optimistic when she stepped out of her apartment, as she had known it would be. Warm sunshine washed over her and set the trees aglow with that fond, nostalgic light that early autumn had. Eloise locked her door and, upon reflection, tucked her phone deep in her bag rather than her pocket.

This was an Eloise problem, not a Jacques Lavesque problem. She would not obsess about it.

She had learned a lot about Kyle in the last few days. There was the drug history, which Krystal had made so much fuss about, but which had not turned out to be much of anything. He had been caught with pot in middle school, and had Tweeted about it on an account that he had since deactivated. Since then, he had passed most drug tests given by the AHL, and had passed *all* drug tests from the NHL—but Krystal had pointed out that there were plenty of drugs that the NHL did not test for, like prescription drugs that could be easily dismissed yet easily abused.

"Krystal, just trust me. He's not a drug addict," Eloise had insisted when they'd spoken the prior night, cradling her head in her hand as she studied Kyle's Instagram.

The conversation had sent her back to an old hell—the many young men and women she had testified against in those dour courtrooms. It came back in taste and touch and smell: stale water in paper cups and stiff Express suiting and damp carpet. There had been a special kind of pain to it all that no one else had seemed to feel, to sit across the courtroom from some nineteen-year-old kid and, in a neutral, rehearsed voice, testify against them and fuck up their life.

At first it had been empowering. Eloise had loved the idea of bringing justice to victims who might have been wrongfully imprisoned if not for her analysis, and for her the world was easily divided into who had done the crime and who had not. Over the years that sense of empowerment and justice had eroded, to be replaced by a hollow grief for how the system had so thoroughly failed some people. She might have her problems with her own family and her own upbringing, but these seemed petty and foolish compared to the childhoods that she learned about in that courtroom. She had been little more than another domino in their inevitable line of tragedy and they had always looked right through her; she was as inherent to their tragedy as the furniture in the courtroom.

She knew what drug addicts looked like, and Kyle did not look like them.

She wasn't concerned about the pot, and she didn't think Kyle was doing any drugs. What *did* bother Eloise was Kyle's disciplinary record, which was peppered with fights throughout middle school and high school. None of them had been ruled assault, all of them resolved with short suspensions of both parties.

And then twined throughout it all there was the tarot deck, a lead fine as gossamer. Eloise had taken out a book called *Tarot: Beyond the Basics* from the public library and whenever she hit a dead end, she found herself idly flipping through it, learning the cards and studying the sometimes-macabre illustrations: twin howling wolves beneath an indifferent Moon; the gimlet-eyed Devil with his human subjects, loosely chained, obedient at his feet; the Sun and its reign over sunflowers and a pure white horse. She always had associated the tarot with women—elderly psychics draped in beads and cigarette smoke; henna-dyed teenagers in secondhand camisoles and eyeliner—and never with men. It seemed a distinctly feminine presence in Kyle's otherwise masculine world.

And then, of course, there was the tattoo, which seemed to best match either the Celtic symbol for Beltane, a festival to mark the arrival of summer, or a strange combination of the Norse rune for *F*, a rune which also meant wealth or possessions. It might be nothing—but he had been so deeply embarrassed by it, and Andrei implied that the tarot deck was private as well. She did not know if it meant anything.

Krystal said she had not been privy to whatever conversations had taken place prior to Kyle signing the contract; she only knew that they had not wanted to sign Kyle, and then Jacques had called a meeting. And then, abruptly, they were signing Kyle for a handsome two-year contract. When she had pressed Jacques to explain his stance, he insisted that he had nothing to do with it and had no influence on the organization, and Eloise suspected this was the first time Jacques had been dishonest or withholding from Krystal, and Krystal had not forgiven him for it.

Eloise boarded the MBTA, jostled between a man and his folding bike, and a little old lady with Trader Joe's reusable bags packed with clothing. Her hand again wandered to her bag; she clenched her hand into a fist before she could check her phone. They would be in practice now. There was no way he would be getting back to her any time soon.

The MBTA took her south to the apartment in Upham's Corner. Kyle had recently moved in, signing the lease shortly after being drafted by the Bruins.

Kyle's building was plain, with faded green siding, on a shabby corner of Stoughton Street. The small number of apartments were situated above a deli and a cheesy-looking hair salon. An Irish flag rippled in the wind on top of the building, and the sidewalk was smeared and stained, with unruly garbage cans cluttered along the curb. She approached, thinking it an oddly practical and restrained choice for a nineteen-year-old who had just signed that kind of contract. She had seen the number—it was a good one.

Eloise tried the front door to the building and was both surprised and disdainful when she discovered that someone had wedged newspaper into its hinge to stop the automatic lock from locking. After slipping inside, she tucked the newspaper to the side of the hall, letting the door close fully behind her.

Sickly sea-green linoleum tile, cracked and grimy, paved the front hall. It badly needed to be vacuumed; grit and dead leaves crunched wetly beneath her boots. Eloise found the silver mailboxes along one wall, and she scanned the nameplates until she found #28—Kyle's apartment number and, incidentally, the jersey number he'd chosen.

And perhaps not incidentally, a number associated with hate groups.

He had scrawled his name in blue ballpoint pen on the nameplate in thin, boyish handwriting. She could tell that he hadn't gotten his mail yet today, but the slit was too narrow for her to learn anything beyond that.

Now what? The first-floor apartments seemed deserted. She had already trespassed; it couldn't hurt to take a look at his door. As she passed apartments, she heard a mix of television and vacuums, but it was otherwise a quiet building, not the kind of place that would appeal to the typical nineteen-year-old boy.

Kyle had no doormat or wreath. Number 28 was nondescript, just the apartment at the very end of the hall. Eloise lingered, not sure of what she was looking for. She peered closely at the door, and realized that it didn't seem like it was locked. That was odd. He was at practice now. It should have been locked.

She set a hand on the knob and applied a little pressure, and then—

A creak on the other side. A breath. Or had it been?

She stilled, holding her breath, but the old flooring creaked beneath her feet when she shifted. Had it just been her own weight?

She wanted to test it, but she heard the shriek of the front door to the building and a brief clamor of traffic, and pulled away hastily from the door. *Time to go.*

On the steps, she passed an elderly man with shopping bags, pretending to be absorbed in her phone, and at the foot of the stairs listened to him walk to the other end of the hall.

Maybe Kyle had a live-in girlfriend that no one knew about and that he never referenced on Instagram. Or maybe he had just forgotten to lock his door, and she had mistaken something else for someone's breathing on the other side. Those were the most likely explanations, and—disappointing as it was—she had learned that ninety percent of the time, the most boring explanation was the truth.

Still. That left ten percent.

After watching his windows for a bit, she left and wandered the neighborhood. She had been taking in the details—the Irish flag; the Celtic cross tattoo; the number twenty-eight appearing on both his apartment number and his jersey; the Norse or possibly Celtic tattoo—and arranging those pieces together with a particular guess in mind.

They formed a pattern: one of a kid raised on a certain type of generational bitterness, a kid who grew up with meaner boys who made worse jokes. Perhaps somewhere along the way, the line between outrageous, provocative humor and genuine prejudice had been crossed. It was hard to imagine the sensitive, observant young man she'd spoken with being so prejudiced, but she had also learned that you never really knew people. The most mild-mannered men could hide devastating secrets, carry unholy grudges, and go about their daily lives without ever giving a hint of what went on inside their heads.

She wandered the neighborhood, not sure what she was looking for, but too wired to settle somewhere. It was better to keep moving; it made it easier to think. The alternative was to sit in her apartment, thinking about her hunger and checking her phone.

The number could be intentional for other reasons. Hockey players were notoriously superstitious. Perhaps Kyle had chosen his apartment specifically *because* it shared a number with his jersey. Perhaps he had not known that the number twenty-eight had any other significance. After all, when she had been scrolling through a database of known hate symbols on Monday night, it had struck her that so many things could be considered hate symbols that it was inevitable that a person would have one associated with them—a frequently-used emoji, or a number at the end of a Twitter handle, for example. And wasn't that the point of them, that they blended in so seamlessly with everything else, just like Kyle so seamlessly blended in with Boston?

After wandering the neighborhood and feeling no closer to understanding, Eloise headed south to Dorchester, consulting Google Maps until she found the Hearst house on Westville Road.

She tucked her bleached hair into her beanie and slowed her pace as she approached. The house was a skinny single on a street full of twins, with pale yellow siding and a slanting wooden porch, its railing like toothpicks. Empty window boxes, a 'Blue Lives Matter' flag, and a grimy satellite dish decorated the second story, and the house was ringed by a tilting, uneven hurricane fence. A slender maple tree, about to blaze into its autumn glory, trembled and rippled in front of the house, glossy leaves catching the sunlight.

It was impossible to tell if anyone was home; the bright sun turned the windows opaque. The house was as plain and unassuming as Kyle, narrow like it was trying to make space for the other houses around it.

What to do now?

Eloise turned around and walked toward Geneva Street, deep in thought. A drill was going nearby, its insistent thunder and rattle somehow harsher in the bright sunlight, and it nearly obscured the feeling of her phone vibrating in her bag.

*Shit.* She was getting a call.

She halted on the sidewalk. *Jacques Lavesque*, her screen told her so indifferently.

"Fucking fuck," she muttered, and then ducked into the Sobrino Market on the corner. She answered on the very last ring, slipping down one of the aisles in search of some quiet.

"Hello, this is Eloise." She pressed her lips together to stop herself from saying *Davies*.

"Eloise. This is Jacques Lavesque."

She huddled by the milk. "Jacques. Hi." Everything else seemed to fade. "Um. How—how are you? I'm guessing you got my call."

"I did." He hesitated and her stomach dropped. There was a dull roar in the background, like he was in a parking lot. "I hope now is a good time."

Eloise squished to the side to allow a construction worker to pass. "It's—sorry—it's absolutely great."

"You sound in the middle of something," Jacques observed quickly. "I can call you another time."

"Not at all, just grocery shopping." She twisted around the tight corner into the produce section. Eloise picked up an avocado and squeezed it, then put it back. Her hand was shaking. "Which I hate, so. Shouldn't you be in practice?"

"We just finished for the day, and now I am walking back to my car," he explained. "I wasn't sure of the best time to call so I just picked now before you would have to hear screaming boys in the background."

"Now is great," she reassured him. "You didn't have to return the call."

"No, I did. I—thank you," he began, "for the voice message. It is funny because I wanted to call you, but Krystal would not give me your number. She said you were private."

"Oh, really?" Perhaps this was why Krystal had not even questioned why she might want Jacques's contact information. Perhaps she had already heard about how unprofessional and interfering Eloise had been.

"Yes, because I'm the one who owes you an apology. I am so sorry, Eloise, for treating you like that the other day."

"No, it's fine—"

"No, it isn't," he interrupted. "You don't have to be fine when someone treats you like that."

"Seriously, I mean it when I say it's fine. I was the one who was poking you," she insisted, ducking out of the way for a mother pushing a stroller. "And I noticed you'd been on your phone and kind of—"

She shrugged, then realized he couldn't see her. "I kind of thought I caught you at a bad time, like you were in the middle of a text fight."

"Actually, that is true." He sounded a little taken aback and she filed that away for later. "But it's still not okay, how I acted. I was angry about—about something else, and I should not have taken it out on you. It's no way to make you feel part of the Bruins, which is something that matters to me, and something that is also my job."

"Well, you don't have to be perfect one hundred precent of the time to make me feel like part of the team. It's not a requirement," Eloise pointed out. "And I was being a jerk too, so maybe we can call it a draw. We caught each other in a bad moment, we both acted in a way that we wouldn't normally..."

The relief was making her giddy. It was okay. She had not burned this bridge—and she did not know why it mattered so much to her. Maybe she just wanted proof that she could leave a few bridges standing; maybe she was simply lonely. "So—so it's fine," she added. "We're good."

"Yeah," he agreed with a laugh, "we are good. And I even learned something about you—you don't like grocery shopping."

"We're really getting somewhere," she said, ducking into another aisle and grinning too hard.

"Huge progress," he agreed. "You know, if you were really sorry, you would give me another fact about yourself."

She toyed with the packaging of a snack pack, relishing the interest in her. She knew it was her ego he was appealing to, knew what he was doing—and truthfully he would have made an excellent investigator—and she knew it was working on her, too, and it was pathetic and embarrassing and the cynical part of her wondered if these were the tactics that had won him the nanny's attention (even as the more rational part of her reminded her that there was no nanny, that that was an invention of her own based on nothing).

On the other hand—she had her own tactics, too. And she wanted something from him.

"Well, since you're sorry too, and we decided it was a draw—how about this? Fact trade," Eloise suggested lightly.

"You want to know Kyle's favorite color," he guessed, and she let out a laugh of surprise. She had not expected him to be a little barbed. "I will text him and ask—"

"No, I want a fact about *you*," she corrected.

"You can Google whatever you want about me—it's all out there thanks to all the interviews and all," he complained. "That is a waste."

"Then consider it a good deal for you," she said. "I want to know how often you get involved in other players' contracts. Krystal said it almost never happens, but I *am* writing a profile on Kyle, and it's no secret that you got involved in that one."

"I was not expecting that," Jacques admitted, intrigued. "Alright, let's see... You're right, I never have gotten involved at all, except when they were going to pass on Kyle, but don't tell Krystal that because we are at a bit of a stalemate there. I don't have any authority or influence with the head office," he reminded her, "so it doesn't mean anything, and I don't know that I influenced their decision at all."

"And what made you get involved in that case?"

"That's all you're getting. Now it's my turn," he said briskly.

"Okay, shoot." She swung into another aisle, further from the cashier's eyes.

"What's your real last name?"

"Jesus—" she blurted.

"I am sure that's not it," he said, and then she was laughing again, drawing the attention of other shoppers.

"It's *Morris*," she protested, still laughing.

"You cannot even answer that one honestly? I'm not going to try and friend you on Facebook, if that's what you're worried about," he teased. "Okay, we'll try an easier one for now. What did you want to be when you were little? When you grew up, I mean. What was the first thing you wanted to be?"

"I..." She hesitated. "Basically—" She thought back to their previous discussions. "You know how your son Peter loves Batman? I wanted to be Batman, basically."

"Batman. You wanted to be Batman," Jacques said in disbelief. "Is this the reason for the fake last name? You have taken this too far—"

"Shut up," she insisted. He was just so *fast*, responding to her more quickly and more immediately than most people did. It felt like a game that she wasn't sure she could win and was so different than the easy, relaxed grace he normally exuded. "You asked and I answered. I wanted to be Batman, okay? I wanted to take down the bad guys, and serve justice, and—and you know, be a hero." She was blushing again. "And since when do I have a fake last name?"

"Since I tried Googling you so I could find a way to reach out to you, and couldn't find anything except an old website."

"I'm—private," Eloise finally admitted. She hoped if she left it hanging, then he might interpret the awkwardness as something ominous or upsetting. "I have my reasons."

"Okay," Jacques said. "I will let you keep your secret identity for now. I should let you go—are you coming to Burnie's party on Friday? As usual you gave a non-answer when he asked."

"Oh, you just couldn't resist another little dig, could you?" She bit her lip, noting the cashier's eyes on her. "I might be busy."

"Gotham can wait. You should come to Burnie's party," he insisted, his voice growing warm again, like he genuinely wanted her to go. And this was his power, she thought, because it really did feel like he wanted her to go, and that made her feel seen. "They're always a lot of fun."

"Yeah, and maybe we can have another embarrassing encounter where we make each other want to crawl into a hole. A real party."

"Another joke instead of a real answer," Jacques noted. "Come to Burnie's party, alright? It will be fun. I promise."

"Maybe," she hedged. "Anyway."

"Anyway," he agreed. "See you on Friday at Burnie's party, Eloise."

At that, she laughed in surprise—he truly was relentless—and then they said goodbye and then she was standing there in Sobrino's Market, and for some reason the world around her looked different.

She could not afford to buy anything to prove she was not there to steal, so she hunched her shoulders and slipped out of Sobrino's, the employee's eyes on her back as she ducked out, and powered down Geneva Street.

She turned back onto Westville Road, trying to get a grip, and almost immediately had to fling herself between two cars, only somewhat hidden between them and by a couple of garbage cans.

"...sick of this, sick of your bullshit. You completely fucked me over, alright?" Kyle Hearst said with more vehemence and emotion in his voice than she had heard yet. "Today really fucking *mattered*—"

The two young men passed. Kyle wore his old Sox cap backwards, the red clashing horribly with his auburn hair, and his companion wore an ancient black hoodie that made his haggard complexion even more wan; he had a black beanie on, too, but it was obvious his head was shaved.

"Whatever, just..." They disappeared around the corner before she could catch the rest of it.

Eloise's palms and knees were stinging from how she'd hit the gravel, her heart pounding.

# Chapter Eleven

They must have been coming from Kyle's childhood home around the corner. Eloise rose from her crouch and hurried down the road, making sure her hair was tucked into her knit hat before rounding the corner and slowing her pace. They had gone into Sobrino's, but there was no way Eloise could go inside again without attracting the cashier's attention and possibly causing a scene.

Had Kyle skipped practice? That was the only way he could be here now, but Jacques had not said anything, even though the subject of Kyle—and Eloise's obvious interest in him—had come up. She lingered by the vivid blue of the storefront next door, and texted Krystal, who replied within seconds. Eloise pictured her enunciating into her Apple Watch while on a treadmill, head to toe in immaculate Lululemon.

**Krystal [12:37pm]**: Just asked and apparently he missed practice today. Coach said he was out sick.

**Krystal [12:37pm]**: ...Why?

Eloise was about to tap out an explanation when the door to Sobrino's swung open again. Both men were carrying soda bottles. Up close, there was an obvious familial resemblance: both boys had the same shadowed blue-grey eyes and the same pretty, thin lips, an un-expected delicateness to the features around the chin. It was definitely Kyle's little brother Patrick, and either he was ill again or something else bad had happened, because he was emaciated—it turned her stomach how his black hoodie draped over his shoulders—and the hollows beneath his eyes looked like bruises. He also had a split lip, and the skin around it was red and angry.

"...don't have time for this shit, alright?" Kyle was saying as Eloise fell into step a few paces behind them.

"Hurr hurr, Kyle's so important now," Patrick said in a mocking falsetto, tilting his head from side to side tauntingly. "Kyle's gonna win all the hockey and marry his boyfriend Lavesque—"

"If Dad knew, he'd kill you, alright?" Kyle interrupted, unbothered by the taunt. "I told you, you gotta keep a lower profile. Stop getting into it at school, or they're gonna take a closer look—"

"Maybe I don't give a fuck what *Dad* thinks," Patrick countered.

They were nearing the house now, and Eloise was about to have to lose them. She was typing the conversation into her notes app, hoping it looked like she was rapidly texting.

"He's such a pathetic beta loser anyway."

"Yeah, sounds just like you, doesn't it?" Kyle said scathingly. "Can't even fucking win the fights you pick. Maybe that tells you that you shouldn't be picking them in the first place."

"Oh, yeah. 'Cause you win all the fights that you start."

"Maybe not, but I never got my ass handed to me by a fucking..."

They were climbing the front steps of the house now. She slowed her walk, eyes on her phone, but the screen door swung shut with a shriek and she lost them.

*By a fucking* what? She wondered if she had been about to hear a slur.

She lingered, reviewing the transcript of their conversation and annotating it, and was rewarded for waiting when the screen door shrieked open again. This time Kyle emerged alone, carrying his soda from Sobrino's and glaring at his phone.

"Hey, man," he said as he made for a silver Honda, holding the phone to his ear. "Yeah, I know, I just wasn't feeling good."

He forced a very fake cough as he paused at the car. Eloise receded into the shadow of a tree as she listened. "Yeah. Yeah, I'm sorry, alright? I can't control if I get a bug."

Kyle paused, hand on his keys, listening and rolling his eyes. He let his head fall back a little, a show of impatience. "Yeah, I get it. I know. I just... uh... wanted to make sure I took care of my body—"

He was interrupted by the person on the phone. "Lunch?" Kyle asked, panicked. "Uh, no, I'm really not... I wouldn't wanna get you sick, man." He forced another fake cough.

Now he was scowling. "Yeah, I know every practice matters. Yeah, I already talked to Coach. Yeah, I *know*." He bit his thin lip and lightly hit the side of the car, a little display of temper. "I *was* sick—I mean I am—no, it's nothing like that. Pat's in school, probably."

It had to be Jacques. The combination of fury and shame curdling Kyle's features was remarkable. You only got that look when you knew you had screwed up with an authority figure.

"Yeah. Sorry. I'm gonna sleep it off, and I'll be there first thing tomorrow," he said in resignation, rubbing at a spot on his window. "Okay. Bye."

He swore under his breath, stuffing his phone into his pocket and unlocking the door. He cast one last furious look at his childhood home before getting in the car. After he had driven off, Eloise looked up at the house, but she couldn't tell what Patrick was doing, and saw no sign of their father—the 'pathetic beta loser,' as Patrick had called him—inside.

She walked back towards Upham's Corner. Kyle had definitely been picking Patrick up from school because he had gotten into a fight, and her gut told her that the fight had not been random. Kyle had parked on the curb outside of his building, and from across the street Eloise glimpsed him in his window, a shadowy figure, but then he pulled the blinds down and she lost him.

·ɔɔ●ᑕᑕ·

Jacques hung up and pocketed his phone, looking around the garage. Pell and Burnie were only just emerging from the building, and were deep in discussion. Pell was the first to spot Jacques and he offered a cautious wave, like he was testing the waters between them.

Jacques lingered, letting his gym bag slide off his shoulder, and waited for the two men.

"Still here?" Burnie greeted when they finally reached him. "Who were you on the phone with?"

"Hearst, and Krystal's intern before that. I wanted to see why Hearst skipped today," he explained. "Said he was sick."

For a long moment, no one spoke, or even looked at each other. Ever since the new lines had been announced yesterday, everything had been wrong between the three of them. After practice, none of them had spoken, and Pell and Burnie had each gone home wordlessly. For four years now, they had all been on the first line together—now, Burnie and Pell were effectively getting a demotion at a point in their careers where those hurt more than ever.

"Ha," Burnie said belatedly. "Calling bullshit on that now. The kid's at home shitting himself over everything."

"That's a gross image, but I bet you're right," Pell said. He glanced at Jacques like he couldn't fully look at him, and raked a hand through his poofy hair. "So, I was maybe a little self-absorbed yesterday—"

"No—" Jacques held up his hand, dismissing it, but Burnie cut in.

"No, we were dicks, dude. You don't have control over who's on what line. It's not your call and we know that," he said immediately. He scoffed. "Still can't believe I'm thirty-nine fucking years old and still getting shafted for Andrei Dickhead Koslov and a fucking rookie, but—"

He halted and shrugged. "Whatever, dude. I thought about it, and Stephy knocked some sense into me, too, last night. Obviously it's got to be you and Koslov on the first line, right? We paid out the ass for that hired gun so we'd better use him. So then that leaves one open spot. And we already know that Koslov and I don't have chemistry—"

"Oh, you guys have chemistry," Pell joked, and mimed an explosion with his hands.

"Okay, yeah, the bad kind," Burnie conceded, "but whatever, it was never going to be me on that line with you two, right? And then there's Pellegrino over here, but Koslov has zero respect for him so that's never gonna work—"

"So it's a wild card," Pell finished for him, holding his hands up.

Jacques got the sense they had been talking about this just now, rehearsing what they would say—and he also heard echoes of their wives in what they said, too.

"So why *not* Hearst?" Burnie continued. "He's fast as hell, he's definitely smart, and he hasn't been around long enough for Koslov to have a problem with him yet."

Jacques looked between his two friends, wordless for how much he loved them.

"We knew it wasn't your fault, and it wasn't the choice you would have made," Pell reiterated. "It's just—fucking Andrei Koslov, right? He ruins everything."

"Well, Lavy might've made the same choice," Burnie said to Pell. "*I* would've made the same choice, to be honest. He and Koslov are fucking monstrous together. Why waste that energy?"

"Especially if it's going to cost us ten million dollars," Jacques pointed out, and both men laughed.

"Anyway." Burnie slammed into Jacques, and Jacques returned the hug. "We good?"

"We were always good," Jacques promised him as they released each other. Pell, a little more reserved with physical affection, offered a fist bump that Jacques returned before slinging an arm around an awkward Pell and giving him a brief, tight one-armed hug. "And it gives us more depth to have two first-line players on the second line," he added as he let go of Pell.

"Yeah, that's what I'm telling myself so I can sleep at night," Pell joked, though like any truly funny joke, Jacques knew that it carried a bitter kernel of truth. "That, and my Koslov voodoo doll."

"Voodoo doll? Is that the thing you stick pins in?" Burnie wondered. "I should get one."

"Ugh, and Juliette was trying to reason with me last night," Pell groaned, fulfilling what Jacques had suspected, "and she was like, 'Imagine how awkward it is for Andrei, he's coming onto a team that basically forced him out last time.' And I was like, he doesn't freaking care, okay?"

"Nah, he likes it," Burnie countered fervently. "The more cucked we feel, the happier he is. That cheap ass is probably celebrating with a single shitty balloon and five-dollar champagne, if he can bring himself to take a break from worshipping at his shrine to himself and rolling around in his stacks of cash."

He suddenly looked at Jacques suspiciously. "Wait. Did you say you were on the phone with Intern?"

"She called me," Jacques explained. "We got into it a bit a few days ago and it was very awkward, so she called to apologize."

"I *knew* it," Pell exploded, pointing at both him and Burnie. "I knew it, and Harper said I was insane, but I knew you guys were in the middle of something weird. She looked like she was about to cry."

Burnie was digging his phone out of his pocket.

"I dunno, Lavy," he said as he scrolled through his missed texts that he had gotten during practice. "If I was getting calls from some blonde, Steph would rip me a new one."

"Yeah, but it's Eloise," Pell said reasonably. "She does not seem interested at all. Plus, she's working for Krystal, so she definitely knows stuff like whether he's married."

"Wasn't talking about *her*. I dunno anything about her or what her intentions are," Burnie said with a shrug, pocketing his phone, "and I'm not talking about Lavy either, because we all know you've never fucked around even when you could have. I'm saying that I think Rachel would have a problem with her."

Pell pressed his lips together, suddenly becoming interested in the ground.

"You think so?" Jacques asked. Burnie scoffed.

"Yeah, dude. Cute weird girl who looks like she'd be a freak in bed, who's making you laugh, making you mad? Yeah. Rachel would have a problem with that. Any wife would. And I'm guessing she doesn't know, because Intern is still alive."

"Don't say that. I feel like you're talking about my cousin or something," Pell protested with a shudder. "Maybe it's because we're both naturally redheaded."

"Ugh. You're like those animals," Burnie said, "you know, those fat Australian animals who just adopt the weird baby animals from other species?"

"Capybaras," Jacques suggested.

"Yeah, those things. You'll adopt anything," Burnie said disgustedly.

"Come on. You adopted Bonehead," Pell countered.

"I know, but someone had to. I thought you'd pick him up and then you didn't," Burnie began, but halted when they all saw Andrei stalking through the doors and heading towards his car.

"Physical therapy," Pell explained in a low voice as they watched him. "He had that spinal injury, remember?"

"Watch that fuck us over midseason," Burnie muttered.

None of them waved when Andrei's gaze fell upon them, but he didn't look away. He held their gaze as he passed. Jacques knew Andrei so well that he could guess what Andrei was thinking, but as always it wasn't obvious on his face.

Pell was, of course, the first to crack.

"Yo, Koslov," he said faintly, lifting his hand in a wave. Andrei rolled his eyes and kept going.

"Jesus, that was painful," Burnie hissed. He glanced back at Jacques. "Have you guys talked about the line change at all?"

"Nah, we haven't." The idea of having a conversation with Andrei was unthinkable, but he couldn't say that. "Not much to say," he added.

*Oh, more 'no comment' bullshit?*

"I guess it's just like old times, right?" Pell said. "You guys played on a line together longer than you didn't at this point. Probably can just leave it to muscle memory."

"Yeah. Alright, well, I gotta get moving. Stephy wants me to pick up the kegs for the party," Burnie said abruptly, a clear sign that he was censoring himself, though Burnie had never been very good at that.

"Good talk, good talk," Pell said, glancing at Jacques a little anxiously. "Right?"

In spite of it all, Jacques smiled.

"Of course. A lot about people shitting themselves, though," he joked.

"Yeah, way too much shit," Pell agreed. "And I'm going to feel bad all day about talking about how Eloise would be in bed."

"Dude, shut up, you've thought about it too," Burnie said distractedly, hunting for his keys in his gym bag. "She has that freaky, kind of witchy thing going. You know that vibe Winona Ryder had, back in the day? That whole deer-in-the-headlights-but-freak-in-the-sheets thing?"

"No, I don't remember that, because I'm not that old," Pell said cheekily. Burnie rolled his eyes. "I personally wasn't alive in the eighties."

"By like a month, fuckface," Burnie said irritably.

Jacques didn't know why he was annoyed; it was an itch that couldn't be scratched because he didn't know where it had come from in the first place. He rarely got annoyed with Burnie, even when Burnie was acting like a jackass, and Burnie hadn't even come close to the level he usually operated at. Stephanie liked to say that his sense of humor could strip the varnish off a boat.

"What?" he added, eyeing Jacques.

"She's part of our team now. I don't think it's right to talk about her like that."

"Dude, do not let Rachel hear you talk like that," Burnie warned, "I'm telling you. It makes it sound like you're into her, especially when I say whatever shit I want about like, Mackenzie and you don't have a problem with it," he added. "Anyway, catch you guys tomorrow." He waved with the fist that held his keys, and started toward his car.

"I'm going to go for a run and listen to a podcast on the reproductive system to repent," Pell said gloomily, digging out his own keys. "Genevieve asked me about the birds and the bees but then *corrected* me on the egg fertilization process."

(Pell's daughter Genevieve was, at eight, smarter than most of the players on the team.)

"She was just testing you," Jacques teased.

"You know, she probably was."

Pell paused, bouncing his keys and biting his lip. "Seriously. You got put in a crappy position yesterday, with the lines thing, and you handled it really well even when Burnie and I acted like assholes."

"I would've had a hard time with it too," Jacques said. "I didn't blame you."

"Yeah, but I kind of wish you did. I'd feel less like an immature jerk," Pell admitted, but he was smiling. "Anyway."

They parted ways, and Jacques got into his own car. He watched in his rearview mirror as Burnie pulled out of the parking lot, then Pell. If he knew Andrei—and he did—he would bet that Andrei was still sitting in his parked car, checking all his bank accounts like a prayer, a compulsion. Last time they had been friends, he was still doing it, even though he had long since made enough money that the amount no longer mattered to his day-to-day life.

His phone vibrated with a new text.

**Eloise ??? [12:56pm]**: okay fine you win (for now)

**Eloise ??? [12:56pm]**: what's Burnie's address?

Fucking Burnie. Jacques locked his phone screen, and pulled out of the parking lot.

·)) ● ((·

It had been an uncomfortable several hours outside of Kyle's apartment. Eloise was stiff and sweaty and had to pee, not to mention her battery was getting low and she was weak with hunger. She had strayed from Kyle's apartment long enough to buy a granola bar at a convenience shop nearby but she had returned in a hurry, and that granola bar seemed like a long time ago now. It was beginning to get dark, the streets becoming choked with rush hour traffic, but Kyle's Honda remained parked on the road, and Kyle had not left his apartment.

Just as she was consulting the bus schedule to get back to Southie, her patience was rewarded: the front door of the building swung open and Kyle emerged. He began walking down the road, sleeves of his hoodie pulled down over his hands, shadowed eyes wary as he walked, slouched and haunted like the Hermit.

She followed him down the road to Dublin House, a faceless brick building nearly hidden by the cars parked in front of it, only identified by the shabby sign declaring that its kitchen was open until eleven. It was a neighborhood establishment, but she could not picture any other Bruins players setting foot in this kind of bar.

The neon edged Kyle in hot pink as he reached a small group of men waiting outside. Patrick didn't seem to be among them. They stood together, talking and greeting each other, until at last they went inside.

Should she risk it? Eloise paced a little on the sidewalk. *Fuck it.* She pushed her way into the bar.

Kyle went to the counter, talking to the bartender across the hideous tile, while his companions chose a table off to the side, hunched around it like vultures. One of them glanced back at her, discreetly checking her out and deeming her unworthy. When he turned back, she caught a tattoo on his neck that looked like two hands, but the hood of his sweatshirt blocked the view. Another hate symbol, very likely. She thought he looked a little like one of the profiles she had seen in association with Kyle's on Instagram, a locked account with the username f3nris_88.

Her phone pulsed, and Eloise slipped to the side of the door, quickly dimming her screen before unlocking it.

**Jacques Lavesque [7:19pm]**: it is out in weston

**Jacques Lavesque [7:19pm]**: 180 meadowbrook road

**Jacques Lavesque [7:20pm]**: you need a ride there? i think travis is also coming from the city and could give you a lift

**Eloise [7:21pm]**: thanks! but I think I've got it

**Eloise [7:21pm]**: what time should I get there?

Kyle was carrying a bunch of beers back to the table. She wondered if he had an excellent fake ID or if being a professional athlete had given him that privilege, as he was only nineteen. He sat down and took a long, long gulp of his beer. He wasn't joining the conversation; the other guys were all huddled around a phone, talking about something on the screen, but he was detached, slumped in his seat, looking around the bar. Eloise turned away just as he glanced in her direction, grateful that she was still wearing the hat.

**Jacques Lavesque [7:24pm]**: 8

**Jacques Lavesque [7:24pm]**: recommend eating a lot of carbs before

She resisted the urge to type back immediately; after all, he had taken a few moments to respond. She just didn't want him to think everything was about him, that was all.

Kyle had returned his gaze to the table. Eloise pretended to text as she snapped a few pictures of the group. She could feel the bartender's eyes on her, but if she went to the bar for a drink, she would put herself too near Kyle's line of sight. She pretended to call someone, acting impatient and annoyed, and then pretended to hang up and swear before leaving.

Out in the crisp evening, it was now fully dark and she was greeted by a blaze of red brake lights. She walked a little ways away from Dublin House before pulling out her phone again.

**Eloise [7:30pm]**: so I heard

She hesitated, thumbs hovering over the screen as she walked. She felt like running and she didn't know why; her thumbs felt clumsy and thick.

**Eloise [7:30pm]**: thanks!

**Jacques Lavesque [7:31pm]**: of course

She stuffed her phone in her pocket, and then, on second thought, turned it off. It was a long walk back to Southie, but for some reason she didn't feel like sitting still on a bus right now. There was a new dressiness to the world around her; the brake lights were rosy and the air had that September bite to it.

Things were starting to matter again, and she did not know how to feel about that.

# Chapter Twelve

F riday arrived and, with it, Eloise's SNAP card came. She spent the morning grocery shopping, torn between relief and shame—and a secret anxiety.

She did not know why she was overthinking this. She wanted to go to Burnie's party specifically because it was a chance to observe Kyle, to see where he went afterwards, to see what he said when he drank too much, but for some reason her stupid brain kept fixating on what she would wear, and on—of all people—Rachel, Jacques's wife, and potentially soon-to-be ex-wife.

Would Rachel be there?

She had not found a way to ask Krystal, who always seemed to be on high alert for any interest in Jacques, whether the separation would become a divorce.

*And why did it matter anyway?* she wondered as she pushed the cart along the aisle. Jacques's marriage had no bearing on Kyle or his life, and therefore it had no meaning to Eloise. But she found herself wondering if Rachel would be there tonight, and then, again, wondering why it mattered. Mostly, she told herself, it was a morbid curiosity about the woman who could turn Jacques Lavesque's head, and a morbid curiosity about whether she might glean anything about the separation from observing them together.

She wanted to ask Lily for advice on what to wear to the party, but she still had not returned Hollis's calls. She listlessly drove the cart with her forearms, trudging down the baking aisle. Maybe another apology was coming—but she did not see Hollis accepting it as graciously as Jacques had.

When she got back to her apartment, having wrestled with her bags of groceries on the bus, it was early afternoon. It was time to start getting ready, and she needed all the time that she could get. She was afraid to walk into this party, a party filled with intimidating men and, likely, beautiful women, all sculpted and tanned and manicured. Her auburn roots were growing in, and she didn't know what was going on with her eyebrows, and the one thing she owned that wasn't pilled or careworn was a slinky past-season Prada dress that probably looked ridiculous on her.

*You know what you have to do*, she told herself grimly, as she so often did.

"Hi. It's Eloise." She stood, phone to her ear, in front of her closet, packed to bursting with clothing that allowed her to become other people—different people, forgettable people.

"Hey, what's up?" Krystal asked.

"I'm coming to Burnie's party tonight so I can observe Kyle," Eloise began. She wanted to seem as businesslike and normal about this as possible. "What's the dress code?"

"Oh, god. There isn't one," Krystal scoffed in disdain. "The rookies' girlfriends will show up in body-con dresses and fake eyelashes. The guys will all look gross in hoodies, except Lavy who will somehow look pulled together yet casual. If I had to guess, Pell's wife Juliette will be in Chacos and a fleece, and Burnie's wife Stephanie will be in leopard print and Louboutins. Personally, I will be wearing my Akris silk sweater and satin midi skirt and matching Chloe platform sneakers—"

She paused, audibly stopping herself from going into further detail on her own outfit. "In other words, wear whatever you want."

"So... black dress and boots would be not-weird?" Eloise held up the dress, still bearing its red 'CLEARANCE' tag from TJ Maxx.

"You and I will probably be the only appropriately dressed ones there," Krystal reassured her. "Why? You don't seem like the kind of girl who worries about that."

"Well, I can't really *afford* to worry about it too much," Eloise admitted, hurt. "I'm not really making hockey player money." Before they could dig into that, she continued. "Thanks, I just wanted to check and make sure it wasn't a formal occasion or something."

"It is an incredibly *in*formal occasion. You will see at least one of them naked at some point. There will be vomit."

"Beautiful. I look forward to it," she joked. "It's been at least ten years since I've been around naked, vomiting guys."

"This will do you for the next ten years," Krystal warned.

After they hung up, Eloise held up the dress and studied it critically.

"Whatever," she said aloud to the dress, shaking it a little. "Stop thinking about it! Pretend it's just another disguise."

Annoyed with herself, she put the dress back in the closet and went to shower and do her hair. When she slipped the dress on and stood on her tiptoes in front of the bathroom mirror, she cringed. The dress was simple, architectural; it left the focus on her face, her hair, her eyes, her arms, like a pencil portrait with the features highlighted with strokes of ink. She was no character, neatly portrayed by silly accessories or stereotypical shoes or a distinctive hat.

She found herself ready an hour and a half earlier than she needed to be, pacing in front of her bedroom mirror and wondering if she was wearing too much eye-makeup or too little, wandering around her kitchen, eating toast with peanut butter and telling herself she was a clown for caring about any of it at all.

Time to leave.

It was a beautiful night: chilly, the sky dark blue and velvety. The bus lumbered past restaurants and twinkle lights, Friday night traffic and Friday night plans, and Eloise watched it all fly past her window with a strange sense of gratitude in spite of all of her many chaotic feelings. She was happy to be out in the midst of all of it, overdressed on the bus in a Prada dress and beat-up ankle boots.

The clutter of the city faded as she rolled into the leafy suburbs. The houses became bigger and farther apart, then receded beyond thick lush walls of green. By the time she got off at Brandeis, it was dark and the world seemed cozy and quiet. She caught an Uber the rest of the way, one that put her bank account further in danger. The car smelled like smoke and air freshener, and she held her bag against her stomach, slightly nauseated.

And then the car was rolling to a stop on a remote road, the trees still thick with summertime leaves. Through a line of manicured firs, a large house glittered with string lights.

"Here is fine," she told the driver. She got out of the car on wobbly legs, clutching her bag to her chest, and tipped the driver as he drove away.

For some reason, she was thinking of the tarot again: this time of the Hanged Man, suspended in space and time, hanging by choice. She drew in a breath and rounded the line of fir trees.

The long driveway was packed with expensive, sporty cars, like Range Rovers and Audis and BMWs, all of them gleaming and new. The large blue McMansion-style house was neatly trimmed with twinkle lights, its windows lit up so that she could see people inside. The front door, flanked by potted mums and tasteful pumpkins, hung open to let in the crisp evening air, and from here she could see the dancing blue glimmer of a pool reflected on the side of the house.

She began walking up the drive, and noticed a car parked at the end, an unimpressive black Toyota, with its lights on. She glanced inside as she passed—

—and Andrei looked up. Too late, he had already met her eyes. She paused as he rolled down the window.

He had been hunched over, forearms balanced on the wheel, and she thought of the Hanged Man again. He was clad in a faded black sweatshirt that strained at his shoulders and fell short at his wrists; his black hair was still damp from a shower.

He looked like he was about to laugh, but he didn't look happy.

"Eloise." Those liquid hazel eyes flicked over her dress, her purse, her styled hair. "I did not know you were coming."

"Yeah, Burnie invited me," she explained, gesturing to the house with her purse and faltering when she realized the gesture didn't make sense. She held her bag against her chest once more. His eyes followed the movement. "What—um—what are you doing out here?"

Andrei set his arms over the steering wheel again, hunching forward as he studied the house.

"If I go in, I have to talk to them, pretend to find them all interesting," he explained. He drew in a breath. "If I do not go in... Jay will think I am a little bitch. He will think he won."

He let out a soft laugh, shaking his head. "The two things I cannot stand the most."

"So basically, you're nervous about going inside," she concluded, and he laughed again. There was that self-consciousness again; he covered his mouth briefly, like he was ashamed of his teeth, but it occurred to Eloise now that he only had good teeth for a hockey player because no one dared to hit Andrei Koslov in the face.

"I'm not nervous," he insisted. "How many of these did I go to the last time I was on this fucking team? They are always the same. Everyone brings their little wives and girlfriends. Everyone gets wasted."

Her stomach clenched at the word *wives*. She did not know why. (Or maybe she did not want to think about why.)

"You don't drink, right?" Eloise recalled Krystal mentioning it. "I guess it's less fun if you're the only one who's not drunk."

"Not anymore," Andrei said with a shake of his head. He looked her over again. "But if you are hoping for something to happen with one of them, tonight is your chance."

"What's that supposed to mean?" she asked quickly, cheeks flushing in the cool air. Andrei's pale lips curved.

"That is a hopeful dress," he said.

"Wow, thanks. 'Hopeful' is exactly what I was going for. You really know how to make a girl feel special," she said with a sarcastic salute. She felt a little seen and not in a good way—this was why it was safer to always be in disguise.

"I have a lot of luck with women," he reminded her, harkening back to their last conversation. "It's a decent dress," he amended. "If you want attention, you will get it."

"Well, gee. Thanks for the support. I really needed to hear that," she said, stung even as she pretended not to be. "So are you coming inside or not?"

Andrei stared at the house again. "It'll be worse if you don't go in," she pointed out, "speaking as someone who also tends to bail at the last second out of fear."

Andrei opened the door to get out, bracing one crummy, filthy sneaker on the driveway, rolling the window back up as he stared up at her.

"I am not afraid."

"Okay, and that's why you're hiding in your car," she said with a thumbs-up. "Got it. Makes sense."

"You are a little bit of a fighter, did you know that?" Andrei sounded amused as he got out of the car. He slammed the door shut. "I hit you and you hit back. This is why Jay likes you."

"I don't think he likes me, but—"

"He does. Everyone thinks he is so soft," Andrei interrupted, leaning back against his car, hands shoved in the front pocket of his sweatshirt. "But what he really wants is a fight. No one understands that.

And who's going to fight him? Pelletier? *Rachel?* She's always got a lot of feelings but she never knows how to fight. She always gives in right away."

Eloise stared at Andrei in faint shock. He did not know what he had done.

She felt like she had been slapped; there was a ringing in her ears as something fell into place.

"What?" Andrei demanded, pushing away from his car as he studied her face.

"Nothing," she said, clearing her throat. Maybe she was wrong. She had to be wrong. "I just don't really have anything to say to that. I don't know him at all, and you know him really well. I don't know Rachel, either."

"No?" His mouth twisted as he prepared to strike. "What about your phone chats? Or was Jay talking to a different Eloise on the phone the other day?"

She just wanted to get away from him. The tectonic shift had rattled her and she was still quaking. Powerful dislike coursed through her as she stared up at Andrei Koslov. She understood now.

"Has anyone ever told you that you're a lot?"

"Boston is boring," he said with a shrug. "It is not good for me to be bored."

"Sounds like a great problem to address with a therapist and a pet," Eloise said. "I'm getting cold. I'm going inside."

"You're still mad that I called your dress hopeful?" Andrei wanted to know. She had almost forgotten about that in the wake of the epiphany that she had just had.

"No, actually. I'm—"

"INTERN!"

Burnie was coming down the driveway, with Travis and Connor at his heels. It was odd to see him out of athletic clothes; he was dressed a little ostentatiously, in blinding white sneakers that she assumed were cool.

"Hey, man," he added to Andrei like a dentist had wrenched it out of his mouth. "You guys made it."

Connor was bright red, his blush visible even in the darkness, as he looked between Eloise and Andrei. "Did—did you guys come together, or—"

"Jesus Christ. Pull yourself together," Burnie snapped at Connor.

"We didn't come together," Eloise reassured Connor before Andrei could speak. "My Uber dropped me off, just now, and Andrei just got here too."

"Oh, uh, yeah, of course," Connor said, clearing his throat. "Do you—uh—can I get you a drink—"

"You're supposed to let her *in* the house first, Bonehead," Burnie said, shooting another wary look at Andrei. "Come on in, guys, I'll get you some beers."

Eloise followed, falling into step with Travis and Connor. Andrei walked behind them, gravel crunching beneath his sneakers. Her palms were damp, her ankles loose and unsteady in her boots. She needed to retreat, to go off on her own and turn over this stone she had come upon. Maybe she was wrong, but—

Then they were in the noise and heat of the party. In the hall, she peeked into the living room and found Krystal perched on the edge of a large, squashy sectional, sipping wine and surrounded by players, but they passed before she could catch her attention.

The kitchen was brightly lit and choked with guests: Kyle was slouched with Ilya, Marcel, and Harper, sipping a soda and half-listening as Ilya—flushed and already visibly tipsy—regaled the group with a story. As he talked and gestured, he glanced self-consciously at a girl beside him whose brown extensions spilled over her tanned shoulders, and who Eloise guessed was his girlfriend.

And there was Jacques, laughing with Pell and two women. He looked over when they entered the kitchen, and his gaze skated over Andrei—like he didn't know him, like nothing had happened, and that should have made her doubt her epiphany but somehow it only strengthened it. Eloise caught his eye and he smiled warmly, offering a wave like he had been waiting to see her specifically, and some of her nerves were soothed even if she knew it was just his charm, his act, his mask.

(Krystal had been correct: he looked unexpectedly sophisticated in a dark sweater and jeans, subtly polished and cool without looking out of place, and she wondered if that too was Krystal's careful training.

(No Rachel, either—at least, she wasn't in this room.)

"Eloise!" Pell greeted, though his eyes were on Andrei as he wended his way around the kitchen island to get to her and Burnie. "Aw, you look so pretty," Pell said, slinging one lanky arm around her in a half-hug as she thanked him. His long, freckled feet were jammed awkwardly into surfer flip-flops and his pressed button-up, untucked, was at odds with his worn jeans.

"We need to get Bonehead that *He's Just Not That Into You* book," Burnie informed Pell, jerking his chin at Eloise. Out of the corner of her eye she watched Andrei slip off and join Ilya, Marcel, and the others. "Kid just made a fucking fool of himself in front of her."

"I'm not sure a book will help," Pell said. "Come on, you need to meet my wife, Juliette, and Burnie's wife, Steph."

He waved to the two women across the kitchen, standing with Jacques, who were intently discussing something in front of a set of ovens. Both were tall, but otherwise they had nothing in common. It was easy to guess who was whom: Juliette's thick carroty hair fell un-styled to her bony shoulders; she had a slightly horsey smile and large eyes, giving her the effect of a friendly, creepy doll. Eloise instantly thought of Sally from *Nightmare Before Christmas*. She was wearing a teal polar fleece, as Krystal had predicted, and was painstakingly, methodically cutting into a tray of something.

The woman next to her, leaning against the counter and looking down at Juliette's precise work, had to be Stephy, Burnie's wife. She was nearly six feet tall, and had the bold, heavily-lidded eyes and broad cheekbones of an Italian beauty. Somehow the spray tan, thick eyeliner, and tight leopard-print dress looked natural on her, and the heavy gold jewelry she wore looked like it belonged at her throat and wrists.

"Meh, they can't hear me." Pell gave in, waving his hand.

"I can fix that. YO, STEPHY," Burnie yelled above the pounding music. Stephy glanced up, arching her manicured brows. "MEET INTERN," he called, pointing to Eloise as Jacques broke from them to join Eloise, Pell, and Burnie.

"Hi, Intern," Stephy called back with a wave, brown eyes flicking over her. "Good dress," she mouthed at Eloise before turning her attention back to what she and Juliette were doing.

"Do they need help?" Jacques asked Burnie covertly. "Stephanie won't let me."

"Nah, already asked," Burnie dismissed. "So you didn't bring some insane boyfriend, Intern?"

"Nope, no insane boyfriend," Eloise said.

"Huh, we were wondering about that, but you're a freak who doesn't have social media so we couldn't tell. Maybe Bonehead has a reason to live, after all," Burnie said carelessly.

"BURNIE," Stephy yelled; she sounded a bit like a seagull. Burnie turned on his heel with a shocking obedience and wended his way to his wife. Pell followed, looking intrigued and amused, leaving Jacques and Eloise together.

God. Eloise took a swig of her beer just for something to do, just for something to occupy the moment. She had noticed his sleeves were pushed up, revealing his forearms which were covered in faded ink, and she didn't want to get caught staring again.

"And your wife didn't join?" she asked at last.

"No, she had another commitment," he said, but he looked away when he said it. The satisfaction—another validation of her theory—was hollow. She tore her eyes from his forearm, and the elegant hand twisted around his own bottle, once again.

He caught her eye, frowning. "Are you alright?" he asked in a low voice. "You seem upset."

She stared at him. If her theory was right... how did he *do* it? How did he stand in the same room as Andrei and act like nothing had happened, like nothing had been done to him?

"Really upset," he added, slate eyes roving over her face. "Did Andrei say something to you outside, or something?"

"No," she said quickly. "No, I'm just—I'm just shy sometimes. That's all."

"Ah, I'm shy too, sometimes," he agreed easily. "Not as much as I used to be. Come on, you will be entertained by Juliette and Stephanie," he said now. He glanced back at her as he touched her back to guide her, then paused; his eyes flicked over her bare arm. She rubbed her skin self-consciously.

"Do I have something on my arm?" she asked, looking down.

"No, it was, ah. Just a freckle," he said. Eloise looked up in time to catch the final twitch of a headshake, but Jacques had already looked away and was gesturing for her to join Burnie, Pell, and their wives.

"Henry, no, stop," Juliette, Pell's wife, was saying anxiously as Burnie opened the oven.

"She's the only one who calls him that," Jacques confided, almost conspiratorially, to Eloise, their arms brushing. They shifted apart.

"Yeah, and I like it," Burnie joked, pulling away from the oven, his face red from the blast of heat. Juliette looked horrified, even as Pell laughed.

"You're Eloise, right?" she asked, turning to Eloise with a smile. "It's nice to meet you. Matt told me you're interning for Krystal. Where are you in school?"

"I'm actually not in school—just a career change," Eloise admitted. "School was more than ten years ago."

"I need your aesthetician's number," Stephanie said loudly, studying Eloise's face.

"No aesthetician, it's just the bad hair," she joked. "There's so much food," she remarked, just for something to say, looking at the kitchen island, which was covered in trays of food: little burgers, pigs in a blanket, pizza, buffalo chicken dip...

"We have a house full of huge guys who like getting wasted," Stephanie said matter-of-factly. "We need truckloads of food to handle it. Even these old guys"—she swept a manicured, beringed finger over Jacques, Pell, and Burnie—"will be sloppy by the end of the night."

"I would like to exclude myself from the 'old' narrative," Pell announced as he opened another beer. "I think I might be the youngest one here, and also, I don't get sloppy."

"You don't, you just get more gossipy and silly," Burnie agreed. "We all get more of *ourselves* when we drink. I get louder, Lavesque gets friendlier."

"How could you possibly be friendlier?" Eloise wondered, risking a look at Jacques. He was laughing, shaking his head, turning pink.

"You clearly haven't seen him play," Burnie concluded, "because you would know. He gets kissy and huggy as fuck when he's happy, and it's the same thing when he's drunk."

"Um." Eloise met his eyes again, trying not to laugh. "Are you *kissing* people when you play? Is there even time for that?"

"Look, we all get a little affectionate," Pell pointed out, gesturing with his beer. "I've kissed a man or two in my career. Usually Lavy, but I've had others."

"Here's the thing about kissing another man in public, Eloise—" Jacques let out a self-deprecating laugh, his seriousness cracking briefly before he controlled his features again. "You just have to go for it, okay?"

"You can't make it look like you thought about it," Burnie agreed.

"Yes, if you make eye contact, or make it seem too thoughtful, then it is weird," Jacques explained. "You just have to go for it and wherever it lands, it lands. Hopefully it's in a normal place like the cheek, but sometimes it's an eye, sometimes it's the mouth, and you can't show that you noticed."

"Yeah, I made eye contact with Simpson that one time before I kissed him, and like, *I* was fine about it," Burnie said defensively, pointing to himself, "but *he* couldn't look me in the eye again for the rest of the whole season. I think maybe that meant more to him than it did to me, but it's an emotional thing, right? When you score a goal."

"Yes, very emotional," Jacques agreed seriously, but he was visibly trying not to laugh.

"I love when they kiss each other," Stephanie admitted fervently. She took a long swig of her martini. "And when they fight. Best sport."

"Who else have you kissed?" Juliette asked her husband with surprise. "I've only seen you kiss Jacques and Henry."

"Well, Simpson kissed me after Burnie kissed him—I think to convince himself it was normal," Pell recounted, "and I've got to admit, I did *try* to kiss Novak on the mouth last year—"

"That beautiful goal against the Stars," Jacques recalled fondly. "I would have kissed him too."

"Yeah, but Novak's not letting anyone get near him, he's so weird," Burnie scoffed. "I fell on him one time and he flipped out at me. Some guys are fucking weird about it."

"Can't mess up the hair," Pell said with a shrug, reminding Eloise of how Andrei had called Matej Novak *Mr. Hairstyle*. She glanced back at Andrei, caught his eye, and looked away again. She wondered if Andrei let anyone kiss him.

"So what was your old career, Eloise?" Juliette asked politely. Eloise got the sense that she was one of those intensely appropriate people, who always reciprocated questions exactly during conversation, keeping track in her head.

"It's boring," Eloise began quickly. They were all looking at her with interest, so she looked down at her beer bottle—which was feeling lighter in her hand than it should have. "I was a bench chemist," she said, deciding on honesty. "So, how it works is, when someone's caught with drugs, they have to make sure it actually *is* drugs before you can do anything else, and I was the person who tested that. And then I'd testify in court that the drugs were, in fact, drugs from a chemical standpoint."

"This explains a lot," Jacques realized. "Eloise wanted to be Batman when she was little," he explained to the others. "It makes sense."

"That's so cool, it's not boring at all!" Juliette said excitedly. "Why would you leave that behind?"

"I just..."

Jacques was half-smiling as he listened, his head tilted.

"There are a lot of messed up things about our justice system, and it wore me down," Eloise said finally with a shrug.

"That's fucking deep, Intern," Burnie observed, taking a swig of his beer.

"So you pivoted hard-left into something pointless and ridiculous after burning out," Stephanie concluded. "Understandable."

"Did you just say hockey was pointless?" Burnie asked his wife archly. She was already back to work, arranging plates to make room for more food.

"I said pointless *and* ridiculous," she corrected him patiently, sweeping her thick brown hair over her shoulder.

"You and Juliette don't take our careers seriously," Pell complained. Juliette flushed.

"I do! I bought that book and I swear I'm going to read it!" she insisted, bright red under her freckles. "And it's not just us. Rachel isn't obsessed with hockey either. I asked her to explain icing to me one time and she just shrugged."

Eloise watched for whether Jacques reacted, but oddly it was Burnie and Stephanie who did—they glanced at each other, so subtly and quickly that she wasn't completely sure it was intentional.

"She doesn't care about it," Jacques affirmed, easy as ever.

It was incredible to her that he could carry on this conversation so naturally. He glanced at Eloise then with an aware look, an acknowledgment that she was staring. "She's very upset about the concussions and that has always been her biggest complaint. She told me the boys aren't ever allowed to be hockey players."

"Yeah, well, fat chance there anyway," Burnie joked, uncapping another beer. "Have you met his boys?" he asked Eloise, continuing before she could answer, "Peter is going to be some kind of fucking poet or lawyer or something. He's so *adult* and *sensitive*. It's bizarre. And Luke is totally going to be a stand-up comic."

"Do either of them show any interest in hockey?" Eloise asked Jacques.

"Well, Luke loves hitting things with sticks," he conceded, "which is most of it."

"It *is* the best," Burnie agreed. "Bells and Loon are like that too. Hitting anything with anything. As long as someone's in pain or something's broken, they're happy."

"Genevieve has no interest. *And* she told me hockey was sexist the other day. I was like, you're eight," Pell said. Juliette winced.

"She's just learned that word, so she's saying everything is sexist," she explained to the group. "Gosh, I just thought we'd have more time before we got there. She asked me if I had ever experienced sexism 'that I knew of' and I didn't even know where to begin."

"We're guessing she's tracking for a major interest in socialism at age twelve," Pell joked.

"What about the environment?" Eloise suggested.

"Been there, done that," Pell said, waving her off. "That was six months ago. I got a lecture from an eight-year-old on why my lifestyle is destroying Mother Earth, which was a humbling experience."

"She called him a 'careless human,'" Juliette added.

Jacques was watching them talk and joke, listening with a smile. *How* was he carrying on like this, with Andrei in the room, mere yards away? She would not have been able to bear it. Eloise finished the last of her beer.

"Sorry, where is your bathroom?" she asked Stephanie.

"Down the hall, past the doors that lead to the pool," she said, jerking her head in that direction.

"Thanks." Eloise dropped her empty bottle in the recycling bin, feeling Jacques's eyes on her, and slipped out of the kitchen.

Everything in the house was brand new and pristine, and decorated in a trendy, cheesy style that Eloise associated with *Real Housewives*, but it was also a cozy, comfortable home. It seemed like a happy place to live. As she walked down the hall, she passed a wall covered with photographs of Burnie and his family on various vacations and holidays. The smiles were genuine, the pictures surprisingly candid and unpolished. It made her like Stephanie even more. She would have assumed that Stephanie would only allow the most Instagram-worthy shots, but every picture here was filled with genuine joy. There was even one from Burnie and Stephanie's wedding, with Jacques as best man, wearing a dark grey suit, his face flushed with happiness.

In the bathroom—all mood lighting and bright granite, with a set of black-and-white prints of the Eiffel Tower—Eloise studied her appearance. She was mostly relieved that her makeup wasn't running and she didn't have pit stains.

She smoothed her hair and then washed her hands, holding them under the cold water to try and cool herself down. She didn't know why her epiphany was bothering her so much; marriages ended for far worse reasons all the time, and she barely knew Jacques, anyway. But for whatever reason, it put a lump in her throat, which grew every time she thought of Jacques being so affectionate with his team, or the way he looked at people like they had *finally* gotten onto his favorite subject when they talked, or the way he so expertly hid any hint of his marital problems.

She left the bathroom but wasn't quite ready to reenter the fray. She could tell that the groups had already shifted in the time she had been gone, and the idea of breaking into a new group—which group to choose? How to make sure she didn't come across too clingy or too awkward? What to talk about even if she *did* break into a group?—was too much for the moment, so Eloise slipped out the French doors and onto the patio.

# Chapter Thirteen

From the patio, the music and laughter of the party was muffled in a way that made the world outside seem like the moon, distant and lonely and indifferent. The twinkle bulbs strung over the pool glowed like planets overhead, and the water cast iridescent spines of light around the patio.

It made her think of the Star of the tarot—stars glistening in dark water, a woman poised before it, looking into the water's depths. Eloise crossed her bare arms over her chest and stood by the water's edge, watching the undulating, shimmering light play on her tights and boots.

Andrei had said Rachel's name like he knew her like Jacques did; Andrei had blown up Jacques's marriage, willfully or accidentally.

She had known it instantly by the way Andrei had said *Rachel*. Never had a single name carried such a twist of familiarity, sex, and contempt at once; it had been a braid of emotion running beneath the sounds. He had gasped that name in a bedroom before; he had cursed that name in frustration before. The shape of the conflict had abruptly revealed itself like lightning flashing on a skeleton. Eloise had seen every bone of the problem for just one instant, every bone that she had been blindly touching, and had recognized the creature.

Suddenly the world became a blur of blue and silver as her eyes burned with tears and her chest became tight. She pressed her fingertips to her eyelids.

It was all tangled like kelp but the overwhelming notion emerged like a shipwreck: Andrei was monstrously selfish, and it revolted her because she was, too. She had glimpsed the monster beneath the bed out there in the driveway, as Andrei had attacked her out of his own anxiety and guilt, and then she had come face-to-face with it there in the kitchen as she had stumbled and choked her way through interactions with Jacques and the others.

And then she had run away when it had gotten to be overwhelming, and meanwhile Jacques was still in there, smiling and pretending to be indifferent to sharing airspace with the man who had ruined his marriage. The maturity and strength and grace of it shamed her. He was giving of himself for the good of the team—she could not recall the last time she had truly given of herself at all.

She saw a wreath, a box, her best friend's face. She saw her colleagues' backs, and the long walk down that hall that she had done by herself, the day she had been fired—because she had been fired, in truth. She had not left in flames like she told herself; she had been *fired*, and maybe it had been in honor of telling the truth and doing the right thing, but she saw now how selfishly it had been done, with no regard for how the truth might impact others. She saw how she had sat in her car afterwards, with the box on the passenger seat, and had realized that she did not have anyone left that she could call to talk about it.

She did not want to be this person anymore. She did not want to sit alone in a parking lot with a box of things that did not matter, with no one to call. She did not want her own problems to take up this much space. She did not want to stand outside alone, too isolated and too at odds with everyone to walk into a party. She wanted to walk into a party because it was full of people she loved, not because she had something to prove.

She startled when she heard the click of the patio doors. When she turned, Kyle was frozen in the doorway, hand on the handle of the French door. The diaphanous light painted him ghostly blue, setting his pale eyes aglow.

"Sorry," he stammered, "I didn't realize anyone—"

"No, no, it's fine," Eloise reassured him, swiping beneath her eyes for any running makeup. "I'm just getting some air. I won't talk if you just need some quiet."

"I just—"

He let the door swing shut behind him, thin lips pressed in a sheepish line. There was a looseness to his movements that told her he was one beer past sober, but not yet drunk. He held up a pack of cigarettes. "Don't tell?"

"I think the smoke will give it away," she pointed out.

"Whatever. Everyone's so fucked up anyway, no one's gonna notice," he muttered, coming to stand beside her before the pool.

There was so much that Eloise now knew about Kyle: his record, his old Twitter account, his relationship with his brother, his fucked-up friends with their neo-Nazi tattoos. And yet after studying him so intensely she still sensed that she was missing something.

He shook a cigarette out of the pack and expertly lit one, then glanced at her. "Want one? I forgot to offer."

"That's okay, but thanks."

She weighed her words as they stood in silence beneath the shuddering twinkle bulbs, doused in chiffon light. Jacques obviously cared deeply about this boy, and that love was a glimmering thread that hinted at what she sensed: something bigger, something that mattered.

"Are you okay?" she asked. "Coming out here and all."

He caught her eye before looking away, exhaling a careful line of smoke.

"Yeah, I mean"—his voice cracked—"I guess you heard the news and all. About me being on the first line with Lavesque and Koslov now."

"No, actually. I've been out of the loop with the team."

Kyle raised his brows. This had to be a big deal. Hollis had talked about the first line of the team, Burnie-Jacques-Pell, so beloved by the Bruins fandom.

"But," she said, gauging his reaction, "that's... a lot? That's big, right?"

"Pretty much," he agreed miserably around his cigarette. "If you ever wanted to get Burnap and Pelletier to look at you like you fucked their wives—"

He noticed her flinch. "Sorry, didn't mean to offend."

"No," she said quickly, "it's fine. I mean, that's got to be really hard. But they're good guys, right?"

"Yeah, and I can handle them hating me, at the end of the day," he said distractedly. "People have always thought I was trash, so like, whatever. A couple of Canadian princes hating me isn't going to push me over the edge."

The bravado was so raw and adolescent.

"And Jacques is a good mentor, and he's protective of you," Eloise ventured. Kyle laughed again, flicking his lighter absently.

"Yeah, he's also a guaranteed, first ballot hall of famer," he countered. "He is a fucking *generational* talent. So is Koslov. They're gonna be on lists twenty years from now. And—and I'm not like that, alright? I'm not even good."

"I've heard diff—"

"No," he interrupted shortly. "Fuck whatever story you heard, alright? I honestly should still be in the fucking AHL. And it's not imposter syndrome or whatever. It's just the truth."

This had been weighing on him; this was a confession, and she was privy to it because he knew she was an outsider, too. They had fled together, two lone wolves beneath an indifferent moon. The humility behind the confession was another hint of that invisible thread that she sensed, but she did not know how to tug on it and test it.

"Okay, so you suck," Eloise said, getting a laugh out of him. "Can you fix it?"

"Yeah, sure! Maybe if I got hit by a lightning bolt of talent or something," he snapped. "Sorry," he said quietly. "Nah, I don't think I can fix it. You either got it or you don't, right?"

She was about to offer a platitude when he continued, the words rushing out in a torrent. "And Lavesque talks all this shit about me being like him, and how I've got captain potential too, and he says this shit but no one else is saying it. He told me he didn't feel like he'd ever be captain of a team, or anything else about where he's at now, and I'm just like, yeah, maybe *you* didn't feel it, but everyone around you did. No one says the stuff about me that they said about him when he was nineteen."

"He's really good at seeing people."

"Yeah, and I wish he'd stop, because sometimes it goes to my head and I forget what the reality is."

He rubbed at the tattoo on his neck self-consciously, grey eyes trained on the chlorinated water. "If I weren't on that first line, I could survive. I could play it out," he continued. "We've got a bunch of shitty players and I could blend in with them. Like, I like Kennedy, but he blows—and I don't like calling him Bonehead, by the way, I don't think that shit's funny, like I just don't fuck with nicknames like that, and I *told* Lavesque that, like privately, and he was like—"

Kyle dropped his voice to a deeper register, adopting an inaccurate facsimile of Jacques's accent. "'Why don't you say something to Burnie, Kyle?' Yeah, I don't know, Lavesque, maybe because Burnap's played in the league for like, eighty fucking years and he's almost as much of a fucking legend as you are? Why don't *you* say something? And then I feel like a little bitch for being mad about it, but then I also feel shitty for disappointing him or whatever. It's too hard."

Just like Andrei, he had revealed so much without ever meaning to, without knowing he had.

"Why don't you like nicknames?" Eloise asked. Kyle shrugged.

"I just don't like them," he said bluntly. "End of story. You want a nickname? What if I called you Blondie every time I saw you? It's not even a diss, and I'm assuming the platinum thing is intentional, but you probably wouldn't like it, would you? And Kennedy *doesn't* like it, and I guess Burnap's trying to let him know that he's gotta perform better, but believe me, Kennedy *knows* he's not great. It's no fucking mystery. Why don't you just fucking *help* him be better, then, if you know so fucking much?"

He coughed a little on his smoke, and then fell silent, shoulders tense. "Sorry," he added.

"I'm not thrilled about the Bonehead thing, either," Eloise admitted. She had not realized she was uncomfortable with it until now. "I mean, I do think Connor can handle it just fine, but I get what you mean. I assumed it was a sports hazing thing."

"Maybe, but it's just unnecessary," he said, waving his cigarette. "That's another reason I'm not meant to be here. I don't fuck with any of that bullshit."

He cast a look toward the French doors, a look that she recognized so well. Everyone was migrating to the living room, toward the massive sectional.

"Looks like karaoke time," he said under his breath. She wanted so badly to be someone who was surrounded by people, rather than isolated from them. And she saw that Kyle wanted that too, that to be out here was his escape but it was also his exile, an exile that did not bring relief.

But she was older, and she knew these things because she had lived them, and he had not lived them yet. He did not know how these little exiles added up, how they could take him in a direction that ten years from now would feel like the wrong one.

"Okay, let's make a deal," she said impulsively. Her words came out fast, before she could walk them back. Kyle was giving her a skeptical look. "Next time someone calls Connor 'Bonehead,' I'm going to say something."

Kyle caught on, grey eyes narrowing in a shrewd look. "And I have to do... what?"

"Go back in there with me," she said, "and sing with me."

"That's some bullshit," he blurted, laughing in disbelief. "Are you kidding me? How stupid do you think I am? That's the worst fucking deal I've ever heard in my life."

"Okay, fine. I'll throw in a slap, too."

He laughed at her, a genuine laugh that was unexpectedly boyish and silly.

"Oh my god. You can't even *reach* half the players," he yelled, shoulders shaking with laughter. "I mean, maybe Burnap, 'cause he's a fucking Lego, but anyone else—"

"Come on."

It was awkward. She wasn't smooth like Jacques—she had to fumble to grab his arm and at first he recoiled, unsure of what she was doing. "We're going in to do karaoke because someday you're going to be captain of this team, and you've got to start somewhere."

*And I think that Jacques is right and you aren't all that you appear to be.*

Her voice wasn't confident. She didn't sound like she knew what she was talking about. But she dragged him to the French doors anyway.

"Can you even sing?"

"Absolutely not. I'm horrible," she told him, pulling the door open with her free hand.

"Awesome. I really feel like this will fix everything," Kyle said sarcastically as she dragged him back into the party.

It was like running into a wall of noise after the peace of the patio. The living room was packed: the massive sectional was spilling over with players and their significant others. Everyone was facing the fireplace, over which hung an enormous flatscreen. Juliette and a rangy, slouching player Eloise recognized as Casper Johansson were focused on getting the karaoke machine connected to the television.

At the far end of the sectional, Jacques was squashed beneath a red-faced Ilya and jammed against Burnie, who was singing off-key into his beer bottle and splashing beer on Pell beside him. Connor and Travis were sprawled on the carpet at their feet, looking fervently at something on Travis's phone.

Krystal offered a prim wave from the closer end, where she was perched next to Stephanie and the delicately handsome Novak—cat-like green eyes and, indeed, excellent flowing brown hair—as well as a slim woman with dyed black hair, studded boots, and an appealingly vulpine face.

"Who's that?" Eloise asked Kyle, nodding to the woman.

"Johansson's wife... A-something. Anita, maybe," he said. "She makes all of Johansson's suits. That's why he always looks so cool."

At the other end of the room, detached from everyone else, Andrei was sitting on a low chair, talking with Marcel and Harper. Across the room, he caught her eye, and Eloise looked away.

"Ah, fuck, he's already noticed us," Kyle complained, but he was talking about Jacques, who reached over Ilya's head and waved at them. "Now I can't escape."

Eloise returned Jacques's wave. She couldn't help but grin at his flushed face. He tilted his head questioningly at her, still smiling, and she waved him off, heat rushing to her face. She felt giddy and terrified and jerky and weird.

*You know what you have to do*, she told herself. *And this time, it's not for you.*

"You can't escape," she agreed, turning back to Kyle. "You're not allowed. And we still have to decide on a song."

"Okay, we have got it," Casper announced to the room in a deadpan voice as the screen flickered behind him. He was almost drowned out by the chatter and laughter. "No one is listening," he complained, lifting a hand up.

"SHUT UP, EVERYONE," Burnie screamed over the chaos, which only made the laughter and chatter bubble up again. Ilya launched to his feet. His brunette girlfriend covered her face and groaned.

"Come on, Johansson," Ilya yelled, grabbing the remote control from a bemused Juliette. "Let's do one together!"

"No, I do not want—ugh, fine." Casper surrendered, holding up his hands irritably as Ilya chose a song. The opening notes of "Take On Me" started playing.

"BOO!" Burnie yelled, cupping his hands around his mouth. Jacques reached over and smacked his hands down, laughing.

"Take... on... me—what are the other words, I cannot read this, it moves too fast," Casper complained tersely into the microphone as he squinted at the screen. Ilya, shorter and burlier, reached up and snatched the microphone from him.

"TAAAAKE MEEEE OOONNNNN," he bellowed, red-faced, as he danced wildly. Jacques and Burnie were singing together, off-key and out of sync. Kyle snorted, grumpily charmed by their antics.

"Oh, fine. I will just make them up," Casper said disgustedly, taking the microphone back from Ilya and singing unintelligibly into it.

"I'm not fucking doing that," Kyle warned her.

"Pick a song," Eloise yelled back.

"*No*—oh, for fuck's sake," Kyle groaned as Travis bounced around to them with an elfish grin and grabbed their arms, dragging them towards the end of the sectional with Jacques and Burnie.

"Were you guys making out—ow," Burnie yelled as Pell elbowed him. Jacques laughed at the look of horror on Kyle's face, his undercut boyishly disheveled in a way that Eloise hadn't seen before.

She was about to drop down beside Connor on the floor, but Travis shoved her and Kyle onto the sofa, sandwiching her between Jacques and Kyle before draping himself across them like they were posing for a sorority picture.

"Dude, get *off*," Kyle yelled, shoving at Travis, but he was laughing, reluctantly cajoled by Travis's mischief and Jacques's laughter. Eloise tried not to think about Jacques pressed against her—the softness of his sweater against her bare arm, or his scent filling her head. It was something a little spicy, a little warm. She wondered if he had chosen it for himself.

"You smell like smoke, but maybe it is your perfume," Jacques said above the music and yelling. He twisted toward her just as she shifted, and his chin bumped her head, stubble scraping his skin. "Oh—sorry—"

"No—I'm sorry—"

"Martin, your fat ass is *killing* us," Kyle was yelling. He succeeding in shoving a laughing (and very lean) Travis onto the floor, where he rolled over, blond hair wild, holding his stomach and cackling. Connor was looking dazedly at Eloise's calves, which were balanced over the edge of the sectional and splayed beside his head.

"I love stockings season," he said vaguely, just as Casper turned off "Take On Me" in a fit of irritation and the room went quiet—which caused the room to explode in laughter again, this time at Connor. Krystal buried her face in Novak's shoulder to laugh; he looked pleased with this development in a feline sort of way.

"Oh my god, he's hammered on hard seltzers just like I said he'd be. This is the best day of my life!" Pell shouted in pure glee. Stephanie and Krystal went to the front of the room, with Krystal still daintily wiping away tears of mirth.

"Stockings season is not a thing, Kennedy," Jacques said, nudging Connor's shoulder with his sneaker. His thigh shifted against Eloise's in the process, rough denim against tights, the friction made more noticeable by her tights. She pretended not to notice, but her whole body was tensed. "There's yoga pants season, or sundress season. That's it," he continued on, like they weren't touching. Maybe he didn't notice it. Maybe he was so affectionate, so physically comfortable, that he didn't notice.

"There's definitely a stockings season. You don't know what you're talking about, Lavy," Stephanie called as Krystal scanned the list of songs. "Not a legs man, I guess," she observed, pulling a theatrical face.

Jacques laughed, his elbow jostling against Eloise's side; he pulled his arm away with a muttered 'sorry.' "Of course I am a legs man," he countered mock-indignantly.

"We all know you're an ass man," Burnie said. "I've totally seen you checking out Mackenzie's ass, I've *seen* it!"

"It's very good, I have looked too, I don't know why you are yelling so much," Casper said to Burnie, shrugging. "But I think even if she were not a lesbian, she would not want you to look at her, Burnap," he added. Stephanie shrieked, seagull-like, with laughter.

"Were you smoking? You smell like smoke," Jacques said again in Eloise's ear, the warmth of his breath rushing over the shell of her ear. She held still. If she turned her head towards him, she'd brush against his neck or face—she wasn't sure but she would not take the risk. Everything was too warm and too close and too loud, and she was trying not to think about Jacques being a legs man. And his leg was still pressed against hers.

"No, Kyle was," she said.

"I can't believe you! You fucking *snitch*," Kyle exploded on her other side. He twisted, the better to put his hands on her head, and made like he was going to push her down, a move strongly reminiscent of Hollis. "Snitches get stitches," he told her in a strangled voice as he tried to push down on her head and she yelped.

"Kyle, those lungs are worth two million dollars, I can't believe *you*," Jacques said in mock horror as he pushed Kyle's hands off her head, trying to save her. Somewhere, Stephanie was warbling the beginning of what Eloise suspected was a Mariah Carey song, Krystal chiming in with less enthusiasm.

"*One* million now," Burnie yelled over all of them as Kyle protested, "It was ONE fucking cigarette!"

"Wait, stop, you're killing her," Jacques said, breathless with laughter. He slipped one hand behind Eloise's back, trying to stabilize her. The dress had a cutout in the back, and the palm of his hand smoothed against her bare skin. Her elbow knocked against his abdomen. "Wait—I can't—"

"Oh shit, sorry, Eloise," Kyle said, pulling away. "I didn't mean to kill you, Krystal's gonna murder me."

"Sorry for snitching," she gasped, trying to wriggle back into a sitting position without hitting Jacques again. Stephanie was still drunkenly belting out her Mariah Carey song, but Krystal had quietly slunk back to Anita and Matej Novak.

"It's okay, but no way am I singing with you now, you snitch," Kyle said after Eloise was sitting upright again, red-faced and sweaty, her skirt riding up. Jacques twisted to look at them just as she was trying to wrangle her dress back down, and his chin brushed her head once more, stubble prickling against her forehead.

"Oh—sorry, Eloise—wait, you guys were going to sing?"

"*Why* haven't we discussed girls in jerseys? Jersey season is incredible," Pell was saying loudly. "And what about baseball hat season, which is perhaps superior to yoga pants season?"

"Matt!" Eloise heard Juliette say indignantly. "You are a *girl dad*, you can't say these things!"

"Gross, you like how she looks in your jersey. I did not want to know that," Burnie complained, and Eloise felt Jacques laughing again. She could still smell his cologne but also his deodorant now, a faint, clean soapy scent, and she wondered if he could smell hers, too.

"It's amazing, she looks so incredible," Pell agreed drunkenly.

"MATT! STOP!"

"What were you guys going to sing?" Jacques asked them again, drowning out Juliette's horror.

"We didn't decide—"

"It has to be something about Boston," Jacques interrupted, "because you are both townies—"

"—I'm not—"

"—No singing—"

"—Yoga pants season is second," Connor was saying from the floor, and Travis was cackling beside him, visibly relishing Connor's hammered state. "It goes stockings season, then yoga pants season, *then* hat season, *then* sundress season—"

"There's no *logic* to that," Travis interrupted gleefully.

"Well, I think you are safe from having to sing," Jacques observed, a smile in his voice, "because I don't think Stephanie will ever let go of the microphone now."

He was right. Stephanie was belting out Mariah Carey with no sign of relenting.

"LAVESQUE." Burnie held his beer bottle up to Jacques's mouth like a microphone. "Only you can settle this. Which is better: yoga pants season or sundress season?" he shouted like he was a gameshow host. His wife continued to belt out "Fantasy," tossing her thick dark hair and dancing as the room cheered.

"Sundress season, yeah," Jacques said in a frank, distracted voice, leaning into the beer bottle, a perfect imitation of a post-game interview.

"You lie like a fucking rug," Burnie shouted into his beer bottle. "I have watched you check out chicks for almost two fucking decades, and you have the *nerve*—"

"—nay, *audacity*," Pell slurred.

"Yeah, whatever, that," Burnie said carelessly, "to sit here, on *my* couch, and pretend to give the classier answer—"

"You have not watched me," Jacques argued, but he was smiling. "I am subtle about it. No one knows when I'm checking someone out."

"Yeah, because you look at *everyone* like you're in love with them," Eloise pointed out. "Maybe that's why you do it. We all thought you were just being nice."

"OH. You're so right, Intern, he totally does that—but I still maintain you've straight-up stared at Mackenzie in yoga pants."

"Yes, I have," Jacques admitted solemnly. "Every time."

"I really need to see this Mackenzie," Eloise decided.

"If you do, you'll fall in love with her, and then Bonehead will have to kill himself," Burnie warned her.

Eloise hesitated.

"You mean Connor?" she asked Burnie, looking across Jacques. Burnie looked at her like she had lost her mind.

"Jesus, are there *two* Boneheads? We're really fucked," he laughed, glancing at Jacques, but Jacques was looking at her. "*Connor,*" Burnie said, shuffling forward so he could kick Connor, "your girlfriend is protecting you."

"No, I just don't think it's that clever of a nickname," Eloise countered, and Jacques laughed as Burnie's eyes widened. "It's not a play on his name or anything. It's not any different than just calling him Butthead or something."

"Burnie, what are you going to do about this? You should feel devastated right now," Jacques said, amused.

"I don't know, but I'm confused and upset and maybe a little into it," Burnie admitted. "Man, you guys all suck. Ruining the *one* bit of goddamn fun I was having. Fine, he's not Bonehead anymore."

"I'm so in love with her," Connor said mournfully, dropping against Travis, who patted him dispassionately on the shoulder.

"I've been waiting for *Kyle* to do that," Jacques said in her ear as Burnie turned his attention to Pell, harassing him loudly about being too drunk to sit up straight.

"Well, we made a deal," Eloise explained. "If he came in here with me and we sang together, I'd say something about the nickname."

They accidentally looked directly at each other. She had been right before; they were too close for it to be normal, but for some reason she didn't look away, and neither did he. His gaze dropped to her cheek, then back again. "What?" she prompted loudly, like it was nothing, like their proximity was some sort of joke between them.

"Nothing," he said, clearing his throat and settling back, arm brushing hers once more.

Two defensemen, Gagnon and Sekelsky, were arguing with Casper who had selected an ABBA song for them ("I don't know this song, dude," Gagnon, one of those men who always looked a little red and puffy, was complaining. "Yes, but I do," Casper said dismissively, "so you will sing it.").

Abruptly it was all too much.

"Wait—" Eloise wriggled forward breathlessly. "I need water or something, let me out—"

"Here—" Jacques's hand was at the small of her back, as Travis gallantly got to his feet and pulled her out of the couch. She swung forward, knocking into him, but luckily no one else other than their little group was paying attention.

"Oh, wow, you're really warm," Travis said, releasing her.

"Because she was buried under four hundred pounds of gross man," Ilya's girlfriend said in a thick accent from behind her high-lighted curtain bangs, brown extensions spilling around her shoulders like furs.

"Two hundred pounds of gross and two hundred pounds of not-gross," Travis decided, narrowing his eyes at Kyle and Jacques. Jacques gasped.

"You think I am two hundred pounds?" he asked in mock disbelief.

"This is the best day of his life," Burnie joked. "He's never managed to get above one-ninety."

"I was at one-ninety-two last season, Buck-Sixty," Jacques shot back.

"I cannot imagine comparing my weight publicly," Ilya's girlfriend said as she texted. "I would have to die."

"You just called me two hundred pounds *of gross*," Kyle pointed out to her, and she shrugged.

"The other one is not so gross, but you are very gross. I hate your hat, it's filthy," she said, still texting. "You should never wear red ever again. It looks horrible with your hair."

"Only Sofia would call Jacques freaking Lavesque 'the other one,'" Travis said to Eloise, and Jacques winked at her. "I have worshiped him all my life and she just called him 'the other one,' I need to lie down or something."

"You're very dramatic about this," Sofia said without looking at Travis. "Maybe try getting a grip."

"I think Travis might be the only one here with a grip," Eloise pointed out. "Anyway. Water."

She swung past Pell, who had a very sober and exasperated Juliette on his lap, and Casper, whose long legs she nearly tripped over.

"Sorry, my wife will want to know where you got your dress," he said from the floor, stopping her by lifting one of his legs slightly. "Just make sure you tell her at some point, I know she is wondering."

"Oh, thanks," she stammered.

"Don't thank me, I am not complimenting it. But if there is a dress, Anita always wants to know where it came from," he said with a shrug, lowering his leg to let her pass.

She had to duck past where Andrei, Harper, and Marcel had been sitting, keenly aware that her makeup was probably melted off by now, her hair was wild, and she was probably shining with sweat. Ilya had joined them, his face still red from singing.

"High-five, Intern," Harper said, holding up his hand as she walked by, and Eloise leaned over to high-five him as she went.

It only occurred to her after she had passed and was nearly in the kitchen that Andrei was no longer sitting with them.

# Chapter Fourteen

The kitchen was quiet and bright, the island piled with decimated plates of food. Andrei stood hunched by the window, studying the screen of his phone as it lit up with rapid-fire text messages, though he made no move to type a response. There was something furtive and sly about the way he was standing and holding his phone, something contemptuous in the set of his jaw.

Eloise paused in the entrance as he looked back at her, simultaneously locking his phone screen. Too late to back out now—but her stomach dropped at the sight of him.

"Oh. Hi. I assumed you had left," she said.

His liquid eyes took in her mussed hair and flushed skin. The tension she had spied in his shoulders earlier was worse now; there was something terrible and animal glimmering in his eyes. The whole kitchen seemed to thrum and vibrate with his soured mood. She was well-acquainted with a certain kind of quiet, bitter anger and knew how it could fill a room like noxious gas.

"I will soon." His eyes raked back to her face. "I think I have done my time."

"Right. Gotcha."

She didn't know what to say. It was hard to look at him.

"Just getting some water," she explained, ducking toward the coolers lining the cabinets. When she had fished a water bottle out, she straightened again, melted ice running down her forearm and dripping onto her dress.

"You are still mad at me," he observed, watching the water running down the heel of her hand. She shook her hand out self-consciously. He slipped his phone in his pocket and moved toward the kitchen island.

The mountain of tinfoil carcasses and plates stretched between them. If she wanted to leave, she would have to push past him.

"I'm really not." She took a gulp of her water, conscious of Andrei watching her, and awkwardly wiped her mouth before setting the bottle down. From the other room, she could hear a Justin Bieber song blasting, and a brief flash of Jacques's laugh.

Anger surged and she had to fight to keep it off her face. "Sorry, I didn't mean to interrupt your text conversation. It looked important," she said. "I just came in to grab some water."

"You want to know if I was texting a girlfriend," Andrei guessed, leaning forward and resting his elbows on the edge of the island. "You can just ask."

"I really just said that because you looked like you were in the middle of a private conversation and I feel like I interrupted it," she said. Her voice was still raw from gulping down cold water. "Not because of anything else."

"No? If I am in the room, you are looking at me." His mouth twisted. "Every time. And the more you drink, the more you look at me."

She had to stifle a laugh of disbelief, and his eyes took that in too.

"Wow. You have *completely* misinterpreted that," she informed him.

"Have I?" he wondered quietly. *He wants a fight, and who's going to fight him?* Andrei had asked her earlier.

*Me,* was the part he had not said.

"Alright. Do you have a girlfriend? You obviously want to tell me about her." Sometimes it was most efficient to just give in, to skip ahead to the fight they were looking for.

"First tell me why you want to know," he countered, "if it's not because you want to have sex with me."

The word hit like a slap in this brightly-lit kitchen.

"You clearly think that's it, so I'm not sure there's anything I can say that will make you believe otherwise."

"You just said it wasn't." He shrugged, a *have it your way* kind of move. "So tell me why you want to know."

"I really was just apologizing for interrupting you," Eloise said and he laughed.

"You were digging for something."

"You know what? Never mind," she said, holding up her hands. "I'm going to—"

"I don't have a girlfriend," he confessed suddenly. He swung around the island with that molten grace that he had demonstrated on the ice, so that he stood before her. "I don't have girlfriends."

"Boyfriends, then?"

"Women always want athletes to be gay," Andrei mused. "I do not know why. I think it is part of some fantasy. No, I do not have boyfriends, either."

"Just hookups, then."

"That is a very *teenager* way of putting it," he decided at last, studying her eyes, her cheekbone, the hair that coiled near her collarbone, her bare shoulder. Eloise had never been so openly perused, and the ruthlessness of it was repulsive. He was checking boxes, boxes that he thought she required. *Yes, I'm the bad guy of your fantasies—is this what it looks like? Am I getting warmer?* "But yes."

"Okay, how would you put it?"

"Just fucking," he said easily, watching for how she reacted. "And yes, I was texting someone I've been fucking."

"Sounds like it's more than just fucking, then."

"Fucking and texting," he agreed. He was faster now, his voice lower. "Have to have some way to get to the fucking part, but if I could skip the texting, I would."

"That would be convenient," she conceded. Her throat was tight with anger, all the worse because she knew that this had nothing to do with her, that she was a rag doll Andrei had picked up, a pillow that he had decided could double as a punching bag. She did not know what had inflamed his anger, but she knew what it felt like to be a substitute emotional punching bag. "So you were putting in a request for the night? Classy."

"Something like that. Why, are you offering? It would save me on driving time."

"You really want to offend me," Eloise said, backing away. He slid forward, bracing his hands on the counter and the island on either side of her.

"You really want to know who I was texting," he countered, "and I am telling you that I'm not going to tell you." He paused. "And also that we could fuck in my car, I guess."

At that her face did grow hot.

"Wow, thank you. What an honor."

"You are very pretty," Andrei decided, giving her an assessing look. "And maybe a little drunk, but not messy yet. One more beer and you would go for it. What," he suddenly asked, tilting his head, "are you still hoping if you sit close enough to Prince Jacques he'll fuck you? He does not fuck around. You might as well let that one go."

"I'm going to leave you to your texting," she said, her face flushed and her voice taut. She pulled back, shoulder bumping the refrigerator. "Please move—"

"You—"

"Hey, what the *fuck*?"

They each froze. Connor, Kyle, and Travis were in the entrance to the kitchen. Connor was deeply flushed, Travis and Kyle wary behind him.

"Is—is Koslov bothering you, Eloise?" Connor asked in a theatrically gallant voice, coming into the kitchen.

"Are we doing this? Is this happening?" Andrei wondered, his own voice low and scathing. He was grinning at Connor as the younger man approached.

"I'm fine, Connor," Eloise said loudly, panicking. She was fairly certain that the one thing that Jacques would hate more than anything would be a scene involving Andrei. "I was just getting some water—"

"You were like *cornering* her, and she's obviously upset," Connor interrupted, moving for Andrei. Andrei ducked beyond Connor's reach with devastating ease. "You're such an asshole," he exploded.

Andrei's eyes were bright with exhilaration. This was what he had been wanting all along. Connor swung messily for him and Andrei carelessly caught his wrist then dropped it, shoving Connor into the cabinets with a *thunk*, making Connor's chin jerk down into his chest with the impact. He stumbled forward, dazed, before lunging for Andrei again.

"Kennedy, for fuck's sake—" Kyle and Travis both grabbed for Connor. Kyle got to him first, flinging his arms around Connor's middle as Connor swung and writhed in his grip.

"No, let Bonehead fight if he wants to," Andrei said slyly—

—and then Kyle released Connor.

"Ah, crap," Travis muttered, limply holding Connor's wrist.

"DON'T *FUCKING* CALL HIM THAT," Kyle bellowed, and then he lunged.

Fist cracked against bone; Andrei's head flew back briefly with the impact of Kyle's fist but he recovered fast and fisted his hands in Kyle's sweatshirt, lifting him up and shoving him with animal strength. The force sent the infamous Red Sox hat flying. Eloise did not know what to do. The two men were a blur as Andrei slammed Kyle into the cabinets; Eloise tried to approach, aware that she was yelling something but not sure what; Kyle was flung against her and they knocked back into the refrigerator together; Connor and Travis were yelling as Connor tried to escape Travis's grip; the breath had been knocked from her; there was another crack and Travis released Connor with a swear, clutching his nose; Kyle slammed into Andrei and Andrei grabbed at the island to balance himself, sending plates crashing to the floor; Andrei got in another hit and Kyle's head smacked against the refrigerator, sneakers shrieking against the tiled floor—

"What the fuck, you guys!?" Burnie was yelling, and then Eloise stumbled backwards, clutching her chest in pain, as Marcel and Jacques wrestled Andrei towards the cabinets and Burnie and Ilya shoved Kyle back. Andrei was breathless and flushed, his hazel eyes fixed on Jacques; Jacques's lip was bleeding and Marcel was hissing something icily at Andrei.

"Koslov was *cornering* Eloise," Connor yelled, still red with fury. "You don't fucking *do* that, you *asshole*, she was obviously *freaked out*," he added over Kyle's shoulder, standing on his tiptoes. Kyle was pressing a hand to his cheekbone, breathing heavily and staring at Andrei with revulsion set in his thin lips.

"Eloise can take care of herself," Andrei said lazily, relenting in Jacques's and Marcel's grip.

"I think it's time for you to leave," Jacques told Andrei. They regarded each other.

"You think?" Andrei let go as Jacques released the fistfuls of Andrei's hoodie he had been holding. Jacques's shoulders rose and fell as he caught his breath.

"Yeah," Jacques said breathlessly, wiping at his lip. "Yeah, I do."

"And we all just do whatever you want," Andrei noted. "Fine."

In silence, Andrei pushed past Jacques and Marcel, and stalked out of the kitchen, all eyes on him. For a moment, the kitchen remained silent after the front door slammed shut. Pell, Juliette, Stephanie, and Krystal stood in the entrance to the kitchen, Pell's hands on his face in silent horror.

"Sorry about the plates, Mrs. Burnap," Kyle said at last to Stephanie. Stephanie arched her brows in shock.

"Oh—honey—it's fine," she stammered. "Travis, let's get you a paper towel."

"Dangk youb," Travis said, blood seeping between his fingers.

"Sorry, Travis," Connor muttered, ashamed. "It was an accident."

"I kgnow, ib ogay," Travis said, patting Connor's shoulder.

"He is worse than ever," Marcel said to Jacques in his melodic, accented voice, which dripped with disgust. "You have to do something about that."

"What? Why does *he* have to do anything about—" Eloise halted when Jacques looked at her, eyes vulnerable with surprise. "Sorry, it's none of my business, I just—"

"No, you're right and you should say it," Burnie said, releasing Kyle at last. "Koslov is not Lavy's responsibility."

"Yes, he *is*," Marcel said mulishly, broad shoulders tense. "He is the only one that Koslov respects, *he* has got to do something about it. Koslov was never this bad before. Hitting a teammate is unacceptable behavior." He glanced at Eloise. "And harassing a woman, too. Just shameful."

"Yeah, you expect the rest of us to be professional," Novak put in from behind Krystal. "Why not him? You never confront him."

"I didn't realize it was only my expectations that were making you behave like a professional," Jacques said coolly, and Novak flushed.

"That is not—that is not what I meant—"

"Just stop talking," Krystal advised him acidly, and Novak was silenced at once. "Alright," she said briskly, shaking herself out a little. "Let's clean up these plates, boys."

Connor, Kyle, Ilya, and Burnie obediently crouched down to pick up the shattered plates; Pell followed Stephanie's directions to get the dustpan and garbage bin. Jacques let out a breath as Marcel wordlessly passed him a paper towel to mop up his split lip.

"Sorry," he muttered, "I didn't mean to call you out like that."

"It is okay," Jacques reassured him, touching the paper towel to his mouth. He turned to Eloise. "Are you alright? No one asked."

"I'm completely fine," she said quickly. Her back was aching from the impact of the refrigerator, but no need to tell him that. "I'm just sorry for the scene."

"It was bound to happen," Jacques said. "I knew it as soon as he came in the door that we were in for something at some point."

"Yeah, don't worry about it, Intern," Burnie said, dumping shards of plate into the garbage bin that Pell had gotten. "That's kind of how he rolls."

"Feels like we're all sleeping on the fact that Killer Hearst over here did more damage to Koslov in sixty seconds than anyone else in the NHL has done to him in like fifteen years," Pell pointed out, handing Kyle a broom.

"Shut up, man," Kyle said, looking down and sweeping plate shards into the dustpan.

"He's got like five inches and fifty pounds on you, dude, way to go," Burnie agreed. "Always the quiet ones, isn't it? Dude's got a fucking temper, that's for sure."

"Bwee herb da gill bilb sirebs," Travis said, pinching his nose.

"We heard the *Kill Bill* sirens?" Pell guessed, and Travis gave a thumbs-up with his free hand as red blossomed on the paper towel. "I can't believe you know *that* movie but you didn't know why Clinton was impeached."

"I lob bintag bovies," Travis said. "Bub not bresidends."

Krystal had made her way over to Eloise, and touched her arm.

"You okay?" she asked in a low voice.

"Completely fine," she reiterated, waving her hands. "Just embarrassed."

"Killer Hearst," Burnie repeated slowly. "Fuck, that's good. Killer Hearst."

"Shut *up*," Kyle insisted, flushing.

"Watch out, Burn, you're next," Pell joked and Burnie cackled.

"What did he say to you, Eloise?" Marcel asked, surprising her that he knew her name.

"Oh, nothing really, just—"

"Tried to get her to have sex with him in his car outside," Kyle interrupted disgustedly.

"*Wow.* Okay then," Krystal blurted in shock. Eloise could feel Jacques's eyes on her but she couldn't bring herself to look at him. *Still hoping if you sit close enough to Prince Jacques he'll fuck you?* Kyle and the others must have heard that too; she was grateful that Kyle had left that part out.

"I know, can't believe I didn't just take him up on that," she joked uneasily, and Pell snorted. "And they say romance is dead."

"Leos love an air sign," Marcel explained. "He just couldn't help himself."

"How did you know I was an air sign?" Eloise wondered. Marcel shrugged.

"Vibes," he said. "I'd bet Gemini if I believed in gambling."

"You play the stock market like it's ping pong, you totally *are* into gambling," Burnie said, rising from his crouch. "Alright, guys, forget about the rest of this, I'll get it tomorrow morning."

The party began to dwindle soon after that; Andrei's rage and Kyle's violence had settled over the mood like fog. Casper and Anita left first, followed by Ilya and Sofia. For a while Eloise sat with

Krystal and Juliette and Stephanie, vaguely listening to them discuss Andrei—"a fucking wrecking ball, and worse than ever," Stephanie said disdainfully. "But he doesn't have any family here, he's probably so lonely," Juliette protested, and Stephanie and Krystal both made noises of disgust and waved her off.

She sensed Jacques across the room, where he stood talking intently to Gagnon and Sekelsky. *Still hoping if you sit close enough to Prince Jacques he'll fuck you?* Shame roiled in her belly and she dropped her gaze. The precision with which Andrei had cut her open made her wonder if anyone else had seen what he had seen. Would they all talk about her after she had left—the silly girl in the dress who had been pressed against Jacques and been too happy about it? She hated Andrei so intensely that it made her want to cry.

Connor and Travis were slouched together on the sectional, with Travis still holding a bunched paper towel to his nose and Connor drowsily putting back more hard seltzer. "Yorb a goob guyg, ag nob a bobeheb ad all," Travis told him.

"Thanks, Travis," Connor slurred. Kyle sat hunched near them, holding a bag of frozen peas Stephanie had given him to his cheek, but he said nothing and just scowled at his phone.

"Shake it off, Intern," Burnie said as he dropped down beside Eloise on the couch, holding yet another beer. "You look the way I usually look after I've had to talk to Koslov, kind of like you want to puke," he explained.

"Yeah, thanks," she said.

"This is *not* reflective of the rest of the Bruins," Stephanie said, touching Eloise's knee and squeezing slightly. "These are good men on this team."

"Believe me, I know. And I'm fine. It wasn't a big deal until they started hitting each other," she insisted. She saw Kyle glance up at her out of the corner of her eye, but when she looked over at him, he was looking at Travis and Connor. "I'm old. This isn't the first time a guy has been weird to me at a party," she added, looking back at the group.

"I'm never letting our daughters leave the house," Burnie said suddenly to Stephanie. She rolled her eyes and sipped her wine.

An hour passed, with the party shifting and evolving and shrinking. Eloise wanted another chance to talk to Kyle, though she was not sure what she hoped to get from him, so she stayed on, even as Krystal left, shooting an icy, dismissive look at a hopeful Novak. Connor, Travis, and Kyle kept drinking. Marcel bid them goodnight, calling her 'Gemini' with a wave over his shoulder.

Somehow Eloise found herself in the kitchen with Stephanie, Juliette, Pell, and Burnie. Jacques joined them, having just walked Gagnon and Sekelsky to the door. They were the last to leave, aside from the three hammered rookies.

"Don't you need a ride home, Eloise?" Pell asked, unscrewing the cap off another water bottle. He was sobering up surprisingly quickly. "Maybe Travis or Kyle can drive you back."

"They are both way too drunk now. They will have to stay over tonight," Jacques said, glancing in the direction of the living room. "I can drive you," he told Eloise, nodding to her. "I have to leave soon, anyway."

"Oh, I can just—"

"You are *not* taking public trans, Intern," Burnie cut in, checking his watch. "It's like two A.M. I don't even think you *could* get back at this point."

"Yes, and it's not safe, even if you could," Jacques agreed. "Let me drive you."

Eloise hesitated before meeting Jacques's eyes. "Are you sure?"

"Yeah, of course," he said easily—but he didn't quite meet her eyes, either.

When Eloise poked her head into the living room, Connor had fallen asleep, his head on Travis's shoulder, and Travis was holding the frozen peas to his nose. Kyle was slouched deep into the couch, staring into space, his cheek and jaw red from the cold of the peas. He was balancing a beer on his chest, his grey eyes unfocused and sleepy. He gave her a listless wave, and she waved back.

"Thank you for standing up for me," she told Travis and Kyle. "And tell Connor I said thank you when he wakes up."

"I'll prolly forget," Travis said sleepily, his voice still heavily nasal but much improved, "but you're welcome, Eloise."

"You didn't do shit, man, it was me and Kennedy," Kyle slurred, rubbing at his face. "Fuck that guy," he added to Eloise.

It felt significant, but she didn't know if it was. She was about to speak, when Kyle's gaze fixed on someone beside her. Jacques had joined them.

"Yo, Cap," Kyle greeted, giving an ironic little salute before letting his head drop back. It was the most effusive she had ever seen Kyle be with Jacques—the result of a significant amount of beer and rage in a very short amount of time.

Jacques was smiling.

"Sleep it off," he told Kyle before turning to Eloise. "You ready?"

"Ready," she agreed.

# Chapter Fifteen

The night air had gotten a bite to it since Eloise had stood on the patio with Kyle. She walked down the driveway with Jacques in silence, arms folded over her chest. The lights on a dark grey Range Rover near the top of the driveway flashed as Jacques unlocked the car.

"I—"

"—You—"

"—Sorry—" they each said, pausing by his car.

"You go," Eloise said quickly.

"I was just wondering if you were cold. I might have a sweatshirt in the car," Jacques explained, gaze clipping on her bare arms again. *Just a freckle*, he had said quietly earlier.

"I'm fine, we'll be in the car anyway."

Jacques ignored her and rooted around in his back seat. Eloise realized she was watching him as he leaned into the car so she looked away, pretending to be absorbed by the night sky and the trees.

"Hm, I guess I don't," he realized, pulling back. "You can just have my sweater, I'm warm anyway," he added, and then he was pulling his sweater over his head, revealing a white tee that looked bright in the moonlight, and it was too late to stop him.

"Oh—thanks."

She clumsily caught it. The soft cashmere was warm in her hands. Had Rachel bought it for him, or had he chosen it himself?

Eloise hastened to the passenger side, trying to climb up without letting her dress ride up again. His car was mostly clean, but there was a toy train in one of the cupholders—and another one in the seat that dug into her thigh when she got in.

"Why, hello, Percy," Eloise said, retrieving the little green train from beneath her thigh. She held it up and Jacques laughed.

"Oh, sorry. That is embarrassing. I used to be the kind of person whose car was always clean, and then I became a father," he said, taking Percy the train from her. "Good eye."

"Thomas the Tank Engine's a classic. My brother loved it," she explained, watching him set the train in the cupholder with the other toy—and a slim plastic card that she realized was a hotel key. There was a duffle bag at her feet that she recognized as the one he had been carrying on the day they had confronted each other, as well as a little Batman figurine discarded next to it, plastic cape tangled with the limbs of a little orange T-Rex.

So he was staying at a hotel. This man whose car was littered with his sons' toys was living out of a hotel. So the separation *was* still on, then, and had apparently not improved. Maybe it was going to end in divorce. She looked around for something else to study, determined not to let her mind linger on that idea.

"My car is never clean, and I'm not even a dad," she added, relaxing a little when she got a laugh for that.

She was still holding his sweater. He had given it to her, so it would be weirder if she didn't wear it, right? She just had to do it, had to pretend it was no big deal. She pulled his sweater over her head and was hit with a blast of his scent: that spicy cologne and soapy deodorant, and the scent of his skin underneath.

They sat in held-breath silence.

He was turning over the car key in his hand. In the moonlight filtering through the window, the fine chain he wore, half-hidden by the collar of his shirt, faintly glinted; the tattoos that snaked up his arms were vivid black against his skin, muscle and bone shifting beneath it with every motion, a reminder of the strength that he downplayed, the strength that had allowed him to match Andrei in the kitchen. Eloise had never had such a powerful sense of being on the wrong side of a locked door, matched by a powerful sense that to even set her hand on the handle would be an intrusion.

"I'm sorry for whatever Andrei did or said," Jacques said at last, surprising her.

*Still hoping if you sit close enough to Prince Jacques he'll fuck you?* She suppressed a shudder.

"I think, based on what I've heard, it was bog-standard for Andrei," Eloise dismissed, hoping he couldn't see her eyes turning a little bright with anger and embarrassment. "And I maintain that it's not your job to police him, so you don't have to apologize."

In the light from the house his eyes looked icy, ghostly blue, like the light from the pool.

"Thanks," Jacques said after a moment. "And thank you for getting Kyle to come back inside."

"Oh, that. He was completely freaking out," Eloise confided. "Sounds like it was for good reason, too."

"The line change?" Jacques wondered, and nodded when Eloise grimaced. He exhaled heavily and leaned forward, bracing his arms on the steering wheel in a startling mirror to how Andrei had sat in his own car earlier.

"That probably feels like shit for you," Eloise ventured. His gaze caught hers again and clung. "You and Burnie and Pell have been the first line for years, right? And then you and Andrei used to be best friends, and Kyle's the rookie that you fought so hard for. You probably feel torn between them all."

Neither looked away. "Not that you have to say anything about it."

"No, you are right," he said, clearing his throat. "It does feel like shit."

The engine turned over and he twisted, bracing a hand on her headrest (she was so *aware* of his hand there), as he backed out of the driveway. His white T-shirt stretched appealingly across his shoulders and abdomen. Eloise looked away.

The street was empty. They drove past massive houses, professionally landscaped and tastefully lit up.

"So," Jacques said, "Southie, right?" They rolled to a stop sign and Jacques took his phone out of his pocket, opening Google Maps.

"Yeah, that's me. Hopefully it's not too far out of your way. Here, I can put my address in your phone," she offered. He passed her his phone, which was warm from being inside his jeans pocket, its screen glossy and new.

"Not at all. I have to be back early anyway because I'm picking up the boys' school things—" he began, then halted. "We're picking up the boys' school things," he corrected, taking his phone back from her and setting it in the cupholder.

"Right, yeah, that makes sense," she said hastily. She felt him looking at her again, but she pretended to be intrigued by the scenery going past the window, though it was pitch-black outside and difficult to see anything.

The hotel key sat between them, a living thing. Had he realized that he had left it out? Did he think she would piece it together?

"So, I told you something," Jacques said after a moment. "A very personal thing, because no one else knows what I think about the new line."

"Let's be clear that you didn't actually *tell* me anything—I just intuited it and you did not contradict me. Is it fact trade time?" Eloise guessed. Google Maps directed him to make a turn. He was a faster driver than she would have expected, and she found herself picturing him as a teenager learning to drive: a snowy, remote parking lot, and maybe his older brother's car. Breath clouding in the air, maybe his skin red and angry from one of his first tattoos. Maybe he and his brother would have fought in the car.

But likely none of that had happened at all. She did not know why it mattered.

"Yes, but I have one in mind," he informed her after the app had stopped directing them. "I want to know why you really left your old job. The one with the lab."

Google Maps said they only had twenty-two minutes to go. Why did he have to drive so fast?

"Wow, starting off with a hard one," Eloise joked. She fidgeted with the edge of the sweater sleeve.

She was thrown back to standing in front of the pool, those spires of icy light cast around her, as she faced the truth of her life. There was the urge to lie, to evade—but of course, Andrei had sliced through to the bone with his comment, and her wish was a silly one. What was the point of wanting someone that everyone else wanted, something that was astronomically beyond her reach? Once again she was watching Jacques skate, envying him for something that would never belong to her.

There was no point in lying to Jacques Lavesque about this, no point in protecting what he might think of her. He was never going to want her whether she lied about this or not. She swallowed her pride and her silly wants.

"I mean, I didn't leave that job so much as get fired from it. So, that's your fact. No one else knows that. Not even my brother, or my dad, or anyone."

Jacques was silent for a moment. His phone screen, still lit up, told her they had twenty minutes left.

"Why did you get fired?"

"Hey. This is fact *trade*, not fact handout," Eloise reminded him.

A laugh of disbelief exploded from him.

"Oh my god. You are so—so *withholding*!" he yelled, motioning with his hands while keeping his wrists pressed to the steering wheel, and then she was laughing, and he was too. "I cannot believe you! I cannot even get *one* personal fact from you without having to strangle you for it!"

"What! You have gotten *plenty*—" she shouted in protest, feeling her own face grow pink too as she tried to stop laughing.

"You are so frustrating," he gasped between laughter. "Why are you so withholding? Every time I try to get a single piece of information from you, you dodge and make some joke. *Hey, Eloise, do you have a boyfriend?* Ha ha, no! No further details—"

"Because there *aren't* any other details and I don't know why you would need—" she yelled over his shouting, but the comment had painted everything in rosy gold. The car might as well have been filled with glittering light.

"*Hey, Eloise, have you skated before?* Ha ha, I respectfully decline!" Jacques continued sarcastically over her protests.

"Oh, because you're so *very* forthcoming," she interrupted with a scoff.

"What! Yes, I am completely open," he shot back, glancing at her, teeth raking over his bottom lip, which still bore a red line from where Andrei had hit him. "What have I not shared with you?"

"Gosh, let's see. Why you got involved in Kyle's contract. How you really feel about Andrei coming back, not to mention what the big problem was between you in the first place," Eloise began, but Jacques scoffed.

"You really need an interview to guess how I feel about that?" he asked in disbelief, brows raised. "How do you *think* I feel about it? I think you were in that kitchen too."

"Well, I'm guessing not great, but I don't actually have any details on why—but that's a bad example." She thought about it and then continued. "Okay, how about this? You didn't tell anyone what you think about the line change, even though technically they should be able to handle it, right?"

"Bad example. No one would benefit from knowing how I feel about that," he said, waving his hand and shaking his head. "You are going to have to do better than that. Next," he demanded firmly.

"Okay—" She halted. "Well. Okay. Maybe that's all the examples I've got, but—"

"No," Jacques protested, glancing at her again. They were pulling onto the highway now; Google Maps said they had seventeen minutes left to go. "You had one more. Out with it. Come on. I am not patient."

"Sundress season," she said. "You were *so* lying about that."

"Like you're lying now?" he laughed. "You are such a terrible liar, I really cannot get over it. You lie as much as I play hockey, but you are so bad at it. And for the record," he went on, "I wasn't lying."

"You just seem like a yoga pants man—"

"I do love them too, but don't try to distract me," he interrupted. "You were going to call me out on something and then you stopped. What was it?"

"You read that wrong—"

"Look, when you're flustered, your neck turns red," he informed her, glancing back at her again. "It's a little spot on your throat that gets red every time. You are so full of shit. Is this a compulsive thing? Is it a power thing?" he wondered. "What happened to you that you need to lie about every single thing?"

"Fine." Eloise crossed her arms, trying to contain this shivery, fluttering sense of joy. She did not know why she was so happy, because technically this was a confrontation, and he had just relentlessly roasted her. She could see the lights of Boston, and she had never been so displeased to see them. "Let's just say that I *didn't miss* the times where you told a lie or withheld the truth tonight—and other times, too. And I'm being the bigger person by letting you get away with your lies, but I *notice*. Alright?"

"Vague," he called her out, shaking his head. "Booooo," he called, cupping his mouth with one hand like a fan in the stands. "Too vague."

"Yeah, kind of like you when answering pretty much any personal question."

"Oof. Was that supposed to hurt me? You are losing your touch."

"You say that now, but you're going to go home tonight and weep softly as you journal about how I made you feel," she informed him, and bit her lip when that got another laugh from him.

"Okay, come on," he said, after their laughter had quieted once more. Fourteen minutes left. "Tell me why you got fired. I will not rest until I know, so you might as well give up."

"Fact trade," she reminded him, and Jacques exhaled, rolling his eyes good-naturedly.

"Fine. What do you want to know?"

Eloise considered it all. The hotel key card was between them. Had he ever brought anyone back to his hotel? She saw him lingering by the door, fishing for the key in his pocket, a faceless woman pressed to his arm. *Are you still in love with your wife? Have you started dating again? How did you find out about the affair, and what do you think of it?*

*...Was there an affair at all? Is that why you can't even look at Andrei?*

"What game did you break your nose at, and who broke it?"

"That's two things," he said. "I didn't break my nose at a game. You should know by now that I do not fight on the ice. It is the most basic thing about me. Now tell me why you got fired."

"Ugh. Fine." Twelve minutes left. Southie was so close. She glimpsed the name *Fairmont* on the key card, then looked away, ashamed for looking. "I'll try to give you the short version, but it's kind of complicated."

She felt like she had had too much caffeine. "So like I said earlier, my job was to test drugs taken off the street, to make sure they were actually drugs. So I would spend all day testing drugs against these samples we had stored in the lab, and then go to court to testify that they were, in fact, illegal drugs."

"Okay," Jacques said with a nod. "Following."

"And—"

Her throat tightened. It was unexpectedly hard to talk about it. She pulled the cuffs of the sweater over her hands, holding her breath until the urge to cry had passed. "And it's very underfunded, so there's not much supervision."

"And we all know you are a troublemaker," Jacques teased, but his voice was soft, as soft as the sweater moving over her skin. She swallowed. "I am sorry, I think I went too far. You don't have to—"

"No, no, it's fine," she said quickly, fixing her gaze on the night rushing past them. "It's just not something I've ever talked about, and it's—it's *so* much more painful than I expected," she admitted with a thick laugh. "Look, long story short, I noticed that the samples that we tested the drugs against were low, even though they should have stayed the same amount. And I started paying attention, and I figured out that the levels changed every time one person in particular worked with them. And it was this really nice man named Charlie who had worked there forever—"

"He was stealing the sample drugs?" Jacques interrupted.

"Yes, basically. And instead of raising it with my boss in a normal way—"

"Is there a normal way to mention that to your boss?" Jacques wondered, an edge to his voice.

"I mean, not really. But I made a formal accusation with no actual proof," she said. "I went over my boss's head and reported it, and there was an inquiry—"

She halted again. "Everything blew up. My boss was totally humiliated by it, because they took a microscope to our department and found all of these things that were like, normal errors, and not his fault, and my best friend Monique got put on a performance improvement plan for no real reason, which hurt her salary…"

"So were you wrong?" Jacques asked after a moment.

Nine minutes from Southie.

"It's probably hard to believe me, but *I know* I wasn't. But I had no proof, and I should have gone to my boss first, but I felt like he didn't like me and wouldn't listen, especially since everyone loved Charlie…"

"And Charlie still works there?"

"As far as I know. He's this sweetheart who has two little girls and a lovely wife, and he's never caused any trouble in his life."

"Except for stealing drugs." She felt Jacques look at her. "I am sorry, but I don't have much sympathy for drug addicts," he confessed. "My brother died of an overdose and I guess I am still angry with him."

It was so obvious that he was giving her something in return; it was so obvious that he was responding to her distress and trying to soothe it.

"I'm so sorry," Eloise said. "Seriously. Having spent so many years in that world, I really get how destructive addiction is. I feel terrible for you and your family." The scenery was growing familiar around her. She wished she lived in Baltimore, in Raleigh; she wished she could have him to herself for hours. "I remember reading that you had a brother who had passed."

"He passed the year I signed with the Bruins," Jacques specified. He made a wrong turn, and she wondered if he knew he had done it. It added another minute. "But it was a very long time coming, and by the time it happened, part of me was relieved, and I think I am still mad at him for that. I don't want to feel relieved that my brother died, you know? It is sort of where my sympathy ends, I think."

He looked at his phone. "Sorry, I think I screwed up," he said, picking up the phone at a stoplight and squinting at the screen.

"Turned too soon. It's fine, it's basically six-of-one," she reassured him as he set the phone down. The trains and the key card rattled as he did it, and she bit her lip, holding in her breath.

Bathed in red light, their eyes met. He knew she had seen the hotel key, just now.

"I—"

The light changed and then they were cast in a green glow. Jacques looked back at the road as he began to drive again. She could see him considering his words, making the trade-offs in his mind for how he might address this.

"I won't tell anyone," she said quickly, looking forward at the dark night. "About the key card. Or about your brother. Especially not the key card, though."

"I forgot it was there," he admitted quietly. He turned onto her street, pitch-black with so few street lamps, and rolled slowly, cautiously, down the road. "Thank you," he added.

"Does anyone know?"

"No. No one knows the whole story. Krystal knows that something is going on, but she's the only one who knows anything."

"That's exhausting," she said. "How long have you been—"

She didn't know how to say it but she did not need to. They crept to a stop on the road and Jacques angled the car to the side, but it didn't matter. It was the small hours of the morning and the street was dark; they were alone in the world right now.

"A few months. Since July."

He turned off the car and then all was silent. "I just—I couldn't stay in the house," he admitted in a sudden rush. He forced a laugh, so desperate to gloss over the anguish in his voice. "I couldn't do it."

His voice was tight with anger and she felt ashamed all over for the assumptions she had made when they had first met, so careless and audacious. She felt shame, too, for the thoughts she'd had when she had glimpsed his tattooed skin through his thin white T-shirt. His heart was breaking and it made her throat go tight. Love was a noose, love was a frenemy, love was faded ink on skin, its bite forever visible. Love was Death as the tarot saw it: skeleton within steel, a breakable body wrapped in inevitability, a shrouded soldier on the march atop the loveliest horse.

"That sounds terrible," she said, smiling softly at him in the darkness, trying to hide her feelings, "and no one ever realizes how *inconvenient* it is to blow up your life, do they? But I guess you probably haven't officially blown it up yet. You can still decide to go home."

"Do you regret it?" he asked suddenly, and her smile had dropped and they were looking at each other again. He held her eyes like a spell but even in the dark it burned to look directly at him. "Blowing up your life."

"Sometimes, yes, and sometimes, no," she said honestly. "But I think two conflicting things can be true at the same time."

"Right." He swallowed; she watched him touch the mark on his lip where Andrei had hit him. "Yeah."

She was doing everything in her power to not let her gaze stray to his neck, to the tattoo peeking out of his white T-shirt. She saw his neck move, muscles contracting briefly as he swallowed again, and for the briefest flash his gaze dropped to her shoulder—bare, except for maybe a freckle there, too—then back to her eyes again.

"I should let you go," she said as he abruptly looked back at the road.

"Yeah. Have a good night," he said, not looking at her, and she told him to have a good night too as she dropped out of the Range Rover and onto the road, awkwardly swinging the door shut and hurrying between two parked cars like she was being timed, and she did not hear the engine start until she had unlocked the front door of her building and the motion-sensor light had flicked on. She waved over her shoulder without looking back, and then let the door swing shut and hurried blindly up the narrow carpeted stairs.

It wasn't until she got to her hallway that she realized she was still wearing his sweater. She unlocked her apartment and checked the window, and watched the Range Rover roll down the rest of the street, briefly pausing at the stop sign before making a turn and disappearing around the corner.

·)·)●(·(·

Jacques dropped his car keys onto the bedside table, then dropped himself onto the edge of the crisply-made bed, mopping his face with his hands. His lip vaguely throbbed where Andrei had hit it, but he did not go and get any ice for it.

He went through his usual bedtime routine. And even though he was exhausted—that stale fatigue that came after drinking so much beer over the course of a long evening—his mind was restless, because the truth was so impossible to overlook.

He spit out his toothpaste, studying his reflection in the dimmed mirror.

He had not thought about Rachel once tonight. This could not be ignored. Until he had realized that his hotel key was sitting in the cupholder for Eloise to see, he had not thought about his wife at all. He had been thinking of so many other things, and most of his thoughts had been those of a single man. When Eloise had come back into the party, with Kyle in tow—visibly awkward, visibly forcing herself despite her discomfort—something in his chest had tightened, and he had allowed it, realizing that he had stopped every other little domino from taking down the line: the freckle on her arm that had caught his eye, the way her words had twisted with remorse in her voicemail, the way her pretty brown eyes fixed on people, the ugly curl of jealousy he had felt when he watched Andrei make her laugh. Each of these he had expertly held still, stopped from tipping over, because it was the right thing to do, because he had promised he would do it—he had made a vow to—even if it was difficult.

And then that last one—he had just let it fall. He had known it was happening. He had done nothing to stop it. Because he didn't want to.

In his mind, his marriage was over. He knew this because he was acting like it was over.

Jacques turned off the bathroom light, mouth tasting like mint and the blood from his reopened cut. His head ached vaguely, and his eyes itched with exhaustion, but he felt strangely clear-headed, too. It was four in the morning now, and he would have to call the boys in a few hours, the way he always did when they stayed with their grandparents—especially now, Jacques was compelled to make sure that they knew he was still *there*, that he was not leaving them for good, he would always be there for them—but this sudden clarity demanded action. There could be no more delay; he had been manufacturing his indecision and in the lamplight of his hotel room it seemed silly, passive, childish.

He went to the desk and retrieved the papers. *An expensive tantrum.* Yes, it had been a tantrum—and he was still so angry. It was ugly, it was wrong, it was imperfect. But he was angry and it was not going away. His marriage—and his faith to Rachel, his respect for her, his friendship with her—had ended the moment he had opened his door to find Andrei sitting at the foot of his front staircase, tying his shoes, Rachel coming down the stairs behind him to plead with him to stay. Jacques had only pretended to be in conflict, because he had not wanted to be the kind of person who could not forgive.

But he couldn't forgive a lie, and he knew this about himself. He did not forgive liars.

He flipped through the papers and then opened his laptop, and, with detached strikes on the keyboard, he started an email to his lawyer.

# Chapter Sixteen

Eloise awoke to grey gloom and still air. Through the mess of her bedroom, her gaze landed on the chair in the corner, where Jacques's sweater was folded.

So much had happened last night, yet the one thing that made everything look different was Jacques's implicit acceptance of what she had done at the lab. For so long, she had assumed that to tell someone the truth of why she had been fired would be to lose them, to lose their respect. *Is there a normal way to bring that up to your boss?* he had asked, and those simple words—a throwaway question—and the lack of judgment in his voice had changed everything. At last, someone was on her side; at last, someone had seen the good she was trying to do, rather than the bad in how she had gone about doing it.

No one had ever seen past her surface before. They had seen her chaos and her scales, but never her warmth or strength. She had been keeping herself in exile for so long—the witch banished from the castle town, the serpentine dragon atop the desolate peaks—and now she was beginning to see that her exile had been, in part, because she believed herself to be deserving of it.

(*People have always thought I was trash, so like, whatever*, Kyle had said, and she had been confronted by a dark mirror: the lonely rebellion, the stung pride. Maybe she had become so entranced by the idea of investigative work because she was waiting for someone to do the same for her, waiting for some knight errant to wander through her woods.)

Eloise sat up, depleted but burned clean like she had recovered from a raging illness. Last night she had resolved to take better care of the people around her—the way Jacques did—and now she knew what she needed to do. She needed to do what he would do in her circumstances.

Eloise rolled out of bed and plugged her phone into the charger that always dropped behind her nightstand. First, she needed some coffee and to find a place that would do same-day dry cleaning. She picked up Jacques's sweater and held it for a moment, then set it down before she could hold it close and breathe in their scents mingled together with smoke and beer. It was a sleeping dragon, around which she must tread with caution—the more she faced it, the more she would be asked to deny it. For a moment, when he had glanced at her shoulder just before dropping her off, it had almost seemed like—

Best to pretend it was not there at all.

Instant coffee made and same-day dry cleaner identified, Eloise sat on the edge of her bed with her phone in hand. *You know what you have to do.*

"So just do it," she said aloud in the quiet of her apartment, and thus she dialed Hollis's number.

"Hey." Hollis answered on the third ring without his usual 'this is Hollis Davies,' his voice wary. Her fingers were thick and clumsy as they held her phone. It had only been a week, and they had certainly gone months without speaking before, but this time she knew it was different.

"Hey," she croaked, then cleared her throat; her voice was still hoarse from last night.

"So you *are* alive," Hollis said. "What do you need this time?"

"I deserved that," she admitted, but he didn't laugh. "I don't need anything—except to apologize."

"Hm, what for?" he began with awful sarcasm. "Let's see. For not calling me back for an entire week? Or for flaking on Dad again? Or for—"

"For being self-absorbed," Eloise cut in. "And selfish."

"Wow." His voice was tight.

She waited for some quip or sarcastic remark, but Hollis gave her nothing. And then she was thinking again of standing there by the pool with Kyle, each of them in self-exile for their own fear. It was time to come inside.

"This isn't me making excuses, I promise," she said. "But I have been really not-great for a while. And instead of opening up, or asking for help, I've just pushed everyone away."

"Yeah, no kidding," Hollis said, his voice raw now. "That's what you always do. And then when anyone else needs anything from *you*, you just... ghost. It's like no one is more important to you than your own feelings. And that—that's shitty. Okay?"

"Yeah." She bounced her leg as her heart raced and her eyes burned. "I know. I'm working on it. I'm going to Dad's today. Even though I really do not want to."

"That's great," Hollis deadpanned. "It's like, really big of you."

Her frustration mounted.

"You know what, Hollis? I don't have the bond with Dad that you have. We can't just talk about sports like you guys can," Eloise said. "We can't really talk about *anything*. He thinks my job is stupid, he thinks I'm a failure and he always has, he thinks everything I have to say is stupid—"

"I don't have a bond with him either, alright?" Hollis snapped. "I just work incredibly hard to make peace with him—"

"Yeah, and I admire that!" Eloise interrupted. "I genuinely do. I think it's something that is really special about you, and it's a quality I wish I had."

"There's no *wishing* about it. You either put in the work or you don't," Hollis said bluntly. "And you never put in the work with anyone, El."

"Yes, I know," she conceded, even though her eyes were beginning to sting, "but I want to. I'm going to try harder with Dad. It's just..."

She swallowed around the lump in her throat. "I think for the past few years I've come to feel like it's not worth it because no one thinks *I'm* worth it."

Hollis drew in a sharp breath like he had been slapped.

"Well, I wouldn't base your self-worth on how nice Dad is to you," he said when he had recovered, "because, as Lily always reminds me, he's not exactly nice to himself either. He treats himself like shit—kind of like you do. No food in the house, no clean clothes, no hugs from friends, no... I don't know, daily joy or whatever."

"Yeah," she said quietly, fidgeting with her charging cable. Here was another dark mirror held up to her: she had been working, all of her adult life, to avoid letting what had happened to her father—losing himself to the grief of being left by the person he had so deeply loved—happening to her.

And in spite of that effort, her life looked a lot like his.

"And—" Hollis's voice was thick now too. "Like I spent a lot of time in therapy about it, and I decided that at the end of the day all that matters to me is how I loved other people. Someday he's gonna be gone, and that's my *dad*, you know? So all you need to do is show him love, and be okay with the fact that he doesn't always know how to show it back."

"That's really beautiful," Eloise said, sincere as she wiped under her eyes, and Hollis gave a wet laugh and sniffed.

"Shut up," he laughed. "Listen," he said suddenly, warmth rushing back into his voice, "you want to come over tonight? Lily's making congee and we're going to get the Halloween decorations down."

"I would love to," she said, trying not to cry. "Congee sounds perfect for this weather. That sounds really great. Thanks."

"Yeah, you need a ride? Your car's still busted, right?"

"I can get there, but thanks. I'm getting really good at the bus system," she joked.

For a moment they were quiet, each pulling themselves together. "Thank you, Holl."

"I'm the best," he reminded her.

"You are. You completely are," she agreed, and at last they hung up.

The noises of wiping her nose and eyes were loud in her silent apartment. It took a few deep breaths to recover.

"Alright," she said into the silence, and she set her hands on her legs, drew in a deep breath, and got to her feet.

Southie was foggy this morning, branches turned black in the damp, red bricks dark and slick. The playground across from her apartment was deserted, save for a circle of old men in beanies hunched over a game of checkers on the sodden basketball court. Eloise carried Jacques's sweater in an old Whole Foods bag and walked past them to the only dry cleaner she had found in the area that could do same-day cleaning.

When she spread out the sweater on the counter for the woman, she had to stop herself from laughing at the woman's reaction.

"This is nice," the woman said admiringly, looking between the sweater's beautiful label—some Italian brand that Lily would recognize—and Eloise's ancient, thrifted Patagonia fleece and bleached hair, her nose wrinkled in suspicion. "Really nice."

"It's not mine, obviously," Eloise agreed with a grin. "Can you get it done today? All I want is to get the smell out of it."

"I can try." She held it up and smelled it. "Smells like a good-looking man," she added with a look before going to her computer to ring Eloise up.

The journey to Chestnut Hill on the green line was faster on a Saturday than on a Sunday, but it still gave her too much time to think as she rocked and swayed with the train, her thoughts irresistibly going to a place she knew they were not allowed. Love was a green meadow behind a locked door, luminous and sultry in summer sun.

Her childhood home looked shabbier in the rain. Eloise smoothed her hands over her bangs, which had gone even puffier in the damp air, before climbing the front steps. She had a flash of watching Kyle climb the front steps of his own shabby childhood home with his brother, and remembered Patrick calling his father a 'pathetic beta loser.' Kyle had agreed with him.

She knew it, with that flash of instinct that she so often had: Kyle hated his father, and this mattered.

She knocked on the door, eyes on the autumn wreath that Lily had picked out: branches of plastic russet leaves intertwined with plastic Chinese lanterns. The front door opened with a shrill squeak, and there was her father squinting at her through the screen door.

"Ellie," he blurted.

Her father was a preview of what Hollis would look like in thirty years: freckled skin gone craggy, hooded eyes heavier, corners of his thin-lipped mouth turned downward. He was Eloise's height, but the fact that she was standing on the porch put her a few inches below him.

"Dad! I thought I'd come over and help out a bit and say hi, since we haven't seen each other in a while," she explained, her voice falsely bright.

He still had not let her in, and his wariness was familiar to her. He was ashamed for her to see him; she had never understood that before. This was the sort of thing that Jacques would have seen immediately. "Can you... let me in?"

"Oh. Sure," he conceded, ducking his head in an obsequious move as he pushed open the door. "Come in. So good of you to stop by and see little old me."

Before, the defensiveness in his voice would have stung her, but now it just made her sad. He was so lonely.

The TV was on in the living room, blaring the highlights of a Sox game. The place smelled like unwashed hair and vegetable soup, and when Eloise poked her head into the living room, she saw a line of dirty bowls and mugs along the end table by his chair.

*"...and the Bruins start their first preseason game in just three days—"* Her stomach clenched, but Dad turned off the TV and studied the remote for lack of anything to do or say. The silence was thick and humid.

"Well!" she said briskly, swinging her arms. "Looks like you have some dishes to do. Let me take care of those before we sit down."

How did Hollis do it? Eloise pushed past her father to collect mugs and bowls. "Are you excited for hockey season to start? The Bruins have a really good team this year."

"O-ho, is someone a sports fan now?" He watched her struggle to carry the dirty dishes, and followed her into the kitchen. The bowls rattled against each other as she walked. Eloise reached the narrow kitchen and wrinkled her nose at the sweet rotting smell of trash that had not been taken out.

"Actually, for work I've had to look into the team," she explained, deciding against sharing how well she had gotten to know some of the men. "Andrei Koslov is back, and he's a legend. They're going for a Cup run with him."

"He's not a legend—he wasn't much without Lavesque," Dad dismissed with a scoff. "He's a hired gun, like any of those big stupid Russian players. He'll do anything for ten million, even if it means coming back to a city that he fucked over—but he's an old whore now, and no one wants him in bed anymore. And Lavesque is probably still injured, and probably will just play through it once again, and that'll get us in a few months when suddenly he conveniently has to sit out a run of tough games. There isn't going to be any Cup run. You should find better opinions to parrot."

She dropped the last bowl into the sink a little more loudly than she might have.

"Old whore? Wow. That is nice," she joked.

"Oh, here we go," Dad said with a roll of his eyes. "Eloise the Feminist, here to educate me."

It calmed her to think of Kyle again. She traced her mental steps back to the flash of insight she had had on the porch, like feeling her way along a dark hall. *He's a pathetic beta loser anyway*, Patrick had said, and Kyle had not disagreed. She now knew Kyle better, knew how he might have taken offense at the insult if he cared for his father at all. He was not afraid of a fight.

"It's not just about feminism," she disagreed, her mind still on Kyle, on the single father who had worked as a Boston cop and who had retired at thirty-five; it was impossible to imagine retiring so young, particularly as she guessed they must have had extensive medical bills from Patrick's childhood illness. And then she was thinking of her own father, glued to his chair in front of the television by grief, and wondered if Jimmy Hearst suffered from something similar, and Kyle had not seen enough of the world yet to forgive him for it. "I think it's just a crappy way to talk about another human being." She paused. "You think Andrei 'fucked over' Boston?"

"Andrei? Are you on a first-name basis with the Bruins?" Dad wondered sarcastically. "And yeah, of course he did. He left Boston at the peak of his and Lavesque's careers, when they were best positioned for the Cup, and any idiot can see that it's because he wanted to be the only special star on the ice. He hasn't aged as well as Lavesque, and he wanted to go somewhere that it wasn't as obvious."

Understanding bloomed in a way that it had not before. Eloise gazed at the suds in wonder.

"So you don't think he was forced out by the organization?" she asked innocently. "I heard he was forced out for being, you know, bigoted."

Dad laughed.

"No. They don't force players out for that kind of thing—just look at Dempsey with the Rangers, and a thousand other players I could name—and at that point he was still good enough that no team with enough cap space would have forced him out. Those rumors came later. I guarantee you he left on his terms and he came back on his terms."

"And you think he left because Ja—because Lavesque was better than him and he knew it?"

"He knew Lavesque's star was still rising and his wasn't. And if you look at how he played in Tampa—sure, he contributed, but he's gotten slower every year. They can't find a player who can handle him on the ice like Lavesque could. You know Koslov used to insist on being the last one on the ice, for dramatic effect?" Dad shook his head. "No, he fucked over the Bruins at the worst possible time—and then suddenly you started hearing those rumors about him. But he played the first twelve years of his career with Boston and you never heard a peep about him being a bigot."

The passion that twisted his voice surprised her, particularly when he had been so critical of Andrei. He seemed ashamed of it now, retreating and turning away from her. Her father had once collected baseball cards, had cared for his collection, had had favorite cards and favorite players. Love was in a deck of cards.

(Was this what it was like to be in Jacques's head—to see the vulnerability in everyone, even when they were challenging, and have your heart broken for it? She was thinking of how he had talked about Andrei's little red book of French phrases and how obviously it had killed him to know that about Andrei, how it had stolen his objectivity from him.)

She looked around the countertops for the sponge, and found one that was crusty and red with dried spaghetti sauce.

"Do you have any other sponges? This one is definitely done," she said, crouching down to look inside the cabinet under the sink.

"It's not *done*, it just needs to be washed," he said defensively, reaching into the sink. "Forget about these—"

"Dad, you can't live like this, you're going to get mice—"

She rose too fast just as he was lifting a mug out of the sink and her head bumped his elbow; the mug shattered on the floor.

"Shit, sorry," she stammered, dropping down and grabbing the dustpan from the cabinet. "I'm an idiot, let me—"

She halted at a strange huffing noise. When she looked up, her father had a hand clapped over his eyes, his thin lips quivering, bony shoulders shaking.

He was crying.

Eloise did not know what to do. "I—"

"Just go," he gasped, turning from her. She stared at his trembling shoulders. "Just go."

"Dad—"

"Get out of my house," he huffed and gasped.

Her hands were so useless and empty; it occurred to her to touch his back but it would mean nothing to him. There was a burning acid in her throat like she had eaten too fast and something was stuck there, an expanding ache that she could not escape.

"Okay," she said quietly. "I'll give you a break. But I'm coming back."

She swept the mug into the dustpan and dropped it in the trashcan. Her father just stared out the window over the sink.

Outside on the sidewalk, Eloise gulped in air and tried not to cry. She hugged her arms around herself and began walking. She considered calling Hollis—she wanted to call her big brother, and have him promise her it would all be okay—but she was sure that Hollis already knew, that to some extent he had been protecting her from how bad things were. What would calling him solve except to make herself feel better?

When she got to the Boston College green line stop, she dropped onto a bench inside the plexiglass shelter and typed *jimmy hearst boston police department* into a browser. The same article that she had read weeks ago came up, detailing Hearst's fourteen years of service, accompanied by a pixelated image of him in uniform: Kyle and Patrick had gotten their thin, pretty lips and shadowed blue eyes from him, but significant weight masked any other familial resemblance. As she had found the last time it occurred to her to research his father, there was nothing else online.

Her phone buzzed and she jolted, and was ashamed that her spirits dropped when she saw it was Hollis—not anyone else.

"As if he would text you," she muttered to herself.

**Hollis [12:36pm]**: how did it go? u still there?

**Eloise [12:36pm]**: eh. just left.

**Hollis [12:37pm]**: bleh. congee?

**Eloise [12:37pm]**: congee.

Eloise locked her phone screen and sat back. A few other passengers had collected on the platform to wait for the train back into Boston; one man wore a scrubby Bruins cap.

She dialed Krystal's number.

"Hey. Do you have a minute?" she asked when Krystal answered.

"Sure. How did last night go—aside from Andrei harassing you, I mean," Krystal self-corrected. "I saw you and Kyle come inside together."

"Actually, really good." The train was approaching; Eloise got to her feet. A soft rain was beginning to fall. "We talked by the pool for a while and I made a lot of progress with him, but I need more one-on-one time. None of my other lines of inquiry have gotten me as far as just talking to him has, but he's so suspicious and cautious."

She leaned against the plexiglass, watching the train approach and considering her words. "I know you guys are about to leave for a road trip, and I was wondering if I could come along? You can give me stuff to do so it's less of a burden on you. I just think I need a little more time with him."

"You don't have a boyfriend or something who will be pissed at you for leaving for a week, last-minute?" Krystal wondered, and got her answer when Eloise snorted. The train slowed to a stop. "You know, Alex *could* use some help," she said thoughtfully. "He's really struggling to have chemistry with the guys."

"Well, I can't promise I'll do any better, but I can run around and follow orders," Eloise offered, queuing up to board the train. "I can take pictures and post things to social media and... I don't know, get coffees for everyone. Anyway, you don't have to answer right now, but think it over."

"Hmm." She heard a tapping sound, like Krystal was rapping a pen against something in thought. "You know what? Let's go for it. Let's see if we can't wrap this up on this trip."

She did not miss the pressure that Krystal was applying. Eloise boarded the train.

"Let's do it," she agreed.

·◗◗●◖◖·

Jacques knew Rachel would be home, because she was getting ready for an event that the non-profit she helped to run was hosting tonight. The boys were with Jeff and Milly for the weekend, and Jacques had FaceTimed with them before spending the rest of the morning shopping for their school supplies. He had texted Rachel to tell her that he wanted to talk to her when he dropped the boys' new school things off, and had gotten a simple *ok* that was unlike her.

Now he drove towards the brownstone that he and Rachel had purchased together—partly with his salary and partly with her family money, a detail that had been meaningless to him at the time but about which his lawyer, Anthony, was deeply concerned. He had so innocently enmeshed his life with Rachel's, thinking it would be forever, and had been so unwilling to let that go. He understood now that he could never again sleep in that bed knowing that Rachel had welcomed Andrei into it. It all seemed so obvious from this angle. He had only been afraid of blowing up his life, afraid of the regret or grief he might feel, afraid of how he might be judged for it.

And he did feel deep grief as he pulled to a stop in front of the house, even as he also knew he could never bring himself to call this place home again. Two conflicting things, as Eloise had said, could be true at the same time.

He turned the car off, grabbed the bags of the boys' school things, and approached. The wreath was different than it had been all summer, than the one burned into his mind's eye.

"Rachel?" he called as he kicked the door shut behind him. Just like that day in July, Rachel appeared at the top of the stairs, this time in immaculate athleisure instead of a hastily-tied robe, all slender ankles and casual elegance. "Hey," he greeted, holding up the bags demonstratively.

"Oh, thanks for doing that," she said as she descended the steps. He considered pointing out that they were his sons too, but instead he forced a smile.

"Yeah, sure. Do you have time to talk?"

It was strange to be so formal with someone he had been through so much with. He knew Rachel's every scar and stretch mark, had gripped her sweaty hand while she had given birth to their sons; he had taken care of her through stomach viruses and food poisoning and bad colds; they had held hands at funerals and gotten mad at each other when it was too hot or when they were hungry. They were like strangers now, strangers who found each other slightly annoying: the seatmate on the plane who won't stop talking, the person behind you in line wearing too much cologne.

"Yeah, I guess," she said with a shrug. "We can go in the kitchen. I actually don't have a *ton* of time. I've got my nail appointment, then I'm dropping things off at the venue and making sure everything's in order, and then I've got to come back here, and then I've got a blowout..."

He followed her into the kitchen, which they had had redone just before Peter was born, a renovation that had been tightly directed by Milly while Jacques had been busy with a series of games leading up to the playoffs, and as a result looked just like Jeff and Milly's kitchen in their main house. Jacques set the bags on the island as Rachel rummaged through the refrigerator for something.

"So?" Her voice took on that falsely bright, peppy tone that she sometimes had with coworkers, her back still to him. "What did you want to talk about?"

There was no easy way to bring it up. Jacques studied her back. He hated her, but he still cared about her, and still felt compelled to protect her from the pain he knew this would cause her.

"Rachel," he said as gently as he could, "I'm going to have my lawyer put together divorce papers. I would like us to get a no-fault divorce."

She did not even slow down or pause in her search. She at last found what she was looking for—a half-finished bottle of green juice—and idly shook the bottle, going to the cabinets to get a glass for it.

"Oh, yeah?" Still that peppy tone, her back still to him. "That's what you've decided."

*No, that's what* you *decided when you cheated*, he wanted to say, but he pressed his lips together until the urge to fire something back had subsided.

"Yes," he said at last, "that is what I have decided."

"And you really can't imagine being, I don't know, an *adult* about it, and just trying to forgive me for this one mistake—the only mistake I've made in our marriage," she continued in that same cheerful, off-hand tone, though her words came out faster in a torrent, like bile, the way they did when she was truly angry. She turned to face him then, her long glossy hair swinging with the movement, her eyes bright and blazing, daring him to hit back.

"If it had been one mistake, I would have forgiven you," he said as evenly as he could stand, "but I don't think it was one mistake."

"Right," she said, nodding, eyes still bright, "and you, for example, have *never* made a mistake in our marriage." She gestured to him with the glass of green juice.

"Not this kind of mistake." He gripped the edge of the countertop and clenched his jaw against the things he wanted to say. It was starting to seep out; he was starting to lose his cool. "Even when I had the opportunity, I did not do something like this."

"You think this was about opportunity?" she marveled, blinking back tears, though she was still smiling.

"No, I think it was very intentional."

"Are you this mad at Andrei?" She suddenly laughed. "Probably not, right? Because he's your *buddy* and he never could do any wrong in your eyes. The rest of us have to be perfect—according to *your* standards—but Andrei? No. For whatever reason, he gets a free pass with you every single time."

"You are right. I'm not as mad at Andrei." He shrugged, his mouth filling with a bitter taste. "Andrei didn't make any vows about how he would treat me. You did. And maybe I could forgive whatever happened between you before we got married—"

She lifted her chin in a rebellious look, and he felt sick. He wished he had not probed, wished he had not searched for an answer to that question that had been lingering in the back of his mind.

"But I can't forgive whatever you let happen with him after we got married. That was," he continued, voice growing tight, "the *point* of getting married. And I tried to get past it, but I just can't."

"Funny timing that you decided this now." She stared at him, mouth twisting with hurt. "I wonder if it has anything to do with Burnie's party. I heard you had fun last night."

Jacques almost laughed at her. He had seen Andrei looking at his phone before and after every practice for weeks, detachedly watching his screen blow up with texts, because that was how Rachel still texted, at thirty-six, every time she had any feeling at all—like she was a teenager going through a breakup. He had known it was Rachel, had known that Andrei could give a one-word response (because Andrei never texted back; he never truly communicated) and Rachel would call that 'talking' and Andrei would know that she thought of it that way, and in his head he would laugh at her for it. And she did not understand this about Andrei. She did not know this. How could she be thirty-six and not know this about Andrei?

It was supposed to be a threat—if he had to guess, Andrei had tossed out some allusion to Eloise and then said nothing else, leaving Rachel to spin her wheels and squirm. Andrei was such a paranoid person; it would have relieved him to, for once, not be the paranoid or anxious one.

"Okay, well, I still would like to pursue the no-fault divorce," Jacques said now, injecting a finality into his voice as he pushed back from the countertop.

"Oh, you're so *fucking* generous," Rachel laughed, genuinely crying now. "What a martyr! Do you want me to clap for you? Do you want an award?"

*No, I want to never have to look at you again*, he thought, but he swallowed that too.

*Oh, more 'no comment' bullshit?*

"I want this to be as easy for our boys as possible," he said. "I don't want them to even remember this when they're older."

"And you always get what you want," she said, unwittingly echoing Andrei's words from just last night.

"You can think of it however you want," he invited, "but I know you want what's best for them too, and I don't think an ugly, long, drawn-out divorce is going to be healthy for them."

"And you living out of a fucking *hotel* for three fucking months was healthy for them? You really think you were being so mature, don't you?"

Her cheeks were wet, her subtle makeup running.

He wanted to say, *healthier than it would have been for them to see how I would behave if I had to sleep in the bed you let Andrei fuck you in*, but this too he pushed down. He stared at her, waiting for discipline to come back to him.

"Maybe not," he conceded. He felt like he was doing post-game media, a microphone shoved in his face, the lights too bright, some salivating reporter waiting for him to make a misstep. Ever since Krystal had started pushing the narrative that he was perfect they had been trying to show that he wasn't. "I have made some mistakes in how I've handled this. I should have been open from the beginning about wanting a divorce."

"Maybe you should have been open years ago, when you stopped even liking me." She wiped her face with the edge of her sleeve and a band of something tightened around his ribcage.

"I always liked you," he said, *until you did this*. It was the truth—from the first time she had smiled at him from across a party, Jacques had liked Rachel. He had liked how brightly she burned, he had liked that she knew her smile was a meteor strike and that she used that meteor strike for good. He had liked how emotional she was, how every high was so high and every low was so very low; he had liked that she was wildly romantic just like he was. She was always alive, and even when she was treacherous she was never really hidden from him because you could not actually hide fire. He had even liked, when he was younger, that she sometimes forced him to reach through her flames, a test of his own boldness, a test of how willing he was to get hurt for her.

The thing was—this was one test too far.

"My lawyer has put together something and I'll review it and send it over, and maybe we can have our lawyers meet and walk through everything together," he said after clearing his throat. "We can figure it out as we go. All I want is for us to figure out a plan that works for the boys."

She said nothing, so he bit his lip and turned from her. "I will be on the road for some preseason games," he said as he made to leave, "but we can talk again next week when I am back."

"Okay."

Together they walked in silence to the front door, as they had done so many times. It was beginning to rain, and the soft hush came into the house when Jacques pulled open the front door.

"Well, have fun on the road," she said, that cheerful tone back. She caught his eye; this too was a reference to Eloise.

"Thanks," was all he said. "See you."

"See you," she called after him as he took to the front steps, his blood pounding in his ears.

# Chapter Seventeen

E loise surveyed her web of people as she ate her breakfast. She had used scrap paper and tape to form the web on her living room wall above the sofa, detailing the groups of people that Kyle interacted with, and what she knew about each one.

The Bruins were the simplest web, as the only one that Kyle had any real relationship with was Jacques—and he was a wall around Kyle, guarding him as best he could. Eloise now knew Jacques well enough to know that he would not let that guard down anytime soon. Whether it was because he knew that anyone who looked more closely would find things unsuitable for public consumption, or simply because he recognized something of himself within Kyle, she did not know yet.

Then there was Kyle's family—his brother Patrick, and his father, Jimmy, and a sister named Colleen, who was in college and seemed like a preppy, social type. Kyle and Colleen notably did not follow each other on Instagram, but Colleen was still active on Facebook and through her profile Eloise had identified a few faceless accounts that could possibly be Jimmy Hearst under different names.

The most likely account had not been on Facebook in several years, but when he had last been active, he had shared links about recent violence against police officers and had been active on multiple pages run by police or former police, leaving cryptic comments filled with typos and links to blog posts—exactly the type of behavior that she knew Kyle would struggle to forgive.

Eloise still could find no evidence that Kyle's father currently had a job, or that he even left the house on Westville Road, and after texting with Krystal, she confirmed that he had never come to any Bruins events either—and had not been there the day Kyle had signed with the Bruins. Instead, 'some woman,' as Krystal had put it, had been there, though Krystal knew nothing about who the woman was and could not remember her name. Eloise had a few candidates for 'The Woman' as she referred to her in her mind, but these were all based on Facebook interactions with Colleen.

And then there were Kyle's friends, the ones who appeared in his Instagram pictures—which were always blurry, intentionally bad shots—and who left likes and comments on his posts that he never replied to. They all had the same look: pale skin covered in bruise-like Norse tattoos, shabby black T-shirts and shaved heads.

It seemed like he had included Patrick in his group of friends, for she now saw (now that she knew what Patrick looked like) that Patrick featured heavily in his posts. Patrick was in the corner of a crooked shot from the Southie St. Patrick's Day parade this past March, his shaved head sickly pale in the watery sunlight; there was Patrick again, looking sheepishly at the picture-taker from a corner of a car on the T, holding onto one of the poles with a black sweatshirt-covered hand. Kyle never bothered to tag anyone and never provided any captions or commentary on his pictures, but Eloise noticed that the man she had seen with him in Dublin House—f3nris_88—was the most frequent.

She had printed out her blurry screencaps of these pictures, using Sharpie to outline their tattoos, and these she stared at now, perched on the edge of her secondhand coffee table. So many of his friends had tattoos of ancient runes, just visible on their forearms or necks, and though his fork tattoo *looked* like a rune, it did not match any of the ones she had found online.

It could have been a mistake—but she doubted it. Kyle was cleverer than that. Andrei had called it: he was like Jacques, so intentional and so watchful. And it was the initial drawing she had done of his tattoo, from memory, that she stared at now in thought.

f3nris_88 might be her best shot.

She dropped onto her couch and opened Instagram. During the first case she had taken on, she had created a burner Instagram and had purchased followers, and had Photoshopped a stock photograph of a smiling, tanned woman in a bikini. She was loathe to use the fake account lest she get flagged as spam and lose the work she had put in, but this might be the perfect use for it—and, she reminded herself, opening f3nris_88's profile, this was her last case anyway.

His profile was still private. Eloise sent the follow request along with a flirty DM, and hoped he was as stupid as he looked.

·)) ● (( ·

"Fuck, it's not supposed to be this warm in September," Burnie complained as they slowed to a stop at an intersection. He raked a hand over his hair, which stuck straight up like a little kid's. "I hate this humidity. When we retire, I'm moving to the goddamn desert."

Jacques waved for the car to go through the intersection first. Burnie's house was only a few minutes away. Soon they would reenter the chaos that was Burnie's home: shrieking, hair-pulling, dolls thrown and tiaras discarded, Stephanie screaming at Bella and Luna while they screamed incoherently, gleefully back. He would not have another chance once they got to the house.

"Yeah," Jacques agreed. "I hate it too. Let's walk a bit."

"Uh-oh. You're not hurting, are you?" Burnie followed Jacques across the road like an outraged goose. "You had better not be running through a punctured lung or something again. My nerves can't handle it, Lavy," he insisted, prodding Jacques sharply in the back. "Remember 2012? We can't do that again. I can't take the stress of wondering if you're secretly about to drop dead on me. I'm too fucking old, do you hear me?"

Jacques had been waiting for the right opportunity for the last forty-five minutes, but it had not come naturally. Burnie had regaled him with the shenanigans of yesterday morning when he had come downstairs to find three hungover rookies in his home: Kyle, grey-faced and anxious, obeying every order from Stephanie, and Connor and Travis in a pile on the sofa, nauseated and surly. Burnie had then moved onto the rest of the team, dissecting how each player had been doing in practices.

Burnie could have kept talking indefinitely, oblivious to Jacques's intentions. Jacques so rarely said what he was thinking; Burnie had come to assume he had nothing to share. He just wanted to tell Burnie about the divorce, and wanted to keep it vague: *everything is fine*, and *it's completely amicable*. He just wanted it done, wanted to control it before it somehow came out another way.

And, perhaps, there were other reasons for wanting to make this change clear—but those were stupid reasons, things he would never actually act upon.

"No, no injury," Jacques said, "but I wanted to talk to you about something."

"You want me to kill Koslov," Burnie guessed. "Look, I'll do it, but I'll need help. He's a big dude, and remember that time I tried to give Crosby a swirly at the All Stars? I had a hard time with that, and Koslov's got like more than half a foot and fifty pounds on that dweeb. I think Bouchie and I could take him together, and you know Bouchie would be down, he *hates* the guy—"

"Burnie, please just listen for a moment," Jacques interrupted. He kept walking, his gaze fixed on a massive, gnarled tree up ahead, its bark turned black in the rain. "This needs to stay between us for now, but I wanted you to know first—"

"Wait, you're not fucking retiring—"

"No," Jacques said, unable to hide his frustration. "Please just listen for one moment. Rachel and I are getting a divorce. It's all fine," he soldiered on quickly, "and it is completely, you know, amicable. But we are getting a divorce."

For once Burnie was silent. The only noise was their footfalls and the distant zip of tires on wet gravel. "And now you choose to be quiet. Say something," Jacques said.

Burnie walked on, looking downward as he thought. He nodded to himself, like he was having some internal conversation.

"She cheated, didn't she?" he asked when he looked up.

Now it was Jacques's turn to look away, to walk in silence. He felt like he had been slapped. He had not been prepared to go there, though now he saw that he should have known how quickly Burnie would intuit the cause for the divorce.

*Oh, more 'no comment' bullshit?*

"No, it is just that—"

"Yeah. Okay." Burnie disregarded his words. "When did it happen? Who was it with? How many times did it happen?"

Jacques could have just told him everything, and for a moment he even pictured doing it. But this might be the single most effective way to ruin any last shred of regard that Burnie had for Andrei, and Burnie's civility toward Andrei was already hanging by one single thread. The line change had done immeasurable damage to Burnie's otherwise bulletproof attitude; Jacques still did not know if it would end up being worth it, and still questioned Duffy's choice.

But he did know that he would not make it worse. He had signed on the dotted line, hadn't he? He had sworn he would put the team first. Burnie might be the oldest player but he was one of the best, and he was deeply respected by the team. If he started having a real problem with Andrei, the rest of them would, too—and then bringing Andrei to Boston at all would be a waste. And then...

*Oh, more 'no comment' bullshit?*

"One of her friends," he lied at last. "I walked in on them this summer, and we have been separated since. Remember that weekend you, me, and Pell went to the beach, and we had to come back early because Genevieve had a virus? I walked in just as he was leaving."

And because it was a detail that killed him, because it was all starting to seep out, he added, "she was asking him to stay when I walked in. It was not an accident. Not just a mistake or a bad choice."

When they reached Burnie's house they kept going. Jacques was grateful that Burnie did not expect him to walk back into Burnie's home, with his rock-solid marriage to a wife he trusted implicitly. He would not have been able to socialize with Stephanie and make a fuss over Bella and Luna, because it was all coming back in a rush.

He had married a woman who would beg Andrei Koslov to stay; he had married a woman who did not know better than that. And he had married this selfish, romantic, fickle fool and *he* had not known better. He had had children with her, he had given her the best years of his health, his career, his wealth. He had endured all of the subtle ways in which he was not really good enough for her, sat at every family dinner table for her, listened to every anecdote about boarding schools and maids and semesters abroad. He had smiled and laughed and asked polite follow-up questions that always exposed just how working-class he actually was. He had bought tickets and homes and cars and baby blankets and parenting books with a person who would beg Andrei Koslov to stay.

"That was in July." Burnie's voice broke. "You've been separated since July... and you couldn't tell me?"

"Burnie—"

"I love you more than *anyone*, Lavy," Burnie went on. "You've been going through this shit for months, and you couldn't tell *me*?"

"I couldn't tell anyone," Jacques reassured him. *Oh, more 'no comment' bullshit?* "I was too angry to talk about it. And I didn't know if I would be able to go through with the divorce, but—"

Jacques decided to be honest about at least this. "Recently I realized I was acting like my marriage was over."

He paused, feeling Burnie's eyes on him. "So it's over. I've just been too much of a coward to pull the trigger until now."

"You're not a coward," Burnie said immediately. "You're not a coward at all for not just blowing up your marriage. You loved Rachel. You saw something in her that I honestly never saw, but that's your talent, isn't it? You saw the good in her and you loved it. You guys built a life together. If Steph did that to me..."

He exhaled with a shrug. "I dunno how I'd react. I know I wouldn't ever trust her again. I don't think I'd ever be able to have sex with her again, for sure. But I dunno that I'd be able to get divorced, either. Jesus. *Jesus.* I can't—I can't fucking believe she would—"

Burnie crouched to pick up a stray pebble, and hurled it at a trashcan with a snarl. It hit the lid with a *clang*, knocked the lid off. His face was red and blotchy with anger.

"And YOU KNOW WHAT? The fact—that she has *two little boys—and she was cheating—*" he exploded as he picked the lid up and slammed it back on the can. "I'm going to fucking neuter this guy—do you know his name—fuck it, you'll never tell me, you're too *good*, I'll just have to torture it out of her—"

Burnie picked up another rock and this time flung it at a stop sign, hitting the 'O' with perfect precision, and part of Jacques could not help but admire Burnie's athleticism, even in this moment. The clang echoed around the street; he picked up another, this time hitting the 'P.' "I'm going to fucking—" He grabbed another rock and made a dent at the 'S.' "She had you and your two—beautiful—boys—"

"Burnie, stop that." Jacques wrenched the rock out of Burnie's hand. Burnie stumbled back, breathless and red-faced with rage. The part of Jacques that maintained his sense of humor even in the worst moments could not help but smile at the idea of how Burnie might have reacted had he told him everything.

"Fuck, don't *you* want to destroy some property? Don't you want to slash the guy's tires? Don't you want to kick his ass? Wait, did you see him? Did you *face* him? What did he do?" Burnie demanded, rounding on him again.

Jacques had to look away again. His grip on it all—on the expectations placed upon him—was slipping.

"Yes, I did want to destroy some property," he admitted, laughing even though there was a searing pain in his chest. "And when it happened I wanted to do much worse than slash his tires. And—"

His words were stifled. He shrugged, shaking his head and avoiding Burnie's green eyes. "Yeah, I did face him."

He could not describe how it had felt to see his best friend—his brother, because in some ways Andrei had absorbed all of the love he had felt for Olivier when he died—sitting on the bottom stair in his house after years of painful silence: the complex mix of relief and grief, for they had not spoken since Andrei had been traded to Tampa Bay, and in spite of it all Jacques had deeply, painfully missed his best friend.

"I just turned around," Jacques confessed. "I did nothing. I saw him, I realized what was going on, and I just turned around and left."

It had become so clear in a flash: Andrei was only back in Boston for hockey; Andrei was coming back to the Bruins; this was the opportunity that Rachel must have been waiting for; this must have been going on, in one way or another, for years.

Even in that moment his responsibilities had chained him. He had to be perfect. He could not react to this either, because to react to this, to fight fire with fire, would be to destroy any final chance of Andrei getting along with the team; it would be to burn down the best chance they would have at a Cup for years (because even in that moment Jacques could admit they *needed* him); it would hurt so many more careers than he could comprehend in that instant. It would be phenomenally selfish of him; it would be a direct refusal of all the duties tucked between the lines of his contract that he had signed all those years ago.

He had faced Andrei, and he had said nothing.

*Oh, more 'no comment' bullshit?* Eloise had asked, not knowing how much that one had killed him.

"I have lost all respect for Rachel," he blurted. It was seeping out again, and he was struggling to stop himself. "I cannot even look at her. Our marriage was over already in a lot of ways," he continued, because for once Burnie was not interrupting, and it felt so good to finally say what had been on his mind for months, churning in his head in the small hours of the night, all that stifled anger, "but I always thought it was fine, that at least we were on the same page about the boys, about our life together, and then—"

He had said his vows and meant them. She had said the vows and—and what? What had that agreement, that *contract* meant to her? What had Rachel been thinking as he slid the ring onto her finger? In that flash it had become so obvious: Rachel had wanted Andrei for years—Andrei, who refused to be loved even by his best friend, would appeal so deeply to Rachel—and the only thing that had stopped her was that until their falling-out, Andrei had loved Jacques too much to let it happen.

"And I guess we were not on the same page after all. I guess it was not enough."

(Did Rachel think he had only been faithful—had only honored that contract—because no opportunity had been presented to him? Did she think he had never had other options, that he had never been approached, that he had never met any women that had turned his head? Did she think his commitment had been a matter of chance rather than choice?

(Did Rachel know that Andrei had never liked her, that he had told Jacques he thought she was a 'selfish slut' and that he had read negative intentions into everything she did from the very beginning? Maybe it was partly an act on Andrei's part to mask their sexual tension, but Jacques saw that for what it was: Rachel was magnetic, and Andrei was filled with contempt even when he did want someone in a basic way, and women always sensed that heartbeat of contempt beating beneath his every word and saw it as a challenge. It was just another thing that had added to Jacques's respect for Eloise, that even when Andrei had been in pursuit of her she had seen through his pursuit and seen his contempt for her at the heart of it.)

"Let me at him," Burnie demanded. "Let me and my brothers fuck him up."

He stood on his tiptoes and gripped Jacques's shirt, looking him in the eye. "You don't even need to tell me the guy's name," he reasoned, his voice suddenly honey-sweet. "You can just give me a zip code and a few hints, and we'll figure the rest out. Arthur's really good with computers, and Ted has logins for all of those white pages sites. He can find anyone."

"Burnie," Jacques said gently, trying not to laugh in spite of everything as he forced Burnie to let go of his T-shirt, "we cannot afford to have you in jail for murder."

"I don't want to *murder* him," Burnie countered patiently, even as he tightened his grip on Jacques's shirt. "I just want to ruin his life, and destroy any chance of happiness or peace or joy, and also haunt his family for generations like one of those curses."

"I would prefer that you be too busy with your own happiness and peace and joy to be bothered with ruining someone else's," Jacques said firmly, as Burnie at last released him.

"Yeah, you *would*," Burnie said, half-exasperatedly and half-fondly as they began running again. Burnie somehow sensed that this was what Jacques needed. "Jesus, dude. Jesus. How can you even fucking look at her anymore?"

"I can't."

They ran. The rain was starting to come down again as they wended their way through Burnie's neighborhood in mindless circles. He could feel Burnie glancing at him every now and then. Burnie was being uncharacteristically cautious now, but people always forgot that he could be incredibly precise when it was asked of him. You could forget that about him, and he would let you. He did not need anyone to think he was smart.

"Look," Burnie panted at last, as they turned onto his driveway and walked toward the garage. "One thing I will say," he said as he input his PIN into the keypad, "and take this from someone who loves you—it was really nice to see you not in Captain mode the other night, even if it was just for a few minutes."

"Captain mode?"

"You know, Team Dad mode. *The* Jacques Lavesque mode. It was like for a few minutes you just let go of all the pressure you're always under and were just *you* again—the kid I remember meeting all those years ago who was always smiling, just this sweet and funny and playful kid who didn't know how special he was. And I know you probably feel bad about the other night, but even before I knew this shit, I was going to tell you I thought it was a good thing. Healthy."

"So—" He considered his words. Mortification seeped in. He had assumed no one would notice. "You think it was noticeable."

"You were jammed against her on the couch, flirting with her and whispering with her. Yeah, Lavy, it was a little noticeable," Burnie said dryly. *Damn.* He could not let that happen again, but then, the only way to stop it was to not interact with Eloise at all, and that— "But like I said, I thought it was a good thing even before I knew about this."

They watched the garage door lift. "You've been taking way too much on the chin lately and just keeping it all in. There's this bullshit with Rachel, and there was Koslov coming back, and I *know* you and Koslov had some falling-out back when he got traded that you won't tell me about," Burnie counted off on his fingers, "and when Pell and I were pissed about the line change, you were just so nice about it and I *know* it was shitty of us to react like that. You should've just told us off."

They ducked under the still-lifting door. Burnie went to the fully stocked garage refrigerator and got them both bottles of Gatorade.

"One of these days," he warned as he opened his Gatorade, "you're gonna blow up, and it's not going to be at someone you want to be blowing up at, and it's not going to be a time you want to be blowing up. And I know you, and I know you'll beat yourself up for it, and there's no need. You've got more than enough on your shoulders."

Jacques opened his own Gatorade and took a long swig. For a flash he pictured just doing it. Just blowing up, just telling him all of it: who Rachel really had been cheating with; what had gone down with Andrei four years ago when he had been traded; all of the thoughts he had been carefully sidestepping about Eloise until she had been pressed up against him on Burnie's couch and he decided to just *not* sidestep them anymore; to just let that glass wobble in place and see if it fell over and crashed. He had glimpsed the freckle on her arm—a pinpoint of dark on otherwise pale skin—and had thought, *fuck*. He was normally so in command of his own thoughts but his mind had kept irresistibly going back to that freckle all night—the wobbling vase, the glassy rattle so audible in his own head.

But none of that was who he had promised to be, who he had signed up to be. *You have to be perfect*, Krystal had said.

"I never saw you that relaxed with Rachel. And if you're not going to be that relaxed around any of us anymore, you *need* a place in your life where you're just you."

"Thanks," he said finally, recapping the Gatorade. He could not believe anyone else had noticed, but he should have known that Burnie—so attuned to him—would pick up on it.

"Good. Listen to your elders," Burnie laughed. "Anyway, let's see if we can trick Stephy into cooking us food."

"I don't think you can trick Stephanie into doing anything," Jacques said, following him into the immaculate Burnap home. Stephanie was in the kitchen making coffee, swathed in a floaty, violently pink robe with gel patches under her eyes when they walked in.

"Hey, Stephy," Burnie said, casually grabbing her backside as he passed. "Lavy's splitting up with Rachel—wait. Where are the girls? It's too quiet." He halted by the refrigerator and peered around suspiciously.

Stephanie dropped the milk frother to stare at Jacques before melting.

"Oh, *honey*." She threw her arms around him, enveloping him in a tight embrace.

"Stephanie, no, I'm too sweaty—" he protested, but she just squeezed him tighter. He relented and returned the embrace, lightheaded from her powerful perfume, as Burnie hunted for his daughters.

"Oh, my beautiful boy. I'm so sorry," she said into his T-shirt, still squeezing him tightly in the quiet kitchen. "I am so, so sorry."

"They're watching *Frozen*—again," Burnie reported disgustedly when he came back into the kitchen. "I don't get it. That snowman is annoying, and none of the songs are any good," he muttered, opening the refrigerator once more in hope. "Also, since when is *Lavy* your beautiful boy? What about me?"

Stephanie pulled back, cupping Jacques's cheek and squeezing his shoulder before letting go.

"You're my man," she said carelessly. "How are the boys? Do they know?"

"Not really. Peter knows something is different, but I don't think Luke does," Jacques explained. "We've been separated for a few months, so I've been living at a hotel. They know that, but we haven't sat them down and explained why yet."

"Oh, god. You've been living out of a *hotel*?" Stephanie gasped, as though he had said *bus station*, or *cave*. "You probably haven't eaten real food in months. Sit down, let me make you something." She frog-marched him to their island. Behind her Burnie did a silent fist-pump of victory, mouthing *good work* at Jacques.

"Uncle Jack?" Bella was clinging to the doorframe, looking slyly up at him. She was clad in an enormous pink tutu and a Pikachu hat. "Where's *Peter*?" she asked flirtatiously, giggling and swaying as she gripped the doorframe.

Luna appeared behind her, clutching a stuffed tiger that was the same size as her. "Peter's here? Where's *Peter*? He's my *boyfriend*," Luna added, and the girls giggled together.

"Peter is at home with his mother," Jacques told them. Bella bounced over, raising her arms at him and making a 'gimme' motion with her hands. He usually greeted the twins by lifting each of them up and kissing them on the top of their heads, and now they demanded it. "No, I'm too sweaty. I can't pick you up. I'll ruin your tutu," he told her, and she let out a howl and kicked the kitchen island.

"I want to play *dragons*," she bellowed, dropping to the floor in outrage. "DRAGONS!" Luna howled in agreement.

"Inside voices, ladies," Burnie said over his shoulder as Stephanie put him to work greasing a pan.

"Daddy's a bad dragon. He doesn't do the roar right," Luna said from the floor. "Uncle Jack is the only good dragon."

"Your dad *invented* being a dragon," Jacques reasoned with her. "He is an excellent dragon."

"Can you occupy them?" Stephanie asked Burnie in a low voice. Burnie immediately dropped to the floor.

"No, I'm the BEST dragon," he growled, crawling on all fours across the kitchen floor. The girls shrieked with delight as he chased them into the living room again.

"Let me help—" Jacques began.

"NO. Siddown," Stephanie ordered. "You and that Kyle kid. I couldn't get him off my goddamn back yesterday. I think he's one of those kids who gets hangover anxiety or something," she complained as she cracked eggs into a pan. "He followed me around like a goddamn shadow until the other two finally peeled their asses off my couch. *Can I help, Mrs. Burnap?* God. You forget how young they are. There I was, checking out his quads, and he's calling me *Mrs. Burnap* and treating me like I'm his best friend's mom."

"Stephanie, he's nineteen," Jacques said, put-off.

"I didn't know! He looks twenty-one, and in my head I'm still twenty-one, too, and mark my words—he doesn't look like much now but he's like you. Give that kid six or seven years and he'll fucking *rule* Boston with those eyes," she protested, throwing her free hand up in the air, then relented a little. From the living room, they could hear Burnie roaring again, making the girls cackle. "So how is Rachel taking it?"

"As expected."

Stephanie grimaced as the kitchen began to fill with the sizzle of eggs cooking.

"I don't think she thought I would really go through with it." He got to his feet and began loading the dishwasher, laughing when Stephanie jabbed him with her spatula.

"So why *did* you go through with it?" she asked in a low voice as she worked. "You know Burn's going to tell me the second you leave, so you might as well just tell me now."

Jacques got out plates. She was right. Burnie always told Stephanie everything like she had given him truth serum; there was no point in saying nothing because as soon as Burnie returned to the kitchen it would be out.

"She cheated," he said, and heard a sharp intake of breath.

Stephanie was silent, her back to him as he laid out plates and forks on the island.

"You know," she finally said in a falsely casual voice, "I do *know* people. You know. Like in the mob."

"You don't know anyone in the mob," Jacques said, setting a hand on her shoulder, "but thank you."

"I absolutely do!" she insisted. In the background they heard one of the girls burst into enraged tears, followed by Burnie apologizing. Stephanie rolled her eyes. "Oh, for fuck's sake," she muttered under her breath. "Let's have babies, he told me," she ranted as she took the pan of eggs to the island. "It'll be fun, he told me. They'll be so sweet, he told me. *Cazzate.*"

"We have an invisible boo-boo," Burnie announced over the wailing, carrying a red-faced Luna into the kitchen. Bella followed closely behind, one small hand fisted in Burnie's shorts. As ever he was unbothered by the wailing and chaos, which infuriated Stephanie like it always did.

"Eat your goddamn eggs before they get cold," she snapped, taking Luna from Burnie. He winked at Jacques as Stephanie smoothed her daughter's hair. "We're going to kill Rachel, aren't we, Luna?" she cooed to her daughter.

"Kill—Rachel—" Luna repeated, nodding as she hiccoughed and sniffled.

"I want to kill Rachel too," Bella intoned loudly from the floor. Burnie grinned.

"Dash my gwirls," he said to Jacques through a mouthful of egg.

# Chapter Eighteen

B oston was waking up around her as Eloise locked her door: ghostly headlights through grim fog, the yodeling caw of gulls over the grinding rumble of garbage trucks. It was still dark, and she could not remember the last time she had had a reason to be out so early.

She was carrying her duffle bag and Jacques's sweater in a paper bag, because she knew she would not have the time—or money—to stop at her apartment again before making her way to Warrior Ice Arena. Like usual she had hidden her bleached hair beneath her trusty black beanie, and had thrown a denim jacket over the Bruins zip-up fleece that Krystal had dropped off yesterday. Before leaving her apartment, she had faced her bathroom mirror and deemed herself sufficiently unrecognizable and undistinguishable—just another figure muddling through the early morning fog, genderless and inscrutable.

Sometime after boarding the bus, f3nris_88 accepted her follow request and followed her back. And as she swayed and rocked with the bus and looked at the drowsy faces around her, she had to hide her exhilaration by twisting and burying her face in the collar of the denim jacket. For a moment she couldn't even look at his Instagram profile.

She had *done* something. She was making something happen. It had been so long since she had had any sense of self-satisfaction, any sense of pride. She had not realized how much she had been craving it—how badly she had needed proof that she was worthy, that this dream was worthy of the effort she had put in.

Before she had recovered, her phone pulsed with a new DM from f3nris_88.

**f3nris_88**: hello beautiful

She already pitied this boy. Only someone incredibly naive or desperate could have believed that a beautiful woman with no Instagram posts had decided to follow him. That pity was quickly obliterated when she opened his profile, to be replaced by disgust.

His name was listed as Rob. Beneath his given name he had 23/16 in a smaller, bolded font. The bus rocked forward and she almost dropped her phone as she tried to scroll through his grid with one hand, the other holding onto the pole.

The very first picture featured both Patrick and Rob (though the comments beneath the post referred to him as Robbie, which she imagined annoyed him). They were in a carpeted basement with dated wooden paneling, and Patrick—uncertain, sallow, and so young—was posed with a complicated-looking rifle, with Robbie to the side, reaching for it in a blur. The post featured multiple pictures, and she scrolled through them: blurry, over-exposed images of boys in a basement, drinking beer and posing with the rifle. *this kid tho*, the post was captioned. Eloise scrolled through the comments but Kyle had not interacted with any of them.

The next post was a selfie. Robbie wore a deerstalker and a drawn expression, like he did not realize his face was in the frame though it was clearly intended to be. In this picture he was shirtless so his tattoos were on display, confirming that he was indeed the one Kyle had gone to Dublin House with, the one who had looked back at Eloise briefly and spurred her to leave the bar altogether.

He had made a few reels as well as a few memes, most of them concerning Boston's Irish population—she assumed the irony of his heritage and his white power tattoos was lost on him. She scrolled back to the earliest post that showed both Patrick and Kyle, a picture that appeared to be taken the same day as the post that she had seen on Kyle's Instagram: by a lake somewhere out west, young men jumbled around the shoreline in shitty lawn chairs and old swimming trunks, pine needles and river rocks. Kyle's expression was opaque; he was looking at his brother, who was red-faced and holding a beer, a single tattoo marring his otherwise pale skinny chest. It was brand new, the flesh around it irritated and red, and it was recognizably a Norse rune.

And then she was thinking of Jacques again, and of his brother for whom his grief was complicated and uneven. Had his brother broken his nose? Was that why he didn't fight on the ice—because his last fight was tied to such grief and regret? Was that why he protected Kyle so closely—because he understood the challenge of having a brother whose life was spiraling just as your own star was on the rise?

Last night she had stayed out late in Upham's Corner, watching Kyle in his apartment. From her perch she had watched him review past Bruins games in his living room—she really needed to find a way to tell him to close his goddamn blinds—and had ruled out the possibility of a live-in girlfriend to explain his unlocked door and the creak she had heard behind it, on the day she had gone to visit his empty apartment. There had been no one else with him all evening, and when she used her camera to zoom in and peer around, she found no evidence of another person living there.

His place was shabby but tidy for a nineteen-year-old's living space, with mismatched secondhand furniture and little clutter or mess. She had watched him move around the kitchen, preparing something via microwave for dinner and then wolfing it down while he hunched in front of a small flatscreen. She knew it was a game from more than five years ago, because at one point the camera had flashed on a sweaty

Andrei slouched in the penalty box. Kyle paused and rewound often, studying Jacques's and Andrei's plays like a suspicious lover.

And then hours later she had watched him tidy the kitchen, dutifully loading the dishwasher and wiping down the countertops, turning off the kitchen light when he went back to the living room. He had ironed something while he watched the game, his eyes trained on the screen as he smoothed the iron over the fabric. He had seemed older than nineteen, self-sufficient and disciplined in the way Hollis was, and obviously happy to be on his own. She had taken photographs, not sure whether these would be enough to assuage Krystal's concerns about a drug problem.

She had thought about this long after the last light in Kyle's apartment had been turned off. In the quiet dark, she had made her way back to her own apartment, a silent shadow slipping between squares of light from the buildings around her.

She wanted to see his father, which was why she was hurrying to Kyle's Dorchester childhood home this morning before she went to Warrior Ice Arena. Her only hope was that she could catch a glimpse of Jimmy Hearst while Patrick got ready to leave for school. She hoped that one of them might open the blinds or keep a light on, and in the early darkness she would be able to see them more clearly. She did not know, exactly, what she was looking for, but she knew she had to see him.

By the time she reached Geneva Street and passed Sobrino's Market, it was just after six-thirty in the morning, and Dorchester was waking up. Traffic was beginning to form on Geneva as she rounded the corner and turned onto the Hearsts' street. The windows of their home were still dark, the blinds closed. No one was on the street, and the nearby houses' windows were dark, so she took the risk and ducked past the hurricane fence that ringed the property, padding on light feet to the side yard. A dog began to bark from one or two houses away, a deep-throated and dark sound accompanied by a chain-link rattle.

Eloise dropped to the ground near the side of the porch, holding still until the dog had quieted.

She didn't have to wait long for something to happen. As the eastern sky grew lighter, an ancient red Pontiac, its headlights dimmed with age and barely illuminating the milky fog in front of it, shuddered to a stop in front of the house. The driver turned the car off as Eloise slowly took out her camera and used the zoom function to get a better view of them.

Her stomach dropped. It was Robbie. Eloise grappled for her phone and opened the message he had sent her on Instagram, rapidly typing out a reply.

**laurenkylie098**: heyyy :)

She sent the message and then, through her camera's zoom, watched Robbie look down and pick up his phone, the screen's glow lighting up his young face in the early morning gloom. She captured a few pictures, then zoomed out to get one of the car as well.

**f3nris_88**: how are you beautiful

She was devising her reply when there was a metallic shriek and then the boards overhead shook with footfalls. Patrick hurried down the front steps, stealing a last look around the street before opening the passenger side door.

"We gotta go, she'll be here any minute—" Whatever else he said was swallowed by the slam of the door. The engine revved, and the Pontiac peeled away from the curb.

Eloise sat back in the damp grass, scribbling notes to herself—Robbie's license plate, the model of his car, and other observations—but looked up when she heard a scrape on the sidewalk.

A middle-aged woman with long, fine dishwater-blonde hair was making her way toward the Hearst home. She was long-limbed but overweight, wearing an oversized Brady jersey that strained at her bust and stomach. She let out a heavy sigh as though she had an audience as she climbed the steps of the porch. When she reached the door, she smacked it with an open palm, rattling the aluminum.

"Hello? Pat? You up?" She moved between the door and window, rapping on the door and ringing the bell. With a disgusted curse she knocked again. "Gonna kill me," she muttered to herself. Eloise held her breath, looking up through the beams at the woman, watching her take out her cell phone. Even from Eloise's vantage point, the ring was audible. The woman swore again and hung up, then sent a text, her nails clacking on the screen furiously.

She stood there, shifting her weight like she didn't know what to do. Then, with another theatrical sigh, she took out her phone again. "Hello? Hey, kid." Her voice softened. "Just thought you should know—I think I missed him. Yeah, no one's coming to the door, and he's not picking up his phone."

Eloise was too far to distinguish the voice on the other end. "Yeah, your dad's not opening the door either. Probably still asleep. I can break in if you want, cook him some breakfast."

There was audible swearing on the other end this time. *Kyle.* "I've told you a million fucking times you can't control other people," she said suddenly, interrupting the diatribe on the other end. "No, don't fucking come here, there's no goddamn point. Pat's gone and you coming by isn't gonna magically make him appear. You're on the road for a few days, right?"

She sighed again. "Just focus on fucking the Rangers up for me, will you? And get an autograph from Fowler for me. I think he's cute." She was teasing now, but Eloise knew that this would not soften Kyle. "Alright, alright," the woman interrupted again, a little defensively. "Bye."

Eloise listened as the woman rapped on the door again, this time with less urgency. She tried another number, and this time let it go to voicemail. "Hey, Pat," she began in a saccharine, sarcastic voice. "This is Caff. You know you're in trouble and if I don't kill you it's because your brother killed you first. See ya."

She hung up and at last gave up on going inside. Eloise snapped a picture of her as she walked away, down the road to one of the twins. This had to be The Woman.

When the coast was clear, Eloise crept out from under the porch, her jeans soaked with dew.

·ↄↄ●ᙅᙅ·

Eloise had the entire journey from Dorchester to Boston Landing—over an hour via public transport—to contemplate what she had witnessed. She had considered pretending to be a solicitor just for the excuse to knock on the front door, but she doubted anyone would answer. She had finally left, with a last look at the 'Blue Lives Matter' flag rippling gently in the wind.

**laurenkylie098**: just moved to boston :))) looking for someone to show me around

She did not know what she expected to gain from this exchange.

**laurenkylie098**: u have some cute friends but your the cutest ;)

She watched the three dots appear and flicker, then disappear.

The players wouldn't arrive for a while—they had already had their morning skate, and returned to their homes to shower and change into their suits—but Warrior Ice Arena was already thrumming with activity when Eloise arrived: staff were buzzing along the halls, toting bins of equipment and freshly laundered uniforms. Polished professionals were breezing in with coffee and sunglasses, taking the elevators to the offices above. She was nearly steamrollered by Dan the equipment manager, apoplectic with stress as he rounded the corner bearing a pair of skates without the blades and, mysteriously, a crusty jock strap. He bowled past her, muttering to himself.

Eloise decided to take the elevator to Krystal's office, and wait there until the other players began to arrive. She walked along a quiet hallway to a door marked with a rose-gold plaque that simply read KRYSTAL TAYLOR—as though being Krystal was her job title, and maybe it was.

When she opened the door, Eloise startled a blond, string-beany man with the boyish energy and precisely gelled hair of a 1950s cartoon, who almost dropped the camera pack he was holding.

"Oh god, sorry. I didn't mean to scare you," Eloise blustered, reaching to help as he fumbled to catch the camera pack. "Something about Krystal's text made me assume you weren't here yet."

"No worries, I'm always early," he stammered, eager to please. "Bleached hair, Bruins fleece—you must be Eloise!" He proudly held out his free hand. Eloise let him shake her hand vigorously, trying not to laugh at his enthusiasm.

"And you must be Alex?" she guessed as he released her hand. *Alex Kash*, she remembered Krystal saying.

"The one and only!" he said brightly. Something about him reminded her of her brother, that John Mulaney-esque staginess that Hollis had sometimes, like he felt the need to perform lest he be disliked. Eloise instantly felt protective of him.

"I was just going to finish wrapping up all the cameras for the trip, but"—he checked an Apple Watch with a Bruins-yellow band before pointing theatrically at her—"*we* have a date. With Jacques Lavesque."

"We do?" She tried to master her features.

"Yup! Gonna get some sweet shots of him in the new jersey while we wait for the other players to roll in," Alex explained, oblivious to her nervousness. He paused, looking starry-eyed. "I can't believe I'm saying that," he added, holding a camera tightly. "I have *worshiped* him since I was, I don't know, in middle school. I had posters of him, I had trading cards of him. And now I'm gonna get to take pictures of him while he babysits his boys. How *insane* is that?"

"His sons are here too?" Eloise wondered, with a jolt, if she might meet Rachel.

"Yeah, just for a little while. Apparently there's a bug going around," Alex said absently, scratching his blond head as he surveyed the many cameras lined up on the desk before them, trailing cables that all neatly led to a power strip. Eloise could see why Krystal had hired Alex—this type of organization would deeply appeal to her. "Alright, I already set up the room, so we should be good here. You can just leave your bags here. Come on and meet him—he's really nice," he added when he looked up at Eloise. "Like, I was *terrified* of meeting him but now we have inside jokes and stuff. He really is that nice."

"Good to know," Eloise said, following Alex as he turned off the lights and locked the door to Krystal's office. She did not bother to explain that she had already met Jacques; Alex had such nervous-puppy energy that she did not want to overwhelm him, or steal his 'I know Jacques Lavesque' thunder. "So! Where are you from?" she asked awkwardly as they waited for the elevator, wishing she had something to hold onto or fidget with.

She should not have been nervous. After all, nothing had changed between them. It was just that *she* had changed.

"I'm from Michigan. Not anywhere that you'd know," Alex added before she could ask. "Middle-of-*nowhere* Michigan. Then I went to North Carolina for school, then I was in Arizona with the Coyotes for years—so I know Babe Fowler really well, and I'm hoping to see him tonight and say hi now that he's with the Rangers," he continued rapidly as they got off the elevator, lugging the cameras and their suitcases. "But then this opportunity came up and I freaked out and applied, even though I knew it was a *huge* stretch. I flew here for the interview and was like, well at least I can try lobster rolls and Dunkin, I guess?"

"Actually, I haven't had a lobster roll in years," Eloise admitted when the elevator doors parted again and they were on the stadium level which overlooked the rink, relieved to have a topic to seize on. "I've lived in Boston my whole life, and I never have any good recommendations for all of that classic Boston stuff."

"That's just how you know you're a *real* local," Alex said kindly. "Okay, we're going—oh! Of course he's already here."

They rounded the corner to an open area by the railing, where a few backdrops had been lined up—one featuring the spoked 'B' of the Bruins logo—and a few cameras on tripods. There was a little pile of hockey pucks next to the backdrop, and a single chair sitting before the 'B.'

And of course, there was Jacques, in full uniform save for his skates which sat beside the chair. He looked bigger in the uniform, more intimidating, and just before he realized they were there she had a moment to observe that he had gotten a fresh haircut, the undercut more precise than before—and also that he was holding one little boy in his arms, and talking gently to another one who was examining one of Alex's cameras.

"No, Peter, that belongs to someone else—" he began, then stopped and turned when he realized Eloise and Alex had arrived.

His gaze flicked to her new Bruins fleece, then between her and Alex. "Good to see you, man," he greeted with a smile that did not quite reach his eyes.

"You too, man," Alex said self-consciously, joyfully, his face going pink. "And who do we have here?" he added, crouching down to Peter's level. Peter dropped his little hands from Alex's camera, looking mortified to be addressed.

"This is Peter," Jacques said, half-laughing, touching his son on his soft ash-brown hair absently, then angling his head and shifting the boy he had on his hip so he could meet his eyes, "and this is Luke. Can you boys say hello to Alex and Eloise?"

"Hi, Alex and Eloise," Peter said politely, regarding Eloise's bleached hair with wary interest. Luke, she now saw, had a red nose and flushed cheeks, and he gave a small groan of complaint before dropping his head onto his father's shoulder and burying his face in his jersey.

"Well, we tried," Jacques said sheepishly, kissing Luke's head. "They are both a bit sick with colds."

"Yeah, I heard you have babysitting duties while your wife's at work," Alex said as he knelt before one of the cameras.

"I don't think it's babysitting if they're my sons too," Jacques said, clearly perturbed. The harshness surprised Eloise. "Their mother should be picking them up soon. I've told them to be good while you take some pictures, right?" he addressed Luke's hair.

*Their mother.* Eloise wiped her palms on her jeans.

"What—what do you want me to do?" she asked Alex, sensing Jacques's eyes on her, but she ignored him awkwardly, unsteadily. There was distance, and she did not know if it was because he felt embarrassed for their late-night encounter or if, since that moment, he had somehow decided that she was not worth a friendship. *Their mother*, she thought again, her keen mind stuck on that phrase. It felt intentional. "I—I can hold your son," she offered vaguely in Jacques's direction.

"No, I don't want to spread their germs and get you sick," Jacques said, just as vaguely. "Alright, we're going to sit at the table and play with trains now, okay?" he told them, carrying Luke and leading Peter to one of the cafeteria tables to the side, which she now saw contained a mess of Thomas the Tank Engine toys and tracks, not to mention a few Batman figurines. Luke let out another noise of complaint but Peter dutifully, politely, climbed onto one of the chairs and helped Jacques situate a very cranky, very sleepy Luke beside him.

"We have to let Daddy work," Peter told his little brother, grabbing one of the toy trains. Something squeezed around Eloise's heart; Peter was so sweet, so polite, so reserved, like his father—but both boys had doe-like brown eyes that she suspected they had gotten from their mother. *Their mother.* Not Jacques's wife—but *their mother.*

"Alright, well, we just want to get some cool shots that we can use for promotional posts over the next few days," Alex explained as Jacques touched Luke's head before coming back to their setup.

"Sure, let me just put on my skates," Jacques said as he dropped into the chair and grabbed his skates. She noticed that his facial hair had also been precisely groomed, another little reminder that he was not only the easygoing, gentle, understanding man who had driven her home—but also a product on which an organization was dependent.

"So first, I wanna get some shots of you just, like, standing in the jersey," Alex instructed. He turned to Eloise, beaming. "I want to get Andrei Koslov in here, too, because the last time they wore these jerseys was when they both debuted with the NHL seventeen years ago. I wanted to get a shot of them together but Koslov said he couldn't come in early, so we can just Photoshop them together later for the 'gram."

Eloise glanced at Jacques and caught his eye as he laced up one skate with brisk, rapid movements, but his expression was opaque.

"Well, the new jersey looks great," she said, just for something to say.

"New *retro* jersey," Alex corrected, and Eloise noticed Jacques's polite expression briefly drop, a flash of annoyance twisting his features. She almost wanted to laugh at him—apparently he didn't like being called old. "Okay—you know what? Why don't you take the pictures themselves, and I'll just direct you. It's good experience, and obviously you have a very photogenic subject," Alex said grandly, stepping to the side and gesturing for Eloise to take his place behind the camera.

Jacques had finished lacing up his skates and got up, setting the little chair to the side and out of view.

"Somehow I don't think our photogenic subject enjoys having his picture taken," Eloise remarked as Jacques straightened and faced the camera again. Over the camera their eyes met.

"It is not my favorite thing," Jacques said patiently, "but I will do it. How do you want me to stand?"

"Head-on, looking at me," Eloise directed, and snapped a bunch of pictures, capturing that quiet defiance he had today. Was he just in a bad mood—like that day they had fought—or was he specifically annoyed with her? "Okay, now let's do some poses. Just sort of do whatever you feel like. Whatever you normally do."

"Alright." He self-consciously turned to the side, crossing his arms, then grabbed one of the sticks off to the side and posed with the stick over his thighs. He was not a natural subject; it was a little bit satisfying to find something he was obviously not good at. She had noticed it on the previous posts on the Bruins' Instagram—he was the one most likely to be featured, but his posed pictures were never as effective as his candid ones.

"Why don't you like having your picture taken?" Eloise wondered as she motioned for him to angle his body toward the rink. Jacques glanced at her without moving his head, then looked back at the rink.

"I don't like my face," he said stiffly, "and, I don't know, I just find it embarrassing. I wish someone else could do this because I know it is not a strength of mine."

"Jacques freaking Lavesque doesn't like his face," Alex marveled, shaking his head. Eloise was beginning to see why he might not have chemistry with the other players, who were less likely to be patient or forgiving of his awkwardness. She had a hard time imagining Andrei, or Novak for example, tolerating him. "Your face is on the side of Boston Garden. Do you not like driving past Boston Garden?"

"I try not to look when I'm driving past," Jacques admitted.

She glanced back at his sons out of curiosity, but they were quietly playing—Peter, she noticed, was working very hard to keep Luke, younger and more emotional, engaged in their quiet game of trains.

"Well, I think you have a lovely face, but I do understand," she said, looking back at Jacques, capturing the briefest flash of surprise on his features. "Okay, try sitting down, maybe."

Jacques obediently pulled the chair back into the frame and dropped onto it, slouching forward. Alex fiddled with the lighting he had set up, giving the image a harsher level of contrast and casting Jacques's carved features in shadow. "Perfect," she encouraged him, but it did not warm him to her.

What had she done? Maybe it really was just a bad mood, she told herself as she rapidly captured images of him. It wasn't like he was being openly antagonistic; he just seemed more detached, more aloof—it seemed like they had never shared that quiet moment of confidence in the car and like his annoyance about having his picture taken was extending to her. Maybe he was ashamed of her learning about his personal business, and she could understand it, but also it was crushing to not have Friday night acknowledged. It had changed her so much; *he* had changed her so much.

"I—" She was about to direct him to another pose when Luke suddenly yelled, "MOMMY!"

Eloise flinched. Kneeling there on the floor, looking at Jacques through a lens, she was able to watch him react to the arrival of his wife. And just like the first time she had met him, she saw the flash of anger, of resentment, before he buried it again and looked to his wife with a pleasantly neutral face—his 'no comment' face.

"Hey, sweetie," came a peppy, cheerful voice, like the voice of the fun babysitter. Eloise pulled back from the camera to watch Luke drop from the chair and run to fling himself at a woman approaching from where Alex and Eloise had come.

And there was Rachel Lavesque, suffusing the air with a soft, sweet, pear-scented perfume.

In person she was lovelier. Everything about her looked so *soft* and touchable, from her glossy fine brown hair that hung in loose, irregular waves, like she woke up with perfect hair, to her minky eyelashes to her delicate shoulders encased in an elegant cashmere sweater-coat. And this was where the boys had gotten their lovely doe-like brown eyes, because Rachel had immediately looked at Eloise and she had been struck by how *pretty* her eyes were, in such an everyday and quiet way.

"Alex, it's so good to see you again," Rachel said warmly, still looking at Eloise as she absently offered a delighted Alex a one-armed embrace. You could have fried an egg on his face, and he did not look directly at Rachel. "And I don't think we've met?" she added, releasing Alex and facing Eloise.

And somehow Eloise knew: Rachel knew who she was—and possibly that her husband had given Eloise a ride home just a few nights ago. Maybe even that Eloise had his sweater in her possession. She wondered if when she had caught Andrei texting at the party, he had been texting Rachel, updating her on the girl with bleached-blonde hair sitting so close to her husband.

"I don't think so," Eloise said, rising to her feet and leaning forward to hold out her hand. Rachel accepted the handshake. "I'm Eloise. I've been interning for Krystal Taylor—"

"Well I *think* I know of her!" Rachel joked, her voice bright, her smile unwavering. There was something blistering, something burning, about her—something just past the line of too much. She seemed desperate for something. "She's been with the team as long as Jacques has!"

*Their mother.* Eloise studied Rachel, her subtle makeup, her perfect hair.

"You're right, sorry. You probably know her better than anyone. I've been doing a social media internship with her—" she continued bracingly, but was interrupted again by Rachel's musical laugh.

"Oh, god. That is adorable—but she must be so hard to work for, right?" She beamed at Eloise. "Also tough to do an internship when you're not a kid anymore, I bet."

Clarity came abruptly. Rachel knew she was losing Jacques, and was striking wherever she thought she might need to. By the stiff set of Jacques's shoulders it was all too obvious that the feeling between them was not a good one, that he had anticipated the poison of this encounter and had been dreading it.

"Actually, I think she's the best boss I've ever had," Eloise said evenly. "And I'm proud that I've got this internship."

She glanced back to find Jacques helping Peter to load the last of their toys into a Batman-themed backpack.

"Here is everything," Jacques said to Rachel, passing the backpack to her. He crouched down in front of his sons. "Are you going to be good while I'm gone?" he asked them.

"No," Luke said, which—at last—earned a real smile from him. He leaned forward and hugged them both; they looked so small in comparison to his padded silhouette. He kissed their heads before releasing them and rising from his crouch.

"Be good," he told them firmly, pointing at them. "Thanks," he added to Rachel.

And then Eloise saw it: the moment where Rachel began to lean forward for some kind of affection, but Jacques turned away like he hadn't seen it. "Back to work," he announced, a cold dismissal, as he glanced at the clock on the wall. "The other guys will be arriving soon. Bye, boys," he told his family over his shoulder.

"Bye, Daddy," Peter said, sliding on his backpack as Rachel knelt to pick up Luke.

"Bye Daddy," Luke added, leaning his head on his mother's shoulder.

"Bye, everyone," Rachel said with a wave of her free hand.

With a last glance at Eloise, Rachel led her sons toward the elevators. Even Alex seemed thrown by the strange tension; he looked anxiously at Eloise, blond brows raised in a *what the hell?* kind of expression.

"Right, let me see what Eloise has gotten so far," he said awkwardly, reaching past her to check the camera. Jacques raked a hand over his hair, a move she was beginning to learn was a giveaway that he was self-conscious. *Their mother.*

Their eyes met briefly. Jacques had to be pursuing a divorce; that dismissal of Rachel said it all. They each looked away.

"This all looks great," Alex said hastily, and both Jacques and Eloise knew that he had not really looked at the pictures. "Why don't we let you go, and Eloise and I will start loading our stuff on the bus? You're right, everyone's going to arrive soon."

"You're sure?" Jacques looked embarrassed; he looked eager to course-correct. "I am happy to—"

"No, it's great," Alex said quickly, waving him off. "I know *you* don't like your face but the rest of the world does. The engagement on these pictures will be awesome. Go, go. You're free!" He waved his arms wildly. "Freedom!"

Eloise watched Jacques unlace his skates, biting his lip, jaw taut and shoulders tight. He was very obviously ashamed of himself.

"Yeah, they really do look great," she added a little lamely. Jacques set his skates aside and got to his feet.

"Thanks." He did not look at her. "Alright, I will see you both on the bus." Eloise could feel Alex looking at her; they watched Jacques stalk off the way Rachel had gone, carrying his skates, rubbing the back of his head with his free hand.

"So," Alex began after they had heard the scuffle of his socked feet on the steps down to the rink level, "*that* was bizarre. You think they had a fight, or what?"

"Definitely bizarre," Eloise agreed as she helped Alex take down the backdrop with the Bruins logo. Her throat was tight. His dismissal had stung; it was hitting her harder than it should have. *Still hoping if you sit close enough to Prince Jacques he'll fuck you?* Andrei had asked. Maybe Jacques had gleaned what Andrei had; maybe he was trying to make it clear that there was no possibility of anything between them. *I already know that*, she wanted to yell at him. She rolled up the backdrop, heart pounding. *Believe me, I am fully aware of that.* "Probably a fight," she agreed before her features could crumple. "He couldn't even look at her."

"Maybe he's mad that he had to watch the boys," Alex guessed as they packed the backdrop and pucks into a cardboard box. "Doesn't really seem like him, though. Honestly I've never even seen him in a bad mood. I wonder if I pissed him off somehow."

"I really doubt that," Eloise reassured him. She was beginning to fully appreciate the pressure that Jacques was under at all times. Alex looked rattled and aghast, hit harder by his poor mood than Eloise would have guessed.

"I don't know. I mean, Krystal said he's *really* funny about pictures," he continued anxiously as they gathered up the supplies and began walking back towards Krystal's office. "Like apparently, shirtless pictures are *off-limits* in the locker rooms before games. He literally has it spelled out in his contract. With all the other guys, they love it, and you know, I used to work with Babe Fowler, and you couldn't *keep* a shirt on that guy... Maybe I pushed him too hard. He was definitely pissed."

As usual, Eloise felt the urge to run from Alex and his emotions. She felt inadequate, as she always did. *You never put in the effort with anyone*, Hollis had said, and it had made her think of Jacques, putting in the effort with every single person and racked with guilt when he didn't.

"I am one hundred percent sure that it had nothing to do with you," Eloise promised. "You were nothing but nice to him. I would bet he feels terrible for letting his mood show."

Alex gave her a grateful smile that almost broke her heart.

"Krystal said you were really nice," he said warmly. Eloise returned the smile.

"Well, only to people who were nice to me first."

Her phone pulsed with a text and she took it out as they waited for the elevator. She had hoped it would be another DM from Robbie—but instead it was Krystal.

**Krystal [10:37am]**: he's here btw, come down to the parking garage

**Eloise [10:37am]**: we'll be right there

# Chapter Nineteen

Alex and Eloise stopped at Krystal's office and loaded up their bags and the many cameras. Alex had assigned Eloise a camera for capturing the players in their suits as they boarded the bus and, later, the charter plane that would take them down to New York.

Weighed down with bags like sherpas, Alex and Eloise took the elevators once more, with Alex, now sufficiently reassured, happily yapping away about tonight's game: how eager he was to see 'Babe' again; how he believed the Rangers should have 'dumped' Dempsey over the summer, whom Eloise belatedly realized was the same player her father had talked about; how excited he was to see Jacques and Andrei play together once more, a legendary duo reunited. Unlike Dad—or many of the fans on Twitter—he saw the reunion as a positive thing, a chance for them to play together after having had years to develop their skills separately.

When they reached the garage level, they found Kyle waiting by the door, reluctantly making small talk with Krystal. He wore an ill-fitting grey suit and the infamous backwards Sox cap, which could not distract from the violet bruise from Andrei that had bloomed across his cheekbone. Krystal was in sunglasses and a luxurious oversized trench coat, bearing a sweating Dunkin Donuts iced coffee (even though Eloise would have bet that Krystal preferred some higher-end espresso, and probably had a gleaming rose-gold espresso machine at home).

"Kyle, you're a Boston local too!" Alex said excitedly, smacking his forehead when he saw him. "I bet *you* know where to get the best lobster roll. Eloise was saying she's lived in Boston her whole life and doesn't know!"

Kyle looked up from his phone at Alex like he had asked him something deeply personal and inappropriate, his thin lips curling and nostrils flaring in disgust.

"No, I don't know where to get a goddamn lobster roll. I'm not a tourist," he dismissed, and looked further offended when Alex laughed.

"See, you're in good company, Eloise," he told her. "And he's even got the accent. *Lobstah* roll! Ha! It's okay, I'll look on Yelp and we can all go sometime."

"That definitely sounds really fun, Alex," Krystal interjected. Eloise would guess that she always took care to be gentle and encouraging with him. She shot a meaningful look at Eloise and Eloise returned a subtle nod. "Actually, Alex, can you help me with this stuff? We'll be right back," she added to Eloise and Kyle.

"Aye, aye, boss!" Alex dropped the camera packs and dutifully took Krystal's iced coffee and suitcase from her. They walked to the elevators, leaving Eloise and Kyle alone in the hall with all of the camera equipment.

"Don't say anything," she warned when Kyle caught her eye. He tugged his earbuds out, the grunge still audibly blasting from them, and together they watched the elevator doors close. "He's really sweet."

"Yeah, and soft," Kyle said. "Like a marshmallow. Good luck to him with some of these guys."

*Mahshmallow.* Eloise smiled and bonked her head against his shoulder, like she might have done with Hollis. It had not been planned; she had felt a sudden rush of affection for him, here early out of anxiety that he would never admit to, and worried about Alex getting along with the guys even though he would never admit to that, either.

"What was that?" he asked with a scoff.

"A sibling head-bonk of affection," she explained, and Kyle snorted.

Now was her chance. "Don't you have things like that that you do with your siblings? Or your parents?"

"Nah. Pat would punch me in the face if I did that, and Colleen's not talking to me," Kyle said. At Eloise's raised brows, he continued. "She's off at Rochester for engineering, big fucking whoop, and she doesn't answer texts anymore. Whatever."

He kicked at the linoleum just as the doors slid apart once more and Connor and Travis entered. For once, Eloise was not happy to see them; she had found a possible opening with Kyle, and she was not sure when she would find it again.

"It's Killer and Eloise! Are you coming with us to New York, Eloise?" Travis greeted. His nose had been taped where Connor had elbowed him at the party. The bruise was the color of a grape and had bloomed beyond the tape, giving him two black eyes. Between that and his slim red suit and his bright, cheerful energy, he reminded Eloise of a cardinal.

"Yeah, just for this trip," she explained. "Just to help get content and get exposed to what it's like on game days."

"Excellent, we can pick your brain on the way to MSG," Connor said, rubbing his hands together. He was wearing a pink Oxford underneath his navy sport coat that made his cheeks even rosier. "We're trying to figure out what Travis should get for Mason's birthday. Mason is his boyfriend," he added.

"Not this again," Kyle groaned. Travis looked genuinely distressed.

"I don't know what to do. He said everything I like is 'basic' or 'problematic.' What do you get for someone who deconstructs everything?" he wanted to know. "He's doing art at NYU," he told Eloise, "so he's smart."

"He's a tool," Kyle said. "You should've stuck with that other guy. Caleb or whatever. The one with the paints."

"You think everyone with an education is a tool," Connor dismissed impatiently, flexing his fingers around the straps of his backpack in thought. Kyle shrugged with a *fair point* sort of look. "I still think if you went down to Brooklyn and waited on his bed, naked except for a cowboy hat, it would be really hard for him to argue with that."

"Aren't cowboys problematic?" Travis asked, chewing on a nail as he considered this option.

"Yes, but it would be subversive—stop laughing!" Connor ordered Kyle. "You haven't come up with any ideas yet."

"Oh, I have something you could give him." Kyle pretended to take something out of his jacket—and revealed his middle finger, earning an eye-roll from Connor. "This dude told Martin he's only dating him and not a finance bro because dating a finance bro in New York is a cliché. Fuck that."

Eloise was beginning to realize just how nervous Kyle truly was. He couldn't stop moving, adjusting his hat or shifting his weight, looking around like he was waiting for a jump scare and drawing in deep, sharp breaths. He only seemed halfway present even when talking, and she wondered if part of his head was still at home—and whatever was happening there—or if part of it was in Madison Square Garden, anticipating the game and his own performance.

"That *was* dickish," Connor agreed, oblivious to Kyle's anxiety. "I did think you should break up with him over that, but I've been there. Relationships are complicated," he finished loftily.

"What do you think, Eloise?" Travis asked. "His birthday is next week, and I don't have anything yet. I'm not afraid to spend on him if it's really good, but any time I spend money he roasts me for capitalism or whatever."

"Yeah, while sitting in his Brooklyn apartment that his parents pay for," Kyle interjected ruthlessly, and she wondered if some of his vehemence was rooted in his anxiety. "Texting Martin on the phone *they* pay for—"

"I'm the worst at gift-giving, but I think I'm with Kyle on this one," Eloise said over Kyle. Travis groaned and let his head fall back, lazy curls ruffling with the movement. "But I'm also very quick to break up with people, so, grain of salt on that. I run at the first sign of trouble."

"I could see that. You're independent. You don't put up with anything," Connor said, scowling when Kyle snickered at him. "Whatever, *Killer*, you're just pissy because you've never had a girlfriend."

"Wow, you really got me with that one, Kennedy," Kyle drawled, rolling his eyes. "Hurts so bad I'm gonna have to sit this game out now," he added—but his voice cracked on 'game' and Travis and Connor guffawed at him as he turned beet-red. He was about to say something when the door slid open once more. Eloise tried to ignore her own mounting anxiety and frustration.

"Aw, it's the kiddos," Burnie shouted as he exploded through the doors, filling the hallway with the scent of Dior Sauvage. He was unexpectedly elegant in a plum suit that brought out the green in his eyes. Pell trailed behind him in dark blue, uncharacteristically aloof, and he didn't make eye contact with anyone.

"Your suit's too big, Killer," Burnie said to Kyle as he swung his duffle bag into Connor's stomach, making him grunt in pain. "You need a tailor."

"Shut up, Burnap," Kyle snapped, earning a look of amusement from Burnie.

"Hey, Pell," Travis called brightly, but Pell moodily stalked past them toward the locker rooms as though he hadn't heard them.

"Eh, don't bother," Burnie said casually. "He's always like this before games, even these meaningless preseason ones. It's better to leave him alone until afterwards. Yo, Eloise, what's with all the bomb equipment?" He kicked one of the camera bags that Alex had left with her. It did not escape her that Burnie had called her by her name, rather than 'Intern'; she wondered what had changed.

"Camera stuff. I'm going to set up to get some pictures of you guys getting on the bus in your suits," she explained.

"And you DINGALINGS aren't helping her carry it?" Burnie shouted at the rookies, making them all flinch. "Get your shit together! Were you all raised in a barn, or what?"

"Sorry, Burnie," Travis muttered. "I feel like a bad Canadian now."

"You're a shit Canadian," Burnie agreed. "Come on, pick this stuff up!"

"You really don't have to—oh," she halted lamely, realizing that they had left her with nothing to carry. "Thanks, guys. It's really not necessary."

"You've gotta get this right, Eloise," Burnie informed her, slinging her duffle over his shoulder and picking up the paper bag with Jacques's sweater. "I got this new Louis Vuitton belt from Stephy for our anniversary"—he pointed at the gold buckle—"and I really want you to feature it. Make it the centerpiece of a great shot, you know? I was thinking a black-and-white shot, maybe with Lavesque looking at me like I just said something really inspiring, or maybe something really funny."

"It's giving Long Island, Burnie," Travis told him as they walked, looking down at the gold LV belt. "I know Stephanie is from New York but are we sure we want to document that?"

"And yours is *giving* fucking bell pepper, Martin," Burnie shot back. "I don't take style advice from bell peppers."

"I told you the red was too much, dude," Connor said to Travis.

"I like it—I appreciate that you took the risk," Eloise reassured Travis. He was quick to sling a lean arm around her affectionately and grin at her. "I didn't know the suits were such a big deal."

"All the teams do it now." Travis gave her a squeeze before releasing her as they reached the parking lot. The enormous black bus that would take them to the airport was waiting for them. Dan, the team's equipment manager, was loading plastic containers onto the bus, looking as usual like he was in the middle of some crisis. "But we have some really stylish guys on the team—like Burnie, and Lavesque—so it's a little competitive now."

"Dunno if I'd call it competitive when the game you're bringing is Bell Pepper and First Time On a Boat," Burnie said with a savage look at Connor. "Okay, what are we putting on the bus and what's staying out?"

Eloise directed Burnie, Connor, Travis, and Kyle to load the cameras and other equipment on the bus towards the front, hoping that that was the right move. "What's this?" Burnie asked after everything else had been loaded onto the bus, peering into the brown paper bag.

Eloise avoided his eyes as she took the bag from him.

"Jacques loaned me a sweater when he drove me home because it was cold," she said, pretending to check inside the bag so she didn't have to meet Burnie's—or Kyle's—eyes. "It looks expensive, so I wanted to return it before something happened to it."

"Oh, precious cargo. That one brings out his eyes really good, too," Burnie agreed just as evenly. Fortunately, Kyle wasn't paying attention to them, and Eloise now saw that the three rookies were deep in discussion, Travis's face flushed and mutinous.

"Don't worry. If he pulls anything, Killer and I will just beat him up," Connor was saying gallantly, reaching to put an arm around Travis's shoulders. Kyle looked torn between agreeing with him and being annoyed by the nickname.

"This Dempsey shit again," Burnie noted under his breath for her benefit.

"The Rangers player? The one who's a jerk?" Eloise recalled. Burnie nodded.

"He's just some punk, but he and Martin've got bad blood apparently from the AHL. Lavy had a whole talk with the kid about it," he explained. "Dempsey kinda sucks. Doesn't have much presence on the ice. I don't think the Rangers played him too much last year 'cause I honestly couldn't even remember who he was."

"I heard he's bigoted."

"A lot of guys are—more than anyone's willing to admit. You get enough freaks together who've been told they're hot shit all their lives and haven't really spent much time in the real world, and you're gonna have some weirdos on your hands," Burnie reasoned with a shrug. "I've seen it my whole career and I think it's a system thing. Kinda why I personally was concerned about Martin coming out before the season started, you know? It's badass that he went for it, but it's a lot to put on the kid in his first full season in the NHL, and there's only so many of these creeps I can beat the shit out of before they just kick me out of the league."

"Do you think anyone here is like that?" Eloise asked. To her surprise, Burnie looked thoughtful. She watched his green eyes to see if he looked in Kyle's direction, but he was looking at the ground as he rubbed his chin in thought. "Like Andrei, for instance... or anyone else."

"Nah, Kozzy's definitely a dick, but never like that. I don't even know where those rumors started." Burnie waved it off. "If there is anyone like that," he decided, "they know better than to show it around Lavy—or me. He always makes it clear that that shit is not tolerated."

"But don't you ever—"

She hesitated, but Burnie was perked up, brows arched like he was suspicious of any criticism of Jacques, ready for a fight if need be. "Don't you ever think that's a lot to put on Jacques, that he's the one who has to drive everything? Like it's amazing what he's done for this team, but—sometimes I just wonder about the cost to him. Like, personally. If it really is a system-level thing, like you say, don't you think that's a lot to ask of one man?"

In her nervousness she found herself talking like Hollis, who talked, as Lily always joked, like a teenager. "Not that I think it's bad that he's created this culture. Obviously, I respect and admire him for it. But shouldn't it be on the NHL and not on one captain, of one team—"

"No, I get you," Burnie said slowly. "And I agree. I do think it's a lot. I worry about him constantly. The minute he showed up on the scene, they started grooming him for leadership. They've been asking that shit of him since he was nineteen, and I don't think it's good for a person," he said suddenly, passionately.

Eloise got the sense he had been dying to say this to someone, holding it back and suffering for it. He was not a man who typically held much back.

"I think it's really bad," he went on. "I would not want a path like this for my daughters. Everything revolves around Lavy, and you can say it's just a stupid game, but it's also *not* just a stupid game—it's also jobs and livelihoods, it's dreams, it's a huge machine, it's a whole fucking religion, and the thing is, he really *is* that good of a person, so it all matters to him, and every time he fucks up it kills him, and the *pressure* of being that many things at once..."

Burnie brought his hands together, forming a tight ball, and shuddered. "And everyone who knew him when he was a brand-new baby is gone, except me and Krystal and Koslov, and we're the only ones left who know that this doesn't come naturally to him. He is the kindest person on earth, but he would never want to be a celebrity, you know? And no one gets that. I mean, I don't think even Rachel ever really—"

Here he halted, a flash of guilt on his face. "Ah, I don't even know what the fuck I'm talking about anymore."

"You're still blaming *him* for it, though," Eloise pointed out. "You're still saying he's putting it on himself. And it's not just his doing."

"Yeah, well," Burnie said with a shrug, "at this point he needs someone who can force him not to do that. That person is not me. He won't let me in anymore. It used to be Koslov, but god knows Koslov fucked that one up."

He lightly slapped her shoulder. "Hey, you okay with the kids? I need to go talk to Dan about my shit."

Burnie obviously felt like he had said too much. She would never have guessed that she would see this man embarrassed or flustered.

"I'm good, thanks." Eloise held up the camera from Alex. "You want me to get your suit shot now?"

"Nah, wait until Lavy's here, I like to take pictures with him," Burnie said, buttoning his jacket. Other players were starting to gather by the doors to the parking garage, all of them in suits and carrying luggage, much of it designer. "Looks like you're up, Eloise."

Burnie bellowed at the three rookies, ordering them to 'look less fucking lame' and 'get on the fucking bus for Eloise,' so she hopped off the bus steps with her camera and tripod and took up a post a few yards away. Connor and Travis walked together, grimacing against the urge to laugh, and when Connor got to the steps he started laughing self-consciously, causing Travis to laugh with him.

Next was Kyle. "Don't worry about your hat," she called as he walked past, and caught him trying not to smile, as she had intended.

Other players took the signal and began filtering into the parking garage with their lattes and Louis Vuitton luggage. Casper, looking surprisingly cool in his custom mulberry suit and gleaming loafers, completely ignored her as he passed; Novak and Harper were next, with Novak devastatingly handsome—if over-styled—in a checked brown suit and Gucci loafers, and Harper in a plain navy suit that did not fit him. Harper pretended to dance when he spotted her, and Novak flashed his most Krystal-worthy smile, making Eloise think of a preening designer cat. Pell stalked past, still moody and still wearing large noise-canceling headphones, and he nodded slightly to her before moving on.

And eventually, Andrei—cheap black suit and wrinkled white shirt, the most 'fuck you' of an outfit she had ever seen—walked into the parking lot, spotted her and stopped.

She had not expected to be nervous around Andrei, but her stomach lurched when she met his leonine eyes. For some reason she thought of the Strength card: a woman delicately prising apart a lion's jaws, her expression peaceful and unafraid.

"I don't do pictures," he said.

"According to your contract, you do," Eloise corrected. Krystal had informed her of this specifically, anticipating Andrei's pushback. "You can just keep walking and I'll get what I get."

"I don't—"

Jacques came into the parking lot in a light blue-grey suit that matched his eyes, mid-conversation with Alex and an older gentlemanly man that she did not know. At the sound of the doors parting, Andrei looked back at him.

"Problem?" Jacques prompted, looking at Eloise. Still there was that distance; once their eyes met his gaze slid from hers, resting in her general direction but not actually on her. It was like he was trying to show that they had no bond, no connection, that to him she was just another employee of the massive Bruins machine.

"No," she dismissed, looking into her camera again. Jacques was only the king because other men had crowned him; she would not make the same demands of him. "You can either look good in this picture or look bad in it, Andrei—and it does not matter to me—but either way I'm getting a picture of you, so you might as well keep walking."

Andrei looked back at Jacques again with an expression she could not read, before shaking his head and stalking past her. She only got one picture of him before Burnie distracted her by exploding back into the parking garage and hurrying to catch up with Jacques.

"Wait, Lavy, slow down. Eloise's got to get the belt," Burnie said, grabbing Jacques's arm to drag him back.

"Of course," Jacques said graciously, and he dutifully walked slowly beside Burnie, both of them looking ahead, deep in thought, like they were thinking only of the game, unaware of any camera. Behind them, Alex was grinning so hard he had a double chin.

"Ahhhhh, they're so cool," he whispered excitedly, shaking his fists and shuddering with delight as the two men reached the bus and climbed the steps. "Also, *you're* so cool. Did you just *totally* tell off Koslov, or what?"

"Well, not really," Eloise said grimly, getting up from the ground and brushing off her knees. "I think I just made him hate me more. Not that that's too much of a loss."

"Ah, I don't know." Alex folded up the tripod absently. "Matt Pelletier was telling me that he's really funny when he's not being mean. He said he used to make Lavesque cry with laughter. Like, red-faced, silent, shaking laughter."

It was this thought that haunted her as Eloise boarded the bus at last, finding a seat with Alex near the front. She had expected the mood on the bus to be boisterous and rowdy, but it was relatively quiet. Most of the players were either listening to music or talking to their seatmate, the first reminder of so many that she would get today that these were professionals, and this was their career. The seat that Alex had grabbed for them was behind Jacques and Burnie, and she saw Jacques had his earbuds in and was focused intently on an iPad screen, watching a previous Rangers game closely. Every now and then, he would take out an earbud to say something to Burnie, but the bus was too loud and his voice was too soft for her to hear.

As the bus rumbled through Boston, Eloise checked her phone, and saw that at last Robbie had messaged her back.

**f3nris_88**: how old are you

Well, at least he was smart enough to check. Maybe he knew her profile was fake and was messaging on the off-chance that he could get something from her.

**laurenkylie098**: 18

**laurenkylie098:** u?

**f3nris_88**: me too

**laurenkylie098**: u look older ;) especially in the pic with the hat

**f3nris_88**: pics

**laurenkylie098**: ???

**f3nris_88**: if your real send pics

**laurenkylie098**: obv im real!!! ur talking to me

**f3nris_88**: pics

His patience with her would run out soon. Eloise closed the messenger and pulled up Robbie's profile, rapidly screenshotting every post and picture in case he blocked her. Her phone vibrated in her hand with a new message and the banner showed a preview.

**f3nris_88**: guess your just a bitch like all females

She rolled her eyes and, angling her phone away from Alex's curious gaze, quickly scrolled through Pinterest until she had found a blurry shot of cleavage that looked low-quality enough to be plausible.

**laurenkylie098**: omg ur so mean! maybe ill just ask one of ur friends instead

She sent the picture and decided to change tacks.

**laurenkylie098**: ur friend with the hat is hottttter than u

**f3nris_88**: that guy is a faggot

She stared at her phone screen in nauseated contempt, then locked it and looked out the window.

"What's up, buttercup?" Alex asked cheerfully. Up ahead she saw Jacques's head turn towards them at the sound of Alex's voice.

*Andrei used to make him cry with laughter.* She could not remember the last time someone had made her laugh hard enough that she had cried—maybe Monique, but Eloise was the Andrei in that scenario, the asshole who had betrayed the other's trust a few too many times.

"You want to see how I edit the pictures for social media?"

"Yes, actually, that'd be great," she said, stuffing her phone in her pocket, and for the rest of the bus ride, Alex eagerly talked her through his editing process.

When they got to the airport, Alex had her crouch at the top of the steps to the plane and capture a few dynamic shots of the players boarding, most of them looking up at the camera sheepishly as they climbed. This time Andrei did not protest; he had cheap black earbuds in and was brooding as he walked, his mind obviously on the game. Burnie slapped her shoulder as he passed, and Jacques seemed to slow as he reached the top of the steps, lingering, like he might say something to her, but then Coach Duffy was coming up the steps too, and the moment had passed. Maybe she had imagined it anyway, because she wanted so badly to go back to the feeling that they had had in the car: that sudden warm intimacy, that sudden glittering sense of closeness.

The loss of that was excruciating, too. But maybe she had done it herself—maybe her feelings had been too obvious. Maybe he was simply drawing a boundary between them. And when the world asked so much of Jacques Lavesque, how could she blame him for putting up even one low wall?

The younger players were silent once they were on the plane, and Eloise used the opportunity of stowing her bag to check on Kyle. He looked paler, his eyes wide and fixed out his window, shoulders taut and hunched. He kept checking his phone before pressing his forehead to the glass and closing his eyes like he might be sick.

Was it just pre-game nerves, or was it something else?

As she settled back into her seat, she caught Jacques's eye once again, but he looked away before she could acknowledge it, like he hadn't wanted her to catch him. And then everyone was buckling in, preparing for takeoff, and once again the moment had passed. Alex was uploading the edited pictures to Instagram, talking her through his process, and she half-listened as she thought about her DM exchange with Robbie and tried not to think about Jacques.

They were not in the air for very long. Soon enough she could see Manhattan below: hazy and cluttered, one of those early autumn days that still felt like soupy summer. Jacques was moving around the seats, crouching in the aisle briefly with different players, but the ambient noise of the plane made it impossible to hear what he was saying.

She watched him reach the front again—he had completely bypassed them—and climb over Burnie to his own seat just in time for their descent to be announced.

"Welcome to New York," Alex sang quietly, bopping his head to a beat only he heard, "it's been waiting for you!"

The wheels hit the tarmac; they had arrived.

# Chapter Twenty

It was chaos after landing. Eloise was once again struck by the professionalism and machinery of the team: the transport of their equipment and uniforms, which Dan, for all of his stress, had obviously nailed down to a regimented and rigorous procedure. They were bussed to the hotel where they would stay overnight before leaving for Philadelphia in the morning, and the players scattered to their rooms for quick naps or downtime before the game.

Eloise and Alex went directly to Madison Square Garden and met a few other Bruins employees, including a puffy-haired, laconic guy named Noah who seemed to be laughing in his head at everything, and a brusque bald guy named Jeff who did not have much time for Eloise or Alex. Eloise followed them around the arena as they discussed their strategy for the game, agreeing on what everyone would capture, all the while checking her phone to see if Robbie had said anything else or blocked her. He still hadn't, but she couldn't decide how to proceed now.

Finally, while Jeff and Noah argued about something, with Alex anxiously trying to mediate, she opened Instagram again.

**laurenkylie098**: rly?

This time, Robbie responded at once.

**f3nris_88**: yea he likes it in the ass

Eloise guessed that this was simply, to Robbie, the most devastating insult that he could think of under the circumstances, rather than an actual comment on Kyle's sexuality, as she had caught him glancing, multiple times, at Ilya's sarcastic girlfriend Sophia at the party. She considered her words, and then typed her response.

**laurenkylie098**: he looks like it

**f3nris_88**: lol

**f3nris_88**: so can i see another pic

**f3nris_88**: maybe something else this time

**laurenkylie098**: only if u tell me what fenris means ;)

She saw the three dots flicker, but then once again Robbie went radio silent. It was lucky timing, because the players were beginning to arrive at the arena and she was needed. She and Alex caught them getting off the bus again at the loading dock, and once again the mood had deepened; even Connor and Travis were too focused to talk, and Travis in particular looked a little limp. She wondered if he was worrying about Tripp Dempsey again, worrying about whether he would be forced to bear the weight of having come out to a league of men who were systematically petrified of being labeled as gay.

As they followed the players up an apparently famed cement ramp from the loading zone to the main area of Madison Square Garden, all was silent save for their footfalls.

"I think Travis is really worried about meeting Dempsey on the ice," Eloise remarked to Alex and Noah later, as they sat in the windowless room where the team would be meeting soon to discuss gametime strategy and review any final notes. Alex intended on capturing a few shots from this discussion, which he had evidently done during his time with the Coyotes.

"I would be too. That guy's gross," Noah said as he plugged his phone into a charger in the wall. "So's Fowler. He always looks like he just got done filming a porno in a motel. It's a team of gross dudes."

"No he doesn't," Alex argued immediately, face going pink. "And Babe's not like that at all. He's so nice. I'm sure if Tripp Dempsey tries to start anything, Babe will stop him. He was always really nice to me when we worked together before. You have to meet him, Eloise, you would really like him," he added. "Anyway, enough of this talk. Here, you take this and go get some shots of the dressing room. Dan should be finished setting it up. Then you can catch the guys doing their last warm-up skate before the actual game."

"Got it." Eloise took the camera from him. She got the sense that Alex had put some work into coming up with simple tasks for Eloise, and she liked him even more for it. "Dressing room, then ice."

"Yeah, it's just a preseason game so this talk won't be too long." Noah jerked his head to the large screen at the front of the room, where Eloise presumed they would review materials as a team. "You won't have to wait long for them to get on the ice."

Eloise went to the Bruins' dressing room with the camera Alex had given her. Dan was still there with one of his assistants, and was currently smoothing a nametag over one of the stalls. Each jersey hung neatly pressed in its stall, displayed so identically that it looked fake.

"Holy crap," Eloise blurted in appreciation. Dan looked up as he pulled back from Andrei's nametag. "Sorry, I just am amazed at how it looks in here. Do you mind if I get some shots for social media?"

"Of course—well—wait—hold on," Dan stammered, fluttering between Andrei's and Jacques's stalls. Andrei was on one side of Jacques, Burnie on the other, and Eloise noticed that the padding that hung beside Andrei's jersey was yellowed and peeling with age.

"There. Try not to get Koslov's disgusting pads, please," he begged, patting Andrei's jersey. He shuddered. "I have been trying my whole career to get him to get new pads. These are from *before* Instagram," he added, holding up one of the shoulder pads. "Literally. I'm not joking. They might be from before Facebook. It's disgusting."

"Actually, I would love to get them in one of the shots," Eloise said. "He's an iconic player and this shows how you put in the work to take the individual players' preferences into account."

"Yeah, he's iconically smelly," Dan muttered. "Fine, just let me spend hours setting this room up and then go and take a picture of Koslov's ancient padding. That's fine!"

"Dan," said his assistant, a sturdy-looking blonde woman in a Bruins cap and small gold hoops, in the tone you might use with a fussing child, "no one is giving you a grade in how AI-generated this room looks, okay?" She shot Eloise a wink. "I'm Nikki. I don't think we've met."

"Eloise. I'm interning for Krystal, and Alex sent me in here to get some shots of the dressing room," Eloise replied.

"Oh, definitely get Koslov's stall, then," Nikki agreed eagerly. "Also, you've gotta come in here after the game and see how all the players leave their stalls. Johansson re-laces his skates with new laces between periods and always leaves the old ones scattered on the bench, and Sekelsky likes to drink a bunch of Gatorades and line up the empty bottles on the bench at the end of the game. He calls them his 'children.'"

"You think he's just this normal guy and then anything he says is completely bizarre," Dan added.

Eloise coaxed Dan into pretending to arrange Jacques's stall while she got some 'action' shots of him. As she worked, Nikki dropped more little factoids about the players: Jacques was only particular about the blades in his skates and preferred an older blade that necessitated an older skate, and the only time he and Dan had ever had words was when Dan had tried to force him to switch to a new skate; Pell ate gummy bears between periods so Nikki always made sure there was a fresh bag in his stall in case he had forgotten.

After she had gotten sufficient material for Alex to work with, Eloise made her way to the ice to wait for the players to come out for their warm-up skate. She walked through the tunnel, hit with a blast of cold air—

—and then she was standing in Madison Square Garden.

All was bright and silent. The screens that hung over center ice were dark; the golden panels of the ceiling stretched out in a sunburst over the stadium in a dome of soaring height. All of the panels that ribboned the seating levels were black, but soon they would be lit up, advertising the Rangers and beer and cars and credit cards, and now she was thinking of what Burnie had said—*it's a whole fucking religion*—and for a moment she could only stare up in awe at the complexity that had been built around such a simple game. It was like walking into a cathedral.

She had never felt strongly about religion, and had always had the sense when she walked into places of worship that these rituals had been built around a human hunger for mysticism and greatness, and then she was thinking of Kyle again—his Catholicism, his tattoos, his tarot cards—and then a new appreciation for Jacques bloomed within her and she took a seat on the Bruins' bench like it was time for prayer.

The rituals, the superstitions, the carefully selected numbers, the mythology and the worship—it was all religion. No one wanted to truly know these men—Jacques's hidden injuries or the sad secrets that Andrei kept or the arcana that Kyle clung to—but they wanted proof that their gods existed. They wanted to see them, hear them, meet them and touch them, wanted to wear their iconography and their names, but never truly know them.

She took out her phone, and saw that Robbie had messaged her while she had been talking to Dan and Nikki.

**f3nris_88**: its a wolf.

**f3nris_88**: the son of loki.

**f3nris_88**: when he was chained he bit the hand off a god.

*And you believe you have been chained?* Eloise wondered. She couldn't find a picture on Pinterest that matched the original one she had sent closely enough, so she pulled aside the collar of her Bruins fleece and snapped a picture of her neck, the ends of her platinum hair brushed aside, and sent it after checking that the picture provided no clues to her identity or whereabouts.

**f3nris_88**: pretty

**laurenkylie098**: ur turn :) show me some of ur tattoos

**laurenkylie098**: what is that arrow one on ur neck?? so hot

**f3nris_88**: its tiwaz. justice.

He sent a blurry close-up of the tattoo which so strongly resembled the one that Kyle had, though it was undoubtedly a different symbol. This one was recognizably a rune and one of the most common ones that she had found.

**laurenkylie098**: ur other friends have it too... except red hat

**f3nris_88**: hes a fucking idiot he got the wrong tattoo

She was about to type out a reply when the soft rush of blades on ice caught her attention. Eloise looked up to see a lean figure skating towards her, in a T-shirt darkened and clinging with sweat, his tattooed arms and neck on full display. There was something sly about his grin and his dark eyes, making her think inexplicably of Peter Pan.

He glided to a stop in front of her, tilting his head curiously. He was handsome in a teenaged girl's dream sort of way—the pretend boyfriend you told everyone you had met at summer camp who lived in Canada: soft brown hair, lightly wavy, and clever brown eyes, and something youthful and boyish about his face. The boyishness, however, was undercut by the sweat, grease, tattoos, and clinging T-shirt.

"Bruins," he observed, bracing a hand on the low boards in front of her, clever dark eyes flicking from her hair to her fleece. "Sabotaging the ice?"

"I'm social media," she explained, holding up her camera. He grinned, leaning forward and hanging over the low boards, close enough that he could have reached forward and touched her. She got the sense that he expected her to be flustered by him. She also got the sense that he was bored and looking for entertainment.

"Nice to meet you, social media," he said. He had a lilt to his words that sounded Texan but she wasn't sure. "I'm Babe. Or Dillon, if you're real mad at me."

"Ha ha," she conceded dryly. "Eloise."

"Like the little cartoon girl," he noted, eyes on her blonde hair. "The one who lived at the Plaza."

"Yes, well, I didn't make that connection until *after* I bleached my hair," she admitted, annoyed with herself for blushing. She was remembering how Hollis had pointed it out immediately when she had debuted her newly-bleached hair, and how gleeful he had been about it. Babe grinned.

"And you had to commit after that," he said. "Obviously."

"Obviously," Eloise agreed, trying not to laugh. "I'm just hanging out here, waiting for the team to do their warm-up skate. Are you warming up?"

"Yeah, I like to come here early, get a feel for the ice," he said, pushing back his slightly sweaty dark hair. She was irresistibly reminded of what Noah had said, and could appreciate the accuracy of it now. "Everyone else's playing soccer inside. Pointless, there's nowhere to send the ball. Hey," he said suddenly, leaning in close again, "what's the word on Koslov?"

"The word?"

"Yeah, like why's he back with the B's?" he wanted to know. He lazily swung one leg over the board and settled into an absent stretch.

"Money, I think, but he hasn't told me anything personally," she said, aware of how closely he was watching her.

"Hm. Alright," he said with a half-shrug. "He was a better player when he was an alcoholic. But you didn't hear that from me."

"I definitely didn't, because that's a really terrible thing to say."

Babe grinned up at her as he leaned further into his stretch. "Oh, don't even get me started. I got more where that came from."

Eloise heard Alex and Noah before she saw them appear out of the tunnel to climb onto the bench. She braced herself to be protective of Alex, but—

"KASH MAAAAANNNN!!!" Babe bellowed with genuine joy, hopping over the boards, and to Eloise's surprise he flung his arms around a sheepishly delighted Alex, and they almost toppled over. "How you been doing? How's it with the B's? How's it working with your hero?"

"I'm just in awe of everything, at all times," Alex said as Babe leaned back against the board, crossing his tattooed arms as he grinned at Alex.

"And you finally got some female company," he said, nodding to Eloise, and cackling when Alex turned pink and Noah rolled his eyes. "The first real heart-to-heart that Kash-man and I had, he asked me about where to meet girls," Babe explained to Eloise.

"Oh, god, don't—" Alex protested, but Babe waved him off.

"What? It was a real good question. I was like, man, you know what, I don't actually know," Babe admitted. "There weren't any women in Arizona."

Eloise could not stop the laugh that erupted and Babe grinned, obviously pleased with himself. "I'm serious," he told her, "there weren't. Just old leathery guys everywhere. No one wears sunblock in Arizona, either."

The Bruins players were beginning to trickle onto the ice—Gagnon and Sekelsky were first, then Casper, looking at Babe suspiciously. Babe waved at him but Casper did not return the gesture.

"That guy is always in a bad mood," he noted as Casper skated on.

"I think he's just Swedish," Alex said earnestly, and Babe and Eloise both laughed. "No! Oh god, no, I just meant that like, culturally, the Scandinavian countries treat friendliness—"

Burnie exploded onto the ice, then Jacques. He looked back at them as the laughter died in Eloise's throat.

"Lavesque," Babe called warmly as Jacques glided to them, wearing a practice jersey and no helmet. He hit the boards lightly. "Always good to see you." He looked back at Eloise. "We really hung out at the All Stars last season. It was a great time. We kicked ass together, too," he added, a point that made Burnie scowl.

"It is good to see you too," Jacques said to Babe, "though I am surprised you are not with your teammates." He raised his brows meaningfully and Babe groaned, stretching again.

"He's always on my ass about not being more a part of my team," he explained to Eloise, rising from his stretch. "Every goddamn time. You know what, Lavy? I hate indoor soccer, and that's all they play, alright? I would way rather chat up a blonde than play indoor soccer where you can't even win."

Jacques, to her surprise, did not seem amused by Babe.

"You are blowing off another opportunity with your team like you always do," he said bluntly. "And you are distracting our team from doing their job."

Babe's brows shot up and Noah cringed as Jacques pushed off from the boards to rejoin Burnie, as well as Pell. Burnie was scowling at Babe and mouthed something that looked like, *mitts off my man,* before skating away.

"Uh—he's been really weird today—" Alex began, but Babe wasn't listening.

"What the hell," Babe said under his breath as he stared at Jacques in wonder. Far from seeming upset or put-off by Jacques's harsh scolding, he seemed delighted. He glanced back at Eloise and gazed at her like he was looking for something. "What the hell."

"Sorry, man. I heard when he gives tough love it's really tough," Noah muttered, apparently melted by Babe's charm, but Babe snickered.

"Oh, there was no love there," he dismissed as he pushed over the boards and onto the ice again. He was still grinning. "That had nothing to do with me at all." He looked at Eloise once more, and shuddered with exhilaration like he had taken a bite of something spicy. "Damn," he said as he skated back to the tunnel leading to the Rangers' dressing room.

"Don't worry, it's really hard to upset Babe," Alex reassured, mis-reading Eloise's silence. "I don't think even Jacques Lavesque being mad at him could bother him, really. But seriously, *what* is up with him today?" he wondered as they watched Jacques skate.

He glanced back at them and Eloise caught his eye, but he did not smile and did not acknowledge her other than that *look*, and then returned to his conversation with Burnie as they skated together. *No comment*, she thought furiously as she watched him.

(Worse yet—why had she found that so... No. She shook her head. She was not going to go there.)

Andrei entered on the ice, then Kyle, who was genuinely pale now, his movements stifled and hesitant. Connor and Travis jokingly knocked into him, but he did not react to them. Soon Jacques joined him and they skated together for a while, deep in conversation, Jacques gesturing as he spoke, Kyle nodding as he listened. Just to distract herself from her frustration with Jacques, Eloise set up the tripod and began taking pictures of the team.

Soon they were being called back to the dressing room. Madison Square Garden employees were trickling in—walking along the stadium seats, looking at the ice—and Eloise followed Alex and Noah back through the dressing room as the players shucked their practice jerseys. She glimpsed Jacques's bare back underneath his padding and she meant to look away, but then he had pulled the jersey off, his hair mussed, and their eyes met, and it was too late. She had seen the tattoo that stretched across the planes of his back, the tattoo she had been wondering about for months, the tattoo that—at least, as far as she guessed—he did not want documented.

In the hall outside of the dressing room, she checked her phone again. Robbie had messaged.

**f3nris_88**: he didnt even get a rune lmao i showed him what to get. and he got something else its not even a rune.

**laurenkylie098**: omg what a dumbass

**f3nris_88**: lol

**laurenkylie098**: why do u all have the tiwaz

She could hear Jacques talking to the team, a pre-game speech, but couldn't distinguish the words. The sounds of other players talking had quieted and now it was just him, the cadence of his words staccato and blunt. She bit her lip and focused on her screen again.

**f3nris_88**: its brotherhood.

**laurenkylie098**: well u shouldnt let red hat into the brotherhood if hes not gonna have the right tattoo

**f3nris_88**: lol

**f3nris_88**: dont worry about him. hes out.

**f3nris_88**: he doesnt know it yet.

Her stomach lurched and she stared at the screen. *Kyle.* She locked her phone screen before she could accidentally type something, and sat with her head in her hands. *He doesn't know it yet.* She thought of him sitting there alone on the bus, pale and checking his phone, and she knew with sudden clarity: Kyle *did* know he was out, and he was terrified. And she was thinking of that rifle in Patrick's pale hands, and now she was terrified, too.

It was getting closer to game time. Just twenty minutes to go. The sense of crowds pouring into Madison Square Garden was building—she could not hear them but the energy of the building had changed, going from the sense of something echoing and overlarge to a thrumming feeling behind her ribcage, an electricity in the air that made her hairs stand on end.

Just when she was contemplating whether she should go into the dressing room, a familiar figure, all in uniform save for his skates, exploded out of it and went into the bathroom, leaving the door swinging behind him.

Kyle.

She went to the door and stilled its movements with her hand. He might simply have to use the bathroom, in which case this was incredibly invasive—but after waiting a moment, she parted the swinging door slightly.

"Kyle?" she called gently. "It's Eloise. Can I come in?"

There was a pause.

"...Yeah," he said at last. "You can."

Eloise pushed into the bathroom. There were a few stalls on the end, and just past them was a large tiled area with shower heads and benches. Socked feet poked out of one of the spaces—Kyle was sitting in the one on the end. She walked to the stall and, instead of opening it, dropped down on the floor on the outside, leaning against the door.

"Hey."

"Hey."

Singing was coming from the dressing room; she thought it might be Burnie belting out a pop song, but from here it was too hard to distinguish. She did not know why but she was thinking of The Hanged Man again, suspended in his indecision, peaceful in his pain.

"Nervous?"

"No, I'm really good," Kyle said sarcastically, and his voice cracked as Eloise laughed softly. "I always sit on bathroom floors when I'm happy."

"I'll make sure to include that when I write your profile," she said. She knew on the other side of the door he was rolling his eyes. She considered her words as she stared at the tile. "I'm worried about you," she confessed.

There were so many thoughts in her head, buzzing like an arena, a chaotic blend of noise and color. She had not had the time or space to sort through all of them, and part of her was ashamed to admit that her angst about Jacques's distance with her was partly to blame. She was distracted; she was hurt; she was focusing on the wrong person.

A soft noise caught her attention. When she looked up, there was Jacques, peering into the bathroom. He raised his brows at her, a silent communication, and mouthed *Kyle?*

She nodded, still gazing at Jacques. For some reason she could not look away, and he held the gaze calmly, listening.

"You shouldn't," Kyle said finally, unaware that Jacques was there. "I'm fine. Just—just freaking out. But it's not—you don't have to *worry*."

"Does praying help?" she asked. She heard Kyle scoff.

"No. Not anymore." His voice was tight.

"What about the tarot?" When she heard him draw in a breath, she added, "Andrei told me you had tarot cards."

Jacques's jaw tightened at Andrei's name, but otherwise he gave no hint of his feelings.

"Yeah, I mean, they're fucking stupid," Kyle said. "I should've known he had seen them... Asshole."

"He likes to reveal people's secrets," Eloise said, "as you probably saw him do with me."

Now Jacques looked curious, tilting his head.

"Yeah. I did. Dick," Kyle said disgustedly. "That was a low blow." He paused before releasing his words in a rush. "I only got them because of Lavesque. He's got a tattoo all up his back—"

"The King of Cups," Eloise finished, still holding Jacques's gaze.

She had recognized it the instant she had seen it just a half-hour earlier. How many times in the past month had her gaze skipped over that very card as she thumbed through that book of tarot, trying to understand its appeal to Kyle?

"You know, I don't think Jacques has that tattoo because he believes in the tarot," she continued. "I would bet it's something much more personal... and probably related to something he feels like he can't actually say to anyone. I don't think it's a belief system for him."

Jacques did not react. The hairs on her skin prickled. She thought of Burnie's words again. "And I don't think that's a healthy path, Kyle—not talking to people about what's going on in your life, not asking for help when you need it."

To her surprise, Jacques smiled slightly. He bowed his head, still listening.

"I'm talking to you now. And I don't need help. I'm fine."

"Not really, though. Right?" she pressed. "Because I don't think you're hiding out here because of game anxiety. I think you're freaking out about something else. I think something matters more to you than your gameplay and that's why you're out here, hiding."

Kyle was quiet. Jacques was still listening, still staring at Eloise. "You don't have to talk about it right now, and you definitely don't have to talk about it to me," she allowed, "but I'm serious, Kyle. You need to open up to someone. You're putting too much on yourself, whatever it is."

Quiet. Then, Jacques pointed at his wrist as though pointing at a watch. *Soon*, he mouthed. Eloise nodded.

"Anyway, you're my favorite player because you're a Boston kid, and you are so much like me in some ways, and I never thought I would give a damn about Boston sports but now I do. So." She leaned her head against the stall. "How about a deal? If you promise me you'll actually get some help for whatever is going on in your life right now, I'll buy you a lobster roll."

He was laughing. "You and your fucking terrible deals. Fine."

She heard the rustle of fabric as he got to his feet, and she rose too. When she looked at the doorway again, Jacques was gone, the door swinging slightly. Kyle emerged from the stall, flushed and hatless, his auburn hair vaguely greasy.

"Shake on it?" she asked. Kyle looked down at his hand and grimaced.

"I was just touching the floor, but whatever," he decided, and he shook her hand, trying not to laugh.

"Game time," she said.

"Game time," he agreed.

# Chapter Twenty-One

Kyle jammed his feet into his skates and scampered out onto the rink, where both teams were doing their final warm-ups, silhouetted by the bright white radiating from the ice as he ran down the tunnel. From the dressing room, Eloise could hear the roar of Madison Square Garden: the warbled blare of the announcer, the rush of the crowd, the insistent thud of a rock song's beat. Noah and Alex were filming each player's entrance, so Eloise watched from the end of the dressing room as Kyle turned the corner and joined the blur of black and gold.

Time slipped by slowly then suddenly, beads along spider silk: now the players were returning to the dressing room, and all was quiet like they were stowaways in the hull of some great ship.

Jacques was checking his tape and laces methodically, like it was a ritual. Beside him, Andrei rested his elbows on his massive knees, utterly and predatorily still as he stared, unseeing, at the opposite wall. On Jacques's other side, Burnie bounced his stick and noisily sucked his teeth, visibly fighting against the urge to get up and bother someone. Johansson was looking mutinously at him, so Jacques set his free hand on Burnie's stick without looking, forcing him to stop.

And then it was time to line up in the tunnel. Jacques lingered by the opening, clapping each man on the arm as they passed. They all seemed to know the order in which they were supposed to go out: Marcel took the lead, massive in his goalie pads, then Burnie, then Pell, then Novak, then Connor, then Travis... all the way to the very end, when every last man had passed Jacques—save for Andrei.

They were the only two that remained. With a final nod, Jacques ducked into the tunnel, and Andrei followed, a routine that Eloise would later learn they had tacitly maintained since their days with the Providence Bruins. She thought of the Hierophant card: two men bowed before the power of tradition and institution, before the power of rites of passage and rituals and the mysticism found within them.

Red and blue light swept over each name, each carefully chosen number—thirteen for Jacques, seventy-three for Andrei—as the two men walked, heads bowed, to the ice. A recognizable pop song was blaring now and she felt the pounding of its beat in her ribs and collarbone like a war drum. She was thinking of church again as she heard the announcer yell, "...BOSTON BRUINS!"

Or maybe not church—maybe something older, something rooted in pagan ritual and wolf-gods and dented armor. From the first time she had seen Jacques he had made her think of some warrior-king, a man meant to kneel on a bloody battlefield because other men had crowned him to do it.

Eloise joined Nikki and Dan at the edge of the tunnel as the lights dimmed and the noise dropped. A spotlight landed on the anthem singer in the corner of the ice as Jacques, Burnie, Andrei, Pell, Marcel, and Kyle took the ice in a line. The Rangers did the same. Eloise spotted Babe, shifting his weight and looking around with an air of entertainment, without any of the sobriety that the other players had.

"Ladies and gentlemen, we ask that you please rise and remove your hats for the national anthem," intoned the announcer.

Everything beyond the ice glowed blue. "Not a bad turnout," Nikki said beside her, scanning the stadium. "Almost feels like it could be a real game."

"So this is unusual for a preseason game?" Eloise wondered. Given that Hollis and Dad rarely watched or even mentioned the preseason games, she had not expected this intensity.

Nikki grinned, raising her micro-bladed brows as she looked back at Eloise.

"Yeah, but it's the moment of truth, right? Do Lavy and Koslov still have that insane power together? Is this gonna be the magic combination that puts the team back where they used to be? Is Andrei worth ten million, worth losing Mäkinen and Simpson? Believe me, they're wondering. We all are."

The players bowed their heads in practiced solemnity. The anthem singer sang, wreathed by motionless New York policemen, their jaws stiff, decorated uniforms glinting. Above it all the banners hung still, though Eloise thought they should have rippled with some medieval, ceremonial breeze. The hymnal of the anthem rose from the crowd around them like smoke, and then—

It was time.

"Alright, back up a little. Don't want you to take any pucks to the face," Nikki said, nudging Eloise further into the tunnel.

The puck was dropped, and the game began.

At first all was quiet as snow after the din leading up to the puck drop, but the noise began to rise again as the players fanned along the ice.

"Well, Koslov's coming in hot, like he always does," Nikki muttered as Andrei thundered past with that fluid fire. "Hope he doesn't tire himself out too much."

Eloise didn't know hockey well enough to follow the game. She tried to focus on Kyle, but her eye was drawn—again and again—to Jacques. He was distinctive among the players in a way she had not anticipated: somehow he was always where the Rangers least wanted him to be, relentless and swift, like he could predict where everyone was going to be; like he saw some invisible hand guiding each player; like he was the tarot's Magician, ruled by spontaneity and intuition. He was so confident, so forward on the ice; he was so at home.

"Icing," Nikki said as gameplay paused and the players gathered around the referee, forming a ragged circle. Jacques emerged from it, loose and confident, as a Rangers player with wide-set eyes came forward. "Blom is pretty meh in a face-off—and everywhere else, to be honest—and Lavy is one of the best in the league. And there it is, he wins again, big surprise. Wonder if he ever loses just for something different," she added absently as the players exploded from the circle, following the puck. "Dempsey with the puck. He's the little guy. And there's Koslov. Dempsey's a moron, you can't pull those moves when Lavesque and Koslov are on the ice—and there we go," she conceded dryly with a shrug.

A red light behind the goal flashed and the crowd booed. The Bruins had scored the first goal of the game. "It was Koslov, handed to him by Lavy," Nikki explained to Eloise, but it was obvious enough when Andrei did a swift loop behind the net, raising a fist in the air, and Jacques glided alongside him with a congratulatory nod. Kyle followed them, anxious and watchful.

"The kid is really struggling to keep up with those two," Nikki observed as the trio skated past them. "I feel like Duffy just put him on that line to shame Koslov into behaving."

"Give him a minute," Eloise hedged. "It's his first NHL game."

"Okay, mama bear," Nikki joked. "Look, most players are not gonna keep up with them. It's okay."

Babe scored the next goal, earning a look of deepest contempt from Nikki and a noise of disgust from Dan for how he celebrated, sliding along the ice on one knee like he thought he was in a music video, shaking his head wildly.

The first period ended, and Eloise listened from the tunnel as Jacques breathlessly addressed the team with rapid-fire words, his grammar and pronunciation suffering for the speed. Here again was a different facet of him, one she had only glimpsed before: the side that had been made captain for his skill and presence rather than his gentleness; the side that did not consider his words so precisely, worrying over their weight and accuracy. Here, she thought again, he was home.

Eloise faced the ice again, crossing her arms.

"You alright?" Nikki asked as she passed a roll of tape to Dan on the bench.

"Just fine," she promised, taken aback that she had been read so easily.

"Cool." Nikki gave her a thumbs-up. "Don't go turning into Dan on me. He's always unhappy about something."

"Shut up," Dan complained from the bench as he taped a stick with precision. "I'm not unhappy—just unsatisfied."

The second period began. The game was faster now, the plays more seamless. Babe got another goal and then Burnie got one shortly after, fuming with spite and assisted by Pell. Jacques and Blom took another face-off and, as Nikki explained, Blom got thrown out for his timing.

"Well, look. You kinda have to cheat if you're going to beat Lavy. I can't blame him for trying," Nikki reasoned as Babe emerged and took Blom's place, grinning like a coyote as he leaned forward. "Ugh. Fowler again. Here we go—oh, not bad for a winger. Fowler actually won that one," she added in surprise as the circle broke and the players fanned out again. "He's so annoying that I always forget he's basically their one good guy."

(If anything, Jacques seemed delighted to have lost; he was grinning as he skated away from the circle to follow the puck.)

The third period was the fastest of all. Andrei and Jacques, as Nikki saw it, had warmed up fully and the Rangers, even with Babe's cheap shots and Dempsey's blunt moves, were not able to get the puck back out of their zone for more than seconds at a time. "They're closing in," Nikki said proudly as she pointed to Jacques and Andrei. "Look at them. They're unstoppable. Look how tired Blom and Fowler are. The Rangers can't keep up."

She was beaming. "They're back."

It was true. Even to Eloise's untrained eye, the Rangers looked depleted, and there was something oppressive about Jacques and Andrei, a claustrophobic force that kept the Rangers frantically dancing in front of their net, never able to push back for very long. "Your baby boy isn't doing so bad, either," Nikki added.

Jacques got the next goal, assisted by Andrei in a move so fluid that even Eloise could appreciate it, a shot that swept through the Rangers like silk. She watched as Burnie and Kyle flung themselves at Jacques, who was flushed and laughing until he looked at Andrei and his smile dropped.

The Rangers were becoming ragged and unruly. There was a minute and a half left on the clock when they pulled their goalie so, as Nikki explained, they would be able to add a player to the ice. "They'll add Fowler. They're trying to at least get the puck back out of the zone and maybe tie it up," she said slyly, "but you're going to need more than an extra Ranger now."

It did push the Bruins back on their heels, back towards the center, as Babe took the ice once more.

And then the magic thing happened: with less than fifteen seconds left on the clock, Kyle broke away from the tussle, and the Bruins on the bench were screaming and pounding the boards with their fists and sticks, and then Kyle fired the puck as hard as he could with a *thwack!* that echoed across the ice, and then the droning noise of the period-end buzzer was filling the stadium and the Bruins were screaming KILLER KILLER KILLER for Kyle, and Eloise watched as Jacques beelined for Kyle and flung himself on top of him—then

Burnie, then Pell, then Connor and Travis all slammed into him, shouting with glee. Kyle disappeared, red-faced and joyful, beneath a pile of his teammates. Marcel skated across the ice, taking the puck from the Rangers' goaltender and holding it up demonstratively for Kyle.

"YOUR BABY!" Nikki screamed, dancing wildly. She reached over to the bench and punched Dan in the arm, earning a shout of outrage from him as he clutched his shoulder, scowling in pain. "THAT'S YOUR BABY! HE SCORED! THAT'S HIS FIRST NHL GOAL!"

It was a blur. The Bruins were trundling off the ice, and crowding in the dressing room. The noise was unimaginable, all these red-faced sweaty men shouting with glee, jumping and dancing around Kyle who was dazed and laughing and red as Connor, and Jacques grabbed Kyle's head and kissed him on the side of his face and Kyle just laughed harder, shocked and disbelieving, and happier than Eloise had ever seen him—and then he spotted Eloise and broke free from Jacques and Burnie and, to her own shock, flung his arms around her so tightly that she thought she might suffocate in sweaty padding and jersey and greasy hair.

Eloise squeezed him as hard as she could and then they released each other, stumbling backward. Eloise caught Jacques's eye over Kyle's shoulder, but she was quick to look away—she knew her feelings would be obvious on her face right now, and there was no need for him to know.

The joy continued into the night. Eloise followed the team to a local chain restaurant for a late-night meal, where they all sat together at one impossibly long table and talked and joked and laughed as they stuffed their faces with pasta, with pizza, with burgers and chicken wings, and more food than Eloise had ever seen anyone eat in one sitting. The giddiness was powered by relief—relief that Andrei had been worth it, relief that the win had not been a close one, relief that the line changes had worked. Even Coach Duffy seemed a little shaky with it all.

She sat with Nikki, Dan, Alex, and Noah, who were all happily trashing the Rangers' gameplay—they were overly-dependent on Babe and, as Nikki pointed out, he would be a free agent at the end of this season; Dempsey had improved since last season and was showing more presence on the ice but was still an idiot—and Eloise pretended to listen while observing the others. Andrei sat at the other end of the table, quietly picking at his food; he was adjacent to Jacques, who was listening intently to Casper beside him. As Casper talked, Jacques smiled and responded, but the effort of it was obvious, and she was reminded of that morning, when he had been so short and brusque with her and Alex, and later with Babe.

No one seemed to think of him. No one seemed to be cognizant of the deluge of emotions he had to be having right now. *Their mother*, he had said before turning from his wife, rejecting her, and then giving his sons away. He and Andrei had walked out onto the ice together for the first time in four years, a reawakening of the traditions and responsibilities that had tied them together for half their lives.

She tried not to watch him. It was his job, she reminded herself. He was a private man, she reminded herself. He did not even let Burnie in anymore. He probably did not *want* his emotions to be acknowledged, or even looked at.

And yet. Jacques happened to look up and catch her eye—and she was about to look away when she saw him bite his lip and look down again, struggling to return to listening to Casper.

*You never put in the work for anyone*, Hollis had said, and she couldn't stop thinking about this as the team wrapped up dinner. It was midnight now, and humid in New York City, and they traipsed back to their hotel around the corner in a long, jumbled line. Travis and Connor were walking with their arms slung around Kyle, and Connor was loudly singing "We Are the Champions," terribly off-key, with Travis and Kyle laughing so hard that they were choking on it. Jacques walked ahead with Burnie and Pell, Andrei close behind them, alone, and Eloise knew that was bothering Jacques too—the uncertainty of being torn between setting the right example and talking to Andrei, versus honoring his own feelings.

*You never put in the work for anyone*, Hollis said again in her mind. She tried to focus on the conversation around her (now Noah and Nikki were trying to give Alex advice on dating that Dan was loudly decrying), but an idea was taking shape in her mind, and as she walked she ran over it, turning it over like a candy in her mouth.

She continued to turn it over after they reached the hotel. As it turned out, she was sharing a room with Nikki, who immediately went to FaceTime her girlfriend in the bathroom, leaving Eloise to sit on one of the beds and stare at the paper bag that held Jacques's sweater.

It would be quick, she told herself. She would pretend to be returning his sweater but would really just acknowledge that she knew a lot was going on for him, that him losing his temper did not bother her, and establish that the boundary he had drawn between them was fine with her and she would not try to cross it; she would assuage any guilt or embarrassment he might be feeling.

She had to do it now. Maybe he would already be showering or getting into bed, but they had only just returned and she might still be able to catch him. Eloise took out her phone.

**Eloise [12:14am]**: hey this is eloise. i forgot to tell you earlier - i have your sweater and am happy to return it now before i forget again, or tomorrow at some point. just let me know.

She dropped her phone and flopped back on the bed—and to her surprise, her phone pulsed immediately.

**Jacques [12:14am]**: i was just about to text you. i wanted to talk to you real quick. meet you on the rooftop? you can get onto it with your hotel key.

Something squeezed her chest as she stared at the text. He just wanted somewhere, she told herself, where he did not have to be Jacques Lavesque for a little while.

**Eloise [12:15am]**: sure.

She left with Nikki still recounting the game to her girlfriend over FaceTime, carrying Jacques's sweater in its paper bag under her arm. The halls were quiet, the noise of Manhattan blotted out, her ears still ringing from the noise and chaos of the game. She took the elevator up to the rooftop. She doubted anyone else would be out there this late, particularly as the humidity was so smothering. A tight coil was forming in her belly and she wished it would stop.

There was no reason to be nervous—there was nothing to anticipate.

The rooftop, lined with a few tables and chairs, was otherwise empty, save for one figure leaning on the railing, looking out over Manhattan. Traffic roared and shrieked down below; the humidity was like a damp cloth, blurring the lights. Jacques was in a slightly wrinkled T-shirt that stretched over his shoulders, his hair still wet from a quick shower. He looked younger than he had earlier—softer, plainer. He turned at the sound of the door swinging shut behind Eloise and she waved, holding up the paper bag.

"Now I cannot believe I was wearing a sweater in Boston," Jacques remarked as she joined him at the railing, hoping that to stand next to him casually would reassure him that she would not interpret any romantic tension from this meeting location. "Burnie was dying earlier, when we were walking back to the hotel. He hates when it's humid."

"I know, it feels like summer here," she agreed. She passed him the paper bag and he took it, peering inside. "I got it dry-cleaned but it was same-day so I don't know how effective it was," she told him as he looked up from the bag. His hair was messy; he had a mark on his cheek that she thought might turn into a bruise tomorrow and she couldn't remember when in the game he had gotten it. "It still kind of smells like smoke and perfume but it's not as bad as it was... I think it's not, anyway."

"You found a same-day dry cleaner?" he marveled, taking the sweater out of the bag.

"Oh, I have one on staff," she joked.

"The bat cave has been upgraded." He pressed the sweater to his face and inhaled thoughtfully. "I can still smell a bit of your perfume," he decided, "but no smoke."

"Sorry," she said just as he said, "No, I don't mind—" and they each laughed, embarrassed.

Silence fell between them, lip-biting awkwardness that Eloise was desperate to resolve. She wanted to get it over with—whatever he had to say, whatever distance he needed to put between them.

"So," she began, casting her gaze past the railing to glittering, damp Manhattan below.

"So. Here, sit down." Jacques dropped onto the bench of the table closest to them, and she followed his lead, surprised. She had not thought this would be a sit-down kind of conversation. "I wanted to apologize to you, and I didn't think I would have time later on the trip," he explained.

Eloise picked at the table, wrought-iron covered in bad black paint. When she looked up, Jacques was raking his teeth over his lip, considering his next words. But she did not want him to weigh his words with her. Even if she meant nothing to him—he meant so much to her. He was worthy of whatever work she put into this bond, even if she was preserving something minor, something small, something that would never become anything else, between panes of glass.

"It's really not necessary, Jacques—"

"No, it *is* necessary," he interrupted her, with some of that strength she had seen earlier creeping back into his voice. "Because I cannot—I cannot really tell you the effect you have had on my life."

Now she looked up in shock. This she had not expected. His gaze was direct, urgent. "When you told me about how and why you left the lab," he continued with more confidence, "it did something to me.

It was like—like I don't know, a switch was flipped. I was able to make a decision about something I had not been able to, before."

That decision hung between them. *Their mother*, he had said. The way he looked at Eloise now was so blazing. Every part of her had been touched by the sun.

"I know we do not know each other very well, but you mean a lot to me," he said, "and I treated you badly today, and I'm sorry. It just—I don't know," he confessed, shaking his head and mopping his face, "I don't know why it started to come out, I was just upset about—about other things, and I just sort of forgot who I'm supposed to be, or something—I cannot really explain it."

"Well," she said, her voice cracking, though he was kind enough not to point it out, "I have noticed lately that I'm most myself with the people who have done the most for me, and sometimes that means I'm a jerk to them. Kind of like how sometimes I've treated you a little rudely and—and you've actually changed me a lot, and done a lot for me, too."

"I haven't," he said in disbelief, but she smiled.

"Everyone always sees the worst in me, and I've never told anyone about what happened at the lab because of that. So when you were so accepting of me about it, so—so on my *side* about it, it just... yeah. A switch was flipped."

She shrugged, trying to swallow all of the emotions threatening to spill over.

His eyes would probably end her. Eloise had to keep talking. The words came out faster; she could not stop them. She needed him to understand that she saw him, that she knew him, that she respected him so powerfully for who he was in the dark, who he was when no one's eyes were upon him.

"And also—since we're here now, I might as well tell you—the way you care about others has changed me, too. I obviously don't know all the details of what you're dealing with privately, and you don't have to share anything with me, but—but I know you're... setting aside a lot of things, with Andrei being back on the team, and I know it must be hellish for you and I honestly don't know what I'd do in your position. Even I can barely look at him, having some idea of what happened, so I have no idea how you're dealing with it. And the fact that you're doing it because it's the right thing, the good thing, even if it's the most difficult thing—it just changed me."

She saw his throat move as he swallowed, saw his chest move with his deep breath, making the soft T-shirt shift along his skin.

"Did he tell you?" Jacques wanted to know, his voice quiet.

"Not intentionally." When he said nothing, Eloise continued. "Maybe I'm totally wrong, and I don't have any hard evidence so feel free to tell me to fuck off, but—just based on the way he said your wife's name in conversation..."

Jacques drew in a sharp breath and covered his face with his hands. Adrenaline coursed through her. She had been right.

He laughed sadly, dropping his hands from his face and shaking his head, his neck flushed.

"You know," he said ruefully, "they should have listened to you, at the lab. You might be psychic."

"Well, it's all because I consulted my tarot deck," she joked, earning a genuine laugh from him this time, and now he was fully flushed with embarrassment. "You might want to consult yours."

"You knew that, too," he noted. "I don't know how you did. My tattoo was never about the tarot."

He looked away, the light wind ruffling his ash brown hair, smiling, and she knew it was over.

She had fought against this all of her adult life—against being consumed by love, against being destroyed by how she felt for someone. But love was rain on the castle when you had prepared yourself for the enemy's fire; it was water seeping between stones, filling your keep with summertime petrichor as you looked up at wet rock and realized you had lost the greater war.

She was in love with him, and it was too late.

"Mad at your mother?" she guessed. "She was a psychic, right? I think I remember reading that." He was still smiling as he looked back at her.

"Yes," he confirmed, "I was nineteen and very angry and only smart enough to know not to confront her about it, but not smart enough to know that I was being stupid."

Eloise thought of her dad sitting in his chair, too afraid of the world and what it had done to him to go outside and greet it, too paralyzed with grief to take care of himself. She thought of how long she had avoided him, how long she had misunderstood him. She thought of Kyle, angry at his father, likely for whatever was happening now with his brother.

"Been there," she admitted.

"Yeah?"

"Yeah, only it's taken me until age thirty-three to get it." They laughed together. "Why the King of Cups?"

"Oh," he began, rubbing his nose in further, brief embarrassment and irritation, "it always stuck out to me. She used it to—I don't know—promise some perfect man to the women she did readings for. You know, they had been unlucky in love, but some man—this magic man, who was kind and gentle and loving and all of the perfect things and would love these women, no matter how imperfect they were—would soon mysteriously come into their lives and everything would change. And these women would buy into it, and she would take their money, but I knew she had ways of making sure that card always somehow appeared in the readings, and anyway our town was so small, there were not even enough men in the town for all of these—these fake promises she was making. And the man she was promising did not exist." Jacques shook his head again. "I was so childish about it. I did not understand it at all."

"So this was your way of saying 'fuck you' to her," Eloise guessed, and he laughed. "It's also a massive tattoo so it's the longest and most drawn-out 'fuck you' I have ever heard," she pointed out, and then they were laughing again, giddy and breathless and red-faced, shoulders shaking with laughter. "More like a fuuuuuuuuuuuuuuuuck yooooooooooooooooou."

"It was so painful, and it took so long, and now I don't want anyone to see it or even know about it. Even at the time, Andrei made fun of me for it for weeks and said it was the most immature thing he had ever seen. At best, they think I really buy into magical cards, and at worst, they make the connection that you did and find out what I really am."

"I understand. I never want anyone to know what I really am," she said, still laughing; but Jacques, suddenly, no longer was.

"You should. You *should* want them to know who you are, Eloise. I still don't understand why you don't."

And now that giddy breathlessness was gone, and they were regarding each other again.

The air had made their skin dewy and damp, and the lights edged his skin, painting him gold. He was the sun and had set her aglow and for the first time in her life she was rising, rising, taking up the sky and surrounded by glittering stars, and he had done it, and she had thought that tonight he was going to construct a wall between them but instead he had beckoned her across the bridge, and—

Later she would not understand how or why it happened. Some invisible hand was guiding her movements. She reached for his cheek just as he reached for her hand, and she surged with that singular joy of skin against skin—and then her hand was on his cheek, his rough stubble scraping her palm as he pressed her hand beneath his, holding it against him, his face tilting as though to press her palm to his mouth, she felt the rush of his breath across her skin and then—

They each dropped their hands and pulled back. Her heart was thumping, her hands were clammy and shaking, tingling where his breath had touched.

"Sorry," they both said. They got up from the table, not looking at each other. Jacques turned away, raking a hand over his hair, looking like he might swear.

"I—I don't really know what that was."

"We should head back down. I am very affectionate when I'm tired," Jacques said as they walked back to the door that led inside.

"Me too, apparently," Eloise agreed, not looking at him as he held the door open for her.

"Don't play hockey," he coached her as they got onto the elevator together. "You will get really affectionate and you will be embarrassed about it all the time. Speaking from experience."

"Oh, good. One career possibility I can check off the list," she said sarcastically as the elevator lurched downward. The fluorescent light was buzzing overhead and she could smell the scent of his skin; they were too close; it was overwhelming. "It was between that and stock market analyst, so this is helpful."

"You might do well in the stock market," Jacques reflected. The elevator pinged and the door slid open. "Being a psychic."

This was his floor. Their eyes met once more as he set his hand on the frame of the elevator to stop the door from closing. It was a gentle reference to their conversation, an acknowledgment of what had passed between them.

"Anyway." His smile was soft, but then abruptly it was gone and he was looking away from her. "See you tomorrow."

"Right." Her mouth had gone dry. She looked down. "See you tomorrow."

Back in her room, Nikki was sound asleep, snoring loudly. Eloise tiptoed around, changing into pajamas and brushing her teeth, hands still shaking and heart still racing.

He was known for his physical affection. She had watched him grab Kyle and kiss him just a few hours earlier; she had watched him touch each teammate on the arm as a ritual.

She crawled into bed, running one palm over the other like a prayer, not sure whether to erase or hold onto the slight scrape of his stubble, his breath on her skin, the feeling of his hand over hers...

And then out of nowhere she was thinking of Andrei again, always orbiting Jacques and never actually touching him, and she was wondering if Andrei had ever lay in bed like this, trying to decide whether to hold onto or let go of the feeling of being touched by Jacques, and that intuition that had been lingering around her about Andrei like smoke suddenly became solid. It was a rock that dropped into her stomach, and above all she pitied him so deeply and thought, once again, that she understood Andrei too well and did not like that she understood him so well.

She had only been asleep for a few hours when her phone vibrated on the pillow beside her, waking her in the small hours of the morning. Blearily she picked up the phone; it was just past five in the morning.

**Krystal [5:11am]**: there is a warrant out for kyle's arrest.

# Chapter Twenty-Two

Drugs had been found in Kyle's apartment. Apparently, his neighbor—that same elderly man that Eloise had seen on the stairs in Kyle's building—had put a tip in with the police out of suspicion. Eloise thought of that day she had first visited Kyle's apartment, and found the door unlocked. She wondered now if Robbie had been waiting on the other side, holding his breath, frozen in place and knowing someone was on the other side. She wondered if Robbie had been the one to plant the suspicion in that neighbor's mind.

Krystal was flying in from Boston along with some of the Bruins' legal team that morning to discuss their strategy. While boarding her flight, Krystal had texted Eloise, asking her to come prepared to the meeting in a few hours with all of her notes on Kyle that she had with her.

Luckily, Nikki had already left to help Dan to pack up for the Bruins' game against the Flyers tomorrow, so Eloise was free to prepare in the hotel room without question or comment. She used the hotel's printer to print out pictures of her wall-web, which she had captured on her phone in case she needed to reference it on the trip, as well as her many notes and other photographs—and her conversation with Robbie.

Now she waited outside the private conference room that had been booked in the hotel for their meeting, holding her old tablet and thick packet of printouts against her chest as she leaned against the wall. Everything had been building toward this moment for months, yet she did not feel prepared.

Someone cracked the door open and Eloise jolted back from the wall, straightening the tablet and papers in her arms. Alex poked his head into the hall.

"Oh, Eloise, you're already here," he whispered in surprise. "Krystal wanted me to go get you." He looked in confusion at the bundle in her arms, but didn't remark on it and instead gestured for her to enter the room.

It was a wall of tension. Kyle was slouched at one end of the conference table, pale and haunted, and he did not even glance up when Eloise entered the room. Jacques stood behind him, mussed hair still wet from a shower and wearing a slightly wrinkled hoodie and jeans, his arms folded across his chest as he listened intently to Krystal. His eyes flicked over Eloise as Alex gently shut the door behind her, and he frowned in confusion.

No. She had not known he was going to be here for this. She had been prepared for Kyle finding out the truth—she had been thinking of it all day, mourning the sibling-like friendship they had formed and knowing she would invariably burn that bridge—but she had not yet thought far enough ahead to the inevitability of losing Jacques.

Well, rather, losing whatever friendship they had developed. It was not like she *had* him in any way.

They were not the only ones here. Coach Duffy and some unfamiliar faces that she assumed were part of the Bruins' legal team also sat around the conference room, gulping coffee and listening to Krystal.

"...and so when he lands in Boston again, he will be under arrest," she finished, glancing at Eloise. Krystal was all polish and confidence now, in an excellent silk blouse and trousers, betraying none of the anxiety or disarray that Eloise had heard in her voice over the phone. "And not only do we have to deal with the matter of a hearing and trial, we also have to deal with the arrest itself, and be ready for that."

Kyle sank in his seat and covered his face with his hands.

"Depending on the bail amount that is posted, he would likely be able to at least play home games," one of the members of the legal team, a slender Black man with horn-rimmed glasses, explained to the room. Coach Duffy nodded thoughtfully. "Our team can work with Krystal's to craft the right statement."

"After the initial arrest, the two major challenges will be the bail hearing and the possible trial," Krystal added as she began to pace. "Ideally, the case is thrown out based on a drug test and the file we will be putting together, but we have to be prepared for the possibility that the case isn't thrown out, and that it goes to trial."

"What goes in the file?" Jacques asked, causing everyone to look at him. "Can it be statements on his character, how he's been in practice, that kind of thing?"

Eloise bit her lip.

"Yes," Krystal hedged, glancing again at Eloise, "and I have a few documents of my own to provide as well."

Eloise's heart was pounding in her ears; a cottony, consuming feeling that made her sick to her stomach. She wanted fresh air, she wanted to sit down, she wanted a cold glass of water. Jacques was staring in confusion at Krystal, clearly picking up on her evasiveness. His shoulders rose up slightly.

"What do you mean?" He kept his voice light, but his posture was stiff. *No no no no.* There was a lump in her throat. She stared at the carpet because it was too difficult to look at him.

"Well," Krystal said slowly, never taking her eyes off Jacques, "back when he was first drafted, you'll remember I had my suspicions about him."

"Yes," Jacques recalled with a tight nod. "I remember."

"And I know *you* felt that my gut sense didn't carry much weight," she continued, her voice growing stronger, "but I've been in this business a long time and my gut feelings don't come out of nowhere, Lavy. So I hired a private investigator to look into Kyle, and we have a lot of documentation on him now."

Kyle's hands dropped from his face.

"You *what*?" Jacques asked Krystal in disbelief. Kyle was staring at Krystal; he looked like he might be sick, and Eloise averted her gaze from him. It was too hard to look at him, to watch him learn how his privacy had been invaded. Krystal lifted her chin as she faced Jacques.

"I hired a private investigator," she repeated.

Eloise realized she was watching the first splitting of a relationship that had been held up by steel for nearly two decades. The cabling was fraying for the very first time. And soon she was going to have that look of disgust turned upon her.

*No no no no no.* He had meant so much to her; he had *changed* her. He had lit her up in the way that no one ever had before. She could not bear to lose him.

But there was Kyle between them, hunched and afraid, and doing his very best to hide how afraid he was. And she might have fallen for Jacques but she loved Kyle and, anyway, eventually this would come out, now that he was here and now that Krystal had admitted to it. It was too late. She had missed her chance to turn around.

She would see this one through. Love was not always romantic; now it was her turn to be the Hanged Man. It was what she admired most about Kyle, that he had willingly sacrificed himself—his reputation, his personal beliefs, a swath of his skin—in honor of someone he loved.

It occurred to her, as she stepped away from the wall, that perhaps Kyle's tattoo was about sacrifice.

"It's me," she said.

All heads swiveled to her. Duffy was in shock, Alex worried and uncertain. Krystal looked grimly satisfied, Kyle was wary—

—and Jacques was cold as ice.

He drew in a sharp breath as though she had struck him.

"Krystal hired me. I have—I have a whole folder of evidence on Kyle," she added, her voice stronger now. Love was sacrifice, and after all that she had learned and all that she guessed about Kyle, he was worthy of that sacrifice—he was worthy of the work. "I'm happy to provide all of it to the legal team, and I am happy to testify. I haven't finished my investigation, but I'm pretty confident in what I have."

"What you 'have,'" Jacques blurted.

"I have a lot of evidence," she replied evenly, gripping her tablet against the urge to crumple, to turn away, to run, to flee, "that Kyle's younger brother is active in alt-right groups and Kyle has been working to control and limit his little brother's activity in these groups. And I have some evidence that they have figured him out, and I believe they're framing him. I've been tailing him for weeks—months, actually—and keeping up with his activity online, as well as the activity of his brother. He has been associating with someone named Robbie, who, I believe, is the one actively framing him. Robbie goes by Fenris88 on social media and I just managed to make contact yesterday. I have the transcripts of our conversation and am happy to share. We talked about Kyle and he implied that Kyle was 'out' of the group."

Kyle was now staring at her in open horror, shoulders drawing up in unmistakable shame. It was horrible to see, so she looked away. She was losing him too. Sometimes love was a closed fist; sometimes it was crumbling ground. "I have a file on him at my apartment in Boston, which has the most detail, but I also have documentation here on my tablet as well as what I've printed out from my phone."

She set the tablet and papers on the table. "You're free to look through it and review my notes and photos, and I'm happy to answer any questions about that documentation. But there's nothing to suggest that Kyle himself is using or selling drugs, and a lot to suggest that he has an enemy."

"Still mad I hired her?" Krystal asked Jacques as Eloise unlocked the tablet. The lawyer with the horn-rimmed glasses took the tablet from her once she had opened the right folder, and began reviewing the contents.

"Worse. I am disgusted with you," Jacques admitted.

Kyle hunched lower in his chair and took his hat off, raking a hand over his greasy red hair.

"He could have told us about this himself. The invasion of a young player's privacy—you know how I feel about that—"

"If you're so against it, then why are you so willing to do it—"

"Because it's my job—but it should not be anyone else's—"

"Jacques, you insisted that this *boy* join our team, this boy with a history of drug abuse and violence, and you expect me to not be ready?" Krystal fired back. "You've got another think coming if you think I'm not going to be prepared for the worst. I don't live in a fantasy land like you do about people—I expect the worst because the worst is usually true."

"'Drug abuse and violence?' He smoked some pot and got into a few fights in school," Jacques said coldly. "I would not call that drug abuse or violence. Are you going to investigate me, too, Krystal? Because you will find worse than that. And then you bring a stranger onto *my* team"—he glanced at Eloise, and she could not glean anything from it—"under some ridiculous scheme so she can invade his privacy, and ours." He shrugged, a move of unbridled fury. "I cannot imagine how you expect me to get past this."

"Well—maybe you do get past it and maybe you don't," Krystal said back, just as coldly, though Eloise knew this was destroying her even if she did not let a flicker of it show on her face. She loved Jacques; she loved him like a brother, a colleague, a close friend—she loved him like family. "I did what I thought was best at the time, and I'm glad I did. Now we have objective evidence that is going to protect this kid and protect our team."

"Kyle could have given that to us," Jacques said, "had you just spoken to him and asked."

"You think so? You think that story would fly if it came from him? I think you sound really naive right now, and I am done discussing this with you." She turned to Coach Duffy and the lawyer. "We have some calls to make."

"Right." The lawyer held up the tablet as he turned to Eloise, and she waved him off mutely, signaling for him to keep it, because she did not trust her voice. "You're coming with us, Hearst. We've got work to do."

Kyle was pale. "Can—do you think you can help Pat—"

"We've got to focus on helping *you* right now," Coach Duffy said, earning a disgusted scoff from Jacques. "But we can talk about your brother, too," he added hastily at the look on Jacques's face.

They filtered out of the conference room with Alex anxiously following, leaving Jacques and Eloise alone with this mustard carpet and fluorescent lighting, and all of his billowing, horrible, awful disdain.

Their eyes met. Eloise gripped the back of the chair.

"I guess I was right," he said quietly as he regarded her. "You are so—so *dishonest*," he continued with a shake of his head. "I was right to not trust you around Kyle."

"Oh, you think I should've introduced myself as Eloise the private detective?" she scoffed, blinking against the urge to cry tears of hot anger. A muscle in his jaw twitched; he pressed his lips together. "You think I should've gone around and told everyone exactly what my assignment was? That would've made a *whole* lot of sense, and, most importantly, *you* would feel better about—"

"I thought you really cared about Kyle, the way I did," Jacques cut in. "I thought you saw him the way I did, I thought you were paying attention to him because you understood him. It made me—"

He looked away. "Never mind."

"No comment, as usual?" Eloise asked as he blurred before her, her last chance to wound him as he was wounding her. "You know, the only person who's more dishonest than me is you."

"Yeah?"

"Yeah. Maybe not dishonest—maybe treacherous," she corrected, wiping her eyes. "Maybe that's a better word for you."

"Maybe you're right," he said bitterly. "But at least you knew my name all along."

He walked past her, then for one burning, blooming moment he paused at the door—he had one hand on the door and she almost thought he might turn, might change his mind, might reach for her again like he had just last night—but then with a last bitter shake of his head and a clench of his fist he left her there in the conference room alone.

Eloise bought a train ticket from New York to Boston that afternoon, after she had gotten a harried text from Krystal that she would swing by to pick up the rest of Kyle's folder tomorrow. There was no need for her to continue pretending to be her intern, of course, so Eloise sat in Penn Station with nothing but her raw anger and grief over Jacques, and her fears about Kyle, while the team prepared to fly to Philadelphia for their game against the Flyers.

She was in agony. Somehow even when she *did* put in the work, she lost people. Maybe she was destined to be alone, aloof, separate from others: in permanent exile, the witch in the woods, that strange pale creature who haunted the trees and sang in the night.

Her phone pulsed with a text from an unknown number, and she unlocked the screen with a sense of foreboding.

**HELLO, FRIEND! This is Alex. From the Bruins! How ya holding up?**

She looked skywards to pull herself together before replying.

**Eloise [12:14pm]**: i've been better, tbh! thanks for asking - just waiting for my train back to boston now

**Eloise [12:15pm]**: how is it there?

**Alex [12:16pm]**: NOT GREAT! Poor Kyle Hearst is definitely freaking out. Krystal is scary. I think it's weird for her and Jacques Lavesque to have a falling out like this.

**Alex [12:16pm]**: Anyway I think you're a totally awesome lady and I'm so grateful you were tailing Kyle Hearst and I just wanted you to know that.

**Alex [12:16pm]**: Shall we get lobstah (ha!) rolls when I get back?

In spite of everything, she found herself laughing on the platform as she tried not to cry. She wiped her stinging eyes.

**Eloise [12:16pm]**: i would absolutely love that. i will ask my brother where we should go - i bet he knows a good place for lobstah rolls!

Alex sent her a series of GIFs from *The Office* to show his enthusiasm, and Eloise locked her phone screen again and put on her sunglasses to hide how bright her eyes had gotten. Her gratitude toward his kindness was immeasurable, and the agony lightened a little. She would have to find some way to thank him later.

Eventually her train arrived, and Eloise shuffled on with the other passengers, still wearing her sunglasses and still checking her phone every three seconds, as though she could somehow miss a text or a call. She watched New York fly past, with no word from Krystal—or anyone else. And as she watched the city move around her, a new fear settled in, joining the many others that brewed within her.

If they had found drugs in his apartment and tested them—what if it was the same lab—what if it was Charlie—

But no, she told herself. That would be too much of a coincidence. And maybe Charlie didn't even work at the lab anymore; it had been a long time, after all. She perused LinkedIn, but he had never had a profile on the website anyway, and she found nothing from her search except that Monique had moved on to a private lab somewhere in Connecticut.

She had no friends that she could reach out to from the lab, and she knew if she cold-called, they would share nothing. They had always been careful to guard the identities of their chemists for obvious reasons, and an anonymous caller would not get any information.

She could wait outside of the lab and watch for him. If Charlie wasn't working there anymore, there would be no need to say anything. Maybe he had retired, or maybe he had been quietly moved into a different position. She looked through social media but found nothing on him or his family; she did find Monique but was quick to click away from her profile, and the surge of emotion made her put her phone aside so she could stare out the window.

Why did she repel the people who mattered most to her?

But she didn't repel everyone. Alex had texted her, and Hollis insisted on sticking in her life, even if sometimes all they had to show for it was sibling friction and frustration. And for a short time, she had been part of the Bruins organization. She had belonged, she had fit in, she had been liked.

And as the world went by in a blur past her, she reflected on the fact that all of her biggest regrets always came down to the same thing: a lack of love, a need to preserve herself and protect herself from the damage that she knew love could do, from the damage that love was doing to her now. Love was elemental; love was destructive; love was warm water that could cleanse you or close over your head. Love was the Wheel of Fortune, cyclical and never static.

When she got back to her apartment, Eloise shed the Bruins fleece she had been wearing. The angry part of her wanted to throw it out, but she was not quite ready to give up the version of herself that she had gotten to experience while wearing that fleece—the version of herself that Jacques Lavesque had given her. She tucked it in the closet beside her black Prada dress—another version of herself that Jacques Lavesque had given to her, a version of herself that was confident and selfless and surrounded by love, a version of herself that she had not known was possible.

She spent some time pulling together her file on Kyle, printing out all of her notes and screenshots and then assembling them in one of her folders, labeling and documenting, working with robotic movements as she contemplated what she would do.

She could just hand over everything and be done with it all—with Krystal, with Kyle, with the Bruins. She could end it all and start fresh, her future a blank slate once again. She could turn around and save herself from this. Eloise was so good at running away, so good at sending herself further into exile; she could always do it again.

That night she got a call from Krystal to arrange a meeting the next day to hand over the folders. Her tone had been businesslike, and now Eloise knew that when Krystal sounded like that, it was because she cared so much it was painful. Krystal also mentioned settling the account, a stray comment that made Eloise sit on her couch numbly until the small hours of the night.

Settling the account—striking the balance, clearing the history. Ending the sentence so that a new one could start. Eloise knew how to start fresh; she had done it before and she knew she could do it again. But her heart ached for Kyle, for the love he had for his brother. She was not ready to end this sentence just yet.

She would see this one through.

Early the next morning she made the trek to the lab that she had spent so many years at, traveling to every morning in her shitty car, Boston going by around her as she listened to music, as she fretted about dating, as she daydreamed about the future she had now. She wore the black beanie she always wore when doing surveillance, and black sunglasses that hid much of her face. She lingered on the sidewalk before the lab, pretending to be on her phone, as she watched the parking lot for Charlie.

And sure enough, the battered gold Buick rattled into the parking lot, and her heart broke all over again as she watched him sit in his car for a moment. When he got out, it was worse: always a portly man, he had dropped significant weight, and was nearly unrecognizable as he made his way to the employee entrance of the lab, skeletal and shadowed.

Eloise made her way back to Boston as she wrestled with her choice. To say nothing would mean that she did not open herself up to possible investigation; it would mean she did not wreck Charlie's life any further than she already had. To say nothing would be to preserve her livelihood and make a cleaner break with the Bruins organization, and with Kyle's case.

But to say nothing also meant she was possibly allowing something to happen to Kyle, something that she *knew* he did not deserve.

For two days, she said nothing. She did nothing. Another man from the Bruins' legal team—a brisk guy in a polar fleece who had little curiosity about her—showed up at her door, and for days afterward, she heard nothing save for a few cryptic texts from Krystal that the investigation was 'progressing' and that Kyle's bail hearing had been scheduled. The rest of her payment was deposited into her account, with Krystal's promise that any further time spent with the legal team would count as billable hours. Eloise stared at the number in her account, a number that it had not seen in a long time—yet a number, she knew, that would not be enough to preserve this version of herself. She should have been working on bringing in new clientele, or applying to new jobs. She should have been doing something, anything.

But instead, she hid in her apartment and did nothing except contemplate all that had happened and mourn all that she had lost. For two days, she lived with what she knew—until at last, on Friday, she sat up on her bed.

She knew what she had to do. She picked up her cell phone, and she called her brother.

"Hey." She bit her lip to stop her chin from wobbling.

"Yoooooo Ellieeeeeeeeee," Hollis bellowed into the phone; he clearly had put her on speakerphone. "I'm in the middle of cleaning my car, because I let Lily eat tacos on the way home when she was drunk last night and then she threw them up, and there's shredded lettuce and vomit, like, everywhere," he explained. There was a plasticky rattling noise and then some cursing. "What's up?"

She methodically ran the cable of her charger through her hand, a grim flashback to just a week ago when she had called Hollis to apologize and promise him that she would do better.

She drew in a breath.

"Hey. Um. So. Can I come over and talk to you about something today? I... I need your advice on something."

"Oh, yeah, sure." He sounded taken aback. The rattling stopped. "Is everything okay?"

"Yeah, it's fine. It's just kind of complicated."

"Alright, well, why don't you come by Dad's? Lily and I are going over there later and I'm gonna make a few meals for him for the week. We can talk while I cook." He sounded cautious. "I'm heading over there around two."

"Okay, yeah." She did not exactly want Dad to hear this, did not want Hollis and Dad to resort to their usual dynamic with her—she was the disaster and they were the two wise men, chortling at her foolishness—but on the other hand, she was desperate, and Dad probably wouldn't even be in the kitchen anyway. "See you then."

They hung up and Eloise looked around her apartment, which she certainly could no longer pretend to afford. She had never decorated it, had never really tried to make it a home, almost like she had known all along that she would have to leave it. Now that she knew the end was near, she wished she had let herself love it a little.

Well. Maybe there was a lesson in there, if she was bold enough to hear it.

By the time she got to her childhood home, Hollis's blue Ford Fiesta was already parked on the street, and Lily was affixing a Halloween-themed wreath to the front door, a Target cloth bag beside her.

"Yo," she greeted in a hoarse voice, glancing over her shoulder as Eloise walked up the front steps. She looked puffy and pale, her black hair greasy. "I would hug you but I might hurl." She narrowed her eyes. "You look worse than me. What's going on?"

"Just a kind of rough few days. I was going to help Hollis cook and talk." She nodded to the wreath, decorated with little ghosts and fuzzy spiders and candy corn. "You need help with that?"

"No, it's just that it's kind of too big for this door and it looks over-the-top no matter where I put it, but I guess a wreath with glittering spiders on it was never going to be subtle," she admitted. "You should head inside and leave me to my suffering. I'm just going to be out here living in denial for a little bit longer." She stepped back from the door to allow Eloise to pass.

The house smelled like roasting chicken. Dad was in his usual chair when she walked in, his eyes glued to the television. He vaguely acknowledged her as she passed, and she wondered if he was simply ashamed about their last encounter. In the newly-gleaming kitchen, Hollis (wearing a navy Williams-Sonoma apron over his chambray shirt) was chopping carrots with surgical precision.

"Ellie! You're here," he yelled over the sound of chopping. "Not that I actually *should* trust you with a knife, but you can chop the bell peppers. We're prepping *snacks*," he informed her, nodding to a green supermarket bag full of bell peppers. "I saw this thing on TikTok? Where she pre-chopped the peppers and then put the hummus at the bottom of the container? And like, it saves time and effort, and I just love that."

Eloise tried not to laugh as she shucked her jacket and washed her hands, which were still a little shaky with nerves.

"Okay, how am I slicing them?" she asked when she had pulled herself together again.

"Long ways, duh. The way you'd want to snack on them."

Eloise washed the peppers as Hollis hummed to himself and chopped. "So what's this about *advice*? I'm so intrigued. You never want my opinion."

Eloise sliced into the first pepper.

"It's kind of a long story," she hedged.

"Well, we've got a lot of snacks to prep. Come on, out with it. I'm dying of curiosity. This is literally the first time that you have ever tapped me for advice, even though I'm probably the smartest person you know."

"You probably are," she agreed with a laugh. "Like actually."

She began chopping slowly, because her hands were shaking again. "You have to promise not to hate me, okay? Because I was doing my best at the time and I—I really thought it was the right thing to do."

Hollis stopped chopping to stare at her, brow furrowed.

"Just—just promise me you're not going to hate me, okay?" She laughed again, a fake sound.

"El, you're more likely to hate me than I am to hate you," Hollis pointed out quietly. "I could never hate you. *You're* always the one who goes radio silent. Not me."

"Yeah, because I don't want you to think even worse of me than you already do." She looked back at the bell peppers. "Anyway." She began chopping. "Here it goes."

At first the words came out halting and awkward: how it had been working at the lab, how she had started paying attention to Charlie, how she and Monique had become friends. Hollis said nothing, just listened as they worked, and soon the words came out more smoothly: how she had become certain of what Charlie was doing, how she had confronted her manager about it, and then how it had all exploded in her face—how she had been asked to leave, how her friendship with Monique had ended, and how that had launched her into her private investigative work.

A few times Hollis paused in his chopping, and she could feel him staring at her, but she avoided his eyes and kept going, kept talking, not allowing herself to look and find out what he really thought. The floodgates had been opened, and her secret was out, and it was stupid but again she was thinking of Jacques, and she shoved the thought of him out of her head. It was over.

And then she came to the present: to her time with the Bruins, to Krystal's ask, to Kyle's secrets and how she had been tailing him and what she had learned about him.

Her throat was getting hoarse and she had run out of things to help Hollis prep, and somehow they ended up at the little kitchen table, sitting across from each other with coffee while she sat with her feet on the wall—in the way that had once infuriated their mother—and Hollis studied her as she talked. It was like a bloodletting, and she did not think anything could have stopped her now that she was going.

When she had finished, they sat in silence. Somewhere a lawn-mower was going, just audible over the sound of the baseball game coming from the living room. Their mugs were empty and the kitchen smelled like chicken and roasting onions. Eloise counted the tiles on the kitchen floor.

"Jesus, Ellie," Hollis said at last. *"Jesus."*

"I know." She toyed with the empty mug. "So I... I think I'm going to have to speak up and say something, right? I mean, for all I know, they've fixed the problem with Charlie—or, I guess, it was never a problem at all and I was the problem all along. But I just—"

And here her voice grew stronger, and for the first time since she had started talking, she faced her older brother. "I know Kyle wasn't doing drugs. I know he wouldn't have them in his apartment. And I *know* he's just made that guy Robbie angry because—"

"You've *got* to speak up about it," Hollis put in suddenly. His brows were knit together as he looked at her, his eyes bright. "Ellie, *why* didn't you tell us about—" He faltered and looked down, shaking his head.

"Because you and Dad have always acted like I'm the failure, the fuck-up, the disaster," she said. "Every time I screw up, every time something goes wrong in my life, you both just... you leap on top of it. Okay? And I was ashamed, and—"

"I'm sorry." Hollis stared at her again. "I never—I guess I thought—I don't know, I guess I thought we were just being funny." He drew in a breath. "I didn't know it bothered you. I really, genuinely thought you knew we were always just kidding. You always act so *aloof*, and like everything's fine, or else *you* make jokes about being a disaster and then I assume it's like a running joke? I don't know. I never thought it bothered you."

He shook his head. "I don't think you're a failure at all. I *do* think you're a messy person," he conceded with a fond smile, "but you're also, I dunno, really brave. And strong."

She did not have anything to say to that. She focused on the table, biting her lip and gripping her empty mug.

"And you do have to speak up. Like, I'm pretty sure you're morally obligated to."

Eloise covered her face.

"Hollis, it is going to fuck up my life. I'm definitely going to lose any possible business if it turns into a big thing, or if I get sued for, I don't know, defamation or something, and I don't have any other clients other than Krystal right now. I have nothing in the pipeline, and no savings left, and I'm also in debt. And I have no way of insulating myself against whatever the fallout is, you know?"

"Sure you do," Hollis insisted. "That's—"

"Okay, you *absolutely* have to speak up, and also, you have to get the Bruins organization to agree to cover any resultant legal fees," Lily said as she breezed into the kitchen.

Eloise looked up in shock.

"Oh, Fred and I were listening in the dining room," Lily explained matter-of-factly as she took their empty mugs and stacked them in the sink. "And stop playing with these, it's annoying me."

Eloise looked over her shoulder. Dad was leaning against the dining room table, just visible over the stacks of mail and newspapers, his back to her. At the sound of his name he pushed off from the table and slipped back to the TV room.

Eloise looked back at Lily, who, in spite of being extremely grey and pallid today, also looked significantly more alive than she had out on the front step.

"You need a lawyer, and you can probably get help from this Krystal woman on that front—maybe you can even consult with the Bruins' legal team," she said, counting off on her fingers, "and they can help you decide whether to go to a media outlet or bring it to court. I mean, it could be like a whole *exposé*—"

"No way, it won't look legit. She's got to do it through the case," Hollis said, shaking his head. "Their legal team will eat that shit up. It will be like Christmas to them."

"Okay, now that you put it like that, I totally agree—and you need to talk to Krystal about how they can help to protect you here. You're definitely going to have to testify on it too, which will be awkward as hell, but better to be awkward than a bad person," Lily concluded.

Eloise couldn't stop grinning.

"What?" Lily snapped.

"I don't know. I'm just happy," she admitted. Lily rolled her eyes, then covered her mouth and went to the sink, holding up a finger against them until the urge to vomit had passed.

"You absolutely should not be happy. You are in a *world* of drama right now and it's about to explode, but whatever, live your life," Lily said breathlessly, mopping her clammy brow. "Now, there's also the matter of your job and income which will *totally* be paused while this is all going down—"

"She can live here."

The kitchen fell silent.

Dad was hunched in the doorway, hands shoved in his pockets. He wasn't looking at any of them, but Lily's eyes were wide as she looked between them, reminding Eloise of one of those Felix the Cat clocks, and Hollis's brows had disappeared under his bangs as he gripped the table, staring at their father. Dad shifted his weight.

"I'm not using her room for anything else," he added with a shrug. And without another word, he went back into the TV room, and the volume of the Red Sox game grew louder.

"Right," Lily said after a moment. "That—that clears that up."

"Y-yeah," Eloise agreed. Hollis was watching her carefully, but none of them knew how to react.

"Okay, we can unpack that later, because I honestly don't even know where to start. Finally, and maybe most importantly, we need to talk about Jacques Lavesque."

Lily pulled the third chair from the table and sat in front of Eloise.

"Wait, what?" Hollis asked, perking up at the name of his hero. Lily rolled her eyes.

"Were you not listening? They obviously had a thing going, and he screwed it up—"

"WHAT? Eloise didn't say that! You didn't say you had a *thing* with Jacques Lavesque!" Hollis yelled as he pushed back from the table, pointing a finger at Eloise. "You just said you had *talked* with him a lot about Kyle Hearst—"

"It was not a thing, Lily," Eloise interrupted. "I mean, whatever it was, it was one-sided, and when he found out my job, he made it very clear how he felt about me. And it was not good."

She couldn't go any further than that. Lily's nostrils flared.

"I hope he gets cancer," she said coldly, tossing her thick hair. Hollis gasped, appalled. "Face cancer, if that's a thing."

"What!? That might be the ugliest thing you have ever said. That is horrifying. Lily, he is *married* with *two sons*—"

"He's getting divorced, actually, if you were even listening to what she was saying—"

"And he's *Jacques Lavesque*, he can't get *cancer*, he has to play hockey forever—"

"He obviously broke her heart, Hollis, so HE HAS TO DIE," Lily bellowed over Hollis's words.

"He didn't break—" Eloise halted at the withering look on Lily's face. "I mean, yes. He completely broke my heart. Worse than it has ever been broken before."

"Pulverized it, didn't he," Lily supplied sympathetically, patting Eloise on the forearm. "Crushed it into the ground. Yeah, it's pretty obvious. So, he needs to die, but also—you need to start dating. You're going to be seeing him a *lot* if this turns into a whole legal thing, right? Oh, god. We need to get to work *right away*. You need to get your roots done"—Lily peered at Eloise—"and your brows, honestly, no offense, and you need to have lots of men blowing up your phone, because he is unfortunately *gorgeous* and that is going to really hurt."

"What's wrong with her brows?" Hollis wanted to know, but Lily waved him off dismissively as she took out her phone.

"I'm booking you an appointment with my girl. And I'm setting you up with my cousin Jeff. He's kind of a himbo, and also he's a couple of years younger than you? But he's big and nice and he will totally treat you with respect. Ooh, and we should set you up with Owen," she added, typing faster on her phone.

"Lily, that's really not—"

"HUSH. You asked for help and you're getting it," Lily snapped. Hollis was frowning.

"Owen is too much of a finance bro," he complained as he rubbed his chin, apparently recovered from his disgust. "He's not going to get Ellie at all."

"Doesn't matter. He's hot and tall and age-appropriate and he'll pay for dinner," Lily said. "This is about quantity, not quality, Hollis. He admittedly cannot compete with Jacques Lavesque, face-wise, but he'll do for now. It's literally any port in a storm. We need her phone to be absolutely *blowing up* for the next few months. She won't even be able to *look* at him when she sees him in court because she'll be too busy dealing with all of the notifications on her phone," she said gleefully. "Ooh, what do you think of Jacob?" she asked Hollis, wiggling her brows.

"Republican Jacob? Or culinary Jacob?" Hollis asked doubtfully.

"Obviously culinary Jacob," she countered, and Hollis tilted his head and rubbed his chin.

"Yeah, I mean, he's a nice guy... I don't know if he's single right now, though, and he's got a kind of annoying laugh."

Hollis and Lily went through Lily's contact list, debating the pros and cons and the relationship status of every male name therein, as Eloise sat there trying to grapple with how everything had changed, yet again, in the space of a few hours.

After a while, she got up from the table. Hollis and Lily were only on S—"What about Spencer?" Lily posed, earning an immediate, "Ugh, no way, he's not getting anywhere near my little sister," from Hollis—so she had a while before they would re-emerge.

Awkwardly, she walked into the TV room. Dad was fixed on the television, but the game was on commercial break.

"Who... who's winning?" she asked, clearing her throat.

"We're slaughtering the Rays," he said without looking up as she dropped into the other chair. On the screen, a woman was gasping with awe as she wiped down her marble countertops in her sparkling kitchen. Eloise noticed there were no mugs around him, but rather a glass of water that Hollis had undoubtedly put there. "But the season is more or less over. It doesn't really matter now."

They sat in silence, watching but not watching the commercial.

"Right. Well. Are you sure you're okay with me moving in for a while? Just for a couple of months, I think. I need to—I need to figure out my career, anyway—"

"Of course I'm okay with it, Ellie. I asked you to." He looked down a little distastefully at his water, and then put the glass back on the side table without drinking it.

The game resumed and Eloise let her gaze fix on the screen without interpreting what was happening on it. She had the vague urge to tell Dad about Kyle, about his love for the Red Sox and the hat that he refused to take off, and then she was thinking about love, and the many ways that it could look, and then she was thinking about Jacques again, and then she was getting choked up so she knew she had to stay silent.

Minutes later, Dad spoke again, after finally taking a sip of the water. "We'll have to clean your room, though," he said, grimacing. "Haven't been in there in years. And it wasn't exactly clean when you moved out, either."

"You really are hating that water, huh?" was all she could ask as she watched him force another sip.

"It has bubbles in it," he complained. "Holl said it would be more interesting than regular water."

She was picturing Hollis buying the sparkling water because he thought it would be more exciting to a recovering alcoholic than regular water, loading it in Dad's fridge, lovingly pouring him a glass and squeezing lemon into it. And she was thinking of Dad in the dining room, listening in on their conversation and concluding that it was time to be a parent again, just for a little while. Love was sparkling water in the refrigerator; love was saved TikToks on healthy snacks; love was an open palm even when it had once been a closed fist.

"Gross," she agreed, and Dad nodded, satisfied, and they went back to watching the game again.

# Chapter Twenty-Three

A few days later, after Kyle had had his bail hearing, Eloise made the pilgrimage to Warrior Ice Arena, this time in a black car that Krystal had hired for her. It was raining today, and the insistent squeak of the windshield wipers and the lurching traffic, slowed by the rain, did nothing for her anxiety, an ever-expanding thing inside of her that made it difficult to breathe. As much as she didn't want to actually get to the arena, she was relieved when they finally reached the parking garage and she was able to get out of the airless car.

She might see Jacques and she might not. She did not know how much involvement he would have in this case, especially as it did not concern him, and especially as he and Krystal were, according to Alex who had been texting her over the last few days, still very much at odds. She also had no idea how the other players, particularly those close to Jacques, would act around her. She gripped the strap of her tote bag as she walked through the automatic doors.

As she walked around the corner toward the elevator, she heard a clamor of voices from the ice. They would have their morning skate now. She paused, listening, and heard Burnie's distinctive shriek, followed by Travis and Connor's guffawing laughter.

She was losing them, too. But maybe she had never really had them—maybe Jacques wasn't the only one who lived in a fantasy world.

She had to keep going. Eloise took the elevator, per Krystal's directions, up to the floor with the head offices and conference rooms. When she found the right one, she drew in a deep breath and knocked on the door.

"Come in," came a cultured man's voice. Before she could turn the handle, the door swung open before her, revealing a long, glossy table. Men and women in impeccable suiting sat around the table with glasses of water and laptops and notebooks. Coach Duffy was absent, but Krystal was there, and Kyle too, as well as the woman that Eloise had seen at Kyle's house—Caff (a nickname for Cathy, Eloise had learned) still in a Patriots jersey, with a denim jacket over top.

She caught Kyle's eye, but as ever, he revealed nothing.

"Eloise, right? Brandon—I didn't get the chance to introduce myself last time," said the lawyer who had opened the door, the same one who had come to New York. Today he wore a burgundy suit and matching glasses. He gestured for her to sit in one of the empty chairs when she nodded, and Eloise took her seat, grateful that Lily had insisted on the mini-makeover over the weekend now that she was surrounded by such polished people.

"Jason Schwartz," said another lawyer, a skinny guy with dark hair who had the rangy body and shadowed face of a long-distance runner. He looked too young to be practicing law.

"Neema Ahmad," added the woman next to him, emerald earrings the size of robin's eggs glistening amongst her thick waves as she reached across the table to shake Eloise's hand.

"Glen," said the oldest one simply—subtly pinstriped suit and poofy white hair—with barely a glance up from his notes.

"Krystal tells us that you had additional context that you wished to add to the case, in addition to the notes you provided," he continued after she had settled down and Jason had poured her a glass of water. "We'd like to run through that as well as your notes."

Eloise accepted the glass of water, relishing the cool feeling of the glass against her skin. She actually *was* thirsty—her mouth was dry, and her stomach was still churning from her anxiety—but she was too nervous to take a sip, because she felt like she was on stage. She still did not know if Kyle shared Jacques's sentiments. She would not blame him if he did, especially as the pictures she had taken of him in his apartment were fanned out on the table between them. She tried to read him, to gauge his feelings toward her, but he merely looked exhausted and apathetic, slouched in his chair and avoiding everyone's eyes.

"Yes, I understand that a drug specimen was collected from Kyle's apartment and will be sent to a lab for testing," she began, conscious of all eyes being on her, "and I used to be a forensic bench chemist, so I know a lot about that process, especially how it's done for cases in Boston."

Caff's plucked brows shot up with interest. Krystal, who already knew what Eloise was about to say, began pacing in front of the wall of windows.

"I was actually fired for trying to call attention to a flaw in that process, one that could potentially lead to wrongful convictions, or wrongful acquittals," Eloise added.

"We're listening," said Neema, leaning forward, pen in hand.

Hours later, Eloise felt wrung out. She had recounted, in nauseating and excruciating detail, multiple times over, how she had been fired. She had had to dig around in her email for records; she'd had to look back through her phone for dates and names. The team of lawyers had grilled her as she had never been grilled before, and though at one point a table of sandwiches and bags of chips had been wheeled in, no one had eaten—these people did not seem to run on food—and now she was limp and drained.

It was still raining as she walked, alone, to the front doors. The car that Krystal had hired was waiting at the curb to take her back to her father's house. She pushed open the arena door and stumbled out into the rain—and looked back when she heard the click of the door again.

Kyle was approaching her, shoulders hunched and hands shoved in his pockets. The rain misted her cheeks as she paused for him.

"H-hey," she greeted hoarsely.

Now was her only chance to explain to him, and she had to seize it, she had to make him understand. "I—"

"Hey."

And then Kyle threw his arms around her for the second time ever, and hugged her impossibly tight, squeezing her until it was hard to breathe. Immediately she had to scrunch her eyes shut against the urge to cry; she returned the embrace just as tightly, and for a moment they stood there in the rain. "Thanks," he muttered.

"Oh. No problem," she joked, grinning into his shirt when he laughed. He released her, visibly embarrassed. Over his shoulder Eloise saw that Caff had come out to join them, lingering by the doors uncertainly.

"Hi," she called to the woman with an awkward wave.

"Thank you," Caff mouthed to her, before slipping back inside, leaving her and Kyle alone together once more.

"She used to be friends with my mom," Kyle explained, following Eloise's gaze. "Now she bugs me about everything like she's my adopted mom."

"She loves you," Eloise said. Kyle rolled his eyes, but the look he shot the door where Caff had disappeared was fondly exasperated and full of love. "Your dad didn't want to join?"

"Getting here would be hard for him; the accessibility's not great." The disappointment in his voice was not hidden, and Eloise guessed that Jimmy Hearst's physical disability was not actually what prevented him from coming here to support Kyle, as she knew that Krystal would have happily moved mountains to make it possible.

"I wasn't sure if you'd be mad at me," Eloise admitted, hugging her bag to her chest, grateful that she could blame any wetness in her eyes on the rain. Kyle scoffed.

"Nah. I mean, it is a little weird that you were following me around," he conceded after a moment's thought, "and it took me a little while to get used to the fact that you know so much random shit about me and that you had all those pictures of my place and all. But I don't think it really changes anything."

He shifted his weight, the way she knew he did when he was nervous, moving around distractedly. "I thought about it a lot. I think if you didn't give a shit about me, you wouldn't have gotten all that stuff."

This simple faith in her—this simple loyalty.

"I was actually planning on dropping the case in the beginning," she told him in a rush of relief. "Because I couldn't afford to keep going. But I started to see you in the way—in the way that Lavesque does..."

It was awkward to call him Lavesque. Kyle's mouth twisted in a sneer.

"Yeah. He's out of his fucking tree," he said with a loose, disgusted wave.

"No, I think he really understood you, and—"

"No, I mean about this." He gestured between them and the building, glancing up a few stories.

"He's got a right to be mad. I did lie about a lot of—"

"Yeah, whatever. It was your job, and if he wasn't so goddamn weird about you, he'd get that," Kyle said impatiently.

"Thanks," she said instead of all the things she wanted to say, and Kyle shrugged. "How are you feeling about all of this?"

He didn't speak right away. Kyle looked around, squinting against the rain, and—like clockwork—he took off his cap and put it back on again. And then his face crumpled and he covered it with his hand, and there was a horrible squeezing sensation around her ribs.

"Okay, not great then," Eloise concluded, just to save him from speaking. He dropped his hand, still looking away from her.

"I'm scared about Pat." Kyle's voice cracked, and the squeezing sensation got worse. He did the cap thing again. He was in agony. "And what the fuck was it all *for*?"

There was such desperation in his voice. She would have given anything to have an answer that would help him, but she didn't have one.

"Yeah. I know," she said sadly, and she reached out and touched his arm. "I know."

"Yeah." He rubbed his face, leaving his skin blotchy and reddened. "Anyway. I guess the next time I'll see you is court."

"Or sooner. You know, Alex really wants to get *lobstah* rolls," she reminded him, "and if you recall, our deal was that if you talked to someone before things got bad, I'd buy you a lobster roll. And since things are obviously pretty bad, I think now you owe *me* one."

"I'm not buying a goddamn lobster roll," Kyle snapped, but he was fighting against a smile. "They're a fucking waste of money. It's just stupid. I'll go with you, but I'm not getting the fucking lobster roll." He faltered. "I just have to check and see if I'm even allowed to go. Thank god they didn't make me wear one of those goddamn ankle monitors."

"Okay, you can get a burger, and Alex and I will get lobster rolls," she promised him quickly, glossing over the terms of his bail. "I owe you a burger anyway, for creeping on you for months."

"You'll owe me more than a goddamn burger if all that creeping doesn't keep me out of jail," Kyle said, and after a beat they both exploded into desperate, pink-cheeked laughter.

Eloise hurried through the rain, coming down harder now, to the black car waiting for her. The car pulled away from the curb, and she watched through the rain as Kyle pushed his way back into the arena—and then, abruptly and intensely, the tears were coming, the tears she had been holding back for days.

They were bittersweet—for all that love would give you and all that it would take from you. She wiped her eyes, reeling with joy and sadness, relief and grief, an overflow of love, and a hollowness of it too.

The time passed. Eloise moved out of her Southie apartment with the help of Hollis and Lily, and back into her childhood bedroom. Krystal called her weekly to give her updates on the case, and soon that evolved into weekly happy hours where they would discuss the case, and the team, and then they started discussing their lives—Krystal's dating shenanigans and her nieces and nephews, and Eloise's latest cases, which were all minor repeat clients and did not bring in enough money to live independently, but which were entertaining and were something to do while she figured out what to do next.

She found out that Kyle's bail had been posted by Jacques, a detail that seemed to infuriate Krystal further. Kyle was indeed on house arrest until the trial, whose date had been set for late December. He was allowed to play home games, but not away games, and as a result the first line had been changed to Andrei-Jacques-Burnie, a detail that, as Krystal told it, was not improving the relationship between Andrei and Burnie. But it didn't matter, because the Bruins were playing like they had not played in years, and Jacques was on fire.

At Lily's insistence, she dated. She finally met Culinary Jacob, who was perfectly lovely but had no interest in her, and Finance Bro Owen, who was hilariously disdainful of her bleached hair and her lack of career. Himbo Jeff was gentle and sweet, but indeed too young for her. She even tried online dating again, but between the fact that she was living with her father and 'between jobs,' it was hard to drum up much enthusiasm for it.

(That, and the fact that every night as she lay in her childhood bed, studying these men and trying to decide whether to swipe left or right, she found herself thinking of someone else, and wondering if she was like her father—destined to be frozen in time over someone who had never felt that way about her.

(Every night she would lock her phone screen and roll over and scrunch her eyes shut, thinking of one man, and then remembering the burn of that man's rejection. Like a sunburn, it was still hot to the touch and so sensitive to even the slightest brush. She could not even hear his name without pain.)

She got lobster rolls with Alex and Travis and Connor, and they brought the lobster rolls to Kyle's apartment and sat around his trash-picked coffee table on an odd assortment of kitchen chairs and ottomans. The case hung like a sword over them, but between Alex's ridiculous optimism and Travis and Connor's antics, it was easy to forget, for a little while, all that hung in the balance.

After that, Eloise made a habit of stopping by Kyle's apartment when he was stuck inside, with coffee or soda or treats that Hollis and Lily had baked. She would sit on the floor and he would lay on the couch and they would talk like twin siblings at night. She learned about his father, lonely and disabled after being caught by a bullet in the line of duty; she learned about how Kyle had watched his little brother become increasingly angry at the world as their lives decayed while others' prospered, with a disabled father and no household income, and a mountain of medical debt that would never go away. She learned about the tattoo that Robbie had insisted everyone in their group get, and how, in quiet resistance, Kyle had altered it to a Celtic symbol for summer.

She avoided hockey as much as she could, and out of solidarity (and a fear of Lily), Hollis and Dad did their best not to bring it up. But it was Boston, and hockey season was in full swing, and the Bruins were—thanks to Jacques and Andrei—finally playing the way Boston fans believed they should play.

She saw something about the Bruins every time she went out, whether it was on a billboard or a television in a bar or on a toque or jersey. Andrei's face, in black and white, was now on an enormous marquee at one of the stations where she often caught the T, and every time she stood by the marquee she wondered if Alex or Noah had taken the photograph, and what they'd had to do to convince him to do it. Every time she opened Instagram or Twitter she saw Jacques's face, even after blocking everything related to the Bruins or hockey.

There was no escaping hockey. Boston had turned its attention to the team that was experiencing a second coming, and for the first time Eloise appreciated just how small this city was and how oppressive it could be. Krystal had once said that Boston fans were like a cult, and never before had Eloise fully understood just how constant their worship was, and how that constant worship could feed into an insularity that felt like the space between a mean-spirited nickname and a slur.

Meanwhile, the trial loomed. As expected, she would be called as a witness. She would be asked to discuss the details of her surveillance on Kyle, as well as the details she had provided about the drug testing.

And even though Eloise knew that she had made the right decision, she also knew that the fallout of this could change her life—for better, or for worse.

# Chapter Twenty-Four

The day of the trial arrived.

Eloise took her time getting ready: she even put on eyeliner in a bold swipe that made her mouth twitch with self-conscious pride when she pulled her hand away and surveyed her appearance. For so many years, she had been dressing to disguise or diminish herself—whether for an investigation, or just because she did not want to be recognized. She had not wanted anyone to know her, but today she would be known. Today she would be Eloise Davies, and her past and present would collide.

And she was at peace with that. The light would be upon her, and she did not know what might come of that. She considered this for a moment, and then added more eyeliner. Whatever came of today's trial, however it came to influence her destiny—she would rise to meet it.

"Um. You look amazing?" Lily sputtered when Eloise came down the stairs in her suit. "Who even *are* you?" she joked.

Eloise grinned as she grabbed her coat from the coat tree.

"Eloise Davies—private investigator," she told Lily proudly. "For a little while longer, at least."

"You don't know what's going to happen," Lily reminded her loftily as she gathered her purse and coat. "This might be the start of a whole new era for your business."

Eloise was so touched by Lily's optimism that she did not bring her down with reality: this was very likely the end of her business, if anything.

They drove in Dad's quaking Toyota to the courthouse, the day unseasonably mild and sunny for December. Neither Dad nor Eloise spoke on the drive, but Lily talked the whole way, and her nervousness for Eloise was like a balm. *I am loved*, she kept thinking as Boston sprouted up around them, traffic and businesses and signage and bus stops.

When they got to the courthouse, the Eloise who got out of the car was calm and collected and stood taller than she had in years.

As a witness being called to testify, Eloise was asked to enter the courtroom from a separate, private entrance, and she bid Dad and Lily goodbye for now—Lily squeezed her tightly; Dad waved without making eye-contact—and was led by a security officer to a windowless room. As a bench chemist, she had always been allowed to sit in the courtroom during the trial, but the judge had ordered all witnesses to wait separately. Eloise entered and surveyed the other witnesses: she recognized one of Kyle's neighbors, the elderly man who had apparently reported the tip to the police, and Coach Duffy, looking strained in a too-tight suit and hunched at the edge of his seat, scowling at a television in the corner that was playing Oprah. When she entered, he offered a quick nod, but did not gesture for her to sit with him.

She sat against the wall and went over her notes in her head, letting herself go into a meditative state. They were not permitted to use their phones and were not given any updates, so she had no connection to what was happening in the courtroom.

She wondered how Kyle was feeling about being forced to take off his Red Sox hat; she wondered if Lily had spotted Jacques yet. She wondered if Caff was anxious or resigned. She wondered if Kyle's father had shown up.

And then her name was called. It was time.

Eloise was led to the courtroom by an older, wispy-haired woman in glasses and a cardigan. Her palms were damp and her heart was shuddering against her ribcage, but her head was clear, and she entered the hushed courtroom with her chin up and shoulders back.

She saw Kyle first, hatless and more polished than she had ever before seen him. He was in a dark, tailored suit that betrayed Jacques's influence. Beside him sat Caff in an ill-fitting cheap black blazer; she looked pallid underneath harsh bronzer and a red lip, and when Eloise looked closer she realized she was gripping Kyle's hand so hard that her knuckles were bleached. When Eloise scanned the rows, she saw no sign of Patrick or his father. On Kyle's other side, the Bruins' legal team—Brandon, Jason, Neema, and Glen—sat in a focused row, impassively reviewing their notes.

There was Pell, brows knit as he offered a bracing smile to Eloise; there was Krystal, who inexplicably lit up and smiled at Eloise like she had done something wonderful, and Eloise wondered if something funny had happened that she would tell her about later; there was Burnie, pressing his lips together like he was physically stopping himself from an outburst; she saw Connor and Travis dressed up in suits like they were at junior prom, eagerly trying to catch her eye, and beyond them Lily and Dad—

—and there at last, at the end of the row just past Krystal and Burnie, was Jacques.

She only allowed herself a glimpse of his soft brown hair and close-cropped beard, his dark suit over his strong shoulders, before she had to turn and take the stand. She went through the motions she had gone through so many times: she heard her name, she placed her hand on the Bible; and then she was sitting above everyone beneath hot, bright lights.

"Please state your name for the court."

She looked first at Kyle, who was wide-eyed and wary, but her gaze was naturally pulled, like instinct, back to Jacques.

He returned her gaze. Even after just a few months without contact, everything about him hit her anew: the curve of his mouth, the asymmetry of his brows that made his face so instantly likable, the romantic precision of all his lines. He looked younger than she had remembered, as though playing with Andrei again had breathed youth back into him. Seeing him was like a slap, like the violent burst of smelling salts, like the salty crash of a wave she had not known was coming.

She saw him take a sharp breath in, saw his throat move as he swallowed—but he did not look away from her.

"My name," she said, "is Eloise Davies."

Her voice rang strong and clear in the courtroom. She fisted her hands on her thighs as she sat up straight and tore her gaze from Jacques.

Her testimony began. The Bruins' legal team took her through what she had provided in the discovery: all that she had learned about Kyle, including his relationships and habits, his school fights and his associations. She had to reveal some unfavorable things that she had found—like that he had been underage drinking at Dublin House—but they had prepared for these details, and took her through them like a well-choreographed dance. Her photographs and her DM conversation with Robbie were shown on a projector and she walked the court through each document, just like they had rehearsed, and the confidence coursed through her like whiskey, warming her rapidly. This was who she was meant to be; this was what she had wanted to do all along.

And then the prosecution began. The prosecutor, a younger lawyer who looked exceedingly pleased with himself and his made-by-Cross-

Fit physique approached her with theatrical leisure, and Eloise glanced at Jacques before she could stop herself. He watched the lawyer dispassionately before letting his eyes drift to her once more.

"I just have a few questions for you, Ms. Davies," the prosecutor confided with a smile, like he thought he was charming to her—or maybe even flustering her. She was reminded of Babe Fowler, and inexplicably had the urge to grin. Babe could skate circles around this man in charm. "Specifically, about your time at the lab."

Beyond him, Kyle's primary attorney gave a little nod, acknowledgment that they had all seen this coming.

"You were employed for—how many years was it?"

"Seven," Eloise said. The prosecutor nodded, pursing his lips together as he reviewed his notes casually.

"Right, right. And you had a nice, steady job during that time. No promotions. Looks like you clocked in and clocked out. You set a boundary and stuck to it. Not one of those over-achievers, would you say?"

"Objection—" Brandon began irritably, rising, but the judge waved him off and the prosecutor continued.

"Didn't make a lot of friends there, either. You were a loner," he posited.

It was incredible that this, of all things, could bother her, could knock down the confidence that had been coursing through her just a few moments ago. Eloise averted her gaze and let it lock with Jacques's.

"I was close with one other employee," she said, "but otherwise, no, I would not say I was close with anyone else that I worked with."

"And are you still friendly with that person?" the prosecutor asked.

"No, not anymore."

"Ah, that's a shame," he said. "When did you fall out of touch?"

She knew what he was trying to do. He was trying to paint a picture of her as a loner, as someone who might have vengefully accused a colleague of something. She had sat through so many trials that she knew all of the patterns of the prosecution. She and Monique used to laugh about their tactics over drinks.

"We fell out of touch in 2020."

She was still looking at Jacques and she did not know why. After all, the last time they had spoken, he had scorned her so completely. But he had also been the first to believe her, to not even question that she had done what she had for good reason. That night in his car had been the beginning of something unfurling in her, something blooming that she had thought was dead. Jacques had done that.

And now she was holding onto that like a lifeline—holding his gaze like she was gripping his hand, and for whatever reason (his innate empathy, maybe; the empathy he could never seem to fully turn off even when it would have protected him), he was holding her gaze in turn, like he was squeezing her hand back. *I know this hurts. I know why this hurts.*

Or maybe she was only seeing what she wanted to see, because his expression bore no sympathy, no warmth or friendliness—but still it was blazing, it was a lifeline, and she would not let it go just yet.

"And that was the same year that you were fired from the lab," the prosecutor said.

"Yes, correct."

He pursed his lips briefly as he nodded and looked down at his notes again.

"And can you tell me more about the accusation that you made?"

She took a breath and went into detail. She had practiced this, she had prepared for it, and the Bruins attorneys had prepared her as well. At each turn, the prosecutor probed and interjected with little questions, all of them designed to reveal her as a bitter, disengaged employee, someone lacking in expertise and ability, someone unmotivated at her job. And strangely, through the prosecutor's questioning, she kept thinking that it was true: she *had* been bitter and disengaged, unmotivated and lost, and no one had known or cared. She had not allowed herself to form bonds—not unless they were forced upon her. She kept thinking that it was true, and also that she was no longer that person.

"So you admit that there is a chance that your accusation was not true," the prosecutor said at last.

"I admit that it was an allegation," Eloise replied. Jacques was still watching her. She was thinking again of that moment in his car, of the way he had swelled with emotion, of the way he had snarled, *is there a normal way to mention that to your boss?* And the confidence returned. "But that allegation was never taken seriously, or addressed in any meaningful way before I was asked to leave voluntarily—"

And here at last it came forth: all of the feelings that she had batted down for years, all of the feelings that she had been denying for years. Yet when she spoke her voice did not waver, her eyes did not tear up.

"—and I will never know for certain that the results of our testing did not falsely convict someone, or falsely set someone free. I will never know for certain if we ruined lives that did not deserve it. And when I brought it to the attention of upper management, no one reacted, and yes, what you've been trying to imply is true—it made me *hate* working there, and it made me distrust the people I worked with, and it made me turn to private investigation, because I wanted to actually *help* people. I had spent seven years watching, firsthand, how our system can fail people when it's too much of a bureaucratic pain to do the right thing."

The courtroom was silent. Kyle was trying not to laugh, overwhelmed by the tension; Krystal was beaming at Eloise with the most radiant smile she had ever seen. Connor was wiping his eyes as Travis rolled his own and patted his shoulder. And Jacques was still staring at her with that blazing look that she could not read.

"That's all," she added, finally looking down.

And then it was done, and she was thanked for her testimony and led from the stand, blood pounding in her ears, knees trembling. Just as strangely, as dreamily, as she had arrived in the courtroom, she left it, and then somehow she was back in that same windowless room once more, purgatory without a phone. Coach Duffy was there and this time he was hunched forward, staring at the carpet. He only looked up and nodded briefly without making eye contact.

It was over. Eloise dropped into one of the creaky chairs and, like Duffy, simply stared at the carpet. She did not know if she had helped or hurt Kyle. She did not know what Jacques had made of her testimony. She did not know what was going to happen next. But it was over.

A long time later, there was a soft knock on the door, and then the same woman who had escorted her to the courtroom poked her head in, glasses turned opaque by the fluorescent light as she leaned in. Eloise and Duffy immediately looked up, the room electric with their anticipation.

"It's over," she said. "The prosecution dropped the charges. You can come out."

Eloise let out a shaking breath as Duffy clapped his hands over his face and leaned back. He was quick to recompose himself, and got to his feet, re-buttoning his suit jacket and reaching to Eloise to shake her hand.

After that windowless room, the main hall of the courthouse felt blindingly sunny, bright, celebratory. The courtroom had emptied and everyone was here in this main hall, standing around looking as dazed as Eloise felt, taking turns hugging Kyle or shaking his hand.

And there was Jacques, waiting separately from everyone else. He turned at the sight of her and Coach Duffy, and her stomach twisted as she drew in a sharp breath, heat flooding her cheeks for no good reason.

"El—" he began, but Duffy, obliviously, grabbed them both by the shoulders, steering them toward where Kyle and the others stood, and the moment was lost.

"I don't think I've ever been so relieved," he was saying as they reached the group. "Jesus Christ."

"Congratulations, Ky—" Eloise started, but was cut off when he flung his arms around her, for the third time ever, and this time was just as unexpected as the first—and just like the first time, Jacques was watching them. This time she looked away, and instead buried her face in Kyle's shoulder and focused on the embrace.

"Thank you," he said under his breath as he squeezed her.

"I didn't—"

"Stop it. Thank you," he insisted into her hair.

They pulled away and Kyle self-consciously adjusted his jacket and hair, looking embarrassed. Before she could fix her own jacket, Caff had stepped forward and awkwardly bent down to embrace her, and Eloise returned it. When Caff pulled away, her face was wet, her mascara running. Krystal passed her a tissue with a sly hand that Caff gratefully accepted and blew her nose into loudly.

"Yes, I think a few thank-you's are in order," Duffy said, holding out a hand to hers once more. Eloise moved to shake it, but Pell swooped in and hugged her. Burnie did not seem to know what to do with himself and instead crossed his arms and looked away with such fervor that his neck cracked loudly.

"Come on, group hug! We've got to celebrate this," Pell ordered, and Duffy awkwardly leaned in and patted Eloise on the shoulder just as she heard a thunder of footfalls and then something hard slammed into her back.

"YAY ELOISE!" Travis yelled into her ear, jostling her against Pell as Connor joined them, red as a pomegranate. "LET'S GO HAVE CHAMPAGNE!"

"You're not old enough," Pell said cheerfully as he released Eloise, "but you can have sparkling cider."

"I'm twenty-one!" Travis protested as Connor took this moment to also hug Eloise. He was holding a mylar balloon that read *Congratu-*

*lations* and it bounced and thudded as they hugged. When Eloise let him go, he turned to a baffled Kyle and handed him the balloon string.

"You've got to be fucking kidding—"

"Look, he wanted to originally do a dozen balloons that all said *Congratulations*," Travis interjected, "and I talked him down from that. This could have been a lot weirder."

Kyle accepted the balloon string, trying hard not to laugh, and tugged on it a few times as he looked up at it, his eyes bright.

The hallway was filled with giddy laughter, and Kyle's snarky comments, and Eloise knew her face was shining as Dad and Lily approached them—shyly in Dad's case, and defiantly normal but a little shaky about it in Lily's case, her dark eyes fixed on Jacques disgustedly as though he had made some tasteless, inappropriate joke. Introductions were made, and Lily was deeply charmed by Connor and Travis, enough to forget to scowl at Jacques.

They walked out of the courthouse in a clumsy stream: Travis looped his arm through hers and, on her other side, Lily did the same, and Caff was crying in earnest as she walked with Kyle and Connor, with Krystal doing her best to help her fix her makeup on the sly, telling her to pull herself together for just a few more minutes, and then they were in the harsh December sunlight, the wind whipping their hair around their faces, and Krystal and Duffy steered Kyle towards the small gathering of media as the rest of them lingered on the steps, giddily recounting the end of the trial, and then—

—Eloise realized that she had ended up next to Jacques and Burnie somehow. She felt Lily and Dad watching them; she felt Burnie looking between them in pained silence, holding his breath.

She had held onto his gaze like it was her lifeline, her saving grace, just a few hours earlier, her feelings so visible in a whole courtroom of people. But now it took everything in her power to look up and meet his slate eyes, made bluer by his charcoal suit.

"H-hey," she stammered, shading her eyes in the sun as she looked up at him. He was close enough to touch now.

"Thank you," he said, and then—too soon—he was walking again, before she could say anything else. Burnie offered a terse, pained nod before hastening to follow Jacques.

"Well, that was super normal," Pell muttered. He touched Eloise's shoulder with a sympathetic grimace. "Just so you know, the prosecutor tried to get his autograph at the end and Lavesque just said 'sorry, no.' I've known that guy for fourteen years now and I've never seen him be rude to another human being, especially not a fan."

"The prosecutor was just doing his job," Eloise brushed it off. "I didn't take it personally."

Pell shrugged.

"Well, apparently Lavy did, so. Just so you know," he repeated. "Anyway, I'm gonna catch up with them." He kissed her on the cheek and then hurried after Jacques and Burnie. Eloise turned, disallowing herself from watching Jacques walk away.

"Ass," Lily said under her breath. "I mean, fine. He is *stupidly* gorgeous, and that smile is *deadly*," she conceded, "and that suit is, like, *perfect*. But he's an ass."

In spite of everything, Eloise found herself laughing—an inane, breathless, desperate kind of laugh that had Dad and Lily frowning at her, and Travis glancing back at them in concern.

"I—I need to go home. And maybe have a glass of wine," she said. She closed her eyes, trying to erase the image of his eyes. "Or two," she added.

"Or maybe the whole bottle?" Lily suggested, slinging an arm around her. "I feel like I need a bottle with a straw. One of those squiggly, loopy ones. I already texted Holl and told him to pick some up after work."

"Is there a place around here you can even buy them? I want a squiggly straw," Travis put in. He beamed at them, his freckled face even brighter in the sunlight. "Go relax, Eloise."

"I will," she promised.

She saw Kyle with Krystal and Duffy and the attorneys, squinting in the sunlight and answering the journalists' questions, the wind toying with his auburn hair, and she felt a pang of the most intense pride.

They slipped off with Dad in tow, Lily blocking view of Eloise before any of the journalists could notice her. Once they had rounded the corner, they all slowed and relaxed as they walked toward the parking lot, the concrete painted rose-gold by the late afternoon sun. The oddly mild wind washed over her, running through her hair.

Dad was the first to break the silence.

"That was Jacques Lavesque," he said dazedly.

Lily groaned.

"That was Jacques goddamn Lavesque. And Henry Burnap. Right there. Talking to my daughter. Matthew Pelletier just kissed my daughter on the cheek."

"*Not* helpful, Freddie," Lily hissed, swinging her purse at him. "Save it for Holl, 'kay?"

"It's okay," Eloise hastily reassured them both. "Really. It's fine."

They got in the car, with Lily and Dad still arguing about Jacques, and Eloise sat in the back seat, watching her phone screen flash with new emails. Distantly, she knew that her life was about to change.

So why did she feel like all she wanted to do was cry? She leaned her head against the window and watched Boston go by.

*I'll be okay*, she reminded herself, vision blurring with tears.

# Chapter Twenty-Five

"You ready?" Anthony asked as they met on the sidewalk before the old brick building. Snow was falling, dotting Anthony's precisely-styled hair and the shoulders of his fine black cashmere coat.

Jacques looked up at the Beacon Hill building, which belonged to Rachel's family's lawyer, one he had visited plenty of times in their marriage for all kinds of things, not limited to the pre-nuptial agreement that her father had had the lawyer put together. At the time, Jacques had been bemused and a little entertained by Jeff's insistence—of course he and Rachel would never divorce; it was a perfunctory but unnecessary step—but now he could wryly appreciate the wisdom of it.

With its glossy black door and stately plaque, he had always been intimidated when he had come here before; it had been just another way in which he had not quite fit into Rachel's world. Now he walked with Anthony to the door knowing this would be the final time he walked up these steps, knowing that this time it was a question of whether she fit into his world—and he knew his answer.

The front vestibule was all marble and lily arrangements and cut glass that winked in the little light from outside, putting in mind a church. Rachel was already there, slender arms crossed over her chest, dressed all in expensive black. From here Jacques could hear Jeff's loud, confident voice from the other side of the door—a quick catch-up with his lawyer while they waited for Jacques to arrive.

In spite of everything, Rachel smiled at him, her eyes wet, and he felt a pang of the old guilt, the thing that had stopped him from pulling the trigger and ending their marriage right away. But it soon faded, and the peace he felt about this decision returned to him. It did not matter, anymore, if anyone else thought this was the right thing to do. It was the thing he wanted to do.

"There he is," Jeff observed, poking his head out of the office. "Ready?"

Rachel nodded; Anthony held up his briefcase; Jacques smiled politely.

It was only the final agreement. All of the work had happened over the last several months, as he and Rachel had negotiated what their lives apart would look like. They sat at a magnificent cherry wood table, and there was a part of Jacques that was tensed, just waiting for Rachel to do or say something to blow it all up at the last second, but today she was compliant. She was tired, worn down, and ready to move on like he was. Their initial meetings had been acerbic and filled with little cruelties that had left him silently fuming, exercising every last bit of discipline he had not to blow up at her, but there was only so long that that kind of animosity could be maintained, even for Rachel.

When all was done he watched her sign Rachel Hathaway, not Rachel Lavesque, at the end of the documents, and he wondered if she felt the way he did: like something had come back to rest, like he could at last let go of the thing he had been carrying.

After it was done, Jacques and Rachel stepped back into the vestibule. Their lawyers and Jeff were tactful enough to give them this moment of privacy.

They stood beneath the little chandelier which, at this time of day, dotted the silk-covered walls with beads of light. There were two mirrors on either side of the hallway, gilt-framed and hanging above slender tables, and through the floral arrangements on each one, Jacques could see their reflections, a million repeating Jacques and Rachels, stacked like a deck of cards being fanned out.

"Wow," Rachel said, always the first to speak. She smiled sadly, tucked her hair behind her ear. "It's just so weird."

It did not feel weird for him. But he sensed that to say that would hurt her, so he nodded. *Oh, more 'no comment' bullshit?* Eloise asked in his head.

The last time he had seen Rachel had been the day they had sat the boys down to explain everything to them—explain their new living situation, explain all of the time they would be spending in cars, being trucked from one home to another, explain all of the time they would have to spend with their grandparents and with nannies and babysitters now. And as they had given them that talk—Luke confused, Peter wide-eyed but quiet—Jacques had begun to see something, a thing he had not wanted to, a thing that sat in his throat now as he and Rachel stood together in this narrow hall.

Rachel shook her glossy hair out, a sudden resolve. "So! You're going to be on the road for a while, right?"

"Yes, a few weeks," he confirmed. It would be the last great push of the season.

"Well—as we just signed on—I will make sure you get FaceTime with the boys," she promised.

"Thank you," he said.

And then her face crumpled, and like clockwork she fell against him. He watched his reflection put his arms around her and they briefly embraced. When she stepped away, her face was red and wet; she looked away, discreetly touching her eyes, trying to save her make-up. Her sadness was still hard to see. He had once loved her—wildly, stupidly, completely.

It was Anthony who saved him. All three men emerged from the office, and Anthony gestured for Jacques, an impatient movement of his hand, and then they were saying their goodbyes, and then Jacques was out on the snowy street, and his marriage was officially over.

"Come on," Anthony said after the door had closed and Jacques had recovered. His Boston accent wasn't strong—not like Kyle's, but more like Eloise's, a subtle flattening of the vowels that always made Jacques smile. "Let me buy you a beer."

They went to a noisy Irish pub near Quincy Market just because this was Anthony's favorite. It was chaotic with the lunchtime rush, wet boots squeaking on tiled floor and a Dropkick Murphy's song blaring loud enough that it was hard to hear. They sat at a table in the corner with two pints of Guinness, which Jacques did not really want, and he took the seat facing away from the rest of the pub in the hope that he would not be recognized.

Anthony sat forward. "Hey. You should be celebrating. I can't believe that went so smoothly—especially with your boys."

The waitress came by with Anthony's sandwich and he took it from her impatiently, already reaching into the basket with his other hand for a French fry.

"I fwought she wash gonna put up more of a fight wish the cush-tody shtuff," he admitted thickly through a mouthful of fry. He swallowed. "Honestly, she should have. Your schedule is way too crazy for you to be a single parent."

Anthony was like this—constantly scattering careless little stinging statements. He couldn't help it; he probably didn't even know he was doing it. He was constantly assessing the world around him, highlighting the practical problems of it.

"You sure you don't want some?" he asked now, rattling the basket in front of Jacques's face. Jacques waved him off.

"Yes, I am sure," he said with a smile. He looked out the window at the street. That sense that he had was growing; it was like being trapped in a room with a wild animal. He could only ignore it for so long before it became ridiculous to not admit it.

Someone passed the window in a Bruins toque, and he looked back at Anthony, who was chewing loudly.

"You wanna know," he began, swallowing and running his tongue over his teeth as he shoved the half-eaten sandwich away from him, "what all my brothers call you?"

It was the very first sign of hockey appreciation that Anthony had betrayed in their entire time working together. Not once had he previously acknowledged who Jacques was to the rest of Boston. Jacques smiled again and leaned forward, setting his elbows on the table.

"No," he said. "What do they call me?"

"Saint Jacques," Anthony admitted. "Now, *I'm* not weird enough to do that. You're just some guy to me. A client. Nothing else. But I *have* watched almost every single game this season—if not the full game then at least the highlights the next morning." He wiped his mouth. "You've been on fire lately. Might be the best year of your career. How's that for thirty-six, huh?"

"Thirty-seven now," Jacques reminded him. Anthony laughed.

"You might as well be twenty-seven, the way you've been playing. We're still gonna be screaming SAINT JACQUES from our seats when you're forty."

Jacques laughed. He knew Anthony thought he was helping, and he knew it was a kindness from him.

"Thank you," he said, and he meant it, but there was that wild animal in the room with him once again, and in the dark its eyes had a phosphorescent and prescient glow. *You know what you want to do*, he heard in his head. *But they will hate me for it*, he said in return.

After he and Anthony had parted, Jacques took the longer way back to his car and looked at the city around him, the city he had called home for twenty years now: the salt-caked remains of Christmastime trimming the brick, the blackened snow, the black and navy coats that choked Quincy Market.

He ducked under the eaves of an older building to get out of the falling snow, and opened a new test.

**Jacques [2:37pm]**: are you still on your church tour?

Kyle texted back surprisingly quickly.

**Kyle [2:37pm]**: yeah going this afternoon why

**Jacques [2:38pm]**: you mind having company?

The church was not empty as Jacques had expected when he pushed open the heavy door. Tourists were pacing beneath the stations of the cross, and taking pictures of the rose window, which left a faintly sanguine-pink glow across the marble floor in the gloom of the swirling snow outside. The air was musty and spicy; the incense and dust tickled his nose.

A lone, lanky figure was slouched in one of the pews in the back—no Red Sox hat to be found this time. Jacques let the door swing shut, letting a burst of flurries into the church, and slid into the pew to join Kyle.

"Hey," Kyle said in a low voice as Jacques settled. He was turning over his Red Sox hat in his hand.

"Hey. Thanks for letting me join you."

Jacques looked around, then slouched forward in a loose copy of Kyle's pose. "So what now? Am I supposed to kneel, or...?"

"You don't have to. It kinda hurts my knees, actually," Kyle admitted. "You can just sit there."

"Okay."

They sat in silence as Jacques studied the stained glass, the marble, the carvings, the soaring pillars. He craned his neck, thinking that Rachel would know all of the technical terms for every pillar, every arch, every carving. And then he was thinking of her wet eyes, and he was thinking of his boys' eyes.

He looked down in time to see Kyle cover his face. They were at the heart of the problem now.

"What do I do now?" he asked gently.

"I don't know." Kyle's voice was muffled by his hands. "It used to just happen to me. I'd be sitting here, just thinking, and then I would have this feeling, this... this *confidence*... and now it's gone. I don't know why. I just want it back."

Jacques was thinking of Rachel again, thinking of that car ride home from Pell's party those years ago when he had first sensed a splitting, a fraying. For the first time, he could think of it without anger. He knew that Kyle had been going from church to church in Boston, refusing to let go of the thing that had mattered so much to him for so long, and he wondered if there had been a first time: a misstep, a pause, a note landing just a little wrong.

"How is your brother doing? I haven't asked, recently," Jacques said. They had not talked much about Patrick, beyond the logistics of the fallout of everything that had happened, including the splitting of his brother's group of 'friends' and the explosion of Patrick's life, which had landed him in a juvenile detention center in Roslindale. Jacques knew that there had been a lot of work with the police, and even with the FBI, but there was so much that Kyle was not allowed to talk about and Jacques often got the sense that he preferred to pretend it was not happening at all.

Kyle did not answer right away.

"I can't stand my dad," was all he said.

Kyle pressed his palms into his eyes, and they sat in silence for a long time, listening to the whispers and scuffled steps of the tourists around them. Jacques studied the stained glass and waited to feel some greater power reach out and guide him, reach out and hand him the ability to do what he wanted to do, but he felt nothing save for a vague awe of the human hands that had built this cathedral and the human mind that had dreamed it up.

"The last time I saw my brother," Jacques began, eyes on the altar, "we were so angry with each other that we broke each other's noses. And I told him I hated him. And then a few days later, he overdosed and died. I went out and got a tattoo that would offend my mother the most, because I hated her too, for letting him turn into that."

"You think I need another tattoo?" Kyle wondered dryly.

Jacques stifled his laugh—this was still a church, after all—and stretched out his arms on the back of the pew, letting one arm rest on Kyle's back slightly.

"I think you need a girlfriend, and a haircut, and a new hat," he said, and now it was Kyle's turn to stifle a laugh. One of the tourists shot them an indignant look and they grinned at each other.

The church quieted again. The choice before him was becoming clearer now. The pews made him think of a courtroom; the podium by the altar was the stand. He was thinking of Eloise again, of the way her eyes had gone wet as she had said, *My name is Eloise Davies,* and how she had kept her eyes on his as she had once again blown up her life.

Yes. He knew the choice he wanted to make. He was only afraid to do it.

*You know what you want to do,* he told himself, thinking of Eloise's eyes, *and it is time to do it—it is time to let them hate you if they have to.*

And somehow in this place of stained glass and spirits, his arm around Kyle, he was at peace with it: at peace with the choice, at peace with the fear, at peace with the fallout. He smoothed his hand along Kyle's back, then pulled away and slouched forward again.

"Sorry. I dunno if this is helping you," Kyle muttered sheepishly. "It's not helping me, honestly. It used to. It really did." He looked up, biting his lip. "I would give anything to get it back."

"I know."

He was thinking of his choice, and all that that choice encompassed. And his eyes burned but he did not fight against it, and he let his vision go briefly wet before at last he blinked, and his eyes were dry again and his mind was clear.

"I understand. But there will be some things that you can't get back—that you shouldn't get back. This might be one of them."

"Would kinda suck," Kyle said, "given I have this massive crucifix tattooed on my back."

"Even if you can't get it back, that doesn't mean it never mattered."

(His heart would bear Andrei's, Rachel's, Olivier's, his mother's fingerprints upon it forever, even after the end of love.)

He felt the sudden urgency of guiding Kyle, of steering him away from the path Jacques had walked, because as they sat there he had the complete and total belief that one day soon—sooner than he was ready for—it would not be his face on the side of Boston Garden, but Kyle's. In this place of faith and unfounded certainty, of jewel-like light and burning incense, he knew it. The Wheel of Fortune would always turn—what had gone up must, inevitably, come back down, and life and death were constantly turning over, spiraling, and he understood now why his mother had always insisted that Death was the most powerful card. Everything ended; everything had to end, in order for something new to begin.

He considered his words. "You do have to find something," he said at last. Kyle did not look up. "To deal with what this will do to you."

He did not know if he meant hockey, or what had happened to his brother, or life itself.

"I know," Kyle said. "Why do you think I'm looking so hard?"

A while later, Jacques emerged from the church to that strangely flat pink light that snowy afternoons got. All the world was quiet for now, save for the scrape of shovels and the muffled crunch of tires on snow. When he checked his phone, he saw that, among missed texts from Burnie and Pell and so many others demanding to celebrate his finalized divorce, Krystal had called him, so he walked back to his car and got in without dusting the snow off of it, and returned her call.

Krystal picked up immediately.

"Hey. Did it happen? Is it done?"

Things were still awkward and uneven between them. He leaned back in his seat, and thought of how much he loved Krystal, how much he had loved her from the very first day he had met her.

"Yes," he said, closing his eyes, "it is all done."

"How did she handle it?"

"Fine. It was all very polite, and over very quickly," Jacques said. He heard her let out a sigh.

"Thank god. What are you doing to celebrate?"

"Ah, I think Burnie has probably organized something, though he told me it would just be me, him, and Pell," Jacques said. "You sound like you are getting ready for something."

"Yeah—" Krystal halted. "Look. I'm just going to be honest with you. I'm going to dinner with Eloise tonight."

Feeling surged in him, and he leaned forward now.

"Oh, yeah? Nice." *Oh, more 'no comment' bullshit?*

"Nice? So are you good with her now?" Krystal's voice was strained with hope, and her words came out in a sudden rush. "Because you know, everything could have gone really badly for her, and I am so relieved that it didn't, and she just signed a lease for a new apartment because she's finally got enough revenue from her clients, so we're celebrating at Yvonne's tonight."

"That is great. I'm glad to hear it."

"You could swing by for a drink, you know," she suggested, so eager for everything to be alright between them again. "Before you go to Burnie's. I'm sure she would be glad to see you, and you both have something big to celebrate."

"I don't think she would be glad to see me, Krystal," Jacques said plainly. "I should let you go—"

"Hey. Wait. You sound not-good," she interrupted. "Are you sure you're good about today?"

"I am," he promised her. "Everything is good." *Oh, more 'no comment' bullshit?*

They hung up and Jacques sat there for a moment, listening to the snow and traffic and wind, turning his phone over in his hands. For some reason he was thinking of Eloise in his car, wearing his sweater. That night, in the moonlight coming into the car, he had noticed that her makeup—too yellow to quite match her skin—had begun to melt off, revealing the freckles and flush underneath, and it had made his mouth go dry and his heart beat a little faster, and he had wondered what it would feel like to kiss her neck, damp hair and soft skin beneath his mouth, wondering what it would take to get her to whisper his name.

He opened his phone and stared at her contact information. He had not deleted it, nor had he amended her name. Not for the first time it occurred to him to call her, to text her. He could have shrouded it under the guise of apologizing for how he had treated her—but he knew what it really was. It was selfish, it was foolish, it was not the way he was supposed to be, it was not who he had promised to be. *You know what you want to do,* that animal told him now, and he said in turn, *but I cannot just do* everything *that I want.* He had already been so selfish with her—from offering to drive her home, under the guise of safety, and then pulling her to the hotel rooftop. He had pretended it had been about an apology, and it had been—but it had also been about putting Babe Fowler and whoever else she liked, whoever else that had made her smile and was not him, out of her head. At times he had been so dishonorable, so selfish, so unlike who he had agreed to be, with her. This would only be more of the same.

*Oh, more 'no comment' bullshit?*

He deleted her number before sitting up and turning on his car.

·ɔɔ●ᙅᙅ·

"You know, I think we're really making progress," Eloise told her father as they surveyed their work.

It had all started on New Year's Day with her childhood bedroom, because it had still been painted a violent purple that she could no longer bear. For a few days it had been stilted awkwardness and long, strained silences as, together, she and her father had taken everything out of the room and laid out drop cloths and other supplies that Lily and Hollis had gotten.

Lily and Hollis had wanted to help, but both Eloise and Dad had turned them down. Astonished to the point of speechlessness that Dad was doing something other than sit in his chair and watch sports, Hollis had not dared to press the issue. Thus Eloise and her father had repainted her bedroom a pale green that Lily had deemed a 'timeless neutral' and Hollis had deemed 'for boring babies.'

They had not talked much as they worked, just painted. Frankly, they had done a terrible job—neither of them knew the first thing about painting, and it had taken so many coats to hide the adolescent purple that the paint had a gooey, clumpy appearance at the corners.

Yet at the end of it, they each decided that the next room that needed to be repainted was Hollis's—still a young boy's light blue—and this time they had gone to the paint store together, with an extremely dubious Lily, and between the three of them they had chosen a pale, warm yellow that would look cozy even in winter. And when Eloise and her father had gotten home, they discussed their approach, and spent hours in the living room reading how-to's on painting. And then they had attacked Hollis's room, and her father had made a stray comment that it was a nice yellow but Hollis would be furious when he found out, and then the floodgates had opened, and they had spent hours painting and talking: about the Red Sox, about Eloise's mother, about Hollis and Lily, about her clients.

They had finished Hollis's bedroom, and had then turned to her father's. He wanted the same pale yellow that Lily had chosen for Hollis's room, and then after painting, her father decided he wanted a different headboard so they had gone to Goodwill together and found a cheap one that Eloise refinished in the kitchen, following YouTube tutorials.

Now they were standing in the living room, surveying their progress. The living room—once papered with a dated floral print that was stained and dark—was now bright and airy, a pale blue that turned periwinkle in the late afternoon light.

"It's progress," Dad agreed, frowning, "but now all the furniture looks wrong."

"Well, we can go to Goodwill again tomorrow," Eloise promised him as her phone pulsed with a text. When she checked it, she saw it was Krystal confirming their plans. "Crap, I'd better start getting ready. I'm meeting Krystal for dinner."

"Oh, the queen herself," he joked as he dropped into his chair and turned on the television.

(Dad had met Krystal recently, and Eloise suspected he found her extremely intimidating, because now he only referred to her as 'The Queen.')

She took her time getting ready, and after some debate—it was snowing, and freezing—she decided to wear her black dress, the one she had first worn to Burnie's party, with thick tights and boots. It was too cold for the sleeveless dress with its exposed back, so she pulled a sweater over top and surveyed herself in the mirror.

She looked, she thought, the way she had that night of Burnie's party, when Jacques had driven her home. And then she had to sit on the edge of her bed for a moment as a feeling coursed through her veins and squeezed her chest until she could not breathe.

She knew he was in the process of his divorce. Krystal had been making comments recently, dropping little updates every now and then, breezing past them before Eloise could ask her not to talk about him. In fact, she was fairly certain that today was the day he had finalized the divorce.

Whatever. She drew in a deep breath and rose, and shook herself out of the intense feeling. This was how she had looked the first time she had felt, in years, like she was worthy, like she deserved love, and whatever else had happened between them, he had still done that for her. This was how she wanted to look on a night where she was supposed to be celebrating her successes: like herself—like the best version of herself.

When her hair and makeup were done—Krystal deserved nothing less than the most effort—Eloise went downstairs, expecting to find her father in front of the television, but instead he was in the kitchen, talking on the phone to, she suspected, Hollis, because his voice was louder than usual and she knew, after a moment of listening in, that they were talking about sports.

She poked her head into the kitchen and waved, and he waved back, and then she took her coat and scarf from the coat tree. Love was an empty chair; love was fresh paint on walls that had not been touched in years.

# Chapter Twenty-Six

Tonight they were playing the Rangers again, the last game against them during the regular season. No one knew it yet, but for Jacques it was yet another little goodbye in a long train that was beginning to overwhelm him.

They prepared for the game, getting dressed and having their usual talks, and like he had been doing since that meeting with Anthony, Jacques told himself he ought to be savoring every second of it, storing every moment in his memories. But tonight the knowledge that this might be his last time against the Rangers—depending on the play-offs—was like nausea. It was distracting and consuming, a thing to be borne until it had passed.

He said some encouraging things to the team. He sought out Travis, who still struggled to keep his cool around players like Tripp Dempsey, and they had a heart-to-heart about staying in control. What normally would have been a free-flowing conversation from the heart was something he had to eke out, and he sensed tonight he was insufficient: they parted with Travis still moody, aloof, sullen. They had talked around the reason for Tripp's behavior, never directly acknowledging the homophobia, and he knew this was a disappointment to Travis. Jacques knew he was failing him. The nausea swelled.

And then somehow they were on the ice for warm-ups, surrounded by a packed stadium. Jacques had thought that once he got on the ice, the nausea would die down and his mind would quiet and his life would belong to him again, however briefly, but instead he was gliding along the ice and wishing he could get away from the lights and the noise and the eyes, wishing he could get away from this thing that he so deeply loved. *You know what you want to do*, he heard again in his head. *But they will hate you for it.*

"Hey, always good to see you, Lavesque," Babe Fowler drawled, knocking lightly into Jacques as he passed.

"You too," Jacques said, forcing a smile.

They skated together for a moment, slowing down as their respective teams buzzed around them. Metallica blared just beneath the dull roar of the spectators and the hush of the ice, the clacks of sticks on pucks.

Jacques meant it, too. It *was* always good to see Babe. He had always liked Babe even if he was a bit of an *enfant terrible*, with his coyote grin and sweaty curls and petty shots. He might be mischievous and a little salty, but he had never once been unkind, and he was a tricky, sly force on the ice that made games more fun.

"Hey. Wait up a sec."

Jacques met Babe's dark eyes and saw the seriousness in them. *Oh, no.* All he wanted from Babe was good fun. Confrontation was caught in his throat as they slowed to a stop and faced each other.

"Heard you're going through a divorce." Babe tapped Jacques's leg with his stick. "I'm real sorry to hear that. Seriously."

"Thanks. It is for the best," Jacques dismissed with a shrug. "Looking forward to tonight," he continued hastily, injecting some warmth into his voice. *Oh, more 'no comment' bullshit?* "I am hoping that Dempsey has grown up a little since our last game."

Babe grinned boyishly (Burnie always called him 'Harry fucking Styles' for that grin), bracing his stick behind his shoulders to better stretch his pectorals.

"He hasn't," he grunted through the stretch, "but keep hoping, Lavesque. That's one of the things I've come to like so much about you. You see potential in everyone—even when it's not, you know, warranted."

Babe skated off on that ominous note, still grinning. Beyond him, Jacques spotted Blom and they nodded to each other, but Blom was never social the way most captains had been trained to be, and did not bother approaching him.

It was fine with him. Jacques skated, still brooding. It might have been his last game against the Rangers anyway, even without all of this. The looming specter of a career-ending injury had been hanging over him since he turned thirty and had started getting questions about *after hockey*. He had had this vague taste in his mouth before, towards the end of every season: was this the end, and he just didn't know it yet?

He had been so afraid of it all ending without him being prepared for it. As it turned out, being prepared did not make it easier. He wished he could be blind to it after all. It was intolerable to wonder if every page was the last and he wondered now if he could have protected himself if he had loved a little less freely. He skated by the pile of pucks, digging deep for some of the usual calm that he felt on the ice—that meditative sense of inner silence that hockey had always given him—but it was a hand grasping blindly for something that he suspected was not there tonight.

"You good?" Burnie asked as he caught up with Jacques. He never wore his helmet during warm-ups and his hair was sticking straight up at the moment. "You look weird."

"I'm good," Jacques lied. *Oh, more 'no comment' bullshit?* They caught up with Pell who was moody and focused as usual, waiting for his turn at the pucks. Jacques watched them all, nearly as self-absorbed as he was today. There was no one who could take over for him easily, no one who was prepared to lead this team and do all of the little things between the lines of the contract. Burnie was too harsh, Pell too focused on his own game-time agitation, Novak too selfish in general. One day it would be Kyle, but he was still simply too young.

The anthem was sung, the puck was dropped, and he was only half-present for all of it. He skated through his first shift, an eye on Fowler and an eye on Dempsey, and felt the power in each stride. His body was not ready for his career to end—it was not *time* yet. He was as swift, as powerful, as precise as he had been at thirty, back when he had smiled at every interviewer's question about his age, a coy smile that always stopped just short of a wink.

(*No, I'm not really thinking too much about the future just yet*, he would always say with an innocent smile. *I think I am still playing strong as ever—but maybe you should ask my opponents if they think I'm getting old...*)

The game was choppy and uncertain, as he had known it would be. Babe was relentless and playful as usual, Blom plodding after him and just barely able to keep up. A penalty was called when Travis accidentally high-sticked Dempsey, who had been head-hunting Travis all of his shift, and Travis was humiliated and defensive about it. Jacques won the first face-off against Blom with a mouthful of bitterness and handfuls of thorns.

Kyle and Andrei were there wherever he needed them, seamless and swift and exacting. Every pass was fluid, every move was intuited, and he had not loved hockey like this in so long. As ever Andrei demanded more of him and it made the game so much sharper, so much better; and Kyle was the third head of the dragon that he had been waiting for all of his career, that rare player who matched Andrei and yet did not compete with him.

Kyle got the first goal toward the end of the period, set up by Jacques and Andrei. Babe, activated as usual by spite, swiftly followed with a cheap shot that got through Marcel's legs—one of Babe's specialties—just before the period ended.

The Bruins returned to the locker room and Jacques said something encouraging to the team, something that rolled off his tongue and that did not come from the heart, because for this too he was not fully present. Duffy had things to say as well, and Jacques half-heard them too, but none of it was new anyway.

(He was thinking of those very first years of hockey: of how he had never been anything remarkable in the beginning, distracted on the ice and more intrigued by the dynamics of the players than whether he could make the puck go in the little net. No one had known at the time that that would be the thing that would make him rise above the other boys; no one had paid him any attention at all. As a result, he had been allowed to fall in love with hockey in peace.

(It had begun on his terms, and no one else's.)

As they sat there drinking water and mopping sweat from their hair, he caught Travis looking down, face flushed, mouth twitching with barely suppressed frustration. If other players like Johansson and Novak failed to take these things seriously enough, then Travis erred too far on the other side, beating himself up for every loss of control, every wrong move—he was so *young*.

"Just ignore Dempsey," Jacques told Travis as they walked back through the tunnel toward the ice. He sensed the uselessness of this suggestion, so he tapped him on the back affectionately, as if that could make up for the uselessness.

"Yeah, he's not half the player that you are, *and* he's a douchebag," Connor agreed fiercely, knocking into Travis, who still looked doubtful and anxious.

"Don't let him get in your head. Just focus on the game. We have seen it a million times with other teams, right? When you let him get in your head, you make dumb mistakes and he profits," Jacques reminded him. "Focus on the puck."

"Okay," Travis promised him unconvincingly as they reached the ice.

"He's already in his head, dude," Burnie muttered behind Jacques as he clipped his helmet strap. They shuffled onto the bench, with Andrei and Kyle and Pell close behind. "Dempsey'll get another penalty out of the kid this period."

"Have some optimism," Pell encouraged. "Travis is resilient."

"Travis is *young*," Burnie said under his breath. Privately, Jacques agreed with him, but he could hardly criticize Travis for not having his head in the game right now. He glanced at the Rangers' bench—Dempsey was chewing on his mouthguard, yammering away at Fowler who was hunched forward, looking hungrily at the ice and not even pretending to listen.

The second period began. As soon as Travis dropped onto the ice for his first shift of the period, Dempsey was tailing him like a goose, yelling something rude and stupid at the back of his head. Travis kept his focus forward but his face was flushed, his eyes bright.

On the bench, Burnie groaned and bonked his helmet on the board in front of them; Pell shifted uncomfortably, mouth twisted in concern.

"He's fine," Jacques told them. "He has to learn."

"He's fine! He's fine," Pell agreed. On Jacques's other side, Andrei scoffed.

"He is spooked," Andrei warned him, and for a blinding, excruciating moment Jacques was thirty again: his sons unborn, his marriage to Rachel still fresh; his career still climbing to new heights; he and Andrei still muttering to each other on the bench without looking at one another, fragments of thoughts that the other stitched together effortlessly.

The passage of time was the worst poison. *You know what you want to do*, he reminded himself. It was time. But it also was not time yet.

Two conflicting things, Eloise had said, could be true at the same time. He was ready to go; he was not at all ready to go.

"That clown is in his head and then he will get into Kennedy's head too, and then we are done."

Andrei was, as usual, right—Travis *was* spooked. Jacques dropped onto the ice with Andrei and Kyle behind him and passed Travis. Travis did not even look at Jacques out of what Jacques guessed was shame, his head held high, chin jutting forward mutinously. Connor, flushed and unruly, bumped into Dempsey to antagonize him and Dempsey laughed as one of the refs separated them.

Andrei shot him a look that he could read easily: *see?* And Jacques stifled a flash of frustration, but this time it was just a little harder to tamp down.

"You have got to get him under control," Jacques told Blom as they circled each other, preparing for the face-off. Blom, impassive and dispassionate as ever, stared at Jacques with those pale, alien eyes.

"He has not done anything wrong," Blom disagreed robotically as he leaned forward, readying himself for the face-off.

And that too caused a flash of rage within Jacques.

"You know why he is doing it," he said as he leaned forward too, as the ref prepared himself.

"I don't," said Blom, and then the puck was dropped and the conversation was over. Jacques lost this face-off, incredibly, and another brick was added to the wall of his resentment. Blom was likely being honest—he was so indifferent to the dynamics of his team, he probably *didn't* know that Dempsey's specific harassment of Travis stemmed from Dempsey's profound homophobia, the homophobia that Jacques had watched the league tolerate, even encourage; the homophobia that Travis had decided to single-handedly fight by coming out over the summer.

(The homophobia that Jacques himself had never directly protested or vocally addressed. He had always told himself that it was his job to set the tone of a team, to lead by example, to lead by control of the culture. He had to be perfect—he had *agreed* to be perfect—and he did not know how to perfectly protest a thing so endemic, so deeply-rooted in the culture of the league, in the culture of professional sports. It did not matter how many times they donned their Pride jerseys and rainbow tape; it had still been a risk for Travis to come out and now he was paying for it.)

And Jacques still felt angry with Blom, a man toward whom he generally felt pleasantly neutral—and that angered him further, a brick wall being built over which he could no longer see. *The least you could fucking do*, he seethed as he stared at Blom, *is try to stop it.*

Dempsey's harassment of Travis had multiple consequences, just as Andrei had predicted: Connor was distracted and angry and was too occupied with following Dempsey when they were on the ice together to properly defend Marcel, which pissed off Johansson and Novak. Johansson played better when he was angry, but Novak played worse, and now Novak was consumed with his irritation toward Connor, and his need for Jacques to know he was irritated with Connor. Their plays were unraveling before their eyes, and there was only so much that Jacques, Burnie, Andrei, and Kyle could do to overcome the rest of the team.

Jacques skated past Dempsey, catching his eye, and Dempsey grinned at him—he knew what he was doing and he knew he could do it. And that bruised Jacques's ego, too, and now Dempsey was somehow in his head as well. He *felt* Andrei looking at him, amused at Jacques's bruised ego, another thing that harkened back to days that were gone, to a house that had been burned down.

Shifts overlapped and soon he was on the ice with Travis again, and for a few blessed moments Dempsey was off but then he trundled back onto it again like a pit bull, broad and stocky, and Jacques wished Travis would just get off the ice and forget about Dempsey—

"Hey," Dempsey scoffed as he knocked into Travis, and Jacques caught the tail end of a harsh and homophobic term. Travis was smacked against the boards as Dempsey laughed.

Jacques had a second to catch the look on Travis's face, and he wished he had not seen it, because he forgot about everything else—the puck, the game, his reputation, all of it. Blood rushed to his head; it was hard to breathe.

*Oh, more 'no comment' bullshit?*

And something in him snapped.

"HEY!" Jacques yelled, grabbing at Dempsey's jersey and holding him as they skated. He saw the baffled faces of his teammates and referees go by over Dempsey's head. "Hey! What was that?"

Dempsey grinned, chewing on his mouthguard as he glided with Jacques, not bothering to wrestle out of his grip. "We do not use that kind of language here in Boston," Jacques yelled.

"Ah, fuck off," Dempsey dismissed with a laugh, shoving him hard away from him.

"I am not kidding," Jacques yelled, looping around in front of him swiftly and grabbing him by the front of his jersey this time. Dempsey could not fight him off. He was bigger than Dempsey—he was bigger than a lot of other players, taller and stronger, even if he let people forget that. "I will not let you use that—"

"Let *go*—" Dempsey snarled, face flushing with his infamous temper. "Fuck off—"

"Not until you—" Jacques began, but Dempsey took a swing at his face and the force of it sent his helmet flying. His cheek throbbed where he had been hit, but it didn't hurt—he was mostly shocked. He had not seen it coming.

No one had taken a swing at him in a very long time. He had not allowed it to happen.

"Get the FUCK off of me," Dempsey bellowed, shoving Jacques as he tried to regain his balance. He didn't know where his helmet had landed, but he was aware that the game had come to a stop around them.

"YOU DON'T TOUCH LAVY," Marcel yelled, skating from the net, but Travis was faster, his face bright red with anger, and he knocked into Dempsey, and that was when it happened.

Jacques saw Dempsey's lips move to form the slur before he even heard it; there was a rushing in his ears. It was like it was happening in slow motion as Jacques dropped his stick, casting it aside, because there was a new flame burning in him, razing any remaining self-control he had.

He should have let it go. That would have been the Captain Jacques Lavesque thing to do. He should have told Travis to forget it; he should have had a talk with the referee. He should have kept a cool head and not reacted to this.

But that was not what he *wanted* to do—and now he was lunging for Dempsey, and then he was knocking into him, and together they went flying against the boards, and he could see the stripes of the referees and he could hear shouting but all he knew was Dempsey, and his own rage, and he knew he should have stopped but he couldn't make himself stop because he had never been so angry and he had never felt so useless; and then someone was pulling them apart, and Jacques realized it was Burnie and Pell, and Blom and Fowler were pulling Dempsey back, one of the zebras skating between them, holding his arms outstretched, and he heard the whistle as he struggled for breath.

"HE SHOULD BE FINED," Jacques bellowed at the referee, but no one was listening.

"Come on, we'll just kick their ass in the game," Pell was saying, looking at Jacques like he was a wild animal and he didn't know what he might do next. "That's way better revenge, right?"

"What'd he say? What'd he fucking say?" Burnie was shouting, hitting his stick against the ice repeatedly, annoying everyone around them.

"Nothing—forget it. He is just a pathetic little bitch," Marcel said, straightening his helmet and skating back to the net.

For the first time in a very long time, Jacques was in the Bruins' penalty box, a thin wall of plexiglass separating him and Dempsey. His cheek was throbbing and his throat felt raw from yelling, and he was struggling to catch his breath.

"Thanks for that," Travis said when he returned to the bench, dropping down next to Jacques. "Really meant something to have my hero defend me like that. Like, I just finished crying. But also, we can't afford to have you not on the ice."

"Yeah, you're right," Jacques agreed, adjusting his helmet, aware of Dempsey looking at him from the Rangers' bench. He felt Burnie slap him on the back and he nodded absently without looking at him.

"Fucking Dempsey," Burnie growled.

Jacques couldn't say anything in return.

And Andrei was looking at him, too, reading him and sensing the change in him like no one else could. In the old days, Andrei would have made a quiet little crack about him being on his period or something similarly juvenile. At least tonight he did not try anything like that, because Jacques thought if he did, he would punch him in the face.

He was struggling to catch his breath and realizing, increasingly, that it was rage and not exertion. He squirted water from his bottle onto his face, and told himself to keep it together.

It was his shift again and he, Andrei, and Kyle slipped onto the ice to replace the fourth line just as Dempsey came back on with Fowler and Blom. And at last everything in Jacques's mind quieted, as it so often did when he was finally on the ice, when he knew he was needed. He caught Andrei's eye and felt that peace deepen, knew Andrei felt it too, that intuition between them. He knew what they would do, knew how they would box Fowler in; there was Dempsey on his left, then behind him, then in front of him, but he was focused on Fowler—

—and then he was blinded by an explosion of pain, the world spinning out of control as he dropped his stick and clutched his face, the impact of his body hitting the ice nothing to the blinding pain in his face, and he rolled onto his stomach, wet heat gushing, blood in his mouth, that coppery taste mixing with the sour green burn of bile. He couldn't stop the gasp from coming out, felt blood dripping from his mouth to pool beneath him, felt the cool rush of the air from the ice ruffle through his hair like a mother's touch; his helmet had come off at some point and he didn't know where it was and he didn't even know why it mattered, and he kept thinking, *you have to get up,* but he was on his knees anyway.

·))●((·

"Holy *shit*," Hollis hissed from the living room.

"What?" Lily called impatiently, and she and Eloise glanced at each other when Hollis squeaked, "Nothing!" in return. "Eloise, don't come in here," he added.

Annoyed, Eloise set down the dish she was drying, having been helping Lily bake cookies for her direct reports. Even as she walked into the living room, wiping her sudsy hands on her jeans, she could hear the commentator saying Jacques's name over the dull roar of the crowd in the stadium. A lump formed in her throat—she didn't want to see this, she didn't want to see *him*. She was about to turn and go back into the kitchen when she saw something that stopped her in her tracks.

There was Jacques crumpled on the ice, braced on his elbows and knees, blood dripping from his mouth and onto the ice. Another player—she recognized Tripp Dempsey—was scrambling to his feet before Jacques as he looked around wildly, sweaty brown curls swinging with the movement.

"Oh," she gasped helplessly.

The stadium was all silent, all held breath, before there was an explosion of movement: Burnie lunged for Dempsey with a roar and was blocked by Babe Fowler; Bouchard and Pell were screaming at one of the referees as Duffy marched onto the ice, terrible and huge in his grey suit—

—but then Andrei ripped off his helmet and gloves and cast them aside, and it was like it was in slow motion: everyone turned to watch Andrei.

Andrei slammed Tripp into the boards before Tripp could so much as hold up his hands. The referees let go of Burnie and Babe to try and pull apart Andrei and Tripp, but neither were big enough to stop Andrei, who flung them each aside like they were dolls. He tore off Dempsey's helmet and discarded it before casting him into the boards with that same terrible fluid grace with which he did everything. He was just getting started, and there was no one on the ice but Jacques who could stop him now.

Players were streaming onto the ice from both teams, circling Andrei and Dempsey warily, but Andrei shoved any assailants aside with a callous, animal fury that stopped the others in their tracks.

Dempsey, pale and panicking, attempted to scramble to his feet as he looked up at Andrei. Andrei watched him dispassionately, allowing him to rise before lunging again and tackling him to the ice—and now it began in earnest as he pinned Dempsey down and punched him in the face.

It was madness. Burnie, Marcel, and Pell were trying to get close to Andrei but he resisted their advances, and they were all so much smaller than him. Babe Fowler was shouting and fighting as Egil Blom held him back; behind them, one of the team physicians crouched beside Jacques, holding gauze to his face and gingerly trying to help him up; the referees were in the tussle now and one stumbled back, clutching his nose after getting elbowed in the face; Tripp Dempsey was briefly visible, flat on his back on the ice, dazed and limp, face shining with blood, as Marcel and Burnie tried to wrench Andrei off of him, with Burnie on Andrei's back, arms locked around his neck; the crowd was roaring; the commentators were speechless and stammering, trying to keep apace of what was happening; Jacques finally got to his feet and furiously shrugged off the physician's help, clutching the towel to his face as it bloomed with blood, leaving a smear of dark red on the ice where he had been taken down by Dempsey's hit—

—and then he skated off the rink without a single glance back at the fight, without a single attempt to stop it. It was as though it was not happening at all.

"Holy shit," Hollis breathed once more. "Holy *shit*."

No one spoke as Andrei at last was peeled off of Tripp Dempsey. It took two referees, an assistant coach, Marcel, and Burnie to do it. Just like Jacques, Andrei too shrugged off the grip of any of the referees and skated between all of them, moving for the dressing room just as Jacques had. The team physicians and referees and players were left to try and help Tripp Dempsey—bloodied and disoriented—to his feet before it became clear that a stretcher would be necessary.

"That—that was unlike any fight I have ever seen in twenty years of NHL hockey," one of the commentators stammered in shock as Dempsey was carried off the ice. "That was the most violent—the ugliest display—Koslov is *certainly* going to receive a hefty fine for that—"

"And a suspension to be sure, which is more crucial, especially if Lavesque's also too injured to play for a few games," the other one replied faintly. Eloise got the sense that he was doing his best to stick to the facts, to not supply his own take. "The only question is *how many* games Koslov will be suspended for, but it's sure to make a dent in the Bruins' season—and potentially damage their race for the Cup."

The game went to a commercial break, and Hollis turned down the volume as Eloise dropped onto the couch beside him, her stomach churning.

"Holy *shit*," Lily whispered from the doorway.

# Chapter Twenty-Seven

His face was throbbing with pain—but mostly he was blind with a rage he had never before known, a rage that buzzed and sparked and stretched its hot, leathery wings.

Jacques stalked into the locker room, hands shaking and throat tight, nowhere to go with this molten, ugly anger. It billowed and expanded as he paced, threatening to take flight, to scorch all the land around him.

He kept seeing Andrei's red face, black hair clinging in sweaty clumps to his cheeks—he would be suspended for so many games—and Jacques knew he was injured too, that he probably would be on concussion watch for weeks, knew he too would be out for so many games—what Andrei had just done—it might cost them the playoffs—and it was his last chance to—his last opportunity—it was *over*—

He could not stand it.

He blindly grabbed a cart full of tape and flung it to the side, sending rolls everywhere, just as Andrei entered. The rolls of tape spilled out between them as they regarded each other.

Andrei. Andrei, who had cost him everything. Andrei, standing there with his split lip and mutinous, glittering eyes, brutal features made even more skeletal and hard by the fluorescent lighting of the locker room. Andrei, whom he had loved like a brother; Andrei, who had been his best friend for half his life. Andrei, who still took from Jacques no matter how much he gave. Andrei, for whom nothing from Jacques was ever enough. Andrei, who was a black hole of rage and want.

Andrei, who had the nerve to stand there before him, shameless and proud, after all that he had burned down.

He hated him. Jacques could hardly breathe for how much he hated him. He knew that the other players were beginning to filter into the locker room, that they would witness whatever this turned into, but he did not care. It was just him and Andrei now, him and Andrei as it had always been.

Seventeen years of making excuses for Andrei. Seventeen years of turning a blind eye, of keeping a shut mouth; seventeen years of making allowances for a man who would take all that he held dear and set it ablaze. Seventeen years of frustration and embarrassment, of tolerating the judgment of others, of feigning ignorance and supplying weak excuses, all for a man who was effectively ending his marriage and his career, the two things he had prized most in his life. This man he called brother—seventeen years of calling him brother—was now standing before him without shame or apology or chagrin.

He had taken, and taken, and taken, and Jacques had just let him. *Oh, more 'no comment' bullshit?* Eloise asked in his head.

Jacques did not care that anyone was watching them. It did not matter anymore.

"Get out of my sight," he told Andrei.

Andrei stared at him and said nothing. He slowly wiped blood from his chin with the back of his hand. Jacques tried to draw in a breath and could not quite manage it.

"Get out of this locker room. Get out of this stadium," he said as he approached Andrei. He took in the exhilaration in Andrei's hazel eyes at his approach. Perhaps a fight was what Andrei had been after all along.

Well, he would get it. Whether or not this was what Andrei wanted—he would get it.

"Yeah, fuck you, Jay," Andrei scoffed. Jacques could not help it—he laughed too, even as it made his head throb more where Tripp had hit him.

"Jay? You think you can call me Jay after everything you have done?"

Why was he smiling? Why was it funny? *Jay*. Only Andrei had ever tried to bring him back to earth with a nickname, yet he had also been the first to call him *Prince Jacques*, the first to crown him.

Jacques reached Andrei and shoved him as hard as he could.

Andrei hit the wall, too stunned that it had actually happened to defend himself in time. *That's right*, Jacques thought viciously as he watched Andrei recoil in shock. *You thought my patience was unconditional; you thought you could just keep pushing me forever.* All the months of stifling himself, of swallowing every burst of rage that he felt whenever he saw Andrei—it was unfurling, a great beast made of ash that had been waiting to take flight.

Andrei was regarding him with that triumphant exhilaration still in his eyes, breathing heavily as he pushed himself off of the wall with strained movements. He was tired from his fight with Dempsey, Jacques could see that much. Andrei was not nineteen anymore; he was not that unstoppable, biblical force anymore. He was no longer fire and flood as he had once been.

"I didn't have to do anything," Andrei said quietly. "You are still so fucking stupid about Rachel. It makes me hate you, sometimes. You've always been so stupid about—"

"This isn't about Rachel," Jacques interrupted. A detached, separate part of him—the Prince Jacques part, the part that was always on alert for how he might be perceived—realized in this moment that the whole team could now guess that Andrei had interfered with his marriage in some way, a thing he had nearly killed himself to keep secret. Now it was out. All that work for nothing, papers scattered in a stream. And now that it was out, he realized how little it mattered that they knew. It had never been the real problem at all; that had never been the real secret. "This is about what you have done to my career. You selfish—"

He could not even finish the sentence.

Before he could stop himself he slammed into Andrei. He heard someone yelling but it didn't matter because he was yelling too, yelling louder—"Fight back, Andrei, come on," and then Andrei was throwing him against the opposite wall, knocking the wind from him, and now they were on the floor, and now Andrei was on top of him, crushing him, but Jacques was bigger and stronger than he ever let on, not so much smaller than Andrei even if he had always made himself smaller, safer, sweeter, softer; and he had seventeen years of unreleased anger, seventeen years of rage and frustration coursing through his veins; and now he was on top of Andrei, and blood and sweat were stinging his eyes as they fought. *It's over*, a voice was saying in his head, or maybe they were saying it out loud, *it's over*, and then they were on their feet again, two unstoppable forces matched against each other, and it was over, his career was ending, and nothing great had come of it, and he didn't know what the point was, and then Bouchard and Burnie were pulling him off of Andrei and he was stumbling backward and it was over.

His mouth tasted like iron. Andrei was on his hands and knees, struggling to catch his breath. The locker room was silent save for their gasping breaths.

"Lavesque—"

"Let go of me," Jacques ordered. He wrenched himself free, heart pounding so hard he thought he might be sick. He stumbled away from Burnie and Bouchard, aware of all the eyes upon him. He looked away, wiping his mouth.

(This, too, Andrei had taken from him.)

He watched Andrei grab hold of one of the benches and struggle to his feet, ominously shaky. His left eye was swollen shut—had Jacques really done that?—and blood was streaming freely from his mouth and nose, smeared across his cheek and into his black hair. He was bruised and fatigued and weak. He was not nineteen anymore; he was not unstoppable anymore.

"This—this is unbelievable," Duffy sputtered, unable to inject enough disgust into his voice to hide his obvious shock. "I don't even know where to start."

"Then don't," Andrei said. He sniffed and wiped his bloody mouth as he stared at Jacques and Jacques stared back. "It is none of your fucking business."

"You're going to be suspended for—for I don't even know how many games, Koslov, and Lavesque probably has a concussion, so I think it is my business," Duffy countered, his voice rising as he spoke, as he fully appreciated the consequences of all that had happened within a mere five minutes. "We discussed this, and you promised me clean games. Dempsey couldn't even walk off the ice on his own—and now you're fighting the captain in the locker room."

Andrei drew himself to his full height as he looked down at Duffy, all contempt and smeared blood. It took effort, maybe all the effort he had left.

"The captain," he said, "was fighting me."

Duffy had nothing to say to that. Andrei scoffed at his silence, his massive shoulders rising with the movement, spraying Duffy's white shirt with a fine spray of blood. Duffy blinked at the spray, gritting his teeth, but he did not move to wipe his face. Andrei turned, mouth twisted in disdain. He pulled off his bloodied jersey and dropped it in the laundry bin, the number seventy-three—spattered with Dempsey's blood—facing the ceiling like a dead body. With one last significant look at Jacques, Andrei grabbed his duffle bag and left the locker room, leaving the team in quaking silence.

Jacques leaned against one of the stalls and put his hands on his knees. The weight of a hand on his back pulled him back to reality—he knew it was Burnie. The shame was creeping in, and Burnie's touch only made it worse. He knew what Burnie would be realizing, knew what the whole team would be realizing, and if they pitied him then he would be sick.

He had done what he wanted—and here were the consequences.

Now that Andrei was gone, no one knew where to look. Duffy was not looking directly at Jacques, like he was too embarrassed to meet his eyes.

"We'll talk later, Lavesque, after you've gotten looked over," Duffy promised him, his tone considerably less confident. "As for the rest of you—back to the game."

Jacques listened to his teammates leave, one by one, as he straightened. He kept his eyes trained on the opposite wall so that he did not have to see how any of them looked at him. In the blink of an eye—as quick as Andrei had gone from nineteen to thirty-seven—it was over. There was nothing left to say.

*Oh, more 'no comment' bullshit?*

He should have said sorry, but he was not sorry. He could not summon any guilt, or any sense of remorse: only the shame that anyone had witnessed it. Now Burnie, Pell, Bouchard, and Kyle remained. Somehow, Kyle's presence was the most difficult.

"How is Dempsey? Did you see?" he asked, blinking when something—blood or sweat—dripped into his eye. Bouchard, cat-quick to recover, cleared his throat.

"He is very bad," he said softly. He glanced over his shoulder, back at the tunnel to the ice, aware that their time was running out. "Lavesque—"

"Forget it. You'd better get back out there," he said before Bouchard could finish. Bouchard nodded and turned. Kyle followed, seemingly sensing that this was a private moment to which he was not invited, leaving just Pell and Burnie with Jacques in the locker room.

They had been with him for so long. They knew him so well—yet they knew so little about him. They did not know him like Andrei had. They had not known this fight was ever a possibility, but Andrei, like Eloise, had known all along: Jacques was this person too. Could their friendship survive this tear, this gash? Or would he lose them too? Maybe this was the first crack.

If so, he could not stand it. He loved them so much. He could not bear it.

"You need to sit down, Lavy. Come on," Pell said in that gentle way of his. He placed a compassionate hand on Jacques's shoulder and guided him to the bench that lined their stalls. "That's it, sit down. You've got it."

Now that he was sitting down he realized how badly he had needed to. Pell stayed by his side while Burnie grabbed a water bottle and passed it to him.

"Thanks," he said without looking at him, without touching the water. He closed his eyes when he felt the weight of Burnie's hand on his head. Burnie's words had come true—he *had* blown up at someone and regretted it—though he still did not know if Andrei had deserved this explosion or not.

Could a wild animal be blamed for being untrainable? It was how they had been made. They had all warned him from the very beginning about Andrei. He was a lion caged in shadow, and when Jacques closed his eyes he knew that that wild animal—with its phosphorescent eyes—had been Andrei all along.

To his surprise, he felt Burnie kiss the top of his head. "I'm—"

"Hey. You're okay," Burnie said, ruffling his hair. "Okay?"

"Okay," Jacques said. When he looked up, he met Burnie's bright green eyes and had never seen them look like that: full of uncertainty and sadness. Behind him, Pell looked fearful, aghast; nothing like the sweet calm his voice had radiated a moment ago. They might be here for him, but they did not know how to handle him like this.

Jacques looked down again as both men turned and left the locker room.

He had wanted them all to leave him alone, but now that they had, being alone with it all was unbearable. The locker room was so silent.

And then he was thinking of Eloise, imagining her sitting alone in her car on the day she had been fired, alone with her unvoiced justifications and her defenses and her rationale, aware that there was nothing she could say that could walk back the choice she had made to blow it all up. And then he was thinking of the look on her face when they had had their final argument, and the fact that she had left Madison Square Garden alone. And then he was thinking of her on the stand again, her back straight and voice clear as she did it all over again.

He covered his face with his hands and leaned forward, elbows on his knees.

"Hey... We need to patch you up a bit, Cap." Moretti had entered the locker room on light feet, and Jacques, hands still covering his face, felt the team physician's hand on his back. "Come on, let's go look you over."

"Yes, of course," Jacques said as he dropped his hands, his voice still hoarse and raw from yelling, and followed Moretti into the office in mute obedience.

Moretti's examination was a blur. Neither of them acknowledged that the fight with Andrei was perhaps the worst thing he could have done after Dempsey's hit. There was no point in saying it. At this point, he knew, and Moretti knew that he knew. This would take him out for a while. In the span of a few minutes, both he and Andrei had seriously damaged the team's chances at a Cup run.

He obediently held still as Moretti shot lidocaine into his brow and his cheek so that he could stitch his wounds closed. He closed his eyes, biting his lip against the pressure of the needle and the burn of the medicine.

"I am going home," he told Moretti, once the physician had finished stitching the gash above his brow. The skin throbbed from the lidocaine and the pressure of the needle, a sensation he was so used to and yet which was claustrophobic this time.

"I think that's a good idea," Moretti said with an uncertain smile. He had nothing else to say to Jacques; he was partly hiding his shock but Jacques could still feel it—that intuition about what others thought and felt, which had served him so well throughout his career, was something that he wished he could turn off now.

Jacques tried to smile in turn but his mouth was throbbing. He settled for touching Moretti on the shoulder as he slid off the table. He knew he should have waited until the end of the game—that would be Captain behavior; that would be Prince Jacques behavior—but there was nothing he wanted more than to get out of Boston Garden.

He changed out of his Under Armour and pads in the empty locker room. He always felt so much smaller in his own clothes after the weight and breadth of the uniform. *After hockey*, he thought, dropping his bloodied jersey in the bin.

He texted one of the admins, requesting a ride home, and after collecting his things he left Boston Garden the back way, where the buses usually arrived. It was cold and damp here in the sheltered area, the distant roar of traffic and rain all around him. But of course—he was not alone. Jacques halted.

Andrei sat on the edge of a crate, slouched like a devil as he looked at his phone.

The exhaustion hit him then as Andrei looked up, the glow of the phone illuminating his harsh features.

"You look like hell," Andrei observed, "...Jay."

If he looked like hell—and he knew he did—then Andrei looked worse. His eye was fully swollen shut now, and blood was crusting along his jaw and around his ear, matting his hair to the side of his face. He should have gotten Moretti to look at it, but then, that would never be Andrei's style.

It occurred to Jacques that Andrei might be waiting for Rachel to pick him up, and he waited for some feeling of anger or betrayal, but all that he felt was the pulsing ache of his injuries, and a hollow sense of loss. Why would you ever love anything? The end of love was inevitable and it burned like lidocaine, leaving numbness and bruised skin in its place, an injury that would be forever visible, a mark of proof that you had been stupid enough, vulnerable enough, to allow yourself to be hit in the first place.

(Love was lidocaine pulsing in your skin; love was a bruise.)

"Andrei," he said wearily, "I am so tired of you."

The thing that happened four years ago was all that was left standing between them right now—that scuttling cockroach, crawling amongst the nuclear waste of their friendship; that thing that had marked the point of no return. Everything else, both good and bad, had been burned to the ground, but this *thing* still twitched and lived between them.

Andrei's bitter laugh, in spite of everything, broke his heart.

"Yeah? I am more tired of you. I am so tired of you, Jay. Somehow in the end everything in my life is about you."

He hesitated, a thing Andrei never did, and it stilled Jacques. "...Like I don't know what is me and what is you."

The raw anger blistering his voice was something Jacques should have expected, yet it still came as a surprise. Andrei *was* anger, he was all anger, but Jacques had always assumed that he had simply been made that way—made from burning matches and spilled liquor and bubbling acid and splintered bone. It had never occurred to him that he had anything to do with it.

"I didn't know you felt that way," Jacques admitted, as something squeezed his chest.

Andrei was looking up at him through the curtain of matted black hair that hung over his eyes, weighed down with sweat and blood and grease.

"Because you are the sun, and the world revolves around you. My world," he added, "has revolved around you since I was nineteen. And I am so tired of it."

"That is bullshit," Jacques said immediately. "Your world revolves around *you*. And I have always accepted that about you—"

Andrei's scoff interrupted him. Jacques braced himself. This, he knew, would hurt.

"It doesn't matter what you thought you accepted, because you were wrong. You were wrong about me, and every time I showed you who I was, and what mattered to me, you turned and looked somewhere else. And when you couldn't turn away anymore, you just refused it. There is no acceptance here—not from you." Andrei shook his head. "You have never accepted anyone or anything, as it really was, in your whole life. Not me, not your brother, not Rachel—not Eloise."

For a moment there was no talking, just traffic and the rain and a rattling vent somewhere, and the distant thud of music from inside the stadium.

"What will you do," Andrei wondered, "when your sons grow up and they disappoint you next? What if Peter isn't the brilliant little boy you have decided he is? What if he is just Peter?"

"Don't talk about Peter."

Andrei rolled his eyes.

"I never wanted him to be my godson, and I hope you figured that out," he dismissed impatiently.

Here again was that twitching, un-killable thing between them, the thing that had been creeping beneath the rest of it all along. *You have never accepted anything in your entire life.*

"Yeah," Jacques said. "I did know that. It killed me. I couldn't ask you to be my best man, I couldn't bring you back into my life, I couldn't ask you for anything, but I thought I could at least—"

"I never wanted 'at least' from you," Andrei cut in ruthlessly. "I am not a dog."

"Then why did you come back to Boston?" Jacques fired back. "If you hate this team, if you hate this town, if you didn't want any of this from me—why did you come back?"

Andrei did not answer. He pressed his palms to his eyes, flinching at the pain, as he leaned forward.

"I don't owe you shit," he said quietly. "Not an explanation. Not a heart-to-heart. You're so mad that I fucked up your little playoff race tonight? You're so mad that I fucked up your stupid little marriage? You have fucked up my whole life. I don't owe you anything."

His phone pulsed with a text to signal that the car was on the way. Time was running out. Was there any way for them to move past this? It was not really tonight that they would have to move past, but rather everything that had come before tonight: all of the little unfairnesses and wounds, the betrayals great and small. And then there was the creature that skittered beneath it, the creature that Jacques had always pretended was not there at all.

Love was an unkillable creature, slinking beneath years of detritus; love was so many words unsaid.

"I am sorry," he said. "For everything."

"I don't want you to be sorry," Andrei said bitterly. "That is humiliating."

The rain fell and the two men considered the smoking ruins of their careers, their friendship, and all of the collateral damage of that friendship, of those careers.

(Love was a bloodstained jersey, discarded in a bin.)

"You don't even know why Dempsey hit me," Jacques said now. "I might have deserved it."

Andrei laughed and shook his head.

"I really don't care why he did it," he said. "It does not matter to me if you deserved it or not."

Understanding was settling in Jacques, a painful understanding that pulsed with the beat of his heart just like his wounds did. When his car had finally arrived, Jacques looked back at Andrei, considering what he could say, how they could leave things, but Andrei was still sitting with his head in his hands.

"I guess I will see you at practice at some point," he said as Andrei looked up, dropping his hands from his bruised face.

"Maybe. Maybe not." Andrei swallowed, looking away. "I don't know what the league will do about this yet."

"You want me to step in?" Jacques asked, and Andrei shook his head. "Alright."

He did not know whether to wave, whether to say anything. Ironically, he thought of Burnie kissing him on the top of his head earlier. His impulse was to do it, to touch Andrei in some way, to acknowledge the depth of their bond, terrible as it was. But that too would have been another 'at least'—so instead he waved, and pushed out the heavy door onto the sidewalk, where his car was now waiting.

He knew Krystal was texting and calling him, frantic with worry, and he had a call from Simpson, who had been traded last year but with whom he was still in touch, and he even had a text from Rachel, but he ignored the calls and texts as the car took him through the inky night toward his new home in Cambridge.

He slumped in his seat and was grateful that the driver did not try to make conversation. He had been stripped down to something that was not even the Jay whom Andrei had so deeply loved, but something plainer, something he did not want anyone to see. He was just stitches and scar tissue now, broken bones and a beating heart; bruised knuckles and split lips and the will to love even when he should have known better.

Now they were in Cambridge and it was quieter, the Christmas lights that should have been taken down a month ago blurred by the rain.

He wanted to see Eloise. It was all he could think about.

"Here we are," the driver said as the black car rolled to a stop in front of his new home, dark in the rain and notably bare of twinkle lights unlike the houses around it. Next year he would put up Christmas lights. Next year, regardless of what his life looked like, he would have the time to put up Christmas lights.

*After hockey.* What came after hockey? It was a black hole.

And yet somehow he had some fight left in him: because he knew what he wanted to do, and he knew it was wrong, knew it was not what he should be doing, but he also knew he was going to do it anyway.

There was no way to protect yourself from love, and after all, this was one thing Andrei had never really understood about him. He might not accept people as they were—that was true—but he *did* love them. He loved them deeply and painfully and stupidly, he loved with abandon, he loved even when everyone told him it was the wrong thing to do. He had loved so many unlovable people—his brother, Andrei, Rachel—and he had loved Kyle and Burnie and Pell and Krystal and their families and their friends. He had loved hockey and he knew he would fall in love with whatever came next, too. He was in love with the world and at times in love with every single person in it. That was real. He had never had to fake his love, not even once.

He was a fool for love: for every painful kind of love. And when he thought of the tattoo that stretched across his back—that King of Cups, that ruler who stayed open to his feelings—he thought perhaps a part of him even at nineteen had known himself better than he had realized. It had not been a closed fist against his past but an open palm to his future.

He would keep falling in love until there was nothing left of him but stitches and scars. He would leave himself open, and he would get hurt every time, because he loved love, and he loved to love, especially those who needed it. And he was afraid of it now—he had been through it enough times to know better, just like he knew to tense against the burn of lidocaine, to be afraid of the pain, to wince and cringe and grit his teeth. He was too old to be fearless the way he once had been, when he had approached Andrei on the ice that first day, when he had knelt down before Rachel and held up a diamond, when he had signed his life away to the Bruins.

"Thank you very much," he told the driver in a raw, quiet voice.

He got out of the car, his duffle bag weighing heavily on his shoulder as he walked up the front path. Inside, the house was cold and smelled damp from the rain. The empty rooms were so loud with his every movement, without furniture or rugs to absorb the noise. His keys clattered on the kitchen counter and his bag thudded to the floor.

Tonight was a night for turning to face things, and he had one more thing left to face.

He knew what he wanted to do, but he had no idea what the outcome might be. He did not know how much damage this might do.

He was a fool, and he was the King of Cups. Jacques took out his phone and texted Kyle.

**Jacques [10:37pm]**: hey, hope the rest of the game went well.

**Jacques [10:37pm]**: Krystal mentioned Eloise had moved. do you know her new address?

He dropped onto the bottom stair in the darkness while he waited for Kyle to text back. His wounds throbbed in time with his heart, which beat a steady tattoo against his ribs, a pulsing reminder of how vulnerable he was.

**Kyle Hearst [10:39pm]**: nah shes still living with her dad rn

**Kyle Hearst [10:39pm]**: its in chestnut hill hold on

Kyle followed with a screenshot from Google Maps with her address.

**Jacques [10:40pm]**: thanks.

**Kyle Hearst [10:41pm]**: np man

**Kyle Hearst [10:41pm]**: good luck

He smiled as he got to his feet and put his phone away, bracing himself against a painful burst of affection for Kyle. He had some missed texts from Burnie, and from Pell, and from Duffy too, and he sent them each a quick message to let them know he would get in touch with them tomorrow.

He had something else to do tonight—one more comment to make.

# Chapter Twenty-Eight

M inutes went by where both teams disappeared to their respective dressing rooms and the broadcast went to a hasty commercial break. When play resumed, both Jacques and Andrei were gone along with Dempsey, and the commentators made no further remarks on what had happened, or where they had gone. It was a gaping black hole in the game that everyone skirted around, a pall that settled over the stadium.

The game ended shortly thereafter with a Rangers win. Kyle scored once more, assisted by Burnie and Novak, but the stadium around him hardly cheered for all that had happened, and then Babe Fowler scored twice after that. Tripp Dempsey's status was not shared, and none of the players—among the Rangers or the Bruins—seemed to know how to act. Goals went uncelebrated, penalties passed with little rebuke, and the game ended on a comma: the players lingered on the ice, looking between each other like they were waiting for a grown-up to come out and fix everything. The camera zoomed in on Pell (pale and anxious) and Burnie (aloof and watchful) and then on Babe Fowler, the last to leave the ice, as he skated in a helpless lap, looking around the ice as though trying to convince himself of all that had happened.

"I can't believe it," Hollis muttered at last, the first to break the shocked silence of the living room.

The highlights played before them, without any of them paying the slightest attention. "Koslov is going to be out for *so* many games. He's completely screwed the team over. I can't believe he did that."

"He knew better than that," Dad said disgustedly. "He knew exactly what that was going to cost them, especially at this point in the season, and he did it anyway. I told you—bringing Koslov back was always going to be bad news. He's bad for teams."

"And then Lavesque starting a fight at all," Hollis continued, aghast, raking his hands through his auburn hair and then mopping his face. "Also, he's probably gonna get put on concussion watch—he's prone to them as it is, and that hit was *something*. He's definitely going to be out for a few games."

Eloise did her best to control her features, but there was a hook in her throat and her hands were clammy. She had not been prepared for what that sight—Jacques bent over on the ice, reeling in pain and helpless as Andrei swept past him and damaged his chances of a Cup run, of everything he had been holding onto—would do to her.

She did not want to feel like this about him anymore. She looked up at the ceiling, aware of Lily's shrewd eyes on her, her vision blurring with stupid, *pointless* tears. Why wasn't there a way to cut out this part of herself, the part that had so foolishly fallen for Jacques Lavesque—the part that was crying over his pain right now like it was her own? She was just like her father, crying over someone who was long gone, someone who did not want her at all.

Dad and Hollis were still running over the fight in shock, and Hollis was Googling to confirm that Jacques had never been in a fight before, so Eloise took out her phone. She could not stand not knowing what was happening, and she knew that Kyle would not judge her for this question. Kyle already knew the truth of how she felt, anyway. He had picked up on it as quickly as Andrei had—perhaps even quicker, his light eyes flicking between her and Jacques that very first day and quietly intuiting what she had not even known yet about herself.

**Eloise [10:13pm]:** hey, I was just watching the game with my family. nice goals - was worried about Jacques. is he okay?

Almost immediately, the three dots popped up. She gripped her phone, clenched her muscles, grit her teeth, as she watched the screen and waited for his answer. Immediately there was regret. This was like a sickness. She should never have asked; he did not want her, had all but *told* her he did not want her; *why* was she even asking after him—

**Kyle Hearst [10:14pm]:** he and koslov just beat the shit out of each other in the locker room and he just left

It was fiction; it had to be something her mind had conjured in the small hours of the morning, something from within those dark hours in which she woke with a start and found herself thinking of him again, grieving the loss of him all over again.

**Kyle Hearst [10:14pm]:** never seen him like this

**Kyle Hearst [10:14pm]:** didn't know he had it in him tbh

**Kyle Hearst [10:14pm]:** also sounds like koslov got with his wife... jesus christ kind of figured he had done something bad but didn't think it was that bad

Eloise waited for another bubble with three dots to appear, but, stubbornly tacit as always, Kyle had nothing else to add.

Every time she blinked she saw Jacques kneeling on the ice in pain, unable to stop Andrei, unable to protect his career, unable to control the feral man he had once called his best friend—

"El, you okay?" Hollis asked, drawing her back to reality.

"Yeah," she said, putting her phone away.

She had to move on. "Yeah," she said more confidently now, "I'm fine. Just freaked out by the fight, that's all. It's hard to see that much violence."

She felt Lily's hand on her shoulder, and she reached up and squeezed her hand to reassure her. "I think I'm going to go up and do some work," she announced, avoiding Lily's eyes. She could feel Dad and Hollis looking at her worriedly, so she smiled in their direction and hastened up the stairs before her feelings could show on her face.

The second floor was claustrophobically warm and she opened the hall window, letting in the damp February chill. Eloise looked into the inky night like she had lost someone in it, pressing her forehead against the icy glass and letting the cold shock her back to reality.

It was all coming back again after months of being okay. She went to the bathroom to take off her makeup, another desperate attempt to shake herself out of it all. For a flash she imagined reaching out: a short text, a quick call. *I know you're in pain and it matters to me.*

But that could not be. She rubbed her eyeliner off vigorously, angrily.

Maybe it would be best in the future if she just avoided anything related to hockey at all. And maybe she ought to give dating a real shot, not just a good-sport kind of shot. She had assumed that time would do enough, but clearly time had done nothing but preserve that burst of sunlight in winking crystal, that uncatchable sense of having encountered something perfect, something magic, something *more*; that glimpse of the wisp behind the curtain, the beauty just beyond the ivy-covered garden door. Now she was just building a shrine to a thing that had never been there at all, worshipping a false god that would only make her bleed.

Years of protecting her heart behind shatterproof glass—and now she was crying in her father's bathroom over a man who had all but told her he did not want her. She was seriously considering reaching out to him.

"I'm okay," she told her reflection: platinum hair with the auburn roots coming in, wild as always, and skin blotchy and flushed with emotion.

She took the rest of her makeup off and ran a brush through her hair when she heard a vague commotion downstairs; most likely Lily trying to explain to Dad and Hollis that Eloise was upset, if she had to guess. She would do some work, and maybe put together a game plan for moving.

"Um. El?"

Hollis called up the stairs; he sounded strange. Eloise closed her eyes and let her head drop back. She did not have the emotional capacity, at this specific moment, to discuss the game with Hollis, which was her only guess as to what he could want. Or maybe someone on Reddit had made a meme about Jacques getting into a fight. Memes were always a strong likelihood with Hollis.

"Yeah?" she called back after a moment.

"Can you—can you come down here?" His voice cracked. He said something else, but she couldn't hear as she dropped her skincare back in its pouch.

"Be right there," she called, irritation seeping into her voice as she set the pouch in its usual spot on the windowsill. What she needed right now was to be alone, to let her face fall the way it wanted, but she could do another few minutes if she had to.

"El?" he called again.

"I'm *coming*," she called impatiently, and she rounded the corner as she rolled her eyes and plodded down the steps—

—and halted halfway down, suspended on the staircase, when she saw why Hollis had called her.

If she had not been so in shock, she would have found the sight comical: Hollis was clutching the front door with one hand, stammering something that sounded vaguely like *you're my hero* and *are you sure I can't get you anything*, putting in mind a wind-up toy caught between two actions. Dad was hunched by the couch, staring at the front door in a stupor.

Lily, on the other side of the living room, had her arms crossed over her chest, her lips pursed and head tilted, torn between arch silence and awe.

And Jacques Lavesque was standing in her front doorway, in the doorway Eloise had gone through hundreds of thousands of times throughout her life so thoughtlessly, never knowing that he would be standing in it. His nose and brow were taped, one eye shadowed with a developing black eye. She wondered if Andrei had done any visible damage from their fistfight, but somehow she doubted it.

(She was not the only one who loved this man—and she had known that from the beginning, now that she thought of it.)

Despite the damage he was as beautiful as ever: those slate eyes, that broken nose, that expressive mouth that was so quick to curve into the half-smile that had hooked her from the first moment.

He was not smiling now. He was staring up at her warily, like she was something wild and dangerous, something untamed and feral—something that could cause him harm.

"Are you *sure* I can't—" Hollis tried again desperately.

"I am really fine, thank you. It is nice to meet you all," Jacques said graciously. Hollis shook his hand mechanically, still staring up at his hero.

"You too," he said, voice cracking again. Lily was too shocked to make fun of him. "I'm Hollis," he added loudly, uselessly, and Jacques nodded, trying not to smile. Eloise got the sense that he had already said this. "And this is my girlfriend Lily, and my dad, and—"

"Please, come in out of the cold," Dad urged Jacques, shuddering to life as he overcame his initial shock. "Jacques Lavesque, in my house—"

"No, it's fine, and I know it is late. I just needed to speak to Eloise quickly," Jacques protested, glancing up at Eloise again. "...If she is available to speak."

"She's, like, actually really busy right now," Lily suddenly burst out, in a tone that made it easy to imagine her as a bossy eight-year-old on the playground. "You should come back later. She has a lot of important work to do, and also, a lot of really handsome men are calling and texting her. Just so you know."

For the briefest moment Eloise and Jacques glanced at each other, a flash of mutual entertainment and affection that they were each quick to bury again. No. She would not do this. Their final conversation was still ringing in her ears; it still rang in her ears whenever the world went quiet enough to let it creep back in. She had loved him and he had hurt her. She would not meet his eyes for a private smile—not like this. She stilled her features, still gripping the banister like she could draw strength from it.

"I just need a few minutes, Eloise," he told her quietly. "...Please," he added.

Everyone was looking at her: Dad with soft eyes of empathy, his brows knit together; Hollis visibly torn between the older sibling urge to set anyone who had hurt her on fire and the ecstasy that his beloved hero was in *his* living room; Lily frowning at her with a warning look. And Jacques with that unreadable expression, one that did not allow her to predict what he might have to say.

The romantic in her—the one she worked so hard to bury—wanted to believe that this would be some rain-soaked confession in which he begged her forgiveness, but the detective in her was studying Jacques's stiff body language, his set jaw, and recalling their last meeting and thinking that, if anything, this was his chance to really vent his spleen. Something in him had broken tonight and he was no longer holding anything back.

Did she want to do this? Was he worthy of the pain this would cause her?

Just like in the courtroom their gaze was connected now, a line of lightning between them that held her in place and made her stand a little taller.

She *was* strong enough. Even Jacques Lavesque, a man who was like the sun, could not hurt her so much that she could not grow back again.

"Okay. Just a few minutes," she decided at last. "We can talk outside."

"It's, like, actually raining—" Hollis began, but she was quick to interrupt as she walked down the stairs.

"All the more reason to make it fast," she said firmly.

# Chapter Twenty-Nine

Eloise grabbed her raincoat from the coat tree and shoved her feet into her boots without taking the time to zip them up properly, and followed Jacques outside.

A light rain was falling, blurring the last Christmas lights on the houses around them. The awning over the front steps partly sheltered them, but the rain would turn their hair wild and sodden soon. After all of Lily's efforts to make sure that Jacques only saw Eloise at her most manicured and groomed, he was now confronting her when she was as vulnerable and bare as she could possibly be.

They turned to face each other, and now she regretted agreeing to talk here because this was still too close. The front step was only big enough for them to stand an arm's length apart, and this close—after so many months of separation—he was too real, too warm, too much. He was looking her over like he was looking for something that was hidden in her, tucked in her smile lines or behind a lock of hair.

"Well," she began, palms up, but he cut in before she could continue.

"I did not come here to apologize," he said. "And I am still angry with you."

She clenched her fists, short nails digging into her palms until it stung. All the frustration swelled up inside her like a balloon—the rejection, the loneliness; the profound sense of grief at losing a connection she had not even had for very long, a connection which had unmistakably transformed her—and then it burst.

"Well, you know what? I'm angry with you too," she shouted above the rain.

When he said nothing, she continued. "You hurt me. When I needed you most, you hurt me."

"You lied to me," he said. "You lied over and over again, and you made me think you cared about Kyle, you got both of us to trust you—"

"I *did* care—I *do* care—"

"And the whole *fucking* time, you were looking for the worst," he finished helplessly.

Even in the dark she could tell he was flushing with his fury. This was the first time she had ever heard him use foul language. She might be at her most vulnerable, but he was too. None of his polish or graciousness were protecting him now; he was not the man whose face was painted on the side of Boston Garden now.

(*This* was the man, she thought, that Andrei had loved from the start—the man who asked too much of others just as he asked too much of himself; the man whose anger sometimes soured and had to be painted on his body because he did not know where else to put it; the man who clung to contracts because he could not trust words.

(In this core way she understood Andrei completely, better than she had ever understood anyone else in her life. She loved this man too. He was the sun: he made things grow and bloom, coaxed beauty from things that looked like nothing—but he could still burn if you got too close.)

"Yes, I was looking for the worst—because it was my *job*," she said when she had collected herself. "I can't do anything about that. Krystal hired me to do that, and it is beyond egotistical that you would think I owed you, in particular, something different from what I owe anyone else. And speaking of trust—you made me feel like you *saw* me, the real me, and you made me feel like you *liked* me. And the minute you actually did see the real me, you couldn't handle it," she continued, her voice rising with every point until she was yelling at him over the roar of rain and cars. "Do you even know the impact you had on me? Do you have *any* idea of how important that was to me—"

"You lied to me about everything!" he reiterated, slicing his hand through the air. "You couldn't even tell me your last name! How far could we have gotten before I found out anything true about you? You lied, and you would have just kept on lying if everything hadn't—"

"You have no way of proving that! You have no way of predicting how things could have developed!"

She paused to catch her breath as they stared each other down. *How far could we have gotten...*

It was impossible; he only meant friendship; he did not mean anything else. "I am *so* sorry that, unlike you, I'm not perfect—"

"You think this was about *being perfect*?" he cut in, yelling above the roar of another car going by, above the rush of rain. "It was about trust. I trusted that it was real, I trusted that you saw things the way I did, I trusted that—that we were the same—that the same things mattered to us—that I had finally met someone who understood me—"

He did not know how his words mirrored the painful thoughts she had been having for months.

"Everything I said and everything I did was real," she told him now. "I don't know if you noticed, but I risked pretty much everything for Kyle and his trial. I had no idea what impact that was going to have on my life—whether I was going to get sued, for example. It's lucky that it worked out, but I was prepared for the worst and did it anyway. And by the way, you are the only one who can't get past this. Everyone else on the team has accepted it! Kyle has accepted it! He accepted it pretty much right away. It's just you now—"

"Yes, they have all accepted it and are fine with it, because they didn't want something more with you," Jacques said, raw and hoarse and vulnerable. "But I did."

Past tense. Tears were slipping down her cheeks, a steady stream of grief, grief that she hadn't really felt belonged to her for months. Eloise turned her back on him to hide her face.

"You really think that I think I am perfect?" he asked, his voice rough from yelling. He sounded exhausted. "Because I don't think that. I—I have not done anything right in months." He laughed sadly; the sound rushed over her like the rain. "It has just been one mistake after another, but the only mistakes I regret are the times we walked away from each other, the times I did not reach out and pull you back."

She stared, without really seeing, at the Christmas wreath on the door, at the little strand of lights that Hollis had twined up the railing.

"I was so worried about doing the right thing. Even when I saw you at the trial, I thought I shouldn't approach you after what I had done. But I don't care anymore. And I don't feel bad for being mad at you anymore, because yeah, you matter to me." His voice was rising again, the words coming out in that staccato she had heard him use during the game, the way his passion overcame his self-consciousness and his caution. "And I don't fucking want you to lie to me again, okay? It pissed me off, and I don't care if you thought it was an overreaction because it is how I feel. I do want you to treat me differently than you treat everyone else. I do want you to owe me something different than you owe everyone else—because I want you. I want you in my life."

Eloise faced him.

She could still save herself. There was still time to turn around. She was a goner in many ways, already in love with a man who burned like the sun. But he was looking at her like she was the moon, uncatchable and silvery and bearing a tidal power that men assigned to witches and gods.

Love had only hurt him and here he was again, battered and stitched and prepared to get hurt all over again. "I want you in my life," he said again, more softly this time.

Last chance.

"I want that too," she said, and watched him let out a breath that fogged in the air, "but I don't know if I fit in your life, Jacques. Your face is on the side of Boston Garden, and until recently I was on food stamps."

"Yeah?" He gave her that wry half-smile. "And I was struggling to end my marriage that should have ended years ago, and you've blown up your life for others—twice."

He bit his lip then, and took her hand, lacing their rain-slick fingers together tentatively and then assuredly. He was not holding back anymore, and when she looked down at their hands—a marvel of skin against skin to her—he squeezed her hand and pulled her closer, a selfish movement.

"My life is about to look different, anyway, I think," he said. "Why don't I show it to you and you can decide for yourself?"

"Different," she said slowly, looking up at him.

"Yeah." He was still smiling. "Come with me—let me show you."

"Okay. Hold on, I have to—"

"Say goodbye to all the handsome men who are calling you?" he cut in, making her laugh.

"Yes, it's going to be a while. I hope you brought something to do."

"I have a lot of Batman toys in the car," he said casually as she poked her head into her father's house.

Hollis and Lily were gone—maybe in the kitchen—but her father was in his usual chair, watching television. He immediately twisted to look back at her.

"I—I'll be back in a bit," she told him with a tentative wave.

He waved too, gave a nod, then turned back to the television. "See you in a bit," he said.

The living room light was warm, and the house smelled like Lily's cooking, and Eloise's own things were scattered throughout the room. It was a powerful reminder of what she would not have if she had not been willing to take the risk with her father, with Hollis.

"Okay." She shut the door and returned to the inky night, and to Jacques. "That should hold them for a little while."

"We need more than a little while. Maybe set Lily on them," he said, taking her hand again—warmth, electricity, the spark of a match—and pulling her down the steps.

"That is incredibly optimistic of you, given that I think we are technically still mad at each other," she pointed out as she allowed him to lead her down the driveway.

He glanced at her over his shoulder, a smile touching the corner of his mouth. "I am sure we can work that out."

"You sound like you have some ideas of how we might," she said as they got into the car.

"A list, yeah," he said, navigating down the narrow street. Now they were both grinning, trying to hold back laughter. "I've had a lot of time to work on it. You want to hear it?"

"Not at the moment." She dug another train out of one of the cupholders and held it up. "I just am not sure Percy is ready to hear that kind of thing."

"You are right, it's not a very polite or appropriate list," he agreed seriously, and warmth flooded through her like the sun had come out.

"So where are you taking me? Or—is that *also* not appropriate for Percy's ears?" she teased, covering the toy train's face.

"It's very appropriate, and it's not far," he promised. "Actually, it is very close."

"What is it, then?" she pressed, watching him as he drove. His skin was still damp from the rain, as she knew hers was, and the streetlamps edged him in flickering blue and gold, painting all of his broken lines with warm light.

"What my future looks like," he explained at last.

"Your future," Eloise repeated, before making her guess, "after hockey."

"Yeah." He cleared his throat. "After hockey."

The weight of his words seemed to take up the whole car. Eloise stared ahead, aware of the animal grief that prowled behind those words.

"I'm excited to see it, then," she said evenly.

They only drove for a little while longer. They passed Harvard Square, and soon turned onto a side street lined with houses that had lush green lawns and spacious porches with fans on the ceilings. Some of the houses were lit up: with tasteful white twinkle lights, or warm lamps along the front path, or cozy jewel-like light from within—but one house, on the very end of the street, was completely dark.

Jacques rolled to a stop in front of the darkened house. A 'For Sale' sign in the yard had been covered with a 'SOLD' sticker diagonally across it. For the first time she noticed the house keys that rattled on the Range Rover keychain.

"Your future looks like it needs a new roof," she joked because he seemed tense, uncertain.

"And apparently a new water heater, and Stephanie has told me the kitchen is very dated and embarrassing and that I need to do something about it right away," Jacques said wryly. "Come on, let me show you."

They got out of the car, and some of their giddiness dissipated as the weight of his words settled around them like the rain. *After hockey. After this season.* Eloise held her tongue as she followed him; he unlatched the kissing gate and let her into the yard, to a mossy, broken slate pathway.

The wooden porch creaked beneath their shoes. Eloise looked around, as Jacques unlocked the front door, at the broad porch. There would be plenty of room for rocking chairs and a hammock; she could easily imagine toys and soccer balls discarded around the porch, could already see those fading with time to be replaced by the boys' bicycles that they'd ride to their friends' houses and then leave forgotten, carelessly, in the yard.

"And probably new locks," Jacques added when the door finally swung open.

They stepped into the darkened front hall, which was narrow and plain, save for a tiny chandelier that was missing a few glass beads and looked like it was an original feature of the house. Eloise could see markings on the walls where a mirror and some art must have been hung by the previous owners, and discoloration on the floor where a runner rug had previously lain. A pair of Jacques's sneakers and his duffle bag sat against the wall, the scent of his aftershave and toothpaste lingering in the air.

"I don't have much furniture yet," he said, shutting the door behind them. "I feel like—well, like a teenager," he admitted.

"Yeah, teenagers often own massive houses in Cambridge," Eloise said. He prodded her lightly in the back, making her skin tingle as she laughed and ducked away, even as she wondered how she might get him to touch her back again. *After hockey. After this season.* She could not get over it.

"Less joking, more walking," he ordered briskly, prodding her again in the back. "You have to tell me what you think of it."

"It's hideous," she said, grinning when she got a laugh from him. "But let me withhold my final judgment until I see the rest of it."

"That is really reasonable of you, Eloise," Jacques said appreciatively, "we're making progress."

"The only question is—where are you going to keep your tarot decks and crystal collection?" she wondered. He pretended to gasp.

"Too low. Never mind, I am leaving you out on the curb with the trash," he said. "Go in here," he directed, placing a hand on her back and steering her through an archway. "This is the living area. Supposedly you are not allowed to have a TV in this room, according to Juliette," he said as they poked their heads into the first room, which was trimmed with dark carved wood and had tall windows looking out on the front and side yards. "And here's the dining room, though I think I won't end up using it too much. I like the kitchen better."

He guided her into the kitchen, and here he flicked on the lights. Stephanie was right—it was bright but dated, all of the countertops and cabinets a putty-brown.

"Oh, yeah, this definitely needs to be redone. Even *I* know that," Eloise said as she walked into the middle of the kitchen and spun around. "The boys can do their homework here," she said as she ran a hand over the island countertop, conscious of Jacques watching her as he leaned in the doorway. "Or here," she added when she saw the breakfast nook.

"I'm sure Luke will," Jacques agreed. "And then he'll leave it there and it will get ruined somehow," he added, looking exasperated.

"You're right. Amd Peter will want a proper desk in his room where he can do everything perfectly," she realized.

*After hockey. After this season.* The urge to comfort him, to hold him, to protect him from what she knew so precisely he was feeling was overwhelming. She turned to him again, beaming.

"Okay, but where does the flatscreen go? Because you'll need a good place to watch hockey."

"I was thinking in here, up on the second floor, but you tell me what you think," Jacques said. He turned off the lights and led her up the carved wooden stairs, which creaked beneath their combined weight, a subtle reminder of their physical closeness.

At the top of the stairs, stained glass windows overlooked the backyard. On sunny days those windows would let in jeweled light and cast colors across the floorboards, little flickers of magic for Peter and

Luke. After admiring it, they turned the corner and entered a room with fusty light blue wall-to-wall carpeting.

"Oh, this is a perfect place. But the carpet has to go. It's just not you," Eloise decided. "Okay, so the television's against this wall, obviously." She splayed her hands, gesturing to the windowless wall. In a flash she pictured a squashy sofa, Jacques sprawled on it as he studied the game, with Luke on the floor by his feet, absently playing with toys as he watched the television, and Peter on the edge, reading a book and half-watching.

And she saw herself there, too—curled up on the other end of the sofa, maybe on her laptop doing some work and smiling wryly along with Jacques's commentary on the game.

"Sofa here," Jacques agreed, "and there is this weird cutout here where I could put a desk. Not that I have ever needed a desk for anything," he added, rubbing the back of his neck.

*After hockey.*

"Meh, details. Not important yet," Eloise joked, breezing past it like she knew he needed her to do. "What about the boys' rooms? Are you going to make them share?"

"No, I had to share with Olivier and we almost killed each other many times," Jacques said. "They're perfect for them. Let me show you."

He led her around the corner. "This will be Luke's room. Lots of windows, closest to the stairs, and it overlooks the street so he can always see what's going on outside," he described as they poked their heads in. "And it is closest to me since he still needs me sometimes."

"Yes, this is perfect," Eloise agreed, peering around the room. It was empty, but it was all too easy to picture bunk beds, and toys scattered across the floor; sunlight falling on a bookcase packed with comics and more toys, a skateboard leaning against the wall, sneakers abandoned across the rug.

Jacques took her hand, fingers slipping between hers, and pulled her to the next room.

"And this will be Peter's," he said. "I don't know why this room has built-in bookshelves, but I think he is going to need them."

Eloise could picture the tidy rows of comics, organized by Peter's thoughtful hands, that would turn into textbooks and fantasy novels; how he would take pleasure in seeing them perfectly aligned each night as he waited for sleep.

"And it's closer to the back of the house, so it'll be quieter," Eloise said.

"Yes, and he's a lighter sleeper, so he needs the quiet most," Jacques added. "And here's my bedroom—it's the only room that has any furniture yet—" They went past a room with a half-made bed and an open suitcase against the wall, beside a dresser that looked out of place and had nothing on it. They glanced at each other, then looked away, but she caught his sly smile just before he turned his head.

"But the room I really wanted you to see is on the third floor."

"An attic room?" she prompted.

"You'll see. Come on."

Hand in hand, he led her up the stairs to the third floor. Here the slender beams of the eaves hung low, a crisscross pattern that made her think of ships and castles. At either end, the arched windows bore the same blue, green, and pink stained glass as the windows on the second floor. They paused in the middle of the room beneath the point of the eaves. The only light came from the streetlamps, which filtered muted, watery color through the stained glass, and left pale jewel-toned patterns across the floorboards.

It was one of the loveliest rooms she had ever been in.

"What will go up here? A guestroom for your mom?" Eloise wondered.

"I don't think so," he said. "There's an empty room on the first floor that could be a guest room, so this room could be anything. Another guestroom. An office. Depends on what I need."

*After hockey.*

That fizzy sense of joy between them had quieted. Eloise looked down at their still-twined fingers, then up at Jacques again.

"But I don't know what I'll need yet. So I am keeping it open."

"Well, except for that kitchen, your future looks good," she said. "Really good."

"You think so?" They were close enough that she could see the freckles in his eyes, flecks of brown within the blue-grey. "You still think you don't fit into it?"

Even in this dark room he was sunlight, almost too bright for her to look directly at him, all the brighter for how she knew he was grieving. Somewhere in the house, the clock struck midnight. This was a witching hour, and Boston always felt its oldest, its most magic, at midnight. And the rest of the world was so far away, and if she was in exile then he was too—the king who had willingly cast aside his crown; the king willingly led by the pale witch deep into the forest, never to be seen again.

"I'm so afraid of how you could hurt me," she confessed.

"You think I'm not afraid that you will hurt me?" he pointed out.

"We probably *will* hurt each other," she agreed. She tightened her grip on his wrist as he pulled her closer.

"Yes," he said, "but wouldn't it be worse if we didn't?"

"So much worse," she whispered, but then he was kissing her, and she was gripping his shirt and his hands were in her hair, and outside the rain gave the moon a halo while it waited for the sun, and the rain came down on the roof that needed repairing, and they were in a room full of pale jewels of light at this witching hour, and Jacques was everything, flooding her every dark room with sunlight, making the leaves unfurl and the buds bloom, and Eloise was so full of hope that she thought she could light up the night sky with her own silver glow.

# Acknowledgements

No story is written in isolation, especially a story about love. These are all of the people whom I love.

Thanks to Maj for being my spirit guide throughout this whole process—from edits to emotional support to practical support every step of the way. MY QUEEN.

Thanks to Meg for the *beautiful* cover, for the years of hockey and Jonsa friendship, and for the beautiful gif sets.

Thanks to Anna for—well, everything. It cannot be overstated: this book would not exist without her. T&C, obviously.

Thanks to Amanda for falling in love with these people like I did, for doing the most beautiful birth charts and divining facets of these people that I had not even seen yet, and for the cards and care packages, the kindness and the transformative friendship. Also, thanks for traipsing around Boston and Nantucket with me.

Thanks to Seraphim for letting me drag her around random patches of Boston in January, oftentimes in the pouring rain, and, in true Jacques Lavesque fashion, so generously letting me ramble about things she already knew and acting like it was new and fascinating to her every time. I have so loved being a Bruins fan with her, and will remember "HAPPY FUCKIN' NEW YEAR" forever.

Thanks to Adrienne for generously responding to my bizarre and increasingly specific questions about the legal process with thoughtful, practical, and interesting answers.

Thanks to Amaati for capturing me in the most beautiful profile picture ever. I have loved her art for so long! That's my face! In her art! AHHHH!

Thanks to Anna and her enormous and wonderful family for the encouragement, support, excitement, and kindness—a fairytale family with fairytale hearts.

Thanks to Catherine for the candle and the reading and the bells. I learned a lot from boldly knocking on her front door at 9:30pm on a Friday night last August.

Thanks to the *many* tumblrinas (they know who they are) for tolerating me and my unhinged and relentless posting about the process of this book and cheering me on every step of the way. The texts, asks, DMs, voice notes, playlist suggestions, and care packages were so inspiring throughout the process.

Thanks to all the readers on AO3 who have left comments and kudos over the years. I have been shaped as a writer and as a person by these interactions—for the better.

Thanks to the Broomall Starbucks, where 90% of this book was written at strange hours of the morning—with me greasy-haired and wearing the same sweatshirt regardless of temperature, slouched in the corner like a raccoon and probably driving away customers. My order was always correct and that corner seat really is perfect. I am sure that my next book will be written there, too.

Finally, thank you to my family. I won't make speeches.

# About the Author

Phoebe is a researcher, writer, adventurer, and hockey fan.
She has been obsessed with making people fall in love since she was six,
and obsessed with hockey since she was twenty-six.
When she isn't writing or blogging about hockey, she can be found
in the woods outside of Philadelphia, or in the corner of your local
Starbucks.

*For more content, including deleted chapters from other characters'
POVs, sign up for the quarterly newsletter at phoebewoodswrites.com.*